BY AMINAH FOX

THE MOURNERS

The Mourners: The Deadly Elite

The Harlots: The Devoutly Corrupt

ALL THE OTHER GODS NOVELS

The Eleventh Hour

A list of content warnings are available on the author's website at: www.aminahfox.com/content-warnings

Ebook Cover design by Atima Kim
Print Cover editions by Aminah Fox

First Edition: November 2025
ISBN Paperback: 979-8-218-70234-2
ISBN Hardcover: 979-8-9870409-8-0

To the survivors, the ones who return, and the ghosts they bring with them

THREADS *of* FATE

AMINAH FOX

Before

Over 1 Year Ago, Halloween

They were everywhere this time of year, pushed out by the rain or construction—her superstitious grandmother would've called it a sign.

So when a rat skittered over Tammy's foot as she stepped out of the Hub & Haven—the on-campus bookstore and convenience store—she didn't flinch. Her tote bag held the textbooks she'd bought, junk food for her and her best friend, and a few Halloween movies that she'd found in the bargain bin. When she'd gone in there'd been a shred of daylight left but now it was night.

Shadows stretched toward her like specters across the cobblestone paths of the Ivy League campus, where the laughter and raucous revelry of Halloween partygoers milled about further away, but their voices were somehow muffled by the oppressive stillness. Most students had chosen the company of costumed camaraderie, leaving the campus desolate, save for the flickering lamps on campus that always made her nervous.

Tammy zipped up her hoodie, the Millfield University Athletics logo barely visible under the dim streetlights. She had been on edge all week and had shrugged it off as stress from studying for finals and the constant pressure of maintaining her scholarship. She had her box braids re-done yesterday. Having her hair done was a familiar comfort after long hours of basketball practice and late-night study sessions. She was glad her caramel skin hadn't lost its glow and acne hadn't cropped up—so in some ways she felt lucky. After all, being an athlete didn't grant her any leniency when it came to academics. So tonight, she would get to relax.

But not before she regretted leaving her letterman jacket draped over the back of a chair in her apartment. If she had known it was going to take so long to check out, she would have asked her roommate to join her, then she wouldn't be walking back alone. After all, her roommate and childhood best friend, Manny, was probably still lounging in bed, watching a movie.

Tammy sighed. She could have called Manny, but it was a thirty-minute walk back to their apartment, and if they wanted to make the party before it got too crowded, she would need to hurry. Or she could head to the western side of campus, make her way to the street, call a rideshare and that was about a ten-minute trek, and in the opposite direction of the bridge she'd normally cross to get home. The ride would take about ten minutes, but it was Halloween weekend so there'd be bumper to bumper traffic.

30 minutes could easily become 50, she thought.

She groaned aloud. She looked around and rolled her eyes at herself.

It's only a thirty-minute walk, Tammy, she thought. *A thirty-minute walk that Manny will be pissed I did alone.* She bit her lip, but then shook her head at herself. *I'll just apologize to her later.*

Tammy started her walk, reminding herself that she was being dramatic. She took this route all the time in the afternoon. Yet here she was, anxiety getting the better of her as she made her way home tonight, her mind racing with thoughts that seemed absurd when compared to what her ancestors faced. What did she have to be afraid of?

As an African American woman, she knew that her ancestors had known the raw, visceral terror of being hunted, of their lives hanging in the balance with every step taken in a world that sought to diminish them. Various forms of prejudice and discrimination still existed, albeit often showing up in subtler ways at Millfield University such as social ostracization. The more blatant displays of racism were more likely to be punished. But during the most pivotal times in her ancestors' history, they were chased by dogs and men, and during the civil rights movement, they were sprayed with fire hoses. She was not being chased; she was simply a young woman walking back to her on-campus apartment presently tethered to the mundane worries of college life.

As Tammy approached the bridge that arched over the campus pond, she admired its sleek design, the wrought iron railings glimmering faintly under the moonlight. The bridge, the Unity Arch, was a favorite spot among students, it was adorned with twinkling fairy lights that draped on the railings, casting a warm glow on the worn wooden planks beneath her feet. There were different countries' flags hung from flagpoles and a few rainbow pride flags as well. The gentle sound of water lapping at the edges of the pond was pleasant, soothing even, and tonight was no exception.

She fished her phone from her pocket, dialing her friend as she stepped onto the bridge. "Hey, Manuela Bella! Get ready for the party!" she exclaimed with a laugh. The nickname—a nod to the moody, dramatic character from *Twilight* that her friend loved to emulate whenever they watched the series together.

"Ugh, Tammy, I don't know," Manny groaned. "I just feel like it's going to be lame. Plus, I heard Ridley is going to be there, and I really don't want to watch him do a keg stand or drag everyone into another game of flip cup. Like regular Ridley, I can handle, but not riled up Ridley. And I'll do shots, but I'm not drinking tequila tonight."

Tammy couldn't help but laugh, her anxiety momentarily forgotten. "You're right; looking after Ridley is always a bit *annoying*. So, why don't we skip the chaos? How about we hit up the pub for trivia night with the gang instead? Good food, good friends, and *way* less keg stands."

"Yeah, that sounds *more* like my scene," Manny replied.

Tammy felt a sense of relief wash over her. Manny's voice always managed to do that to her.

"Wait…how are you getting home?" Manny asked.

"Umm…I'm walking, *but* it's okay, it's nice out anyway. I'm practically halfway home," she said as she continued across the bridge, taking in the fairy lights.

"You could've told me!" Manny said. "Dean and I would have come, so you wouldn't be walking back *alone*. That's so not safe Tammy."

Tammy scoffed. "Well, I didn't know we wouldn't be going to the party tonight. Which means we'll have to do the group costume *tomorrow* night."

"Don't try to change the subject."

"I'm hardly trying to change the—" A fluttering sound came from behind her, and she froze.

A chill ran down her spine and she glanced over her shoulder, but all she saw were the colorful international flags flapping gently in the breeze.

It's probably just a bird, she reassured herself, shaking her head.

"Anyway, I'm almost across the bridge, so I'm going to hang up. I'll see you when I get home," she said, walking faster. "Love you. See you soon, Manuela Bella!"

"Love you too, Tammy Tams! Don't let any weirdos convince you to do a keg stand!" Manny joked before hanging up.

As Tammy walked briskly across the bridge, the rustling sound came again, louder this time. Her heart leaped in her chest, and she quickened her pace, the comforting lights of the campus square ahead urging her forward. But the sound seemed to be following her.

Enough of this, she thought.

She stopped and spun around, her voice trembling as she shouted into the darkness, "Whoever that is, knock it off!"

The silence that followed was almost mocking, pressing in on her from all sides. Just as she was about to turn back, a bird darted out a nearby tree, its wings flapping frantically before vanishing into the night. Tammy let out a shaky breath, her nerves still on edge, but she forced herself to focus on the familiar path ahead. She made it across the bridge and continued through central campus, the buildings, smaller at this distance, but shadowed under the moonlight. Luckily, the fountain at the center provided a marker for her.

Ten minutes to home, she thought.

And even less if she ran.

The sound came again, even closer now, like a whisper of movement just beyond her sight. Panic set in, and she ran, her footsteps echoing in the deserted square. Her breath came in short, ragged gasps as she approached the fountain.

Skidding to a stop, she dared a quick glance over her shoulder, her eyes straining to see anything in the dark. "Who's there?" she called out, but no one answered.

She turned her head left, then right, searching for someone. But no one was there.

But when she turned again, something struck her from behind, knocking the breath out of her. She stumbled forward, her scream strangled in her throat as she fought to regain her balance. A sharp pain shot through her leg, and she gasped, catching herself as she collapsed against the fountain edge. She coughed, her mind reeling with shock and confusion. Tammy tried to stand back up, but couldn't. Her ankle was twisted at an unnatural angle, and bile rose in her throat at the sight of her bone pushed through the skin.

Tammy's vision blurred and stung with tears, the world spinning in a disorienting blend of shapes and shadows. She turned around and squinted into the darkness, trying to make out her attacker, but all she could see was a looming, dark figure, its form shifting and indistinct in the dim light.

She tried to move, but for a moment she couldn't. She couldn't focus, though she knew she didn't have much time. Tammy grunted as she flipped onto her belly and pulled herself into a crawling position. Wincing at the pain going through the entire left side of her body, each movement worse than the one before.

Then a searing pain slashed across her back. She cried out, the sound piercing the night air, and fell to the ground, her hands clawing at the cold, hard concrete. Tammy reached behind herself instinctively and hissed the moment her fingertips met the painful slivers on her back, wetting them with blood. She managed to lift her head up and saw a university emergency phone by a nearby bench.

She tried to crawl away, her ankle weeping blood, leaving a trail of scarlet in her wake. She could feel the warm, sticky blood trickling down her back, mingling with her sweat. Her fingers pressing into the ground, desperate for any traction to pull herself forward to escape her attacker. Tammy didn't dare look back at them again, she couldn't think between her own ragged breathing and the sound of her heart pounding in her ears.

But before she could make any real progress, a hand clamped around her ankle, yanking her backward with terrifying strength. She screamed, her cries echoing into the night.

Chapter 1
Manuela Bella
Sunday, September 8th

Everyone begins at the end. The end of an uncourteous labor, after nine long months, bloody, bruised, and screaming. They can't walk or crawl. Not *yet*. *Yet* would be too much. Their mother's bosom there to comfort them, less rough than concrete or the asphalt of a deserted road, smoother, warmer too.

Hospital lights differed from high beams, though burned just as bright. Two shadows dangle above them, stagnant. For her, in her earliest days, one was Mother, the other, Father, still blue-gowned, lovingly gazing down at her. But on that dreaded day, the shadows were empty, hollow, husks on the ground, no longer who they used to be. A body bloodied, bruised—had she screamed? She couldn't tell her. The midnight darkness was too thick; perhaps each breath she'd taken had been like morphine, her windpipe strangled, though she could hear the distant howls of dogs. Police dogs. So, maybe Tammy had made it to one of the university emergency phones on campus. After all, they'd found blood there too.

Manuela Bella—that was the last thing her best friend said to her. It was an affectionate pet name that Tammy had given her for her love of all things supernatural. Even teen flicks that others didn't enjoy quite as much—she watched them for the worlds their author's built. Books turned into movies were some of her favorites. There was something for everyone in fantasy—and *horror.* She and Tammy were slasher flick fans as well, but unlike Tammy, Manny mostly wanted to understand the villains' reasoning behind their actions. What could lead someone to doing something so heinous? Or was monstrous a better word?

But in real life. *Them*, the murderer, the monster, whoever, they had been, took joy in disemboweling their victims like freshly slain pigs, and then hung them up somewhere for all to see like macabre sculptures, displaying each new masterpiece without any fear of repercussions—and Millfield University had been their grand exhibition. But they didn't show those images on the news. Manny had seen them on a table in a police interrogation room, that was, before her lawyer, her cousin's ex-boyfriend, Johnathan Cassidy tapped the silver handcuffs on her wrists with his ink-stained fingers, and said, "Manny, we can leave now."

She was Manuela D. Webb. She had sat in an interrogation room for three hours at 24-years-old, as an African American girl suspected of killing her roommate and childhood best friend, Tamara "Tammy" Moore—she was a suspect for all of two weeks—and they kept calling her Manuela. But if they knew her, they'd know she was Manny, and in those weeks she'd felt outside of her body, when she'd been her own personal narrator, recounting every detail of her day: the morning, the evening, that night—what she and Tammy had talked about over the phone.

In the end, she would repeat, "I wouldn't kill *anyone*. I'd never hurt Tammy." That was old Manny. Before Old Manny had trauma, but she had also had Tammy, but of course that was before.

Before it happened, Old Manny hadn't minded listening to politicians or biased newscasters making fools of themselves on television. She cared more about what she'd wear on her twenty-fifth birthday, because that was meant to be the pinnacle of her twenties. Everyone told her that 25 was going to be a great year. But now, she was 25-year-old Manny, and her frontal lobe had developed, and she'd gone through extensive therapy processing her past traumas, including her confusion around her friend's murder. Seeing as, Tammy was the first of many murders on campus that year.

The infamous 'MillU Murders,' as the media had dubbed them, had fueled the 'media and violence' debates, but back then it had been an election year. Violence was a major topic on college campuses, mainly gender-based violence and gun violence. She had experience with the former. But that's all they had meant to the media. They were just topics of conversation, and nothing came of those discussions. Nothing managed to dampen Millfield University's esteemed reputation.

Manny had chosen to finish her final year of undergrad online—only to apply to the same university's graduate program. But what else could she do? Millfield University was an ivy league school. If she wanted the best chance at a job after graduation, she would find it by graduating from here. And she didn't hate the location either—Toronto, Canada. She was from the states, and this was her first time living outside of the US.

Everyone those murders had impacted was left to pick up the pieces, and the victims were nothing more than golden plaques on benches, and a commemorative composite photo right by the main entrance of the Tremont Hall. An image of thirteen students using individual images, together side by side in little oval frames, their names under each photo. And Manny stood in front of it, staring at Tammy's photo. She was frozen in time, her bright smile, glowing caramel brown skin, and perfect box braids didn't quite capture the bright future her best friend had had ahead of her.

She would have been an amazing poet, Manny thought. *She should still be here—I should have gone to the Hub & Haven with Dean.*

They should be standing here together. Instead, Manny stood there alone, the weight of her responsibilities pressing heavily on her shoulders. When she was an undergrad, Tremont Hall, was just yet another large, ancient building on campus—its corridors were a maze that she'd imagined rivaled most greek labyrinths she'd read about as an English major, and at night, its Gothic architecture casted long, ominous shadows under the flickering lamps outside. *Shakespeare would have loved this place,* she and Tammy would joke. The joke never got old—and now neither would Tammy.

Today, as a graduate student, Manny found herself equally troubled by Tremont Hall's corridors, and she still needed to find the associate dean's office to discuss her reassimilation into university life. Due to Associate Dean Shepherd's concerns about her well-being, which she knew came from a good place. He was a busy man, he used to be an English professor, he'd taught her short stories workshop in undergrad—but now he was the Associate Dean of the Faculty of Arts & Science. His office was in the most complicated building on campus, and she couldn't begin to think of which way to go, so instead, she walked to the easiest place to locate in Tremont Hall—the library.

By the time, Manny reached the ornately carved door of the library—which she had discovered in undergrad was the easiest place to ask directions—she wanted to go home. The door creaked open, revealing the brightly lit interior, rows upon rows of bookshelves, with numerous titles, some focusing on subjects like knowledge or power. She stepped inside, the scent of aged paper and leather a comforting, albeit deceptive, familiarity. Eventually, she found a student library assistant, who was sitting behind the circulation desk with a smile plastered on his face.

"Hi, do you need some help?" he asked kindly.

"Yes, um…" Manny began, her voice echoing slightly in the vast library. "I have a meeting with the associate dean. Can you tell me how to get to his office?"

The student nodded, a gentle smile tugging at his lips. "Of course. The associate dean's office is on the north side of the building in the administration wing. You'll want to head out of the library and take a left. Go straight until you reach the main hall, then follow the path to the right. The administration wing will be on your left. It's the one with the large stone archway."

Manny thanked him, glancing around the library once more. She was surprised there weren't any students in the library. It was the largest library on campus, and there wasn't even a tour going through it. She turned to leave, the directions clear in her mind but a strange unease settling in her stomach. The student's eyes followed her as she exited, his smile fading into concern.

She hated when people looked at her like that.

* * *

The grand foyer in between the two wings was quiet, the usual bustle of students and faculty was noticeably absent. Manny glanced around, the warm lighting reflecting pleasantly across the marble floor. She spotted a sign pointing toward the Administration Wing and started down the corridor, her footsteps echoing as she walked.

The corridor stretched out before her, lined with portraits of stern-faced deans and benefactors from ages past. The air was cool and carried a faint scent of floor cleaner. Manny's eyes flicked to the plaques beside each door, searching for her old professor's name.

At the end of the corridor, she turned a corner, following the directional signs. The building seemed to stretch and twist in the warm light, every turn revealing another seemingly identical corridor. The fluorescent lights overhead did little to dispel the shadows lurking in the corners.

Then she finally passed through a set of double doors, entering the administration wing. The walls here were lined with more contemporary decor, a contrast to the austere portraits she'd seen earlier. A few offices had their doors ajar, soft murmurs of conversation drifting out. She caught snippets of administrative chatter, the mundane discussions of schedules and paperwork oddly comforting in their normalcy.

Finally, she found the door marked "Associate Dean's Office," and noticed herself in a hallway mirror.

Her caramel skin had surprisingly held onto its glow through her sleepless nights. But the dark circles under her eyes were barely masked by concealer that had begun to fade due to Millfield's humidity. She had forgotten to apply setting spray this morning, which had become a crucial step in her routine. Her curly hair framed her face, softening the intensity of her dark eyes, which held a mix of warmth and weariness. In truth, she hoped the associate dean wouldn't notice how disheveled she was. Or that he was at least too polite to mention it.

Taking a deep breath, she pushed open the door to the office and stepped inside.

The executive assistant sat outside the main office, in a small, cluttered space with filing cabinets and stacks of paper that she was going through. A middle-aged woman with glasses perched on the edge of her nose looked up from her desk.

"Can I help you?" she asked, her tone brisk but not unfriendly.

"Yes," Manny replied, trying to steady her nerves. "I'm here to speak with the associate dean. Can you let him know that I'm here?"

The woman nodded, her fingers tapping a few keys on her keyboard. "Ah, yes! Manuela Webb…" she trailed off and then smiled at her warmly. "Welcome back!"

"Thank you," Manny said, feeling a bit more at ease.

"He's ready for you now."

Manny nodded. Then pushed open the cracked door of the associate dean's office, and stepped into a warm, inviting space, with shelves lined with academic texts and a large window overlooking the campus. The associate dean, Dr. Alan Shepherd, rose from behind his desk, a kind smile spreading across his face.

"Manny, it's good to see you," Dr. Shepherd said, extending a hand. "I'm glad you're here."

Dr. Alan Shepherd towered over her at six feet, his presence always commanded respect. His skin was a rich, deep brown, and his eyes, warm and thoughtful, were framed by a pair of stylish, dark-rimmed glasses. His close-cropped hair, peppered with strands of gray, added a distinguished air to his appearance. He wore a tailored navy blue suit that complemented his broad shoulders and athletic build, and a crisp white shirt and a burgundy tie completed his ensemble. Despite his formal attire, there was a natural warmth to him that put people at ease.

His face, though often serious, could light up with a smile that revealed a set of perfectly straight, white teeth. He had a calm, measured way of speaking that conveyed both authority and empathy, making him approachable despite his impressive credentials.

“I know it’s difficult this time of year…with Tammy gone.”

That’s an understatement, she thought dismissively.

She hated when people said that. Tammy isn’t gone. She’s dead. She was murdered in cold blood and her killer was never caught. But she never said that out loud—no matter how many times she thought it.

“Thank you, Dr. Shepherd," Manny replied, shaking his hand. “It’s good to be back.”

“Please, have a seat," Dr. Shepherd gestured to a leather chair at a table near his desk. “How have you been holding up?”

“It's been…hard,” Manny admitted, settling into the chair. “Finishing undergrad online was challenging, but I managed. And I’m back now.”

She didn’t want him to pity her. Everyone always seemed to pity her.

Dr. Shepherd nodded sympathetically. “I checked in with the rest of your friend group as well. It's been a tough time for all of you. And of course, if you need any support, don't hesitate to reach out.”

“I appreciate that,” Manny said, nodding at him. “I think being back will help me move forward.”

That wasn’t entirely true. But it wasn’t entirely false. The fact of the matter was she needed her degree, and she needed to take on teaching hours to become a professor.

Dr. Shepherd leaned back in his chair, his expression thoughtful. “The new semester starts on Monday. Are you ready for your classes?”

“Mostly,” Manny said, managing a small smile. “I’m really looking forward to the occult studies class. I picked it because Professor Moreau is teaching it. I've heard great things about him.”

“Beau Moreau is one of the best,” Dr. Shepherd agreed. “I’ve heard he’s challenging but incredibly insightful. You'll learn a lot from him.”

Manny hesitated for a moment before speaking again. “I do need to work on my personal portfolio, though. Everything I've written since...since Tammy's death has been *dark*. I think it’s mostly been my dreams that are causing my writer’s block.”

Dr. Shepherd's face softened. “Dreams can be powerful, especially after a traumatic event. Sometimes, writing them out can help you process what you've been through."

Manny nodded. "The dreams are always the same. People standing above me in the dark, but I can't see their faces. And the sounds they make…" She trailed off, noticing the way he was looking at her. "But they're just dreams after all.

Dr. Shepherd leaned forward. "That sounds frightening, Manny. Have you spoken to anyone about these dreams?"

"A little," Manny admitted. "I've been writing them down, but it just makes them feel more real. Dr. Carter said she has been in contact with the school to let them know about things."

Things being her recently diagnosed post-traumatic stress disorder, and all the work she'd been doing to improve her mental health. Dr. Evelyn Carter believed that they could get her back on track, and Manny appreciated the woman's optimism. But wasn't optimism mixed with a healthy dose of realism part of every therapist's job? Manny mostly was hoping to prove she could take on more than the 3-course load they were giving her. She still qualified as a full-time student so they wouldn't take away her scholarship, but since she couldn't take four courses, it could take her an additional year if she didn't take classes in the summer for her two year program. And Dr. Carter would frequently remind her that her mental health should be prioritized over her coursework. But that was easier said than done.

Dr. Shepherd nodded."I'm glad you're seeing a therapist. It's important to take your mental health seriously, especially if you want to start teaching. Once Dr. Carter gives the green light, you'll be able to get those teaching hours in. Until then, focus on your workshops and electives."

"I will," Manny said.

"Remember, my door is always open," Dr. Shepherd said, standing up. "Take care of yourself, and I'll see you around campus."

"I'll try," Manny said softly. "Thank you, Dr. Shepherd."

Manny left the office feeling a mix of relief and lingering unease. The new semester was just days away, and while she was grateful for the support, she couldn't shake the haunting images from her nightmares.

She left the administration wing, retracing her steps. The building's labyrinthine layout was a bit less daunting, each step bringing her closer to her destination and, she hoped, some peace and quiet.

* * *

Manny walked upstairs to her apartment and unlocked her front door and entered, the click of the lock a welcome sound. Her apartment was modest but cozy, with wood flooring that extended throughout the living and dining areas as well as the bedrooms. The living room was furnished with a comfortable, well-worn brown velvet couch and a low coffee table cluttered with books and papers. A large, soft rug in muted green tones covered part of the floor. Shelves lined one wall, filled with a mix of novels, academic texts, and framed photos.

To the right, the dining area was simple, with a small wooden table and three benches creating an "at-home dining booth" as Tammy had called it. To the left of it was the kitchen, which had cool, gray tile flooring. It was compact but efficient, with dark granite countertops, white cabinets, and stainless steel appliances.

Manny moved into the living room and sank onto the couch, feeling the weight of the day settle over her. She glanced around the apartment, her eyes lingering on the door to what used to be Tammy's room. The door was ajar, and through the gap, she could see the beginnings of what would eventually become an office. The room was mostly bare now, Tammy's family had taken her belongings, but they had left Manny a few photos of the two of them together. Those photos now sat on her desk as silent reminders of the past.

The apartment was filled with memories. The walls of the living room were adorned with framed photos of happier times—pictures of Manny and Tammy at various university events, laughing with friends, or simply hanging out together. The wood floors creaked slightly as she shifted on the couch. Their kitchen had been a place of shared meals and late-night talks, and now it was tinged with a sense of loss.

As Manny sat there, the apartment felt both familiar and unfamiliar. It was a place of refuge, but also a space filled with memories that haunted her as much as they comforted her. She could feel Tammy's presence in every nook and cranny. The transformation of her room into an office was slow, deliberate, a way of moving forward without forgetting.

Manny's eyes rested on the photos Tammy's family had left her. She reached for one, the image of the two of them smiling at a mix-and-mingle campus event that Gamma Phi Beta had held, and it brought a bittersweet smile to her face. The 2-bedroom apartment was hers now, but Tammy's spirit would always be a part of it.

As Manny sat on the couch, lost in thought, the familiar buzz of her cellphone jolted her back to the present. She glanced over at the coffee table, where her phone vibrated against the wood. With a sigh, she reached for it, already anticipating the message.

Unlocking the screen, she saw a text from her friend:

Grant

Hey, just wanted to let you know, Dean and I are heading to the pub now! Shantelle got us a reservation. We can't wait to see you! Wade might be late, because he has practice.

Manny groaned, the sound escaping her lips before she could stop it. She had hoped to ease back into campus life without a grand welcome, especially since she was the last of her friend group to arrive. She wasn't ready to face the excited chatter and the well-meaning questions about how she was doing. The thought of reconnecting with them after everything felt overwhelming.

She ran a hand through her hair. She knew they meant well, but the idea of seeing their sympathetic faces made her stomach churn. She wanted to be okay in front of them, to smile and laugh as if everything were normal, but the shadows of their shared past wouldn't leave her alone.

Wade might be late—of course, he'd be late. He had every right to be late. He was going to propose to Tammy last December. This year was hard for him. He sobbed at Tammy's funeral. He got in on the same basketball scholarship Tammy did. And he wasn't the type of guy to just up and move on to the next girl. Wade was a genuinely good guy, and he'd lost the love of his life. Tammy had been in their lives the longest. In many ways, he and Manny were in the same boat. He'd lost his soulmate, she'd lost her platonic soulmate—so not *entirely* the same, but a little.

Manny sighed and leaned back against the couch. She stared at the ceiling, thinking about her next move. She could ignore the text, pretend she hadn't seen it, but she knew that would only prolong the inevitable. The last thing she wanted was for them to worry more than they already did. She couldn't keep making excuses forever.

Reluctantly, she stood up from the couch, setting the photo down as she prepared to face the inevitable. She took a deep breath, steeling herself for the moment. In a way, forcing herself to remember everything Dr. Carter had taught her. She would take a shower, redress in something nice for the pub and join the people who cared about her, and take her first steps back into a world she was trying to rejoin.

Chapter 2
Sunday Night, September 8th

When she considered coming back to Mill U last spring, she thought that getting back into the swing of things would be easier and give a sort of structure to her day to day; she wanted to forget for a while. Forget the person she would call for every event in her life, whether it was school-related, or some terrific writing breakthrough with a fictional character—talk for hours about how she was finally able to let her character speak through her. Whether it was big or small—Tammy wanted to hear it all. But she would listen to Manny go on and on about it. Those phone calls are gone now. Manny had gone to therapy at least once a week to spend time discussing all of her trauma—and her guilt for not going to the student store with Tammy that day.

Beyond that, was the pub, "The Black Stag," it was only a few blocks away. But from where she stood at the top of the hill, she could see it, a squat building of old brick and stained wood, its windows fogged and streaked with glittering rain, glowing faintly from the light inside. Its name painted in bright yellow letters on the building. There used to be a sign above the door that creaked on rusted hinges whenever it swayed.

A few strands of hair clung to her face, as she made her way down the street, cars roaring past in the opposite direction over the gleaming black cement roads. Puddles reflected the dim glow of streetlamps and shop signs like tiny, fractured mirrors. Gutters were overwhelmed with water, choked by branches and debris, causing murky streams to slither down the edges of the road. She was about three-quarters down the first block when she finally pulled her coat tighter around her, silently cursing the cold autumn air.

Yet despite the dreary weather, the buildings still managed to shimmer. Neon signs, their colors muted by the mist, flickered and cast their hues across the rain-soaked surfaces—pinks and purples, greens and blues—spilling across the streets like splashes of spilled paint. High above her, rooftop bars with fairy lights, and customers under an awning talking, laughing, clinking glasses to a day's end. Probably sororities and fraternities meeting up after a long hot summer—most of them came back with travel stories or new people added to their networks—they always settled at that bar, the Globe. They loved it there like her friend group loved The Black Stag.

By the time she reached the third block, the sidewalks felt narrower, as if the world around her was slowly shrinking. She shook herself, trying to focus and ignore the nausea swirling in her stomach. Then nearly jumped out of her skin when a rat scurried over her foot, its tiny paws sending a shock through her system. Manny stopped to find her bearings, staring down the alleyway the little pest had gone down, noticing a statuesque silhouette leaning against an apartment building's ladder. For a moment, she was positive they were looking at her, and she wanted to move, but felt frozen. She didn't know why, but something about the stranger made her uneasy. Manny squinted at them, trying to make out their face—for a moment thinking, or perhaps hoping, they were hurt and simply needed help. Those alarm bells going off inside her head that were slowly giving her a headache, or a migraine given the burnt toast smell, were actually telling her this person, whoever they were, needed her help.

But then she was jostled, and a sharp pain shot through her shoulder.

Manny turned to see a kind-looking around eighteen-ish boy blushing.

He gave a soft, "Sorry," and followed it up with. "My friends were being stupid."

Then he rushed ahead to a group of his greek letter-jacket wearing friends, faceless with their backs turned and dripping Mill U ballcaps, laughing when he reached them.

Probably in undergrad, she thought, rolling her eyes at the back of their heads.

Somewhere, the low hum of a car engine rumbled, cutting through the patter of rain. Manny looked back down the alleyway, but whoever had been there, was gone. The silhouette, and whatever strange allure they had left with them. Smells of damp concrete and the faint, smokey scent of the city's breath, returned.

Manny shook her head at herself. *Clearly, they didn't need any help,* she told herself. *They were probably just some creep.*

When she was finally inside the pub, she was thankful for its warmth and loud music, the low hum of voices mixing with the clink of glasses and the crackle of a fire burning in a stone hearth at the far end of the room. The space was lit with warm lighting coming from the golden sconces that made the place feel alive with energy, buzzing with conversations and laughter that managed to echo off the wooden beams above.

Its decor was worn but charming in its own way. Dark mahogany panels lined the walls, polished to a dull gleam over years of wear, while mismatched framed pictures—some of stern-faced men in old-fashioned garb, or old drawn advertisements, others of beautiful land-scapes—all hung at odd angles.

There were low-hanging lanterns above giving an industrial-feel to the place, their brass fixtures tarnished and aged. The booths, tucked into the corners, were well-worn, the leather cracked and soft with age. There was a certain intimacy to the space, like it was built to encourage long nights with friends or lovers.

It took her a few minutes to spot her friends, and a few more to navigate around the drunken pubgoers to reach the table. They had settled into a half-booth table near the back of the pub, the cushioned curve of the booth pressed up against the far wall, while the other half was filled with sturdy wooden chairs.

Most of them were there—Shantelle "Telly" Hicks, Grant Altman, and her boyfriend, Dean Altman. Two people were missing—Wade Greene and Isla Thomson.

"Baby!" Dean said, the moment he looked at her.

He got to his feet and hugged her tightly. She hugged him back, as he placed a kiss on her forehead.

"I'm so glad you're back," he said, stroking her back.

He was one of the tallest men in the bar: a handsome, thin, lively guy, six-foot three, fair-skinned Caucasian, with feathered, wavy brown hair, a strong jawline—the first time they'd met, she thought he had an artistic look to him befitting his major. He was pursuing an MFA in Poetry, and going on that first date with him was probably one of the better decisions she'd made two years ago.

About a few weeks in, when she knew it was serious, she had explained her sexuality—where she fell in the asexual spectrum—how she had feelings for him. He didn't whine about her sexuality hampering his needs; that was a green flag. She didn't want to date anyone that complained about her sexuality or made jokes about it. She heard enough commentary from other people about her sexuality—graysexuality. Whenever she tried explaining it people acted like she'd said she loved pineapple on pizza. They would give her the *oh-you-precious-delicate-flower* face—the one they used when they thought they were being supportive but actually they were mentally patting her on the head like a confused kitten too stupid to chase a string. It was always followed by the same tired lecture about how *everyone's a little picky sometimes.* Talking about her sexuality with allosexuals felt like handing them a map they refused to read — all cheerful nodding, no real understanding. After a while, she stopped bringing it up.

Still, she was grateful, she had found a handful of people that didn't need her to be anyone other than who she was.

"I guess you got caught in the shitshow outside?" Grant asked, looking at her bleakly.

Manny laughed and nodded. "Unfortunately, the *shitshow* decided to meet me," she told him, letting Dean take off her coat for her. "But I guess it couldn't be avoided, at least it isn't snowing yet."

The *shitshow* was the rain, and Grant was her first friend in the Mill U Queer Student Society. Grant had said that was their name since Millfield University had a hierarchy whenever there was 'alliance,' 'association' or 'club' for student groups on campus specifically.

Grant was a proud bisexual man: an adopted, intelligent, spiritually in-tune, dark-skinned African American with a buzzcut, and an avid book reader. He had a naturally chiseled jawline and was six-foot-one, and between his personality and height, he often made women swoon, though he preferred to date men. Still he was the best person anyone could meet when opening up about their sexuality, he was accepting of those who accepted him. He was the younger of the Altman brothers—Manny hadn't known they were siblings until he told her. He'd said it apologetically, seeing as he hadn't told her before she had started talking about her crush on Dean. And Grant had called him his brother, though he had complicated feelings toward his adoptive parents, he did love them—perhaps Dean more so, but Dean was hard not to love.

Shantelle grimaced. "Ugh, *girl*, don't put that into the universe," she said, scrunching her nose and knocking on the wooden table. "I haven't ordered my new coat yet, and I need to be mentally prepared for when Isla starts asking me to go caroling in November."

"You're going this time?" Manny asked, hoping she looked as visibly confused as she felt. She slid into the booth and Shantelle shrugged in response. In a way that said, *maybe, who knows.* It was a mystery that would probably elude them both until the moment Isla asked came.

Shantelle, or *Telly* for short, hated the cold. It was one of the first things Manny had learned about her in the short stories class they took in undergrad. She was double-majoring in undergrad at the time. Back then she was an overachiever, but had stopped overwhelming herself after Tammy's death. She also was a witty, creative, unequivocally beautiful, dark-skinned African American, and a computer science whiz. She has a closet fascination with the occult—that she's hid from her mother as the Hicks' Christian family values didn't align with learning anything about it. But she had managed to swing getting an elective class with Manny, Grant, and Dean this semester, and a different writing course next semester.

Those classes made Manny hopeful. It meant she wouldn't have to sit alone, or try to awkwardly establish a new friend group.

"When is Wade coming?" Manny asked.

No one answered. They all hung their heads as if saddened by the thought—or maybe in shame.

Eventually Grant spoke up. "I don't know—" he trailed off for a moment looking over at the bar. "He said he wanted to practice a bit more before the season starts…he's not exactly been the same since Tammy."

"Well, the love of his life died, you can't expect too much from him," Shantelle said softly, and then she let out a long sigh. "Isla won't be coming—sorority duties and all that. They're at The Globe, as always."

Grant rolled his eyes. "I'm surprised she still hangs out with them after what they said about *scholarship kids*."

Shantelle shook her head. "She's too sweet for her own good sometimes," she said. "Probably a southern thing."

Manny nodded in silence. Though she had been hesitant to come here, she had wanted to see all of her friends. Tammy would always be missing, but she could appreciate who was here. Or at least that was how Dr. Carter had explained it.

"I'll go get us food then," Dean said with a smile, standing from his seat. "Cheese pizza, right?"

He was looking right at her with a toothy grin on his face.

"Right," Manny said, giving him a quick kiss.

"Awww," Shantelle said with a smile, as Dean walked away blushing. "I missed seeing you two around. It almost feels like the old days."

Her heart gave a painful twist.

"Yeah, the old days," Manny repeated, trying to hold her smile.

She couldn't help but stare at the vacant chair beside Grant—Tammy's chair.

The old days, she thought.

Before the gaps in their lives, before the weight of everything had come crashing down her. Even the pubgoers laughter was quieter somehow, as though it echoed from a time long gone. She remembered it all—the long nights spent talking until the sun came up, milling about Millfield, the reckless certainty of youth that everything would always be the same. But time had its way of carving into things. Life had taken a toll. The memories were still there, but everyone, they had changed. All of them.

Chapter 3
Cultural Histories of the Occult and Forbidden Knowledge
Monday, September 9th

It would have been more practical to ask someone for directions rather than wander around for almost thirty minutes trying to find the classroom. But eventually she found it, or the building at least. Winthrop Hall stood out like a sore thumb compared to the rest of the campus' classic architecture—or perhaps 'classic' for Ivy League universities. Most of the campus was constructed from red brick with ivy climbing up weathered walls and arched windows.

But this building which housed her Occult Studies class—or the more accurate course title, 'Cultural Histories of the Occult and Forbidden Knowledge'—was a sleek and modern, angular structure made of glass and steel that gleamed in the sunlight, which was a stark contrast with the timeworn brick buildings around it. The walls, made almost entirely of reflective glass, cast back the image of the surrounding campus as if trying to blend in, but it only highlighted its differences. It almost felt cold and distant, clinical even, all sharp edges and harsh lines.

Inside, the white painted walls were mostly bare, save for a few abstract art pieces, and the fluorescent lights above humming softly, casting a cool, impersonal glow. There was a sense of disconnect. But Manny supposed it made sense, seeing as the Occult Studies class was technically thrown under a branch of anthropology that existed on the fringes, exploring the strange and mystical practices that other disciplines dismissed. Since the course was an outlier, why shouldn't the building be?

The course description described it as more than just studying ancient rituals or mysterious practices—it was about challenging the established order, questioning what was accepted as "normal" in academia and society alike. She could appreciate that.

And when Manny sat down in the auditorium, she was thankful she was only the tenth student to arrive. She chose a seat in the middle row, close enough to stay focused but far enough from the front to avoid attention.

As more students trickled in, the hum of conversation rose as they too settled into their seats. Then her phone buzzed in her pocket, and she went to check it:

Shantelle
Almost there, I think. I stopped to get coffee and got you some tea. Who the hell designed this building?

Manny sighed and took a deep breath. *At least Shantelle is almost here.*

She could relax knowing that she wouldn't be alone for long. It was enough that she could see a few people from old classes pointing and whispering.

To make matters worse, two girls—both in green sorority hoodies—sat with their backs to her, their voices just loud enough for her to hear. A pale-skinned girl, her dirty blonde, highlighted hair curled to perfection, leaned over to speak to her friend.

"I mean, I'm just saying maybe we can get something out of it. Like all the girls—we can say we're in mourning for at least a few weeks, right?" Her voice oozed with insincerity. "I mean Yasmin was a Kappa. Maybe we could use that to get the professors off our backs a bit this semester."

The blonde's friend, a brown-skinned girl with ombre-dyed hair, nodded absently, texting on her phone. "I dunno, Ophelia. It's not like we knew her," she said, finally turning toward her. "She just sort of died or *whatever*...like why was she even out that late? Brian offered to walk her home."

Manny's stomach twisted, but she tried to keep her expression passive, lowering her gaze to her notebook. She didn't know these girls, had never spoken to them. But the way they spoke about their friend, 'Yasmin'—like her death was something to gossip about, or that they could use to their advantage. Isla was in their sorority, but didn't act like this.

"I mean, who even cares, Priya?" Ophelia stated, almost too cheerfully. "Yazzy wasn't that involved. If she had shown up to The Globe last night, it probably wouldn't have happened, you know? Like, no offense, but...it was completely preventable."

Last night? This was only last night, Manny thought, staring down in her notebook.

Their indifference gnawed at her. It was the fourteenth murder after almost two years—didn't that bother them? She stared at her open notebook in front of her, eyes tracing the blank lines, trying to ignore their conversation.

"You're so right," Priya said, setting her phone down. "We all know how long *you know who* used that excuse." Priya pointed behind her—at Manny.

Manny's heart sunk in her chest. They knew who she was, and she wanted to scream in frustration. But what did she expect? She had been led out of the school in handcuffs.

Someone politely saying, 'excuse me' pulled her from her thoughts. She turned just as Shantelle swept into the room with her typical energy. Shantelle was a morning person. Dressed in a baggy sweater and ripped jeans, she had a cupholder in one hand with two cups, and her backpack slung over her shoulder.

A small wave of relief washed over Manny. Shantelle saw her and smiled as she made her way down to the row.

"Well. they don't call her *Manny Manslaughter* for nothing," Ophelia whispered, and Manny knew her face dropped, because in that same moment, Shantelle's foot 'accidentally' caught on the corner of Ophelia's chair.

Then in one smooth motion, Shantelle stumbled forward, spilling both drinks—and their sticky contents—on the two sorority girls.

"Oh my God!" Ophelia shrieked, jumping up as coffee splashed onto her lap. "My laptop!"

The blonde stared in horror as her screen began to fritz.

"Oops," Shantelle said with a casual shrug, straightening and wiping her hand on her jeans. "My bad. Guess I tripped."

Priya let out a whine, gathering her things and standing up. "*Seriously*? My hair's soaked!"

Manny bit her lip, trying not to smile. Shantelle slid into the seat next to her, feigning innocence.

"Accidents happen, you know?" Shantelle whispered, then turned back to the girls. "Really, I'm so sorry about that. Total accident."

Ophelia and Priya glared at them. "We need to move. I can't deal with this right now," Ophelia snapped.

They gathered their things, bemoaning their frustrations, muttering until they were well out of earshot. Manny was grateful to see them go, and for the moment that felt like a victory. But then she caught herself, and Shantelle cocked a brow.

"What's wrong?" Shantelle asked.

Manny paused, trying to find the words. "Do you know someone named Yasmine that's a Kappa—I mean, like them."

Shantelle paused, chewing on her lip as she did.

"You mean Yasmine Brewer?" Shantelle asked, tilting her head slightly. "I mean I saw her at a few Black Student Society meetings. She was always complaining about the Kappas—said they rarely select Black students. Why?"

Manny lowered her voice. "She's *dead*."

Shantelle blinked, appearing taken aback. "Where did you hear that?"

"*They* were talking about it, before—" Manny paused, and sighed. She would have thought that by now, that gruesome nickname would be gone. She shook her head and continued. "They wanted to use her death as an excuse to get extensions."

"Damn…people can't even Rest In Peace anymore. Do you know what happened?"

"No, I don't know, but don't you think it's weird?"

Shantelle shook her head silently. "Well, people don't have any sense of empathy nowadays."

Manny nodded, staring down at her notebook. But she couldn't help but think of the stranger in the alley.

Could I have prevented it, Manny thought. *I could have gone to the police.* She shook her head at herself. *And told them what? Oh, hello officer, I think I saw someone in the alley by The Globe and it made me uncomfortable.*

It wasn't the best story. She was in the area on the same night that Yasmine died, and she had already been suspected of a murder before. Though she had been proven innocent, she wasn't sure she wanted to take her chances.

"Do you think it's weird that the school hasn't said anything?" Manny asked hesitantly, looking at Shantelle.

"Not really," Shantelle said, her expression hardening. "If it's true I doubt they're going to share anything yet. They don't want the campus in a full-blown panic." Then she let out a long sigh. "And they're an ivy, they can't have it getting out that a Black student is dead until they know something. Then they'll probably issue one of those 'we're working with the authorities' statements. If it's true, I can see if the society can drum up some sort of support for Black students. But realistically, I don't think we'll get coverage like Natasha did in undergrad…"

Manny remembered the Natasha incident—she was a white-passing mixed African American student, she'd gone missing for a weekend during undergrad. Low and behold, she'd been with her boyfriend in the next town over, completely fine. But the reaction? The all-campus alerts, the round-the-clock television coverage from Millfield News, the urgent emails about "student safety"—there was an immediate response.

But then, again, Natasha's family was wealthy and more well-connected. Unlike Tammy or Yasmine.

Shantelle sighed, her expression softening. "Look, I get it. When my cousin was shot, people barely batted an eye. They just assumed he was part of a gang because of where he lived. It didn't matter that he was a straight-A student, that he had plans for college. All they saw was... someone they could dismiss."

Manny looked at Shantelle, and immediately felt guilty. All the things people had said about him online. How Shantelle had kept it together, and it still amazed Manny to this day.

Shantelle continued. "They don't understand that when someone like Yasmine dies, it's not just a headline. It's... it's personal. And they sure as hell don't care like they did for Natasha."

Manny nodded, trying to think of what she could do. There had to be something more she could do.

Then it dawned on her. *Dr. Shepherd.*

She could ask Dr. Shepherd if he knew anything. He was the associate dean now, and he had said his door was always open to her. Maybe he could tell her something.

"I could ask Dr. Shepherd," Manny said, thinking out loud.

Shantelle raised an eyebrow. "You sure? He'll probably have to feed you some bureaucratic nonsense about 'not wanting to cause panic' or 'respecting privacy' now that he's associate dean."

"I know." Manny took a deep breath, feeling the familiar knot of anxiety tighten in her chest. "But I can't just...let it go. I have to do something. Yasmine deserves that much."

Shantelle studied her for a moment, then nodded in approval. "All right. If you're serious about it, I'll go with you. I don't want you to go alone."

Manny was about to respond when someone sat down beside her, and she turned to see Dean. Grant and Isla were directly behind him.

"So, what are you two talking about?" Dean asked with a cheerful smile, giving Manny a kiss on the cheek.

"Everything all right?" Grant sat down and exchanged a look with Shantelle. "You good, girl?"

Shantelle shrugged.

"You need coffee?" Grant asked, cocking a brow. "What happened to your pants?"

"Long story," Shantelle said.

Isla walked over to the seat next to Shantelle and sat down.

"Yeah, you smell like coffee, what's that about?" Isla asked.

Isla Thomson was sporting a cheery smile and her sorority hoodie: her pretty doll-like face was framed by her shiny blonde hair with black bangs. She was naturally statuesque, bright-eyed, and a proud Scottish American with pale-skin. She was from Houston and had come to Mill U on a scholarship in their undergrad, Shantelle had been her roommate, and she had added numerous southern phrases to Shantelle's vocabulary.

"I spilt some on those girls over there," Shantelle whispered to Isla.

Isla nodded slowly and then shrugged. "Hmph, I'm sure they deserved it."

"They were using *that* nickname," Manny explained to her.

"Then they *definitely* deserved it," Isla said, pulling out her laptop from her bag.

Dean grimaced. "I'm sorry. I can come to class with you next time," he said, glaring in the girls' direction.

"Damn you got her laptop too," Grant asked, looking at Shantelle amused.

Shantelle nodded.

Grant nodded back. "So, what *exactly* happened?"

Then Shantelle explained the little bit she knew of the conversation, as at the time the *Manny Manslaughter* bit was all that had mattered to her, and the moment she spent deciding between their drinks and Manny's good name. The latter had won. Manny explained what the girls, Ophelia and Priya, were talking about. This brought a look of disgust across everyone's faces.

"And I was thinking about talking to Dr. Shepherd about it after class," Manny finished. "If anyone would know, he would."

"You think he'll tell you?" Grant asked in disbelief. "I mean, yeah, they have no respect for the dead. But that's *if* she's dead. I don't think the Kappas really pay attention to their littles—remember Natasha? And Dr. Shepherd's great and all, but he just got promoted. I can't see him helping."

Manny sighed and shook her head. "I can at least try asking him."

They stared at each other for a long time, communicating wordlessly. Grant wanted to convince her it was a waste of time. But Manny wasn't going to give up so easily.

A loud slam drew her attention to the front of the auditorium as a tall man, walking with an effortless grace waltzed into the room, and began writing his name on the board. Professor Beau Moreau was a distinguished man: porcelain white skin, smooth and flawless, marble-like with a chiseled jawline to match. When he turned around, it was impossible to tell where he was looking, but when his eyes briefly passed over her, a shiver ran down her spine.

His hair was dark, nearly black, and perfectly tousled in a way that suggested he hadn't tried at all, yet it was somehow flawless. He tossed his coat over a chair at his desk, and his vest was cut in a way that accentuated his broad shoulders. On top of it all he had the faintest hint of stubble on his face, adding a rugged edge to his otherwise polished appearance, and it only made him more handsome.

"Damn," Grant said, saying what she was thinking.

Professor Beau Moreau sat his briefcase down on the desk and cleared his throat, scanning the room with a stern but detached expression.

"Good afternoon, everyone," he began, his voice carrying the kind of authority that made even the noisiest students fall silent. "Welcome to Cultural Histories of the Occult and Forbidden Knowledge. I am Professor Beau Moreau—but we're all adults here so you can call me, Beau."

Manny looked down, staring blankly at her notebook, the lines on the page swimming in and out of focus.

God, am I having a panic attack, Manny wondered.

It wouldn't be the first time she had one. She hadn't quite figured out how to stop them yet.

"Since it's our first class, we'll just go through the syllabus, I'll answer some questions and we'll get out of here early," Beau said, looking around the classroom again. "Does that sound good to everyone?"

Heads bobbed around the classroom in agreement. With that he passed out the syllabus, the papers shuffling around until one landed on Manny's desk. She could hardly manage to focus on it. In fact, she was actively trying to, but her thoughts kept going back to Yasmin Brewer. When would the school announce something? Anything? Her pen hovered above the page, but she couldn't bring herself to write.

"This class," Beau was saying, his voice finally pulling her attention back to the front of the room, "is about more than just the supernatural. It's about understanding belief systems, the power of ritual, and the way venturing into the unknown has shaped human history."

His words should have intrigued her. A few years ago she would've been excited to get into a class like this. But today, she just felt withdrawn.

Her heart pounded in her chest. *Manny Manslaughter*—would she ever get rid of that dreadful nickname? Everyone knew she didn't do it. Though Tammy's killer was never caught. It was clear it wasn't her. She still wanted to scream, to make them feel the way she did—lost, angry, hurt.

She gripped her pen tightly. *Going to the associate dean makes sense, doesn't it?* She thought, questioning herself.

A chime from someone's phone pulled her from her thoughts. A ping came from another student then another. Notifications pings echoed all throughout the classroom and students checked their devices. Then an unmistakable *brrr* came from her phone on her half-desk.

She picked up her phone, and turned on the screen. The subject line of the email stood out immediately:

Campus Safety Advisory

Dear Students,

In light of the recent and tragic loss of one of our own, Yasmine

Brewer, we are working closely with local authorities to ensure the safety of our campus community. We have been assured that the ongoing investigation into her death is high priority, and we ask for your cooperation as we navigate this difficult time.

Thus, we are advising all students to take extra precautions, particularly in the evening, and to avoid isolated areas on and off campus. We strongly recommend walking in pairs or groups and utilizing campus security services when possible. Please report any suspicious activity to campus security immediately.

We understand the impact this has had on many of you, and our campus counseling services are available for anyone in need of support. Additional campus safety patrols will be conducted, and we will provide further updates as needed. The safety and well-being of our students remains our top priority.

Thank you for your understanding and commitment to keeping our community safe.

Sincerely,

Eugene S. Hargreaves

President

Manny could feel a pit growing in her stomach. She wasn't sure whether she should be grateful for the confirmation or not. Yasmine had died. But there was no utterance of a *how*—even more so, she wanted an answer as to *why*. Them advising students to "walk with a buddy" was practical, but still didn't feel like enough.

"Well, at least they have her name in it," Grant said.

The words stung. But he was right—they hadn't put in Tammy's name when she'd been murdered.

Chapter 4
Monday Evening, September 9th

Manny had an easier time navigating Tremont Hall that evening—power walking in a way that drew a few sideways glances, though no one stopped her. Although she could partially attribute that to being on her phone, reading about Yasmine's death, where the body was found though the details were limited. Which was to be expected—she had just died—they still needed to notify her family. But she could also attribute it to the sheer nervous dread of the moment being equally etched on her face as it was in her frantically beating heart. When she reached Dr. Shepherd's office in the administration wing, she was glad when his executive assistant quickly ushered her inside.

"Oh, Manny, what a wonderful surprise," Dr. Shepherd said with a warm smile. "What brings you in today?"

He gestured at the seat in front of his desk and Manny sat down in it.

Manny paused, her fingers curling tightly around her messenger bag's strap. "I actually wanted to ask about something." She hesitated, then pressed on. "I wanted to know if you'd received any updates about the investigation into the MillU Murders—after what's just happened to Yasmine."

Manny paused, and Dr. Shepherd's expression shifted, suddenly taking on a composed, measured look that she'd seen before.

"The girl they sent the email out about?" Manny asked.

She thought gently probing him would work—maybe he wouldn't deflect. But then again, maybe he would.

Dr. Shepherd took off his glasses and cleaned them, sitting down at his desk. His neatly pressed suit wrinkling as he did so.

But his expression faltered for a moment—so brief that if she hadn't been watching closely, she might have missed it. He knew something.

"Ah, yes. Yasmine, truly tragic. They don't tell us much, but there's no new information. I'm not sure what else I can say, but the authorities are handling it, and we've been advised to let them do their work."

Manny frowned—Grant was right, he wasn't going to be any help. "I understand, but don't you find it strange? The news says they found claw marks on Yasmine—just like Tammy."

Dr. Shepherd shifted in his chair, his fingers steepling together. "So, this is about Tammy....you know, Manny, these things take time. I assure you, the school is doing everything it can to support the investigation." His eyes softened and then he said. "Have you thought about calling Dr. Carter and seeing if she could move up your next appointment? I know this must be hard for you…"

She knew he meant well, but his words still stung. Manny forced herself to ignore it and press on. She could hardly believe this was the man that stressed the importance of Black student empowerment a Black Literature course years ago.

"Yasmine Brewer," Manny repeated, feeling her pulse quicken. "Was found behind a dumpster in an alleyway. She was a Black student, who went to our school. Don't you think it's odd for there to be fourteen deaths—most of which have been Black students only a little over a year apart? Tammy and Yasmine both had claw marks on their back. I mean wouldn't that at least hint at the same murderer?"

Dr. Shepherd shook his head dismissively. "The authorities don't believe there's any connection between the MillU Murders and Yasmin's death—in fact, it was the first concern most Black professors raised. But it's just an unfortunate circumstance—wrong place, wrong time."

Wrong place, wrong time? He must be joking, she thought.

"Wrong place, wrong time? Do you hear yourself?"

"I understand your frustration," he said quickly, his tone dismissive, almost bored. "And your concern is valid, but the police are handling it."

The idea that it was merely coincidence—that Yasmine had just wandered into an alleyway and met a tragic end—seemed too convenient. There was no reason for anyone to go down that alley to get back to the university. She was supposed to be attending a sorority and fraternity social at The Globe. Why would she take a detour down an alleyway that's almost five blocks away from that bar?

Manny nodded slowly, and hoped it looked like she was agreeing with him. "I see. Thank you, Dr. Shepherd."

He gave her a small smile, clearly relieved the conversation was ending. "Of course, Manny. If you need anything else, my door is always open."

Manny stood and gave him a polite nod before turning toward the door.

As she left, their conversation repeated in her head, and she still couldn't shake that the two murders were connected. Was she just being paranoid? Making connections that simply weren't there? Maybe she should talk to Dr. Carter. Maybe she did need another appointment. And yet, though Dr. Shepherd had said all the right things—none of it felt right.

She couldn't shake the feeling that something was very, very wrong.

* * *

When she stepped outside, she sighed and immediately wished she had brought her umbrella. She hated when the weatherman got the forecast wrong. Manny looked for her friends, and smiled when she spotted them waiting by a brick tunnel in between two buildings. They were huddled together under the overhang, staying dry. Shantelle was talking animatedly to Grant and Isla, and they laughed. Though Isla kept looking up at the sky as if she was willing the rain to stop any second. Next to them, her boyfriend, Dean, was leaning against the tunnel wall, staring at his phone. Of course, he spotted her first.

Manny smiled at him and waved. But as Manny walked toward them, she found herself slowing, as she noticed something unusual. It wasn't anything about her friends, or the bridge itself—but a spot nearby a lamppost, where a weathered plaque was set into the brick wall. She had passed under this bridge dozens of times before in undergrad, but this was the first time she'd seen it.

There were plenty of commemorative bronze plaques around campus, but something about the symbol underneath these funders' names confused her. It was subtle. But now that she was standing there, the symbol seemed to shimmer faintly beneath the water droplets. Its design resembled runes or an ancient sigils, though she didn't know its meaning.

"Hey, baby, ready to go?" Dean asked, pulling her from her thoughts.

Manny turned, and stared at him blankly. Her friends were still huddled beneath the tunnel, waiting for her. Now each with a look of concern on their face.

Dean's arm wrapped around her waist, and he pulled her in close. "You all right?"

"Yeah, girl, what are you looking at?" Shantelle asked, walking over with Grant and Isla.

"Just… something weird on the wall," Manny replied, uneasily as she stared at it.

Dean glanced over his shoulder at the plaque and shrugged. "Oh, that? Yeah, those things are all over campus. They've been there forever."

Manny bit her lip. "Really? I've never noticed that symbol before."

"Yeah, there's a bunch near those really old buildings on the northside of campus, too," Dean continued, unfazed. "I remember because one of those religious societies was petitioning to have them removed."

Grant laughed and smirked. "Of course, they did," he said, rolling his eyes and then he looked at Manny. "Maybe they're warding off witches…" he said, playfully nudging Manny. "You know, the school's founder was descended from Salem witch hunters, right?"

Manny stared at him. "Wait, what?"

"Yeah, it's a whole thing," Isla chimed in, with her thick southern accent. "They tell the freshmen about it in their cohort welcome presentation session. I saw it five times in August when I was working in the auditorium."

Manny shook her head. "Are you sure?"

"Okay, enough with the spooky, occult talk," Shantelle said. "Can we please get out of this rain and to the pub? I'm starving and I could use a triple cheese pizza."

Manny's stomach growled and she nodded in agreement. Dean took her hand, and they made their way to the pub. After a while, she was back in the moment, the air filled with laughter and talk about the rest of the week's classes. And she decided if she was still concerned about the sigil-looking symbol tomorrow that she would look at it in the library. Besides, she didn't have class on Tuesdays or Fridays; that had been her gift to herself.

Chapter 5
Tuesday, September 10th

Manny blinked awake, faintly registering the soft light filtering in through the curtains, the remnants of last night's rain still clinging to the windows. Beside her, Dean was still fast asleep, his arm draped over her waist, holding her close. For a moment, she considered staying there, letting his body heat slowly lull her back to sleep. But she wasn't tired, in fact, her mind was already racing—switching between snippets of her conversation with Dr. Shepherd and the strange symbol—and she wasn't sure how much longer she could bear it.

Slowly, she shifted, carefully lifting Dean's arm and sliding out of bed without waking him. His hand twitched but stayed limp as she moved, giving her just enough room to swing her legs over the side of the bed and stand up. The wooden floor creaked under her bare feet, but Dean didn't stir. Manny considered giving him a kiss on the cheek, but didn't want to wake him. Instead she smiled down at him before putting on her slippers, grabbing her phone off of the nightstand and padding quietly out of the room. She shut the door behind her and sighed.

Her apartment felt still with only the faint hum of the fridge and the occasional drip of leftover rain from the gutters outside to keep her company. So, she started off her day as she normally would: she went to the kitchen, filled the electric tea kettle, switched it on to bring it to a boil, and looked at the time on her phone.

7 o'clock. Tea first, then the news.

She needed to know if there had been any updates on Yasmine's case.

While the kettle warmed, Manny opened the gallery app on her phone, swiping until she reached the photo she'd taken outside last night.

And there it was, the symbol, protruding from the metal with unnerving precision, still bothering her as much this morning as when she'd first seen it by the bridge.

What the hell is going on, she thought.

She'd noticed it when they were on their way up to her apartment, after their pub run—that same symbol, or something close to it, had been woven into the treelike design of the lamp post outside her on-campus apartment.

The kettle whistled, snapping her back to reality. She shook herself, and tossed a tea bag into a mug. She had slept well, but she could already tell it was going to be a rough morning.

Manny poured the hot water into the mug, watching as the dark liquid bloomed and swirled, filling the air with a rich, cinnamon scent. She sat down on the couch, cradling her mug, and reached for the TV remote.

Clicking it on, she flipped through channel after channel until she reached the morning news. Her breath caught in her throat when a segment on Yasmine flashed across the screen, though she wouldn't have known it was her without her name underneath a smiling photo of a girl. It was a selfie, maybe from her instagram, but she was wearing a t-shirt with her sorority's letters.

Manny turned up the volume, until she could actually hear the news anchor. She was olive toned with freckles and ginger hair, with a grim expression on her face.

"...Authorities have yet to release any updates on the murder of Yasmine Brewer, the MillU sorority student found dead earlier this week. Investigators are reportedly still combing through evidence, but no suspects have been named. Students at the university are advised to stay cautious and avoid walking alone at night."

She almost groaned aloud—the news anchor was basically echoing the email they'd all received. All the same canned warnings, no real answers. Manny frowned, gripping her mug tighter.

"...now here's Larry on the scene. Larry..."

Another news anchor appeared on-screen, at a different location—the alleyway. He was standing in front of police tape, and seemed ready to repeat the exact same things the previous news anchor had.

"...here behind me is the alley that..."

Manny's heart dropped. The news anchor's voice seemed to muffle as the camera panned to the alleyway.

No, it can't be.

She couldn't zoom in on her tv screen, but between the image on her phone and the one on-screen, she didn't doubt it—they were the same. The exact same symbol.

"...authorities say that someone spray painted this symbol in the middle of the night," news anchor Larry said, pointing to the symbol on the wall. "But they haven't had any luck catching the perpetrator. Or linking them to Yasmine's murder..."

What the hell is this thing? she thought, staring down at her phone.

She needed to find out more about this symbol.

Setting her mug down, she grabbed her laptop from the coffee table and opened it. She typed in a few quick search terms: *ancient symbols, university symbols, occult markings.* Page after page of results blinked into view, most of them irrelevant. But after a few clicks, she finally stumbled onto something that made her pause.

A website, old and poorly formatted, detailing obscure markings found at certain universities with historic ties to the occult. Manny slowly scrolled down the page until she reached a grainy image of a symbol that looked similar to the one she'd photographed. According to the text it was some kind of warding.

The text beside it read:

Ancient protection symbol, believed to ward off or trap malevolent spirits. Some debate on the intended usage. Often associated with Christian Wiccans and secret societies dating back to the early-18th century. Creator: Unknown. Time of creation: Unknown. See Symbols and Runes.

Manny's skin prickled as she stared at the screen. She looked out her living room window, staring at the lamppost outside.

"What the hell?" she whispered to herself.

Something strange was going on—and it had to be connected with at least Yasmine's murder. Bile rose in her throat. Something *was* very, very wrong.

Behind her, she heard Dean stirring in the bedroom and glanced back at it. What would he think of all this? Would he think she was going crazy?

She was sitting here, combing through poorly maintained websites and cryptic forums, searching for this sigil—Sigil of the Warden, or the *Wardens' Sigil* in modern language. And according to more obscure sources, it was far older than the university itself. But before she could go down another rabbit hole, she heard the shower in her bathroom start.

"Baby, I'm just going to shower, I'll be right out," Dean shouted.

Manny hesitated, glancing between the door and the screen.

That'll take a good 30 to 40 minutes, she thought. Which at the moment was a good thing.

So, she shouted back, "Okay, my love!"

She typed *'The Wardens' Sigil'* into a search engine, and new articles appeared. The sigil appeared in ancient texts, particularly tied to a language that was mentioned several times across various arcane forums—*Enochian.*

Manny grimaced at the page, she'd never heard of it. She clicked through a few more articles until she found an explanation. *Enochian* was a language believed to be the 'language of angels,' developed in the late 16th century by the occultists John Dee and Edward Kelley. It was supposedly used to communicate with higher powers, particularly angels, and was often linked to rituals involving protection, summoning, and control.

As she scanned the pages of dense text, the disquieting sensation in her stomach spread. *If* this sigil wasn't some decorative emblem placed on plaques or sporadically around the university. It was something more important, and if these sources were right, it was tied to powerful Enochian magic—magic designed to bind or trap entities. The so-called 'Wardens' Sigil' had reportedly been used in the past by secret societies to "guard spaces" and to keep unwanted forces at bay.

She opened a new tab, typing in the university's name along with the founder's.

The MillU website had a waxed poetic biography about the university's founder, Ezekiel S. Abernathy—he had built the institution from the ground up in the mid-1800s. He was a wealthy industrialist with connections in politics, known for his philanthropic work.

Manny clicked through another set of search results until one particular link caught her eye—a link to a blog post from an amateur historian detailing Abernathy's alleged involvement in occult practices. According to the post, Abernathy had been part of a secret society called 'The Wardens of the Gate,' a group that had supposedly dabbled in Enochian rituals to gain power. The blog claimed that Abernathy had embedded Enochian symbols into the architecture of the university, ensuring that certain places on campus would remain "guarded from malevolent entities and evil spirits."

She craned her head, overwhelmed by the information. Could all of this be true? Or were these just wild conspiracy theories? And *if* it was true—what the hell did it mean? What was Abernathy so afraid of that he'd practically decorated the whole university in this sigil?

Manny leaned into the couch, trying to process it all.

Rituals to bind or control malevolent entities, Manny thought, shaking her head at herself. *This is stupid. If he was doing this, which one was Abernathy trying to do? And was it failing or succeeding?*

She couldn't imagine this man trying to destroy the university he built. So, maybe he was trying to lock something away, and maybe those sigils were failing. But it wasn't like she would even know where to begin.

And then there was Yasmine. Was her death a coincidence? Or was it somehow connected to that malevolent entity, possibly leaking out?

A chill ran down her spine as she looked at the sigil again. Then shook her head at herself again.

It could've been a conspiracy theorist that had spray painted that sigil into the alleyway, Manny told herself. *Or it was some undergrads playing a prank and seeing if anyone buys it. Or there was some murderer on the loose that was going back to his crime scenes to spray paint symbols on the walls like a calling card.*

Manny rolled her eyes at herself. People back in the 18th century were suspicious of witchcraft. There were people suspicious nowadays about witchcraft. It was hardly something she needed to worry about, especially in her first week of classes.

* * *

She and Dean spent all afternoon together, cuddling and watching movies. She didn't mention the sigil or any of her findings. She decided that she couldn't tell him without some sort of concrete evidence. But thought it might be fun to bring up to her friends, as a *hey, look what I found* sort of thing. Shantelle and Grant were interested in spiritual things and this seemed right up their alley. She texted them to meet her at the Black Stag to hang out—and invited Wade and Isla too. Dean had two evening classes, so she doubted he'd show up.

"Hey, you made it!" Isla called out, scooting over to make room for Manny in the booth.

Manny slid into the booth, dropping her bag onto the floor. "Yeah, I couldn't think of anything to do," she said. "I was glad when Dean got up. He said he might swing by later."

Grant grinned. "I still don't know how you manage to get him up so early. He sure as hell doesn't when he's in our apartment."

"Well, what can I say?" Manny shrugged. "I guess I'm like a weighted blanket. Except for this morning…" she said, trailing off.

"Oh no, bad dream," Shantelle asked, reaching for her drink. "Please tell me you didn't fall asleep to one of those true crime podcasts."

Manny rolled her eyes, but she still smiled. "No, not this time. And that was one time, and it was an accident. It was just that thing I saw on campus yesterday." She said, pointing at Grant's fries, and he pushed them toward her. "That weird symbol on the plaque, it's not random. I looked it up. It's called the Wardens' Sigil. Apparently, it's tied to some old Enochian magic."

Her friends exchanged concerned glances, but none of them said anything.

Grant raised an eyebrow. "Wait. Magic? On campus? Are you feeling okay?"

Manny nodded, her voice picking up. "Yeah, I just found it weird. I saw it on a lamppost outside my apartment too. And there's some weird connection to the university's founder…"

Someone laughed behind her, as he sat his drink on the table. "Don't tell me that occult studies class already has you four talking about conspiracy theories," the familiar voice said.

Manny smiled up at him. *Wade.*

She hadn't seen him since Tammy's funeral. Today he looked more like himself. Wade Greene was tall: he was about six foot five, handsome, dark-skinned African American with an athletic figure that could be attributed to him playing basketball most of his life. He had gotten a full ride scholarship from MillU and had been on the team since undergrad. Tammy used to say, *I'm sure he'll get scouted, they'd be stupid not to scout him.* And she wasn't wrong, he was a great player. He was kind-hearted and gentle, and he'd loved Tammy with all his heart. He'd wanted to marry her. She could still remember how giddy Tammy would get whenever she'd talk about him—and the way he looked at her. Wade was such a good man, he deserved whatever success came his way.

"It's good to see you, Wade," Manny said, smiling up at him.

Wade nodded. "Good to see you too! Glad your back," he told her, sitting down beside Shantelle. “Now, what are you guys talking about?”

“Some old symbol around campus,” Shantelle said, brushing it off. “Apparently it’s linked to Enochian magic?” She turned toward Manny, and she nodded. “I mean, it sounds cool and all, but what’s the worst that could happen? Abernathy rises from the grave and decides to pop in as a guest lecturer in Professor Moreau’s class?”

Manny couldn’t help but laugh. “Yeah, you’re probably right. I’m sure it’s nothing,” Manny rolled her eyes at herself again. “If it’s still bothering me tomorrow, I’ll swing by the library or something—maybe there’s a book that can clear things up.”

“That’s the spirit,” Shantelle said, raising her glass. “Or you could leave the ghost hunting until after midterms.”

They all laughed and clinked their glasses. For the rest of the night, Manny tried to push the thoughts of the sigil and Ezekiel Abernathy’s supposed involvement in secret societies and Enochian magic to the back of her mind. She could deal with it tomorrow.

But as she sat there, ordering rounds of drinks with her friends, listening to them joke about their professors and complain about upcoming projects, she couldn’t stop thinking about the sigil. And though she tried to ignore it, every instinct, every nerve inside her body was telling her something was going on—and she needed to find out what.

Chapter 6
Wednesday, September 11th

The Tempest, Macbeth, even *A Midsummer Night's Dream*—all focused on mystical forces, interwoven into the human experience. And as the teller in the bookstore portion of the Hub & Haven sat them down in front of her, ringing up her booklist, Manny couldn't help but think she should drop two of her classes—her occult studies and her Shakespeare early-1900s class. She wanted to put this whole sigil thing behind her—it had already taken up two nights in her life, and she couldn't let it take up anymore.

Every Wednesday Manny attended her Shakespeare early-1900s class—she had added it to her class schedule because, in her mind, it would round it out, and her Women's Fiction class was every Thursday. Every Friday she was going to see her therapist Dr. Carter, and that'd be the hardest part of her week. Because they would talk about everything that was going on with her. If she was capable of describing everything bothering her, and then pinpointing the source of her problems, but that was a big *if*—given she was currently in the midst of it. Then her nightmares would come back, and so would those horrible, macabre images of Tammy.

Luckily, when she left the Hub & Haven, she considered taking the long way around to avoid going through central campus, but it was the fastest route to the Abernathy Library—and she'd have to pass through it eventually if she wanted to be on time for her class Thursday.

Manny took a deep breath, clutching her shopping tote tightly, and slowly made her way across the bridge. There were students lounging along the railing, some leaning over the edge to watch the slow-moving river below. On warmer days there were friend groups huddled together, laughing and taking selfies, sometimes there were couples gazing out at the autumn trees lining the water. Occasionally there were a few art students sketching the view for whatever art class they were taking. As she passed, she overheard fragments of conversations about rumored pop quizzes, weekend plans, and upcoming parties.

It was almost pleasant how normal everything was. There were the usual impromptu picnic set-ups near the fountain, and students that were perched on the edges, undeterred by the overcast sky. Some were dipping their hands in the water to rinse them from whatever they'd been eating.

Manny studied the students around her, briefly wondering how many of them knew that Tammy had died in the exact spot they were comfortably lounging in. That there was a plaque right near the fountain's base—or if it simply hadn't mattered when they sat down. It was just another plaque they'd happened to see, or not see, probably never noticing the epitaph: *beloved daughter, devoted student...*

It had probably gone without ever being read by anyone but those who Tammy mattered to—and she didn't know why it bothered her just that it did.

* * *

When students first entered the Abernathy Library they'd see portraits of esteemed alumni, antique globes, and displays of rare manuscripts encased in glass. The library itself had multiple floors of bookshelves and sitting areas, though the top floor still managed to have large arched windows to bathe it in natural light, lending indoor lighting and desk lamps adorning every wooden table to provide light for visiting students. Then there were other nooks and crannies that created intimate study spaces, many of which were already in use.

Manny was surprised to see so many people in the Abernathy Library.

She was lucky enough to reserve a study room for three hours. Albeit, half the time, the Abernathy Library's study rooms weren't being used for studying—at least the ones on the second floor—she'd learned that her freshman year at MillU. Particularly, about how the second-floor study rooms were notorious for their frosted windows, suspicious muffled giggles, and the occasional thunk of something hitting the table—the latter two details were likely to be ignored. Student library assistants weren't paid enough to care if someone's conjugating verbs or just…*conjugating*. Today, she planned to hope to God the soundproofing held up. She was here for research, not a live demonstration of *Fifty Shades of Coursework.*

Manny was hoping that if she found anything in that time, it would at least be useful. Luckily, she hadn't heard anything, so far. So, she sat her bag down on the floor and shut the study room door behind her—not that it mattered much in terms of privacy.

She took out her laptop and opened it. Re-opening her web browser to the school library's web page to continue her search, though she decided not to log in, in some ways worrying that this web search would be linked to her search history. The last thing she needed was something setting off the system, and someone alerting Dr. Carter—though she wasn't sure if the school kept track of students' search history—better to be safe than sorry.

Manny sifted through dozens of articles, hoping to uncover anything linked to the strange symbol and the town's history. Finally, an article caught her eye: *A Legacy of Curses and Mischief: Occult Practices and Folklore in Millfield* by Celia Morales, PhD. Celia was an Afro-Latina scholar who had been a beloved faculty member of Millfield University—before her sudden passing, unsettlingly the same year Tammy died. There was only one other author of the article—Beau Moreau.

Well, at least I know who to talk to, Manny thought, staring at Beau's name.

But when she clicked on the link to the article, a paywall blocked her from viewing it. Manny groaned aloud.

Looks like it doesn't matter, Manny told herself, and sighed. *Well, if anyone asks, I'll just chalk it up to being in Moreau's class.*

She quickly logged in using her student ID, and clicked the link again.

This time the article loaded, and she began reading the article. At first she didn't find anything interesting, then she paused on information about the town's founder: Nicholas F. Abernathy, his involvement with a woman, an outsider, rumored to be a witch, before his marriage to a more "acceptable" bride. As the story went, the spurned woman, seeking vengeance, had cursed the town and the founder's bloodline, promising suffering and misfortune for those connected to him. Though the Abernathy family still managed to thrive and notably became the wealthiest family in the province. However, the curse, Morales argued, was believed to have embedded itself in the foundation of where the university was eventually laid, with its reach extending through generations.

Or more lengthily:

> *The rumored witch's curse is said to predate the establishment of Millfield University, reflecting a longstanding cautionary tale against the pursuit of forbidden knowledge. The Abernathy Witch is left nameless, neglected and subjected to no other importance outside of her connection to him. Perhaps this is why the curse annihilated those associated with him.*
>
> *Folklore surrounding the curse emphasizes the Abernathy witch's vengeful nature, specifically preying on students and scholars, which aligns with themes from the biblical story of Adam and Eve. Much like the serpent in Genesis, which tempts Eve with the fruit of knowledge, the curse is believed to lure individuals into transgressing boundaries of acceptable knowl-*

edge, symbolically punishing them for their intellectual ambition. Historically, accounts and folklore frequently center on the tragic fates of female students, archival records reveal that male and possibly non-binary students were also among its victims. This discrepancy raises questions about why the narratives and documentation of the curse's impact emphasizes female victims, even as the curse itself is believed to have affected all knowledge-seekers, regardless of gender.

Though Morales also doubted the unnamed woman was a witch at all, stating:

Historical records indicate that most individuals accused of witchcraft, particularly women, were not practitioners of any occult or supernatural arts. Instead, they frequently possessed characteristics or lifestyles that diverged from societal expectations, marking them as targets in a climate of suspicion and superstition. Many of the accused were outspoken women, reclusive women, or women who defied traditional gender roles and norms, traits which made them more vulnerable to charges of witchcraft.

Furthermore, personal rivalries and grievances also fueled accusations. Envy of a neighbor's physical appearance, resentment over unreciprocated romantic or sexual advances, or even a person's rumored or actual romantic interest in a member of the same sex could quickly transform interpersonal tensions into allegations of witchcraft. Men and women alike might have made these accusations, but women were disproportionately accused and punished. In such high-stakes environments, accused individuals were often pressured to implicate others to avoid or lessen their own punishment, leading to a devastating chain reaction where accusations spread rapidly through communities.

Leading these so-called 'witches' to more likely be individuals whose nonconformity or mere existence posed a perceived threat to the social order, as communities projected fears of supernatural influence onto those who were marginalized, outspoken, or otherwise at odds with prevailing cultural values.

But there was nothing on the witch herself. No description of her, not even a name. At least if there were a name, Manny could research her. Find something, *anything* on her. But if there were anything it'd be in the town records, which meant a trip to the town archive.

Do I even want to go to the town archives? Manny thought, rolling her eyes at herself. *I don't have time for this.*

She bookmarked the article, and got onto her therapist's website. Scrolling until she found the patient login, and logged in to create an emergency meeting time. Luckily, she could have one within the next few hours, which was only for an hour—and she had two left in the study room. Though she didn't have any use for them. So, she gathered her things, made her way back to her apartment, turned on Millfield University's streaming service—MillU TV—and started adding the entire Scream series onto her watchlist, and let them play.

* * *

Manny had made it halfway through the movie, eyes drooping slightly from staring at her laptop for too long, but nothing she couldn't handle. Unfortunately, at some point, she must've dozed off, because she woke to the glare of her laptop burning into her retinas, and half-wondered if she was back in the police interrogation room. But, no, she was still half-wrapped in her blanket cocoon and vaguely remembered falling asleep. Although, now there was some marginally recognizable romcom she considered so saccharine it should come with a warning for diabetics playing on her MillU TV streaming browser. Definitely not from her watchlist.

She was working her way through the *Scream* series—for educational purposes—because it's always good to know what not to do when a masked murderer starts a killing spree in your quaint little town. Except the school's streaming service, as it's prone to do, must've decided to take one of its patented "detours." A quick switch from campy slasher horror to swooning leads about to undergo their miscommunication trope.

Squinting at the screen, Manny groggily attempted to close the tab with MillU TV streaming service, but as she absentmindedly tapped the spacebar to pause the Movie-That-Shall-Not-Be-Named, she managed to open the wrong window entirely, and Dr. Evelyn Carter, her therapist, popped up on her screen.

"Shit," Manny hissed, wiping the drool from her chin. Dr. Carter craned her head. "Sorry, Dr. Carter."

Manny muted the browser MillU TV was still streaming on.

"It's all right, Manny. What's on your mind today?" Dr. Carter asked, probing gently.

Manny hesitated. Dr. Carter's expression was a mix of shock and concern, though that didn't surprise Manny. Her hair was probably doing its best impression of a bird's nest, and she was still clutching a half-empty can of Coke like a life preserver.

Give me a break, she thought. After all, she was still waking up. But she also wasn't quite sure what she wanted to talk about. None of her worries were going to make sense to the average person today.

"I don't know if you've heard, but a girl died on campus—Yasmine Brewer…it made me think of Tammy. And it's been over a year, but it still feels like…like it just happened."

Dr. Carter nodded, her eyes softening. "Loss like that doesn't follow a timeline. You went through an incredibly traumatic experience, and it's natural for it to linger, especially when other stressors come up. It's normal to create those connections."

Other stressors. She meant coursework—of course, Dr. Carter would think it was university-related stress.

"It's just lately, things have felt off," Manny admitted. "Like something is wrong, you know?" She paused, trying to decide how much she should tell Dr. Carter. She didn't think it was worth mentioning her search history over the past two days. But she didn't want Yasmine's death to trigger her—to make everything go back to the way things were when Tammy died. Back when she was spiraling, when she was living outside her body. The waking dreams that landed her in the middle of a street and then on a hospital watchlist. "And…I guess I just don't want to lose control again."

Dr. Carter nodded thoughtfully, perhaps even encouragingly. "You're not losing control, Manny. What you're describing—struggling with unresolved emotions, and dealing with those memories are all what we're working on now—this is all part of healing from your trauma. What you've been through isn't something many experience, and certainly isn't something you should deal with alone. Which is why it's good that you reached out to me. Have you considered also talking to your friends about how you're feeling?"

Manny glanced sideways at her screen. The romcom couple is mid-kiss now and the lighting was soft and golden. Even the music was uplifting—according to the captions. Then she looked down at the table, she wasn't sure she wanted to bring up Tammy with them, they had all dealt with it in their own way. She was the only one not moving on, and now she was bringing up Yasmine's death constantly.

"A bit," Manny lied, keeping it vague. "I don't want to burden them, though. And I don't think… I'm *not sure* they'd understand," she said, correcting herself.

"I know that you would rather handle things on your own, but it's okay to rely on others for support. Just because they might not understand everything doesn't mean they don't want to be there for you," Dr. Carter said, giving her a warm smile. "And you also need to take steps to take care of yourself. It's important…" she hesitated, trailing off for a moment. "Have you been getting enough sleep?"

Manny shrugged. "Yes, I have."

There's a beat of silence, just long enough for Manny to contemplate closing the tab and pretending this never happened. She'd never scheduled an appointment—or maybe she could email Dr. Carter afterward claiming her laptop disconnected mid-call. But before she could reach for the trackpad, Dr. Carter said, "And what about *the* dreams? Have you had any more of those?"

"No, I haven't," Manny answered. There were bits and pieces of the last dream she'd had that concerned Dr. Carter: a heavy, rusted iron door with words carved into it in a language she didn't know, distant, disembodied voices merging together in a distant, rhythmic chant, and the chanting growing louder as she ran. Or at least she thinks she was running. But no matter how hard fast she did, how desperately she tried to get away, the darkness just stretched on forever.

God, no.

"Everything has been normal on that front. I just…fell asleep on the couch. I'll book another session later. Promise."

But the memory of it made a shiver go down her spine, and Manny hoped Dr. Carter wouldn't notice. Dr. Carter gave her a look that said *I don't believe you, but fine*, and Manny hastily clicked out of the call before she could pry any further.

This is why she needed tea at night. And maybe a new therapist.

Chapter 7
Thursday, September 12th

Manny's footsteps seemed unnaturally loud as she made her way down the corridor, past rows of heavy oak doors, each marked with shiny brass nameplates.

She often avoided this building, though it loomed like a fortress on the edge of the quad, and was the most common stop on every Millfield University campus tour for its gothic arches framed by narrow, leaded windows that were surrounded by weathered brickwork. Ivy clung to the walls, twisting up to the gabled roof, as though nature itself was trying to reclaim the place. Inside, the building was dimly lit and eerily quiet—a silence disturbed only by the faint creak of old floorboards and the distant murmur of professors and lecturers alike. Professor Beau Moreau's office was at the very end of the hall.

Luckily for her, his door was cracked. Unluckily for her, he was there. She pushed the door open, and noted his office was nicer than others that she had seen.

There were tall windows casting natural light across a room that felt more like a private study than a university workspace. Everything was meticulously arranged; no piles of papers, no clutter, just an elegant expanse of polished surfaces and carefully placed artifacts. A large, stately desk sat near the center, its mahogany surface bare save for a vintage brass lamp and a single open book, spine gently cracked, as if waiting for his return. A few feet behind it, dark wooden bookshelves lined two walls, filled with books and what she imagined were rare academic texts.

Beau Moreau stood near one of those bookshelves, leaning against the windowsill with a casual grace about him. His dark hair seemed darker in this light and fell in soft, unruly waves around his face, casting complementary shadows over his sharp features. Despite the soft glow from the afternoon light, there was a subtle sheen about him —like he was made of glass—giving his skin a faint iridescence she assumed came from her own grogginess. He was dressed in all black, each piece immaculately tailored. Though the sleeves of his shirt were rolled up at the wrist, revealing two admittedly impressive arms.

"Excuse me, professor…um Beau," Manny said, hovering in the doorway of his office.

Beau looked up from his book, and for the first time she took notice with piercing clarity. His eyes were almost black. They flicked over her with a knowing look, as if he could read every thought in her sleep-deprived mind. He tilted his head, studying her with an amused smile that just barely reached his eyes, triggering something within her that made her stomach clench.

She'd read about him, of course, in her late-night research. Beau Moreau was something of an enigma in the academic world—an authority on ancient rituals, lore, and cryptids who, unlike many of his colleagues, held Indigenous knowledge in high regard. He had studied across continents—from dimly lit libraries in Spain to ancient ruins buried under Mediterranean cliffs—and received awards for his research. Yet here he was, holding office hours on a Thursday afternoon, as if blissfully unaware, or simply uninterested, in the acclaim attached to his name. In addition, he was the only surviving author of *A Legacy of Curses and Mischief* and her occult studies professor, which meant she needed to speak with him. Especially if she wanted to have a relatively normal semester.

And though already remarkably nervous, Manny found it somehow more remarkable that Beau Moreau was even more handsome up close.

"Have you been standing there long?" He asked in a way that told her he already knew the answer.

Manny wasn't sure which would be more embarrassing: explaining she, a graduate student, was still nervous to talk to *any* professor, or that she was in fact checking out her professor.

Manny let out a nervous laugh. "Sorry, I don't do this often," she said, when a small, more confident part of herself had wanted to say, *I don't usually check my professors out, nor was I trying to.*

But saying that could be helped, while her awkward ogling of her occult studies professor was already a few seconds in the past and she intended to leave it there.

"Yes, I suppose most students don't want to appear too eager," Beau said. "But I'm glad you're taking an interest in the class…" He paused in a way that said, *And your name is?*

Manny shook herself as if she were freeing herself from a trance. "I'm Manuela Webb, Manny for short."

"Well, you don't have to stay outside, Manny," Beau said with a smile. "You can come in, I don't bite."

Manny stepped inside and shut the door behind her. Beau gestured toward a chair across from his desk and she sat at it. He sat on the other side of the desk and smiled.

"So, is there anything concerning you about the course?" Beau asked.

No. She had asked herself approximately five times if there was anything remotely academic that could justify this visit. But she knew there wasn't. She was here because she wanted to know what he knew about the witch. And yet, now that he was asking her what she needed, she realized she had no idea how to broach the subject without sounding as strange as she'd felt Tuesday, stumbling through the subject with her friends. This time, she was hoping, or perhaps begging herself to find a better way to ask that didn't make her sound like a conspiracy theorist in desperate need of answers. Maybe she could try to sound like an interested student that had read his work ad nauseam, at a relatively sensible pace, rather than binge reading numerous articles either solo or co-authored by him until approximately 4 am this morning.

Beau tried again. "Are you concerned about the amount of reading or the final research paper?"

She couldn't name two things she was less concerned about. Manny was sure she would enjoy the readings given the clear grasp he had on the concepts and practices, and she had never gotten less than a B on a paper at Millfield University—which surprised her most days.

"Not that paper, per se." The words were out there. She hadn't said them intentionally. In fact, they had definitely slipped out of her mouth. Those were the kind of more passive comments she might make after a shot or two of tequila.

Beau studied her intently, as if trying to gauge what she was asking from the look on her face.

Clearly dissatisfied with what he found, he asked. "Which one?"

"A Legacy of Curses and Mischief," she answered more nervously than she'd meant to. She cleared her throat. "I know it might sound strange, but I wanted to know more—about who the Abernathy Witch was, and the curse that's supposedly connected to her…I really found the connections to feminist theory interesting."

Beau nodded slowly. "Ah, Arabella Crayton—the men back in the early days weren't too kind to her," Beau explained calmly, stirring his coffee absentmindedly.

"Unfortunately for her, Nicholas F. Abernathy took a liking to her, pretended to court her, deflowered her—and cast her aside. Though he accused her of witchcraft, and before they burned her, she cursed the town and his society."

"So…do you think he believed in the curse?" Manny asked hesitantly, trying to think about what she shouldn't say. "I looked into his society—and there seems to be a lot of Warden's sigils around the university—like he or Ezekiel was afraid of it."

Beau rested his chin in his hand thoughtfully. "Yes, I suppose so," he said, staring at her, clearly intrigued. "He was quite interested in Enochian magic. No idea what he thought he was warding against, but you know, men of that time—I'm sure they would've thought they were keeping out something that was *otherworldly*, or perhaps if they had hoped to imprison something *dangerous*…" he looked slightly amused by the thought. "But, of course, it's all just folklore—keeps the tourists coming in. Capitalism influences a lot of things in culture, but I won't bore you by droning on about that."

He gave her another warm smile and this time she returned it.

"So…should we be bracing ourselves for an uprising of were-wolves and vampires next? Maybe stock up on garlic and stakes?" Manny joked.

If there wasn't anything else she could do, she could at least make a good first impression with her professor.

Beau shrugged. "I mean sure garlic has its uses, though it's more myth than fact..." he trailed off, and wandered over to his bookshelf. "Fire, however, works well on witches, werewolves, and vampires. But with vampires, you definitely need to be more thorough…lore says the most powerful ones can rise from ashes—a bit like a phoenix."

Manny laughed nervously. "Really…like a phoenix?"

Beau nodded. "Yeah. Scholars theorized it would be best to make sure there wasn't even the smallest piece of a vampire left intact, or the vampire could potentially regenerate," he explained with a smile. "A friend of mine found a few old accounts of severed heads that reat-tached and bodies reformed from a single drop of blood. Witches are believed to be the same—makes sense though, the stronger the being, the harder it is to stop them."

Manny shifted uneasily in her seat suddenly very uncomfortable with the prospect of dealing with an immortal witch or her curse. It took her a moment to realize Beau was studying her.

"Is something wrong? I sometimes forget that students don't always… share my sense of humor."

She shook herself. "Yes, sorry. No worries, Professor. Just… hoping we don't get any unexpected visitors."

That brought a smile to his face.

"Yes, we wouldn't want that, Manny," Beau said with a chuckle. "Would you like a cup of tea?" He asked, gesturing toward an appliance on the bookshelf. “I suppose I should’ve offered when you first arrived.”

“No, it’s all right,” Manny said, though she wasn’t sure she was actually okay. “I’m sure I can do a bit more research of my own into it. Thank you, Beau.”

“No need to thank me, Manny,” Beau told her as he clicked the appliance on. “It’s always nice to meet a student with actual interest in occult studies…I can loan you a few books on the Abernathy Witch. Just be sure to get them back to me.”

* * *

Though her messenger bag was heavier due to the books, she felt lighter and rushed to meet with her friends. They had made plans to walk together afterward, and she was thrilled when she saw Grant waiting for her outside.

He was leaning against a wall with his arms crossed, looking every bit as relaxed as he always did. His face lit up as she approached, though his brow arched at the look on hers.

"So," Grant began, hands slipping into his pockets, "how was your talk with Professor Beau? Did you learn any dark secrets about Millfield?"

Manny sighed, rubbing her temples. “Apparently, the town’s founder probably ‘deflowered’ a witch—and supposedly her curse is what’s causing all the deaths—or that’s how the lore goes.” She shrugged, feigning nonchalance. “You know, just typical cursed-town lore.”

Grant let out a low whistle, clearly amused. "And did he tell you how to lift the curse, or just how to kill this witch—if she’s still alive?"

“Unfortunately, just the last part,” she replied dryly. “But he had some... pretty specific methods.” She shivered, remembering the way he’d described burning a powerful being. “Anyway, where’s everyone else? I thought we’d be meeting up to go to the pub.”

“Oh, they’re all busy,” he said. “Wade’s got practice, Dean is writing a paper, Shantelle and Isla are brainstorming ideas for their group project for another class. But I'm free, and I think I know a good next step—if you're up for it."

Manny raised a brow. "What do you have in mind?

"There's a local historian we could visit…" Grant shrugged and trailed off. "She's… a bit of an eccentric lady, *witch,* whatever—but she knows the town's lore better than anyone else." He grinned, a mischievous glint in his eyes. "Besides, if she tells us anything too creepy, we can head straight to the pub afterward. I'm definitely not facing anything supernatural of sound mind or on an empty stomach"

Manny laughed and shook her head at him. "All right. We can pay her a visit—and if things go south, I'll buy the first round."

"You've got a deal," Grant said, throwing his arm around her shoulder.

Chapter 8
Friday, September 13th

It was moments like this where she would often remember that time was a fickle creature. When it was generous it breathed life into the world, healed dying continents and restored balance to nature. She had always believed they should be grateful for the life they were given as everything in the material world could be taken away. Last summer, she'd stood on the beach by the shore watching as the frothy surf flowed up over the sand, brushing the tips of her toes before retreating back to the ocean's depths—at the time, she couldn't help it, in spite of everything she was coming to terms with, she could still admire nature's beauty. But in this moment, Manny would be far more thankful if her life and her person weren't standing in front of a shop called the *Bewitchery.*

The *Bewitchery* was tucked between a shuttered bakery and the *Pat's Bits and Baubles* thrift store, the latter of which, Manny used to spend Saturdays perusing the aisles, finding little treasures. Today, however, she stared at the neon sign of the metaphysical shop and thought that if Tammy were beside her, she would have laughed at the thought of going inside. She was skeptical of anything "spiritual," as was the rest of the Moore family. Tammy's aunt Geraldine had made a point to mention it to Grant at the wake, she'd said, "Tarot readers are good at reading people, not *cards*…they're just scammers with candles and crystals, selling hope to anyone willing to pay for it. And you're handing them hundreds to tell you things you already know."

It led to a longer, unsolicited, and unnecessary lecture, which none of them, especially Grant, had paid any mind to. He had generously written it off by saying "People do strange things when they're grieving"—and they'd all expected Aunt Geraldine was likely doing the same.

A bell tingled as they opened the door. As they stepped inside, Grant pulled out his phone to check his text and Manny stared in astonishment. She had immediately noticed the faint smell of dried herbs wafting through the air, a curious mix of sage and something *metallic*. From the outside, she had assumed they were going to a small, cramped space, and she would have to deal with her claustrophobia. What she found instead was a much larger, more cavernous space, albeit cluttered with shelves that seemed ready to buckle under the weight of the bones, skeletons and jars of mysterious contents they bore.

There were windows obscured by hanging bundles of lavender, thistle, and rosemary, casting misshapen shadows across book displays, jars, and tarnished trinkets.

But there was also music with chimes and baritone singers, which barely masked the creak of the old wooden floorboards—Manny quickly decided the *Bewitchery* was equal parts novelty and mysticism. From the strings of amber and purple lights patterned in constellations on a ceiling, that was at least five stories up, casting a soft glow within its walls, walls that were painted a rich navy color. A few lamps posted around the shop flickered, giving the space a living, breathing quality, its walls subtly expanding and contracting as if drawing breath.

Manny half-wondered if the air was getting thicker with each imagined exhale, or if it were merely a mix of incense, beeswax, and something earthy that might've been moss. But still her throat tightened as she looked around at the shop, which seemingly was caught in some slow, unending sigh.

Then Grant stepped in front of her, and she nearly jumped out her skin.

"When I called earlier, she said we would meet her at the cash register," Grant started, not remotely noticing Manny's reaction. "Then she'll take us downstairs to the reading room."

Her heart was still pounding against her ribs. "God, you scared me," she blurted, her voice shaking despite intending to sound annoyed. Manny pressed a hand to her chest, trying to calm down. "You really shouldn't sneak up on people like that."

Grant rolled his eyes at her. "Manny, I stepped away for a second," he said, shaking his head at her.

Manny stared at him, hoping she looked as annoyed as she felt.

"Okay, okay, *I'm sorry...*" he said, stressing both words, as if trying to sound more sincere. "But, hey, the register is just over there. I'll even let you ring the bell."

Manny rolled her eyes. "I'm not a *toddler*. You ring the damn bell."

They walked over to a counter draped in a green velvet cloth with gold patterns and crowned with a cash register so old it seemed more decorative than functional. Behind it, a small shelf displayed delicate glass bottles and vials filled with liquids that shimmered.

Grant rang a small bell on the counter. "Hello!" he called out, then spent twenty seconds drumming his fingers on the counter and ringing the bell again. "Trish, where are you at?"

"Gimme a sec, Grant!" a woman's voice called back from somewhere far away.

Manny heard the clang of bottles then heels on hardwood floors, and before long a door behind the counter creaked open and a tall, regal woman stepped out into view. She was young—early thirties, maybe—and exuded a confidence that seemed carved from years of dismissing what anyone thought of her. Her jet-black hair was gathered in a messy bun and her V-shaped bangs only added to her striking looks. Small silver hoops glinted on her earlobes, and her dark lipstick was a shade too bold to be called anything but intentional. She wore a long green velvet dress and a warm smile on her face.

“So, this is the one asking about the Abernathy Witch?” she said, gesturing toward Manny. “For what? A paper or something?”

Or something, Manny thought, but she didn’t want to sound crazy. She already felt crazy enough, chasing answers to questions she couldn’t quite solve by normal means.

Trish's black-painted nails tapped idly on the surface, her rings clinking softly with each motion, waiting for her answer.

"Yeah," she said quickly, though her voice wavered slightly. She was glad Grant hadn't told Trish the real reason. “I need to research local lore—and Grant says you’re a *historian*.”

Trish's lips curled, her catlike eyes, flashing mischievously, as if she wasn’t entirely convinced but didn’t care enough to pry. “Histori-an...that's sweet,” she murmured. "I've heard 'witch' often enough, but I prefer spiritualist, but it does keep the Karens away from the shop."

Manny nodded in response. And she half-hoped she could convince herself this was all purely some academic exercise.

There’s no way in hell the university is cursed, she told herself.

“All right, come on then,” Trish said, gesturing for them to follow her.

They followed her down a dark staircase that led to the basement, and Manny half-expected something to jump out at her. But to her surprise, the basement was relatively normal outside of the corner set up for tarot reading.

It had a low ceiling with a single dim bulb, giving the room a certain ambiance for tarot reading, which probably made it more real for buyers. Shelves lined the walls, packed with dusty jars of herbs, bones, and strange talismans. There was a faded rug underneath a table with a velvet tablecloth, and a waiting tarot card deck. She grabbed the cards, pulled the tablecloth off the table and messily folded it before setting them aside and sitting down.

“Take a seat, I’ve got to grab the book,” Trish told them, pointing to the two mismatched seats on the opposite side of the table. She went over to a bookshelf and began searching for whatever book she was looking for.

Manny and Grant took a seat, and she gave him a look that said, *thanks for not telling her.*

To which he made one back that said, *don't mention it.*

Then a book slammed down onto the table and they both jumped. "Here we are…" Trish began, flipping through the book. "The Abernathy Witch. She was powerful, cunning, and wronged in every way a woman could be wronged in those days…When the town's founder courted her—lured her in with promises, a bit like a few of my ex-boyfriends—"

"Yes, I know," Manny said, interrupting her. "I'm sorry, but I was more interested in the curse. I've heard about that part of the lore already."

"Of course, you do. But I was getting to that. You see, because no one ever cares as much as they let on. They stripped her, bound her, and burned her alive. History says her screams could be heard for miles, and when they finally faded, the sky itself darkened as if mother nature herself mourned the witch's death...but I bet you didn't hear about one thing."

Manny leaned forward. "What?"

The spiritualist's lips curved into a grim smile. "The *child,* of course."

Manny recoiled. *Child.* Her heart gave a painful twist.

"She was pregnant when they burned her."

"But wouldn't the fire—"

"No," Trish interjected, waving away her thought. "Her child's bones didn't burn…at least that's what the church records say. But even they weren't sure if it was an act of God or the Devil himself." She said, leaning toward them. "The reverend overseeing her burning believed the curse might be embedded in its bones, so he bathed them in holy water, and kept their skeleton in a sacred space. But some say her curse seeped into the child's remains, like venom, bearing all their mother's pain. Leaking, festering, perhaps *waiting* to release."

Release. Was that why Abernathy had put all of those symbols around the university? Was he trying to keep it out?

Manny gave herself a brisk inward shake and said. “Has anyone tried to get rid of it? The *curse*, I mean.”

“No,” Trish said, tapping her finger on her lips thoughtfully. “But there really are only two ways to break a curse like that. Either find a witch strong enough to lift it, which could be dangerous, if you don’t know who to trust—and I certainly couldn’t do it. Or two…” she paused, her gaze locking onto Manny’s. “You do this ritual, and you’ll have to burn the remains at the end—and I’ve got it *somewhere*… hmmm…where did I put it?”

Manny’s throat was suddenly extremely dry. “Burn the bones?”

Could she really see herself doing that? Desecrating remains due to some strange feeling she was having in the pit of her stomach? It was a sigil put around the university by some religious zealot. A religious zealot who would no doubt do the same to her.

But her intuition wouldn’t let her ignore it. Something was definitely wrong.

A heavy thud pulled Manny from her thoughts.

“Jesus, Trish,” Grant snapped.

Trish laughed. “Oh don’t get squeamish now, Grant,” she said, her voice low, as she handled the old leather-bound book as if it weren’t already cracked and blackened as though someone had tried to burn it. “That can come *later*.”

Trish opened the book, its pages groaning as she flipped through them, each one brittle and yellowed with age, covered in inked illustrations and looping, near-unreadable script. She paused at a page darkened with fingerprints, perhaps ash or dried blood. “There,” Trish said, poking a drawing at the center of the page.

Manny stared down at the intricate diagram of symbols with instructions. It depicted a crude drawing of a pile of bones encircled by jagged markings, possibly sigils and dripping candles. Then the ingredients required: *blood, black salt, snake’s venom, graveyard dirt*—and three options for purification. Those three options: *sage, salt or holy water.*

Trish’s fingers traced the symbols, her voice dipping further into the macabre. "Oh and about the blood. It can't be just *any blood.* The ritual demands it come from someone who shares a connection to the curse—someone who shares similar ancestral blood, but they don't have to be the *same bloodline.* But the witch was African American—or well, *mixed.* But I'd guess you'd handle that?" Trish said, gesturing toward Manny.

Manny scoffed. Trish said it so matter-of-factly, as if asking for a charger or a glass of water.

"Wait, what?" Grant blurted out. "Seriously, Trish? You better not be just trying to sell shit."

"No, I'm not, dumbass," Trish said, smirking as she leaned against a wall. "Curses are like scars—this is about resonance. *Balance*. Her blood, the Abernathy Witch's blood. Whoever is stupid enough to try it would need to sever that tether. One of your parent's is white, right?"

That question was for Manny.

"No…my nearest white ancestor was a slave master," Manny told her.

This information seemed to make Trish uncomfortable. "All right, well, I hope your *paper* is worth all this," Trish said. "Let's go upstairs. I've got everything you need behind the counter *and*—you can borrow the book."

Chapter 9
Friday Night, September 13th

After their conversation with Trish, they walked back to campus so Grant could grab candles from his apartment. She had half-considered leaving a note for Dean to let him know where they were going, but she didn't want to worry him. What was she supposed to say: *Just decided to pop out to the graveyard with your brother for the evening. Be back soon, kisses!*

Dean loved her unconditionally, but even she had to admit that sounded insane.

Millfield Cemetery was on a long sloping hill, and its iron gates never quite closed properly, still the hinges creaked as they entered. Despite most of Millfield being well kept, the cemetery was overrun with weeds and tufts of grass. Open graves were six feet deep and awaiting new arrivals. A few broken angel statues' faces had smoothed from decay, and if they'd ever had an angelic expression, it'd been lost through the years. But there was one statue reminiscent of the Winged Victory of Samothrace, and Manny hoped that was a good sign.

There was an abundance of leafless trees with skeletal branches, their twisted limbs reaching toward the night sky. At the far end of the cemetery stood the crypt, an imposing structure half-sunken into the hillside. That was where the remains would be, but Manny couldn't bring herself to look inside. Its door, which had previously been reinforced with iron bands, now was slightly ajar. So if anything was seeping out, it probably followed the fog hiding her feet. Above the entrance, a worn inscription carved into the arch read: ABERNATHY.

"You ready?" Grant asked, handing her a flashlight.

Manny knew she wasn't, but she nodded anyway and took it.

When they stepped inside, she swore the temperature dropped a few degrees. Niches lined the walls, holding crumbling caskets and urns alike—but no bones, yet. Cobwebs were suspended everywhere, but most of the spiders appeared to be dead, or perhaps killed by a larger member of their species.

The longer they walked through the crypt, the more nauseous she felt. Manny wished she was one of those girls who was unfazed by cemeteries, even though she loved horror movies. But she had been raised by a reasonably superstitious African American family—it didn't matter if someone asked her mother or father's side. Both would reasonably say not to mess with the *dead* or *dead things*. Don't go into graveyards after dark, be that as a young woman, or on the off chance *something else* might follow you out. They also reasonably believed if people can believe in heaven, they should also believe in hell—and all its demons.

But Manny took comfort in what they'd learned from the book. There was plenty in the book about removing a witch's curse inside:

> *To sever a curse from its host one must call upon the forces that bind blood to spirit and spirit to earth. This ritual must be performed under a waning moon, when the veil between worlds thins, and a forsaken curse's hold is at its weakest.*

There was a waning moon tonight. They were already in a cemetery, so they wouldn't need to search far for graveyard dirt. Grant had a blessed stake; he intended to inscribe the symbols in the circle which in the book looked jagged, almost violent in their design, each shape spiraling outward like a shark's teeth. And when they had the remains, they would place them in the center, arranged carefully, to *'not disturb the salt line,'* or the ritual would fail.

Manny could spend all night listing off the instructions—she'd practically memorized them. Hell, it was her blood they'd be using. It made sense for her to at least *know* what she was getting into.

She stopped abruptly, and Grant turned around, giving her a look that said, *'Are you all right?'*

But it was as if something were calling to her—that was to her right.

Manny slowly turned her head, using her flashlight to see the contents of a glass case beside her. It almost reminded her of a museum case—except, of course, they were in the Abernathys' crypt.

Its glass pane was smudged with decades of grime. Inside, perched atop a faded velvet cushion, was a child's toy—a worn doll with a porcelain cracked face. Its glass eyes stared blankly, one slightly askew, which reminded her a little of Chucky. The doll's hair was coarse and brittle, likely made from human hair, which was common practice in the past.

The once-bright curls were dulled to a sickly brown, and a portion had unraveled, hanging in tangled wisps over its chipped features. Its dress, though tattered, still bore traces of once-white lace and embroidery. Beneath the case, a tarnished brass plaque gleamed faintly in the flickering light: Miriam Abernathy, 1794.

The doll's placement felt almost reverent, but the case's neglect hinted at how long it had been since anyone cared to remember Miriam.

Beside it, another case was somehow more unsettling. Behind the pristine glass lay a small skeleton, its fragile bones bleached white and arranged with painstaking care. The tiny figure sat upright, its hollow eye sockets gazing forward, as if in silent vigil. Its ribcage was too small, its delicate fingers given an eternal curl.

A silver chain dangled around its neck, the pendant bearing faded scratches that, if she pictured it correctly, would match the Warden's sigil. Beneath it, a plaque with a short description—*Cursed child of the witch*—as well as a small crack between its glass pane and where they stood.

If there is a curse—this has to be where it's coming from, she thought, convincing herself.

"It's cracked," Manny told Grant, who was now standing beside her.

Grant nodded. "Good enough for me," he said, pulling a crowbar out of his backpack.

He placed it in the crack, and it scraped against the glass in a way that sent chills down her spine. Grant gritted his teeth, steadying the tool as he wedged its flat end between the seam of the frame and the pane. As he applied pressure the glass let out a growl-like groan in protest like thick ice about to crack underfoot.

Shit, it's going to break, Manny thought.

The glass resisted, warping and bending ever so slightly under the strain. But then, Grant shifted his weight on the bar, straining against it, then there was a sudden loud *crack,* and the seam gave way. The glass pane splintered—not in clean, uniform pieces, but in jagged shards that gravity plucked free, one by one, two by two, each slicing through the air before shattering on the stone floor.

Grant sighed in relief, and said. "It's open."

"I can see that."

She stared at the small skeleton, and swallowed.

The bones aren't going to collect themselves, Manny, she thought, scorning herself.

She moved mechanically, gathering the fragile, chalky remains and placing them gently into the burlap sack. The bones were lighter than she expected, but, honestly, she wasn't sure what she'd expected. She'd never as much as picked roadkill up off the road.

She swallowed hard, trying to steady her trembling fingers. Was this how graverobbers felt? Or were they more enthusiastic about it? Rather than revulsion, they likely felt some sort of thrill, since their greed blinded them to any wrongdoing. But it was easy to justify any act when someone attributed it to a greater cause. Wasn't that what every dictator throughout history had done? Claimed their theft had meaning? That their actions were righteous?

Either way, she knew she wouldn't forget the hollow rattle of bone clacking against bone as she dropped each piece into the sack. These bones had belonged to someone's child. She tried to shake it off, telling herself that someone needed to end the curse though she was still worried about whether there was a curse to begin with.

It's just nerves, Manny. Just nerves, she told herself.

Reminding herself again and again. But no matter how many times she did, she was still putting a baby's bones into a sack.

Her fingers hovered over a tiny rib, no bigger than a twig, and she wondered how it had snapped off when all the others had remained attached to the sternum. She imagined it could have happened during handling at some point, after all, Abernathy hadn't handled the witch with care—he probably cared even less about his unwanted child's remains.

Was she thinking about this too much? But how could she not? She was a young woman with her male best friend, looting an infant's cursed skeleton under the cover of night—and was about to burn said skeleton to stop a curse.

When she finally did a final sweep of the case to make sure nothing was left, and they left the crypt, she felt dirty. A feeling she could only describe as being somewhere in between seeing literal dirt on her hands, but nowhere near close enough to embodying Lady Macbeth.

But she would still have plenty of time to get there—the night wasn't over yet.

They walked until they reached a well-lit spot beside a tree directly under the waning moon, where Manny could set down the burlap sack and Grant pulled the book out of his backpack. She could faintly hear Grant flipping through pages as she stared down at her hands. He was drawing out the circle and sigils on the ground, while she sat there, essentially useless until it came to her part in the ritual.

The text outlined every step down to the last detail. Step 1: Preparation —the circle must be drawn with the necessary sigils, then they need black salt mixed with graveyard dirt following the circle's lines. She was confident in Grant's ability to draw them—spirituality and witchcraft where he thrived. He set the remains in the circle's center and took a deep breath.

"Almost ready," Grant said, lighting a few of the candles he'd brought with him.

Next, the instructions became more macabre:

From the living must be drawn the blood of kin. It need not be of relation, for blood knows balance. But blood must be spilled upon the remains to awaken the tether, to bribe the curse and call it forth.

Manny's stomach churned at the thought. At first, she wasn't sure where to make the cut, but knew she wanted it somewhere she could explain away. Her thigh was obviously a bad idea, if she and Dean decided to be intimate. Slicing her hand open was a better decision—she had done so more than once while cutting an apple. It was the easiest to explain away, and she didn't imagine they would need a lot of her blood.

"Okay, ready?" Grant said to her, looking at her.

He had the blade in his hand. All she had to do was take it.

Manny swallowed and took it, and Grant began speaking in Latin, a language she neither knew, nor was she sure she was ready to hear.

Manny took a deep breath, steeling herself, and took a step toward the circle, careful not to disturb it. She held her hand over the remains, and pressed the blade to her palm. As Grant continued the incantation, she slowly drew a line across her palm, tears welling in her eyes as it slit open. Cutting through her hand like butter, pain spreading the moment through it. She balled her hand into a fist, warm blood washing between her fingers as she bled.

Watching as it trickled down onto the small skull made her skin crawl. Grant continued muttering the incantation.

The book said:

As the blood spills, the fire must be lit—a flame fed by the oils of hemlock and ashen wood. To this flame, add some of mother nature's protection: sage, rosemary, and a single blackthorn. Let the smoke rise, dense and dark, as it seals the circle.

Grant struck a match, continuing to read off the latin words in the book, and she swore the flame grew for a moment. Her hand trembled as more blood spilled from it.

There was a warning at the bottom of the page:

Speak the words with conviction, or they will have no power. Do not let it sense your weakness. Do not bend to its will. Do not break in fear or strife.

Finally, Grant threw the match onto the remains, and in that same moment, thunder clapped in the sky, as if God himself was watching. However, when she looked up—she didn't see clouds. But when she looked back down, the bones were burning and there was an intense metallic smell wafting through the air.

Is that...my blood? She thought. *Holy shit. Is the curse—real? It has to be.*

She could hardly believe it.

Shit, what did the next paragraph say, she thought, but she couldn't seem to remember it.

Then it hit her. The worst of it wasn't over:

The incantation calls to the curse, drawing it forth from its vessel. The curse's tether will resist, will lash out, and the fire must be kept strong. Feed it if you must, but do not break the circle.

She wasn't sure how one fed the curse, but from what little she did understand, she wasn't supposed to move. Which was easier said than done with how large and hot the flames were getting.

But more importantly, was the final instruction:

After the tether is broken, the vessel will turn into ash, consumed by purifying fire. Scatter the ashes beyond the circle. Only then will the curse be severed. Should any remnant of the vessel remain, as will the curse, its power diminished but not undone. Failure is not an option. Most curses, once provoked, will not rest until they find a new vessel to tether onto—be it relic, bone, or flesh.

She couldn't believe they were doing this, but they were—and clearly she wasn't going insane. There was a curse, but there wouldn't be one after. They would stop it.

Grant shouted something else in latin, then his eyes met Manny's. "Okay, Manny, step back!"

She did as she was told, and in that same moment, the remains erupted, surging upward into an all-consuming inferno, clawing toward the night sky. Transforming into a twisting and writhing column, radiating heat. Like a fiery tornado, it spiraled higher and higher, until it was pure chaos. It tried twice to break free, slamming against whatever invisible barrier held it inside the circle. It roared and crackled, making an almost guttural, feral sound that made her teeth vibrate and her brain scream, *RUN*. Manny could hardly believe her eyes, as the fires licked at the circle's edge. No matter how hard the monstrous flames searched for an escape, they couldn't find one. Then Grant recited more words switching between Latin and some other language, raising his hand as he did so. But as he brought his hand down, the flames died down, letting out a high-pitched whine, like a tea kettle on steroids—which was almost loud enough to make her regret the decisions that led them here—but slowly the flames subsided until only ash remained.

Manny held her hand close to her chest, ignoring the textures of old and new blood mingling on her hand. And as Grant scattered the ashes, she sighed—it was over. They'd done it.

"Is that everything?" Manny asked Grant, hoping she hadn't forgotten something.

Grant didn't answer immediately, presumably going over the steps again in his head. Then he read over the page in the book and looked back at her.

He nodded.

Manny sighed in relief. “Thank God.”

Grant looked past her, over her shoulder, and said. “Oh shit.”

“What?” she asked, turning only to have her heart sink in her chest.

A distant flashlight beam sliced through the cemetery, and a deep masculine voice shouted. “Who’s out there?”

Her breath caught in her chest.

“Manny, we’ve gotta go. Now.”

She barely managed to get the knife in his backpack as Grant shoved the book inside, and barely closed it before beginning to run.

The flashlight's beam flitted wildly across the headstones behind them, and she could hear the security guard's heavy boots pounding after them.

They ran toward the cemetery’s entrance, and she didn’t dare to look back, focusing only on her breathing and the uneven ground beneath her feet, weaving through gravestones as she followed Grant.

But her foot caught on something—a root, or maybe a broken stone, she couldn’t tell—and she stumbled forward. Arms flailing, trying to catch herself, but she landed hard on her front, knocking the wind out of her. But she found the strength to turn herself over, and stared up at the sky, before realizing with nauseating horror—she’d fallen into a grave.

Its edges loomed a few feet above her, she was surrounded by walls of densely packed, cold soil.

“Whoever’s out there, you’re trespassing!” the security guard barked, the beam of his flashlight sweeping through the graves just a few yards away.

Her breath caught in her throat. She pressed herself flat against the bottom of the grave, dirt and dampness clinging to her clothes. She didn't move; maybe out of fear of being caught, but more than likely from shock.

I’m in a fucking grave.

She saw the guard's silhouette pass above her, and heard his boots crunching on loose gravel just beyond the grave. Then let out the breath she'd been holding, her pulse racing as his footsteps faded.

She stayed where she was for at least four agonizing minutes, staring up at the moon.

As if grave robbing wasn't bad enough—now I'm hiding in a grave.

Manny slowly got to her feet, her legs trembling as she stood. Her head throbbed as she hoisted herself out of the grave, and half-limped back to the Millfield Cemetery entrance, all the while hoping the guard wouldn't circle back.

Chapter 10
Saturday, September 14th

A stomach-churning aroma that would repel even the most unseemly creature breached her senses. Manny jolted upright, gagging, her eyes burning from the sudden light. She gulped down air as though she were a newborn taking its first breath. When her body finally caught up with her, the world around her was in a haze. However, as she blinked, slowly her vision cleared, revealing the culprit of the grotesque smell. It was a small bottle with ground herbs that she faintly remembered Grant purchasing at the *Bewitchery.* Currently Grant was placing its cork back in, and looked surprised, as if he hadn't expected it to wake her.

Manny glared at him. "You complete ass!" she said, hitting him with her pillow.

"Welcome back to the land of the living," Grant said, laughing at her. "You sleep all right?"

"I fell into a grave last night—how would you sleep?"

Grant's mouth dropped open. "Seriously? How the hell did you manage to do that?"

"We were in a cemetery…with *open* plots."

"Oh, come on, no need to get snappy," Grant told her.

Manny laid back down. She was still tired, but at least she could consider last night a success. Mainly, because if she couldn't, the dull ache in between her shoulder blades would have been for nothing. Her entire body was sore, she supposed in ways that could be expected after falling into a grave. Every step through the cemetery, every second she'd spent putting fetal bones into a burlap sack, played on repeat in her head like a macabre slideshow.

"You're gonna miss breakfast if you don't get moving," Grant said with a cheeky grin, his voice carrying the kind of relentless energy only morning people possessed.

"I'm up," Manny mumbled, though she didn't sit up. "You can see that I'm up," she assured him before rolling over and burying her face in a pillow.

"No, you're not," he said, sitting on her bed. "Come on, Manny. Today's a good day. No creepy rituals, no graverobbing. Just pancakes, cappuccinos, and quality time with friends. You need it. So, get up," he told her, using his hands to shake her a little.

Manny sighed and sat up. "You're awfully chipper for someone who spent most of his night in a cemetery."

Grant shrugged, his grin widening. "What can I say? I've got a knack for compartmentalizing."

She rolled her eyes, and swung her legs over the side of the bed. "Fine. Let me get dressed."

"I'll wait in the living room," he said, standing up and backing toward the door as though she might attack him like a rabid animal. "Don't take too long. You know how Wade gets when he's hungry."

"How did you get into my apartment by the way?" Manny asked.

Grant muttered something under his breath.

"What was that?"

He poked his head back into her room. "Dean let me borrow his key. He was worried about you when you didn't text him back last night. But don't worry—I didn't tell him anything," he explained with a shrug. "I figured I'd let you do that."

Manny gave him a thumbs up, and stretched, letting her back and shoulders crack and pop as needed. For a brief moment, she let herself believe that today really could be normal—despite last night.

I'll tell Dean later, maybe, she told herself as she changed out of her pajamas and pulled on a sweater dress and fleece leggings.

She glanced down at her phone. The screen lit up with several text message alerts over a photo of her, Tammy, Dean and Wade from their junior year in undergrad. Her chest tightened. But she shook the thought away, grabbing her coat from her closet.

Today's a good day, she told herself. *We broke the curse. There's nothing to worry about.*

She rushed to the bathroom, quickly brushing her teeth and putting on makeup before walking out into the living room, where Grant waited by the door, his coat already on.

"You should probably wear a scarf," he recommended, tossing her a scarf from her coat rack.

Manny caught it, and quipped, "Thanks, Mom."

* * *

It had taken them longer than she would have liked to get to *The Black Stag*—but it was Saturday. What else could she expect? The streets were always crowded on the weekend. They were lucky the others had arrived earlier and gotten a table. But it was too early in Millfield for anyone to be drunk just yet. They would easily get a ticket for disorderly conduct from the police. The smell of bacon and coffee hung in the air, inviting and oddly comforting, and Manny was starting to feel normal.

The moment they stepped through the door, they were greeted by a loud whistle from Wade, who was already sitting in their usual corner booth with the rest of their friends.

"Well, look who finally decided to show up!" Wade shouted.

"Some of us like to sleep in, Wade," Grant shot back, steering Manny toward the table.

Dean grinned, raising his coffee mug in a mock salute. "Of course, morning people are the real heroes, though. Aye, Grant?"

Grant nodded, barely glancing up from his phone, muttering something incoherent. But as Manny slid into the booth next to Isla, she noticed Dean's phone buzz, and then noticed Grant and Dean exchanging a look.

She wanted to believe they were texting about something else, but considering all their family was healthy, it was safe to assume it was about her. She half-wondered, half-wished to avoid thinking about where she would even start to explain to Dean what they'd been doing last night. She tugged her scarf loose, trying to internally shake off any thoughts about last night.

"So," Wade began, leaning forward with a playful smirk. "Grant says you two had a little...adventure last night."

Manny stiffened. Grant gave her a knowing look, as if to say, *Play it cool.* Unsurprisingly, Dean was glaring at Wade, likely due to wanting to discuss it privately. Though Wade occasionally liked to stir up trouble—that was the way things were.

"It wasn't anything too crazy…or *adventurous*," she said quickly, waving a hand dismissively. "Just research stuff—for Professor Moreau's class. I just wanted to get ahead."

"Research, huh?" Wade's eyebrows arched. He seemed to be trying to put two and two together, and couldn't quite work it out. But it was clear he wasn't convinced. "What, you two doing some spooky witchy manifestation ritual on the night of the full moon?" He joked. He wasn't big on spirituality. "You know most of that stuff isn't real. I mean…thinking things into existence, really? That's psychological meltdown stuff."

Grant set his phone down. "*Breakdown*," he corrected. "The term is *psychological breakdown*, dumbass."

"Either way, it's ridiculous," Wade scoffed, shrugging. "You could probably half-ass that class and get an A. I mean what's he going to grade you on…whether or not you can do a seance?"

Manny's jaw tightened, and heat began creeping up her neck.

But before she could snap back, Dean said, "You don't have to believe in any of it. Manny is trying to get ahead in her coursework—"

"Yeah, maybe you should try it too, *jackass*?" Grant interjected, glancing at her as if to say, *I've got your back.*

Manny couldn't decide if she wanted to yell at Wade, thank Grant and Dean, or disappear entirely. Instead, she stood up. Deciding if anyone ever did find out about what had happened in the cemetery, or that grave robbers had struck the Abernathy's crypt, she didn't want to say anything, and that included to Wade, who was the biggest skeptic of anything supernatural. Wade and Tammy were mutual skeptics throughout their entire relationship, though Tammy had left Grant alone, when she was alive.

"I'm going to get a London fog," Manny announced, not waiting for a response.

She sidled her way to the bar, navigating around patrons and ignoring three middle-aged men leering at her like she was the burger of the day. She ordered her London fog quickly and the bartender nodded agreeably and began making the drink. He had a few other orders, so she expected it'd take a while. Surprisingly, some pubgoers were already ordering morning beers, though she had expected the mimosas that were going out. There was a mimosa special on Saturdays meaning all of the moms' groups were present—working moms, single moms, and sorority moms—which brought a disproportionate influx of men into the pub. Though she wasn't sure how many were making passes at women their age, or if they were searching for twenty-somethings.

"Mind if I sit here?"

The man's voice was smooth, low, and disarmingly calm. She didn't get a chance to answer before the man sat down on the stool beside her. Everything about him seemed wrong, yet impossibly right at the same time—but she couldn't quite explain why. To make matters worse, a sharp pain went through her head, which she assumed was likely remnants of her unfortunate burial plot landing last night. She considered calling the bartender back and asking for her London fog in a to-go cup. Thinking if she had to choose between enduring a headache while fending off a strange man at the pub or heading home to nurse an oncoming migraine, she'd choose the latter.

But when she looked at him, she froze. Her foot lingering on the lower rung, ready to go. But she couldn't.

There was a flirtatious, borderline sensual smile on his face. She blinked, somehow forgetting how to speak. And if it was a mouse it would've bitten her; he was breathtaking in a way that felt wrong, almost painful to look at—it was like she was staring into the sun, knowing she needed to turn away or she'd be blinded. High cheekbones framed a straight nose, and his jawline could have cut glass.

Black hair swept neatly back framed his angular face, with a jawline that could've cut glass, and his eyes—almost silvery—caught hers and held them. His hair had a similar, lesser silver sheen, as if it had been dusted with stardust. He was tall, pale, broad-shouldered, with an athletic build that suggested strength, but his movements were languid, fluid, when his hands moved as he spoke, like he wasn't quite bound by the same laws of physics as everyone else. And he had said something else, but she hadn't heard it.

"Sorry," Manny said slowly. "What did you say?"

The man's lips curved into a smile. "You look like someone with a lot on their mind."

She blinked, unsure how to respond. "I guess so."

He tilted his head and studied her in a way that made her feel exposed. His eyes seemed to shift colors, darken subtly, though she could attribute that to the light.

"Rough week?"

"You could say that."

His gaze was both inviting and predatory as though he were sizing up. She was worried she was getting paranoid. He was another male patron at the bar, maybe even a tourist given his accent. Besides, her friends weren't far. She could leave the bar whenever she wanted—though she wasn't sure why she wasn't.

But then, the bartender—her saving grace—sat the London fog on the counter. That was her exit. "Well, I have to get back to my friends," she told him. "Nice talking to you."

She didn't move. She *couldn't* move. Why *couldn't* she move? Was her anxiety getting the better of her? Maybe it was something she should bring up in her next session with Dr. Carter.

"You know I've never seen you around here," he said, his tone conversational, as if ignoring what she had said. “New to town, or just exploring the local scene?”

Manny blinked again. Her neck constricted, she didn’t want to speak to him, but then she said, “I’m a grad student,” suddenly wanting to explain herself. “My friends and I come here *sometimes*.”

Sometimes was the smallest white lie she could manage. She wasn’t sure why, but she’d answered him. In fact, part of her wanted him to keep asking her questions.

“Ah, a young scholar.” He said, nodding, as if that explained everything. “Always searching for something—knowledge, experience, maybe a little trouble.” He winked, a flicker of amusement on his perfect face. “But what are you looking for?”

She hesitated. “Just…hanging out. It’s been a long week.”

What the hell is wrong with me?

He picked up a glass of Guinness she hadn't noticed the bartender bring to him, and sat it down with an almost theatrical casualness. "Something academic, or *personal?* Though I suppose that's maybe a bit much to tell a stranger…”

"I'd say so," she said, her voice more defensive than she intended. She sipped her drink to hide how uncomfortable she was, but he didn’t take his eyes off of her. “Do you always talk to strangers like this?”

“Only the interesting ones.” He leaned closer, lowering his voice. “And I suppose I’m interested in you.”

Her breath hitched, her pulse quickening. “I find it strange,” she said, breathlessly.

Am I having a heart attack, she wondered. She was a little lightheaded. *Is this guy even blinking?*

“But I suppose curiosity can be a dangerous thing,” he said, his voice dropping just slightly. “Sometimes you find more than you bargained for.”

“That sounds like something out of a mystery novel,” she said, forcing a small laugh.

He chuckled, his eyes glinting with an emotion she couldn’t quite place. “Life is full of little mysteries, isn’t it?” His gaze dipped to her hands, her fingers were fidgeting with her mug.

"You all right, Manny."

Who said that? She opened her mouth to respond, and an arm wrapped around her shoulder. She looked up to see Dean with Wade sauntering up beside him.

Dean's eyes narrowed as he sized up the stranger. "Is this guy bothering you, my love?"

Manny looked at Dean, then at the man beside her, who was now smiling lazily, completely unphased by their arrival.

"Yes," she blurted, as she shook off whatever had come over her.

The man laughed softly, standing from his stool. "Apologies. I didn't mean to upset anyone." His gaze darkened as he looked at Manny. "I hope we meet again, *Manny*."

As he walked away, Manny took a deep breath, her heart was pounding in her ears. Something about the man—who hadn't bothered to mention his name, and now knew her's was—off. Unnatural. His smile appeared both inviting and unnervingly predatory. She used to be able to tell creeps off or give them her frostiest glare before they spoke to her. And yet, in that moment, her anxiety hadn't gotten the best of her. It had been some time since she'd frozen like that. Perhaps it was the way he'd questioned her—like he was interrogating her. Pulling her right back to her time in the interrogation room—those grisly photographs of her best friend's dead body. Bile rose in her throat.

"You okay?" Dean asked, his arm having slid down to wrap around her waist as he sat down on the stool beside.

"Yeah," she lied, her voice quieter than she meant it to be. "I'm fine."

Dean kissed her on the forehead, trying to comfort her. His face said it all. He didn't believe her for a moment, but they'd talk later.

Wade moved closer, hands stuffed into his jacket pockets, his expression uncharacteristically sheepish.

"You got a sec," Wade said softly, standing far enough away to give her space.

Manny nodded, letting go of her mug, and turning to face him. "Yes, Wade?"

He hesitated, scratching the back of his neck. "I…I know I've been an ass lately. To you. About all this stuff with Tammy."

Her chest tightened at the mention of Tammy. God, she missed her.

"It's just all this spiritual stuff is weird to me," Wade continued, his voice dipping lower. "and I guess—seeing you get so wrapped up in… *everything*, it worries me, okay? I don't want to lose you, too."

Manny was taken aback. She had never expected Wade to be so raw. He rarely let his guard down, and when he did, it was usually to Dean.

"You haven't lost me," she said quietly, crossing her arms. "But it'd be nice if you laid off a bit. It's just research. I'm not planning on pulling out a Ouija board any time soon."

"I know." His gaze dropped to the floor, and for a moment, he looked more like a little kid than the confident guy she knew. "It's not fair. I'm sorry. I guess I've been so caught up in trying to move on that I didn't stop to think you might need more time… or a different way to deal with *all of it.*"

'All of it' seemed to be his way of talking about Tammy's death. She was getting tired of dancing around it.

"It's not about *time*, Wade," she said, shaking her head. "Tammy's gone. One day she was there, the next she wasn't. Grant was just helping me with something important—I feel like it helped. But I want answers."

"I get that now," he said, stepping closer. "And I support you, Manny—and I'm glad Grant helped figure whatever it was out. I am. Even if I don't fully get it…I promise."

She studied his face, searching for any sign of insincerity, but all she saw was Wade—Tammy's man—the same man who, despite his flaws, really did care.

"You mean that?" she asked softly.

"Yeah," he said, with a small hesitant smile. "I mean it. And I really want you to come to my game tomorrow. I want you there because it's been different not having the whole gang there, and it hasn't been the same without you."

Manny smiled. "Okay, I'll be there. Even though you're an insensitive ass sometimes."

Wade laughed. "Fair enough. I'll try to be less of an ass. Deal?"

"Deal," Manny agreed.

"See, all fixed!" Dean said, triumphantly, as if he'd mapped out the whole interaction in his head. "Now we can have celebratory drinks."

"We haven't won the game yet, Dean," Wade said, shaking his head at him.

"But you will! Stop doubting yourself, you're the best on the team," Dean told him, signaling the bartender. Then turning back to them. "Mimosa and a beer. We're going to celebrate with the crew."

Wade's face contorted and he laughed. "When the hell did you start saying *crew*?"

Manny laughed at them both, as Dean went into his brief explanation of adding words to his vocabulary. Not because he wanted to be cool, but because language was an art form. This would eventually lead to his 'arrogant creative writing student' impression, which she wholeheartedly loved when he did. And maybe, just maybe, she could relax, for now.

Chapter 11
Tuesday, September 17th

Claustrophobia is thought to be an irrational fear of enclosed spaces, though it always seemed completely rational to Manny. And if it stemmed from fear, it seemed to evaporate the moment she felt safe and she always felt safest with Dean, even as the gymnasium buzzed with energy—with everyone cheering, their feet thumping in a ceremonious march driven by the cheerleaders, the basketball players' sneakers squeaking, and the giddy conversations of students in the stands—Manny felt untouched by her claustrophobia. She sat wedged between Dean and Grant, her right cheek painted with Wade's jersey number in a bold, messy blue scrawl. Dean had insisted on painting it himself, and though the 24 on her cheek wasn't perfect, she liked it when his fingers brushed against her cheek. Hers did the same when she'd painted a '24' on his cheek. She didn't realize how much she'd missed being near him. It made her feel even worse for being away for so long.

"I think we're going to need a selfie to commemorate this," Grant declared, pulling out his phone. "The people need to know how ridiculously good I look today."

Beside him, Shantelle rolled her eyes but leaned in anyway, her braids framing her face perfectly. “You better tag me this time. Last game, I looked amazing, and you *cropped* me out.”

"Yeah," Grant muttered, waiting for everyone to get in position, Manny included, before snapping a few quick selfies. "Last time, I was mad at you for stealing my paper idea.”

Shantelle scoffed, “That was ages ago.”

Grant swiped through the photos, probably thinking about which ones to post. “Okay, these four are good. Posting to SnapFlare *now*.” He typed quickly, the sound of his thumbs tapping the screen barely audible over the crowd.

Moments later, his phone buzzed with notifications. “Wow, that was fast,” he said, scrolling through the likes. His face faltered, though, as he paused on a notification. “Great. Guess who decided to DM me?”

Manny leaned over, peering at the screen and grimaced at the name. “Is that the guy you were supposed to go on a date with last year?”

Isla raised her eyebrows. “Gavin? *Really*?”

“Ding, ding, ding. We have a winner,” Grant said, dropping his phone into his lap. “Apparently, ‘sorry something came up’ is supposed to make up for me sitting alone for two hours at *Pasta Paradiso.*”

Manny held back a smile—Grant’s over-exaggerated Italian accent always made her laugh.

“He’s trash,” Shantelle said firmly. “*Block him.*”

“Agreed,” Manny chimed in. “He didn’t deserve you to begin with, Grant.”

“You’re too good for Pasta Paradiso anyway. It’s always full of wannabe rich idiots,” Isla added. “Next time, go to a steakhouse. At least then you get steak, not *flavorless* pasta.”

Grant chuckled, his expression softening. “You guys are the best. Fine, he’s gone.” He made a dramatic show of blocking Gavin’s profile, then raised his hand, adorned with a 24 painted in glittery silver paint. “Okay, I’m channeling all this negative energy into supporting our man, Wade. We don’t dwell on negativity—we thrive.”

Isla gasped. "Oh, that reminds me! Leila and our fellow beyhive gals said tickets go on sale today!"

Grant smiled. “If you manage to buy them, I’ll go with you."

“Oh, definitely,” Isla said, sealing it with a high-five.

Manny smiled, grinning at the two of them. For the first time since she’d come back, she felt normal—like she could just exist and focus on therapy and healing. Nothing was going to stop her now. She glanced at Dean, he was chatting with a couple of guys sitting in front of them. His face paint was smudged slightly, but he looked endearingly boyish. She reached for his hand, and he squeezed hers—she loved when he did that.

The guys he was speaking to were wearing binoculars, explorer hats and sweaters embellished with fraternity symbols. Their faces were painted in animal patterns to match Millfield University’s new mascot—the blonde guy with a Scottish accent had cheetah print face paint and his friend, a guy with zebra stripes on his face, used his pale skin for contrast.

The "Explorers" was Millfield University mascot’s rebranding, which was a major development in Millfield as a small town. Prior to its rebrand, it was a more offensive caricature of indigenous people that had been swapped out after years of protests. But the school had wanted to maintain a theme engaging 'historical roots,' leading to a forced connection to “explorers.” The change hadn't been too much trouble for the university, and their cheers hadn't grown any quieter since then as a few locals had inferred to a *Millfield News* reporter in frustration over ‘cancel culture’—though, as with most sports teams, there was no intention of ending any sports at the university. Except for the chess team, but that was because no one had shown up to watch chess competitions.

The university’s all-male theater society—the MillU Players—seemed to manage better than both them and the film society. The Scottish blonde, who was half-sloshed, held onto his empty plastic cup and kept rambling to Dean.

“But Andre—*Dre* didn’t come back last night,” he said, wide-eyed and jittery. “It’s just weird, you know? Ramirez wouldn’t be late to soccer practice, but he didn’t pick up his phone either. We’ve got a game on Wednesday. Plus, Yazzy died last week, and like...the cops haven't found anything. My dad's a cop. Back home. He says stuff like this doesn't happen by chance, and that the MillU Murder's killer might be back."

The other guy nodded along, smearing his zebra—or liger?—face paint further with what she hoped was water in his sports bottle.

But he had a point. Missing roommate, dead student, no answers? Sounds like the start of a true crime documentary—but Dean's attention was already back on the game.

"All right, let's go!" Dean shouted, accidentally nudging her. "Sorry, baby, Wade's got the ball now."

Manny turned her attention back to the basketball game. Wade weaved through the opposing team's defense with ease as the game clock ticked down, the numbers glowing a fiery red. Only ten seconds left.

"Come on, come on," Grant muttered, leaning forward.

Manny held her breath as Wade dodged one last defender and launched the basketball into the air. It seemed to hang there forever before it arced perfectly through the hoop. The buzzer sounded, and the crowd erupted, everyone leaping to their feet in unison.

"YES!" Dean screamed, high-fiving Grant before turning back forward and pointing at Wade.

On the court, Wade was mobbed by his teammates and lifted up into the air like a king. Manny cheered loudly, knowing her voice might be a little hoarse tomorrow. Her heart was pounding in her chest, and for one brief moment, everything was perfect.

Then a high-pitched wail broke through the veil of cheers and Manny lost whatever marginal glimpse of perfection she might have experienced. The crowd's exuberance died down instantly, replaced by a ripple of murmured confusion. She scanned the basketball court, eyes searching for the screamer, and found her.

A cheerleader, blonde, bowed, and ponytailed, stood near the gym entrance, her silver pom-poms trembling. Her porcelain doll face was pale, she was pointing to her left, but she wasn't saying anything.

Manny wasn't sure who was the first to look. At first, she couldn't see much behind Dean, but whatever it was, stood near the double doors. She put a hand on Dean's elbow and moved him slightly to the right, and her heart dropped. A lone person—a boy in a Millfield University letterman jacket was stumbling forward.

Manny's stomach twisted. She could barely manage to understand what she was seeing; it was like something from an Edgar Allen Poe novel, or maybe worse. His brown skin was streaked with mud. One arm dragged lazily, while the other was bent, his hand clutching his neck, as a dark, glistening liquid seeped through his fingers. *Blood.*

"Oh my God," the Scottish blonde said breathlessly. "It's *Dre*."

Manny couldn't move as she watched the boy—Andres "Dre" Ramirez—stagger a few more steps into the gym, muddy footprints trailing behind him. Underneath his letterman, a soccer jersey—number 17—was soaked.

Manny grabbed Liger Boy's binoculars, ignoring his protests, and tried to get a better look at Andres. Her hands trembled, but when she focused the image in the binoculars, her breath hitched.

The gash on his neck was jagged and impossibly deep as if something had torn into him with claws— or *teeth.*

Her mind reeled. *Could it have been a wolf?* She internally shook away the thought—there wasn't a forest near enough for him to have walked here. Was it the curse? Had they not gotten rid of it? She had been there when it was broken—she'd spilt her blood to make it happen. And since witches were real—but witches didn't leave wounds like that. What then? A werewolf? A vampire? Had they accidentally summoned something worse by burning the Abernathy Witch's unborn child's bones?

Andres swayed, his legs barely holding him upright. Blood dripped steadily from his neck onto the glossy gym floor, but he didn't move. Manny wasn't quite sure whether he knew where he was. Was he in shock? His wide, unseeing eyes scanned the crowd as if searching for something—or someone.

Thump—his body hitting the floor was nauseatingly loud, echoing in their shared stunned silence. Blood flowed onto the gymnasium's vinyl floors from the gash where his aorta would have been. A gush of crimson, horribly dark, still washing down his neck. Then the cheerleader's sobs filled the void—then the screaming started.

"He's dead!" Someone yelled.

Pandemonium erupted. People surged toward the exits, shoving and trampling each other in their desperation. Players on the court froze for a moment, then ran toward the fallen boy, their sneakers squeaking against the blood-slicked floor.

"Move! Everyone move!" one of the coaches bellowed, his face twisted with panic as he sprinted toward the fallen boy.

Manny had yet to leave the stands. Then someone firmly grasped her arm, pulling her toward the stand's stairs. "Come on, baby, it's all right! Hold onto me," Dean shouted over the chaos.

"But—" She twisted, trying to get another look at Andres, trying to understand how this could have happened.

Grant appeared on her other side, blocking her view, his face contorted. "Manny, go!"

She let herself be pulled along, her heart pounding in her chest. Around them, people screaming, crying, and pushing in all directions. Somewhere, someone tripped and fell, and she heard a low *thud* followed by a loud shriek of pain.

As they got closer to the exit, she glanced back one last time. There were people behind them—students, faculty, pushing and shoving. Behind them, coaches and security guards surrounded something—she presumed, the fallen boy.

Her eyes burned with unshed tears. She didn't know why she was crying. Whether it was claustrophobia—or disbelief.

This can't be a coincidence, a little voice inside her head told her. *It can't be. Whatever had killed him, sent him here.*

Then she had the most unsettling thought. *What if this was a warning?*

Chapter 12
Wednesday, September 18th

The administration didn't mention anything about the basketball game that night, but all classes were canceled Wednesday morning, nonetheless. Manny noticed the police presence on-campus had noticeably increased this morning. At least from what Manny could see from her apartment bedroom window. As soon as she opened her eyes, Dean was nuzzling her neck—fast asleep beside her—it was nice. Despite the events of Tueday night. Sadly, she couldn't bring herself to stay in bed. She found herself wandering out into the living room dressed in her long white nightgown, checking on the rest of her guests.

Luckily, they were already awake. Isla sat cross-legged on the couch, scrolling through her phone, while Shantelle lay against one arm of the couch, wrapped in a blanket, staring blankly at the Millfield News channel. Grant was sprawled out in an armchair he'd brought over from his apartment across the way, and was fidgeting with his hoodie strings. Wade was half-propped up in a sleeping bag on the floor. No one wanted to be alone last night.

Grant gave her a nod of acknowledgement when he saw her. Manny nodded back and made her way over to pour herself some tea—luckily, they'd left enough water in the kettle. As she was pouring, her phone buzzed in her pocket, and a notification popped up. She half-expected it to be Dean asking her to bring him something back to the bedroom.

Instead she unlocked her phone, clicked the notification, and dropped her phone on the counter almost immediately. It wasn't Dean. It was an email from the university.

She stared down at the email on her phone screen with a solitary heading from the *Millfield University Gazette*:

CONGRATULATIONS TO OUR BASKETBALL TEAM! GO EXPLORERS!

Her stomach twisted. *What. The. Hell.*

"Look at this," Wade said, holding up his phone to the group. "Coach just sent an update. They're moving practices off-campus until further notice."

Grant scoffed, looking at Wade's phone. "That's all they had to say?"

"Well, what else were they going to say?" Wade asked, shaking his head.

"No, he's got a point," Shantelle muttered, nodding her head. "They're probably still taking pictures of his body, and all they have to say is 'we're moving practice'—his bloods probably not even buffed out off the floor yet…but that sounds like administration's doing. Nothing stops them—not even a student dying."

Isla shuddered. "I doubt they'll say anything. I can't even imagine going near the gym right now."

Manny didn't say anything—she didn't want to. She couldn't get the image of Andres' lifeless body out of her head—the way his eyes were staring at something and nothing at the same time.

Grant broke the silence. "So, are we just gonna ignore the fact that this is the second student of color to die on this campus? In a semester? And the police still don't have a clue of what's going on?"

"It's suspicious, yeah," Shantelle admitted. "But what can we do about it? It's not like we're detectives."

Isla chimed in, “It’s more than suspicious. It’s *horrifying*. And it feels like no one’s taking it seriously—except us.”

"Do you think... it could be connected to the curse?” Manny asked, though she wasn’t sure whether or not she was asking Grant, or everyone in the room.

Grant snapped his fingers and pointed at her.“Maybe...maybe I didn't do it right. I’m not a witch—maybe we unleashed something. Maybe it is Abernathy’s curse—it’s gotta be something...”

Shantelle rolled her eyes. “Come on, Grant. You really think a make-believe curse is behind this? It's probably, oh, I don’t know, a racist psycho on campus or something.”

“It could be both,” Grant shot back. “I mean—Andres is *Afro-Latino.* Plus, his neck was practically torn open. Could be a racist witch for all we know.”

Shantelle sighed, looking around for support. She landed on Wade. "And you? What do you think?"

Wade hesitated, he stared at the news, then at Manny, and back at Shantelle. “I don’t know,” he admitted. “I didn’t even know there was a curse—but there’s definitely something...off. We need answers… also…what do you mean you didn’t *do it* right? Do *what* right? What were you guys doing?”

Grant rolled his eyes at him, then said. “You know what else is *off?* The Abernathy Witch. Trish said she was Black, or *mixed*, or whatever. But why would her curse target her own people? Doesn’t add up, right?”

“Yeah, that’s shit,” Shantelle said matter-of-factly.

“Well, the witches in movies don’t always make sense,” Wade countered, piquing everyone’s interest. “Maybe it was a self-hatred thing. Or maybe...it’s one of those ‘whatever you give comes back tenfold’ kind of things.”

“So, you think she targeted Abernathy with the curse—and Black students got hit with it instead?” Grant said, seeming to consider Wade’s suggestion. “It’s possible.”

The room was silent for a few moments. Perhaps in surprise of Wade being receptive to Grant's musings about spirituality and the occult. Or in deep thought of whether or not these two murders could be linked a potential serial killer, who was just getting started. Either way it was becoming something of local concern, considering the news ticker along the bottom of the screen. And Manny was just grateful Wade hadn't pressed further on the subject of what she and Grant had been doing.

But she was just beginning to wonder how many murders had to happen before anyone considered the possibility of a serial killer—when Isla spoke, her voice cutting through all thoughts of anything outside of Abernathy's curse being the next logical option.

"So, what do we do? Sit here and wait for another email warning us to travel in groups or?"

"No," Manny said, reaching a resolution. "We go to the library. We research. We figure out what's happening—before it happens again."

"Sounds great," Grant said, standing up and stretching. "The last time I played Scooby-Doo, I was a kid. But *fair warning*—I'm not splitting up to search for clues—that's how people die in horror movies."

Despite the laughter his comment drew, there was still some tension in the room. Perhaps in fear of whatever they might find and perhaps whatever came next.

* * *

Manny wracked her brain for answers. She had never been this annoyed. She remembered one of her undergrad creative writing professors revering this place, calling it 'a place to better understand the writing prowess of the greats.' Unfortunately, Manny hadn't gotten to partake in any of that, she had slowly become so enraged she wanted to take a step outside to remove herself from Millfield University's Rare Books Library due to a student clerk at the desk saying they needed to fill out a form to view the books, then following up with refusing to allow them to fill out the form for this library's special library card—because Grant had stood her up twice.

"You don't remember me from sophomore year, do you? You stood me up. Twice," she'd said.

So, now, instead of looking at any rare books she desperately needed or pulling her hair out, she stared at a preserved outfit of one, Nicholas F. Abernathy. And she had acquired some reverence, mostly for the man's audacity, seeing as the bastard had the nerve to deflower a woman, have her burned at the stake to protect his reputation, and—to have bad taste in shoes.

She could see inside the rare books' library through the museum-like preservation glass. Apparently, his clothing was back to back with another one of his ancestors, though there weren't any fashion students to observe them today. The poor clothes had to settle for her—a creative writing student researching the occult.

Wade walked over to her. "Well, I guess we aren't storming the occult section after all."

"Oh, Grant couldn't manage to sweet-talk her into letting us into the library?" Manny asked.

"Nope," Wade answered. "At the moment, Telly is talking a librarian out of Grant being banned from the one place that might help us."

Manny tilted her head, looking past the clothing, spying the section from here—in bold white letters: OCCULT. It was annoying she wasn't allowed in. A younger Manny would've kicked up more of a fuss, but she didn't want to be banned either.

Then someone tapped her shoulder and she turned around.

"Come on, Tasha said we can go in…but just you and me," Shantelle told her.

"Okay," Manny agreed, following her.

She did wonder what had come to pass between the three at the circulation desk, but Manny decided it was best not to ask. It was better to get in and get out before Tasha could change her mind.

The Occult section, though visible from behind Nicholas F. Abernathy's outfit, was tucked away on the far side of the library. It was dimly lit, the shelves lined with leather-bound books that looked like they hadn't been touched in decades. But when she got a good look at the shelves, her heart sank.

Almost all of them were empty.

"What the hell?" Shantelle muttered, staring at the shelves. "This is supposed to be the most comprehensive collection in North America, isn't it?"

Manny nodded.

"Where the hell is the rest of it?"

Manny crouched down by a lower shelf, pulling out a single book with a bat embossed on the cover. She flipped it open and sighed.

It had torn pages, and entire chapters missing. Someone didn't want anyone reading it. Or they took out everything they needed.

"This can't be all of it. Someone must've moved the rest," Manny said.

She sounded more confident than she was.

"Great…let's hope Tasha will be a bit more cooperative—if Grant hasn't managed to piss her off more than when I left," Shantelle said.

Manny knew she was partially joking, but she still hoped against hope that there would be something they could look at. When they approached the desk, there was a new student clerk there—she had brown skin, dark blue hair, and was painting red nail polish on her fingernails. Her name tag read: Louise.

"Hmmm…" she said, acknowledging them.

"Would it be possible to access the *rest* of the Occult section?" Manny asked kindly.

She shook her head. "Nah…if it's off the shelves it's restricted to faculty use only, or in course reserves. Either way, you can't check it out, *sorry*."

The '*sorry*' was less an apology and more a *this conversation is over*, which bothered Manny. But she didn't feel like arguing.

Shantelle wasn't as easily moved. "Can we get access from a professor?"

Louise bit her lip, thinking as she blew her nails. "Maybe…you'd have to ask your professor," she said in a bored tone, as she examined her nails again. "That it?"

"Yes," Manny said before she gave Shantelle a look that said, *what are you doing?*

Shantelle gestured for her to follow her, and Manny did.

"What about Professor Moreau?" Shantelle asked.

Manny shrugged. "I mean, maybe."

She wasn't sure she wanted to re-involve her professor—she'd already had one awkward interaction with the man, and she wanted to keep her embarrassment this semester to a minimum.

"I did ask him a little about the Abernathy Witch before I went to Grant," Manny explained, mostly feeling grateful that she didn't blurt the information out. "He'd written a paper about her with someone."

Shantelle thought about it for a moment, but seemed to decide not to question her. "Well, why not go back and ask him? See if he can find anything useful about it…" she trailed off, rolling her eyes at herself. "And I'm not saying I believe in this *curse*. I mean, I believe in God, but I also believe the devil exists. So, maybe you should ask Professor Moreau."

Manny hesitated, biting her lip. "I don't know…wouldn't it be weird?"

"Weird or not, he's our best shot," Shantelle told her.

"What about not splitting up?"

"That was Grant's idea. Not mine," Shantelle said, brushing it off. "Sometimes you have to divide and conquer. The rest of us can check out the Abernathy Library and see if we can find anything there."

Manny nodded. "Fine. I'll try to get a meeting with him, but we meet back at mine to regroup."

* * *

Manny didn't know if it was appropriate to be the kind of teacher's pet, who immediately placed a request with her professor for an emergency meeting after a student had died on campus. She had never been any form of a star pupil before, but pretending to be one, while other students were mourning, left a particularly bad feeling in her stomach. But she had learned something new about herself. She was good at lying over email. That is, she managed to write a convincing enough email:

Request for an Emergency Meeting

Dear Professor Moreau,

I hope this email finds you well. I wanted to reach out regarding my research paper. As you know, I've been focusing on the Abernathy witch legend, but I've run into some unexpected setbacks. Of the key resources I'd planned to use, including your paper, I couldn't get a hold of, as some of them are either damaged or incomplete, and I'm concerned this might significantly impact my ability to stay ahead in your class.

Would it be possible to schedule an emergency meeting to discuss alternatives or other potential resources? I understand it's early in the semester, but I'd like to stay proactive to ensure I can address my concerns sooner rather than later.

Thank you for your time and guidance. Please let me know if there's a spot available in your schedule.

Best,

Manny Webb

Course: Cultural Histories of the Occult and Forbidden Knowledge

After she sent the email, she'd assumed she wouldn't hear back from him for quite a while—what professor would be checking their email when classes were cancelled—it's practically a day off for him. Though apparently Beau Moreau was the exception to this rule, as he replied in under an hour—thirty minutes to be exact.

RE: Request for an Emergency Meeting

Dear Manny,

Thank you for reaching out. I appreciate your commitment to

staying ahead in your studies—quite commendable for this early in the semester.

I have some availability this afternoon before 5 PM. I have an appointment at 6 but otherwise a mostly open schedule today. If you'd like to swing by my office, we can discuss your concerns and work through some potential solutions.

Looking forward to helping you sort this out.

Best,

Beau Moreau

Associate Professor, Department of Esoteric and Arcane Studies

Millfield University

Office: Whitlock Hall, Room 312

Email: bmoreau@millfieldu.edu

Office Hours: Tuesdays & Thursdays, 12—5 PM (or by appointment)

That had led her to standing outside his office door, checking the time on her phone, wishing she were anywhere else. But still she knocked on the door, and Beau let her in.

His office was dimly lit, the evening light filtered through the blinds onto the bookshelves.

Beau returned to his desk, not waiting to see if she would follow. To her surprise, he even looked good in this lighting. His crisp, white button-up shirt hugged his frame, the sleeves rolled to his elbows, his forearms flexing subtly as he moved, stacking papers neatly. His shirt was tucked into tailored slacks. There was something effortless about his appearance today—like he had just stepped out of a vintage editorial, refined but not contrived. His dark hair was slightly tousled, as though he'd run his fingers through it in thought moments before she'd entered. His expression was calm, almost unreadable. It gave him a kind of quiet authority that made the room feel smaller, or maybe it was just her heart hammering in her chest.

Manny hesitated for a fraction of a second in the doorway, realizing she was staring at him—quite noticeably—*again*. Her throat was dry, but she masked it with a polite smile and walked to the chair opposite his desk, the sound of her boots muffled on the carpet. Staring absent-mindedly at his coat on the coatrack by the door, trying to pretend she was easily distracted. She wasn't ogling him.

He glanced up as she settled into the chair, his eyes meeting hers for a moment longer than expected. Perceiving her with such clarity that made her feel as if she were being observed—but she internally shook away the thought.

It's probably just nerves, she told herself.

"Ms. Webb," he said, his voice smooth, a baritone that carried just enough warmth to be disarming. He leaned back in his desk chair. "I appreciate you reaching out. What can I help you with?"

Manny hesitated, and chose her words carefully. "For my paper, I wanted to include how the media portrays supernatural creatures—like vampires and werewolves—and compare it to historical accounts. Specifically, whether certain abilities, like glamours or telepathic manipulation, have any basis according to research."

Beau raised an eyebrow, his expression shifting between curiosity to amusement. "*Interesting* angle. Let me guess: you got inspired by all those shows and movies people are obsessed with these days?"

Manny forced a laugh. "No, well, not *entirely*," she said, like a teacher's pet would. "I thought it might be interesting to examine how these tropes tie into larger themes. For example, could a glamour or similar ability have influenced how the curse spread or was perceived? Were they ever under any impression that the Abernathy Witch was a vampire? If she was able to seduce him so easily…like addressing an angle that might've fit back in the day—like what if it was more than just her witchy behavior or her *feminine wiles.*"

Beau nodded thoughtfully. "Well, you're certainly ambitious. As it happens, I know the university has a few texts on the occult."

"Yes…I'd looked into them in the rare books library."

"Oh, you did, did you?"

That brought a smile to Beau's face.

"Is there any way I could get your permission to see them? I would read them in the library—which I think is all they allow anyway—if you were able to get me access," Manny said, the words rushing out of her.

Beau tilted his head, studying her. "That depends entirely on which texts you're looking for?"

"Oh!" Manny said, straightening up. "Lycans and Laments: The Forgotten Histories and The Vampiric Veil: An Analysis of Power Dynamics…and there's a few on witches…" she paused, pulling out her list. "The Witch's Mark: An Analysis of Fear, Power, and Persecution, and The Bewitched Mind: Cultural Fascination and Fear of the Feminine Mystique."

He chuckled. "Well, you certainly picked the heavy hitters. I read those for my own research. Those aren't exactly light reading."

"I think I'm ready for the challenge," Manny replied.

The professor leaned forward. "Tell you what—I'll approve access to the books for you. But I'll need a detailed outline of your paper's direction by the end of the week. Fair enough?"

Manny nodded, relief washing over her. "Fair enough. Thank you so much, Prof—Beau."

Beau scribbled a note on a slip of paper, then looked at her. "I'll send you an email with a completed request form for you to bring to the rare books librarian. She'll get you sorted. And, Miss Webb?"

"Yes?"

"Be careful," he said, his voice dropping slightly. "The Abernathy curse has a way of...consuming people."

Manny swallowed but forced a smile. "I'll be sure to keep that in mind."

She had tried to keep her tone light, but was sure she'd come across nervous. As she left his office, her mind buzzed with questions. The most adamant of them: *What did he mean by consuming people?*

Chapter 13
Wednesday Evening, September 18th

Vampires are undead humanoid creatures sustained by the consumption of vital essence (generally but not limited to blood), often targeting the vulnerable or isolated. Their existence is marked by compelling others telepathically (see: compulsion), which they use to lure prey. In some accounts, vampires are bound by ritualistic behaviors, such as needing to be invited into a home or avoiding sacred symbols (or sigils). However, older, pure vampires are said to be less restrained, capable of walking around in daylight and resisting many traditional weaknesses. Immunity to sunlight is rare, as it is an inherited trait common throughout certain vampire lineages, as some descendants have evolved to endure it...

—Southern Nocturnal Entities: An Encyclopedic Guide to the Occult By Eliza Harrow

It was the only excerpt of Eliza Harrow's *Southern Nocturnal Entities: An Encyclopedic Guide to the Occult* still stuck inside her head as she dragged her corkboard out of her bedroom closet. She would spend half the night grateful to Eliza Harrow's scholarly research, if she had the time, but she was still stuck on the general thought of vampires having children.

It's not like they were signing up for PTA meetings or baking cupcakes for school fundraisers. She couldn't imagine a vampire with a diaper bag slung over one shoulder, fangs glinting in the sunlight, while kid Dracula played soccer. Do they have sex like regular people? Thinking about that, in itself, was absurd. And yet, the idea of descendants meant they must have some way of reproducing. The more she thought about it, the more questions she had. Also, if vampires had families—if they have bloodlines—then they couldn't just be monsters lurking in the shadows. Could they be? It made them feel...*permanent*. Not because they're *immortal* but because they're not going anywhere. Like they've been here long before humans and would still be here long after.

Of course, before she could mull over that any more than she already had, Dean had grabbed the other end of the corkboard to help her lug it out into the living room—the corkboard was heavier than she remembered.

But it was massive. It took up nearly half the wall by her "small space" dining table, and she'd forgotten how heavy it was until she'd hoisted it onto its hooks. She hadn't used it since her third year in undergrad—when her biggest worry was a creative writing project that required her to map out her dreams on a vision board depicting her next five years. Back then, it had been covered with pictures of London, a clipped-out quote about publishing her first novel, and magazine cutouts for a stylish, chic lifestyle she'd wanted to have.

Oh, how things had changed.

Red threads stretched taut between locations on an enlarged Millfield University's campus map combined with a larger Millfield town map she'd printed both out and pinned them on it: the alley where Yasmin "Yazzy" Brewer's body was found, the gymnasium where Andres "Dre" Ramirez-Carr was pronounced dead on the scene (according to *Millfield News*), and the bench where they'd found Tammy. And maybe Tammy was a long time ago, but Manny couldn't ignore that it might've been where it all started. Or maybe it was just where it had started for her. Each location linked to a photo of the victim—their smiling faces, once full of life, full of promise—and now they were a statistic.

Beside the photos, Manny had pinned sticky notes with scribbled notes about each student. Anything that might lead to a connection: Andres was a soccer player, a member of the Black Student Society, keen on Political Activism, and a First-Generation university student; Yasmin was involved with her sorority, the Queer Student Society, had received a volleyball scholarship, and volunteered with the town over's soup kitchen; Tammy was a member of the Black Student Society, a student activist, received a basketball scholarship, and volunteered with the Young Writers Chapter in town.

Manny still wasn't sure if Tammy matched the pattern—she hadn't been bitten, but she did have a claw mark like Yasmine, but not a bite like Andres. Or not one that Manny was aware of.

Manny frowned at the corkboard. Her handwriting was haphazard and growing more illegible with every minute she'd spent hunched over the table jotting down notes. From Wade's joking, 'my precious' comment, in reference to Smeagol, she could safely assume she looked obsessed—or *possessed.*

Maybe I have lost my mind, she thought, folding her arms as she stepped back to check if the corkboard was straight. She swore it was tilting.

It resembled corkboards from old detective shows—a tool for hunting serial killers. But this wasn't that, and the reality of it made her stomach twist. What was she doing? She wasn't a detective or a journalist. She was a grad student. And yet, here she was, stringing together clues about dead classmates, piecing together their lives in a way that was invasive, or borderline voyeuristic.

Her gaze lingered on the faces of the victims. They smiled back at her, oblivious to what had become of them.

She shook her head at herself. Luckily, everyone else was too busy to notice.

Grant was grimacing at his laptop screen, his brow creased as he continued scrolling through news articles, his foot tapping against the floor. Isla was doodling in her notebook, probably taking a break from jotting down notes as she had been for an hour. Shantelle sat cross-legged on the carpet, her laptop balanced precariously on a coffee table cluttered with notes and empty coffee cups. Wade, who had made a coffee run earlier, was now ordering a pizza, instead of reading any more about werewolves—because he *'just couldn't do it'* at the moment.

"So, Andres would be the third victim, in the last two months," Grant said, suddenly looking up from his laptop. "The first was Donny C—police found him a few days ago. He was washed up by the ravine. But he doesn't really fit. Everyone else shares the same basic profile—Black, brown, queer, or marginalized in some way. Activists, serving the community in some way." He pointed to his screen, showing a picture of Donny C, with an accompanying Millfield News headline. "Andres was supposed to be camping near the same ravine with some friends. But all the *'friends'* he had with him have probably lawyered up by now—I doubt any of those parents want their kids getting in trouble."

"Donny C? Like 'D.C.' Donny C? I didn't know he was missing," Wade said, scratching his head. "I just thought he was sick or something."

Shantelle cocked a brow. "I didn't know you guys were close."

"Well, he's been the team mascot for like three years," Wade answered. "I'm not going to be the basketball player that's a dick to the guy that basically ushers in school spirit."

"Maybe the killer thinks they're easy targets," Isla suggested, twirling her pen. "Yasmine and Donny C weren't exactly popular."

"*Maybe*...but Andres was MVP last year for the soccer team—he's on like every ad they put out," Wade said, shrugging at Isla's suggestion. "Dude was about to be a male model. I can't believe he's dead."

Grant rolled his eyes. "*Okay*, before we start theorizing about *why* they were killed, let's talk about methods. Like gee, I don't know: Both Yasmine and Andres were somewhere dark when it happened, both of them had gaping wounds on their person—neck or chest, respectively—and what leaves a wound like that? Oh, *right*, vampires!"

Isla laughed, her shoulders shaking and her head thrown back, but her expression faltered when she noticed Grant wasn't laughing. "*Oh,* you're serious?"

Grant glared at her. "And why not? We're sitting around reading occult lore—and every culture has some version of vampires as a myth. And given everything else going on at this school—mysterious deaths, Abernathy's secret society—are vampires really the most far-fetched suggestion?"

Isla pouted in his direction. It was a rhetorical question. But a valid point. They were sitting here, sifting through a pile of books they'd lent from the library, while Manny had spoken to Professor Moreau. And she was still waiting for him to send her that form.

"Or werewolves, depending on the mythos," Shantelle interjected, having spent more than a few hours reading *Lunar Beasts: Truths and Myths of the Werewolf Legends.* "Werewolves would kill their victims by ripping out their throats or eating their hearts. In that show, Supernatural they ate hearts."

"So, *theoretically*, since we're hypothesizing about mythical creatures now..." Wade started rubbing his temples. "Should I expect Bigfoot to be lurking around the quad?"

"I'm not saying it's *definitely* vampires," Grant shot back, clearly defensive. "But what else explains the pattern? The victims' wounds? The fact that no one hears or sees anything? I've never heard of a witch or warlock going out their way to bite into someone's neck with their teeth."

"It could be a serial killer with a twisted sense of theatrics," Wade countered. "And haven't you heard of the bystander effect? Happens all the time—sometimes people just stay out of it. Maybe you should take that visit to New York, you'd find out then. Why are we immediately jumping to supernatural nonsense?"

"You said you'd keep an open mind," Grant snapped back, irritated.

Wade rolled his eyes. "I'm ordering pizza."

He pulled out his phone and punched in a number. Shantelle waved Manny over, and she walked over to her. She sat, pointed her finger at a passage in *Lunar Beasts: Truths and Myths of the Werewolf Legends by Anstasia Wei*, and tapped the page.

"Do you at least see my point," Shantelle said.

Manny stared down into the book, and read it:

> *Werewolves, or lycanthropes, are known for their predatory nature and violent attacks on humans, which leave behind distinct puncture wounds and claw marks. This is why it's important to differentiate between a vampire attack and a werewolf attack, as it's common for these two natural enemies to be mixed up. For example, one clear distinction between a werewolf's bite is its massive size, which is often much larger in both length and width. Full moon transformations are common, but most pure lycanthropes can change form at will, blending into society while carrying out their hunts.*

Manny re-read the passage three times. There was nothing in there about them drinking blood, however, there also was very little information available to the public about the students' deaths online; or at least, *not yet.* In fact, she would have loved for it to have been a serial killer, and it have nothing to do with lore involving a werewolf or vampire. She'd not bothered to read through the first volume of Eliza Harrow's *Monsters of Midnight: A Comparative Guide*. But she couldn't imagine a werewolf drinking blood any more than she could imagine a lion channeling its inner mosquito. Though facts were facts, and at least, for now, one of their victims had been bitten and two had claw marks on their back—so a werewolf couldn't be written off their suspect list.

"A werewolf would just tear someone apart, wouldn't they?" Grant said finally, gesturing toward Shantelle. "If they were hunting, they must've been hungry...otherwise there wouldn't be anything left."

Manny closed her eyes for a moment, trying to weigh their arguments rationally—but there wasn't anything rational about any of this. "Okay, stop," Manny said, and they both turned to her. "We don't know what we're dealing with, *yet*. And if we keep arguing over lore, we'll never figure it out. Let's focus on the facts: their marginalized victims with different types of wounds, and there's a curse on campus—possibly Millfield itself. That's what we have right now."

Isla raised her hands in mock surrender. "I'm team hybrid. Why choose?"

Manny sighed, shaking her head. "Let's just keep digging. We'll figure this out—one way or another."

She flipped a few pages of the book, looking for something she could compare it to, and then her phone buzzed. A single notification, an email from the BSS, the subject line was:

BSS Emergency Meeting—Attendance Urgent

Manny clicked it and read the email immediately: *We need to band together to address the university's failure to protect us. Meeting tonight, 8 p.m., BSS lounge.*

She looked around the room, noticing most of her friends receive the same email. "Guess our little research session is over," Grant said, shutting his laptop. "I'm going to try and wash off the rest of this paint and put on something warmer. Meet you guys downstairs."

Shantelle frowned, but she didn't look up from her phone. "Everyone's probably scared. Who wouldn't be?"

The Black Student Society, BSS, for short, was one of the most outspoken groups on campus, often working with other societies to organize protests and call out injustices. And Manny would guess, they'd decided it was high time for them to step in.

The Marshall Burns Building had the Cultural and Community Center on the ground floor. It occupied a relatively large space, where students could sit on bean bags and socialize, or they could meet and enjoy movies or guest lectures on the projector. Bright, open, and impossible to miss. It wasn't tucked away in some forgotten corner or the basement where the ceilings leak, and the Wi-Fi barely works. There were beautiful big glass windows and sleek furniture, a kitchen no one's figured out how to work yet, and walls that are constantly plastered with posters and flyers for events and meetings.

It's a big deal. A win for everyone who spent years making noise about how BIPOC students needed more than the occasional lip service. But it's also kind of messy. Shared spaces meant shared politics, shared histories, and all the shared misunderstandings that came with them. But it still felt like a community—not perfect, not without its faults—but still a home base for anyone who needs it. Whenever there wasn't a meeting, it was used for socializing, and made a lot of cross-cultural events possible.

Manny and her friends slipped into the room, finding seats near the back. Dozens of students crowded into the space, their faces a mix of fear and determination.

At the front of the room, BSS President Kaeri Masters, stood with her braided hair pulled back into a bun. Her brown skin reflected the light as she clapped her hands together to draw everyone's attention.

"I'm not going to waste your time," she began, her voice steady and clear. "We all know why we're here. Two students are dead, and the university's response has been a joke. If we don't look out for each other, no one else will."

Shantelle shot Manny a look, as if to say *I told you so.*

"Some of you might think it's just coincidence," Kaeri said, scanning the room. "But this isn't the first time students have died on this campus."

Manny's heart sank in her chest. Most of the newer faces in the room seemed confused, but it wasn't as much of a mystery to those that had been around.

"What do you mean?" a student called out.

Kaeri shifted nervously and said, "Tammy Moore was killed a little over a year ago on Halloween—she was the first victim in the *MillU Murders,* but her death was pretty much ignored by administration—it took several other students' deaths and one body hanging off a statue in the quad for them to say anything—a total of thirteen students died. To make matters worse, the police never caught the killer—and we don't know who they are or if they're back—but we are going to look out for our community. That being said, everyone needs to be careful." Kaeri glanced over at Manny. Then she turned back to the room. "A few of our brothers and sisters involved with the National Pan-Hellenic Council have brought up the idea of forming a system as a preventative measure—"

"So, your solution is the university's solution?" another student said, scoffing at the idea.

"No," Kaeri said. glaring at them. "This is being done by the BIPOC student societies. We're protecting our own in this, because we don't know what's going on."

Another shouted. "But wasn't Donny C white?"

"Maybe they killed him because he was dating that Indian girl," a soft voice answered.

"Please, Donny C doesn't even fit the M.O.," a male voice retorted. "That's True Crime 101. He's not a minority. If a serial killer is targeting Black students, he's targeting Black students."

"But Andres was mixed."

"Okay, quiet down. Quiet down!" Kaeri said, sternly, pulling their attention back to her. "The bottom line is we need to be careful, and if you use this QR code, you can report on this app we've created to stay connected with each other. Our representatives, including three black faculty members, will be there to advocate for you, if any of your friends go missing." Kaeri said, assuring them this was the solution. "We'll report it to the police so we can have a record of their disappearance, and go from there."

Students began raising their hands. Manny sighed, scanning the QR projected on the board, and downloading the app. There wasn't much else to do besides listen to the students try to ask the same questions she'd asked Dr. Shepherd and end up with more of the same answers. But she decided to sit through it.

"That's all for tonight. Stick together. Watch your backs," Kaeri said.

All that was left to do was for them to leave.

Chapter 14
Thursday Morning, September 19th

She had another nightmare last night, a dream Dr. Carter would probably be interested in. Manny woke up from it covered in sweat, even though the room couldn't have been colder. The dream itself was disturbing: a poorly lit lecture hall, blood splattered on the walls, elongated teeth, and a voice whispering *'blood is devotion,'* before something lunged at her throat. And she was convinced that if Millfield's serial killer wasn't a vampire—it was someone truly demented. She would've been a wreck if Dean hadn't stayed the night—mainly rooted in his concern about any unspoken feelings she had about the mere mention of Tammy.

Manny had assured him she was fine, and more than okay. Last night, as they lay with their legs tangled together, she found herself grateful that in that moment, he seemed to know exactly what she needed.

In so many ways she felt lucky. His arms woven around her, keeping her warm, they always found her, even when she didn't even know she needed finding. He would reassure her, wipe away her tears—always making her feel seen and safe. He wasn't perfect—she knew that—but she didn't need him to be.

And the sex—that was undeniably good.

It was as if he had memorized every inch of her, and didn't act as though she were a clock radio that needed tuning—or spent time creating too much friction. It was never rushed, or awkward—he wasn't in a hurry to get it over with. He took his time, like she was something worth savoring, worth cherishing.

Through all the chaos, he had never thought of her as 'too much,' or 'not enough,' which had been the repetitive, unfortunate nature of her previous relationships. To top it all off, there were those men who just wanted to take her out to see if they could *'bone an asexual,'* as if she weren't a person, but instead a potential prized notch on their bedpost.

Unfortunately, her morning gratitude was cut short by a flurry of notifications lighting up her phone screen. The app, SafeCircle, according to its 'about' channel, is designed to provide a secure space for marginalized students to share information, organize protests, and support one another, while 'allowing real-time communication in its channels, providing the most up-to-date information. And it was more than apparent, the app, SafeCircle—as Kaeri had claimed at the meeting last night—was active and working.

All her notifications came from a new post in a channel labeled 'missing students' linked to an article:

MILLFIELD NEWS

LOCAL UNIVERSITY STUDENT'S BODY FOUND ON NIGHT BUS

The body of a young African American woman that was discovered on a night bus last week's family has given us permission to disclose her name.

Winona Thomas, a queer African American student, an active member of the MillU Mathletes, ranked at the top of her class was discovered on Marble Road. Just last week a local hiker contacted authorities upon noticing an abandoned bus near a path to Abernathy Falls. According to police, the 22-year-old, who had been missing for over 72 hours, is believed to have boarded this bus early Sunday morning to return home. When she didn't make it there, her parents called the police.

Police confirmed that the bus, which had been found hours before, was covered in blood, but Winona's body was later recovered a short distance away near a tree.

Initial reports indicate that the victim was drained of blood, with no signs of a struggle, further complicating the investigation. Meanwhile, Millfield Police Chief Martin has stated this may be the work of a satanic cult or a death cult, though they're unsure if Winona was in contact with any known groups at the time. The discovery has raised alarm among students, who are still reeling from the recent string of similar deaths. University officials have yet to release a statement about the case, but sources suggest that they are working closely with law enforcement to investigate the matter further.

Campus safety concerns have escalated as the student community demands answers. Winona's death marks another chilling chapter in what many now suspect could be a targeted series of attacks on Millfield University's students. Millfield Police Department gave no further comment.

Manny reread the words, 'drained of blood' several times, but only needed to read 'no signs of a struggle' once. They'd written Tammy off as being potentially in a 'drunken state' at the time—*It was Halloween, maybe you met up with her to pre-drink, maybe she'd already had a few—and she punched you. Maybe you fought back*—she could still hear the policemen's voices in the interrogation room. Or referred to it as being an 'opportunistic murder' in Yasmine's case. Or failed to cover it at all. She considered taking a guess at how they would get the media off this one. Or were four bodies too many to sweep under the rug? They would have to admit there was a predator walking through their streets. A night stalker. And an alarming thought popped into her head: *A vampire.*

Chapter 15
Midnight At Anselm Library
Friday, September 20th

Her living room was a mess of half-empty tea mugs, short and long cut red thread, and crumpled papers. She'd connected faces, dates, and locations, but every time she got closer, she found something else that didn't make sense. Maybe none of it ever would. It was like she was trying to remember a half-forgotten dream.

Every detail turning over and over in her head again and again:

Donny C stood out. His profile didn't fit the pattern. Tammy was outspoken at campus protests; Andres Ramirez-Carr organized rallies against discriminatory hiring policies for students; Winona was suing the university for mishandling her sexual assault case. And Donny? Outside of his scholarship and the fact that he was potentially white-passing, he was...*ordinary.* A ghost in his own story. All of the others were visible minorities. It was strange—but wouldn't that matter to a serial killer? Wouldn't they choose people that no one would miss?

She kept asking herself those questions when she'd logged into the Millfield Library database again. The search results were endless—academic papers, yearbooks, and campus newsletters, all useless. But then she stumbled onto something: a scanned Millfield News article from the 1980s.

Mysterious Deaths at Millfield: A Look Back

The words blurred together as she read them, the same sinking feeling in her gut. The article described students disappearing or being found dead—same MO. Marginalized students, their deaths ruled suicides or accidents. Though them being 'suicides' was different. But what stood out most was how the university handled it. They'd sealed the records—and she couldn't help but wonder why?

Money, maybe, she told herself. *They wouldn't want something like that easily accessible to students.*

She texted Grant then, thinking maybe, if there were anything left to find, maybe they could find it together.

* * *

Their walk to Anselm Library was quiet, save for the faint, chirping of crickets echoing through the night. Between the frigid winds whipping through her hair, carrying the earthy scent of freshly cut grass and the faint sweetness of blooming jasmines from the nearby garden beds. Fireflies flickered in and out of view, each tiny glowing orb, hovering lazily near the bushes lining the library's stone path.

Flying buttresses arched gracefully from the base to the upper levels, giving the structure an almost weightless quality despite its immense scale. Heavy, iron-bound doors sat beneath a pointed arch etched with an inscription: "The Mind is a Tower Unto Itself."

It was the largest library on MillU's campus, it was twelve stories high, consisting of books in the east wing along with reading areas for students, and faculty offices in the west wing. If she had to pick between Abernathy Library and the Anselm Library—there was no competition. Anselm was beautiful, there was no denying that, but she also had so many memories inside. Good ones, mostly. Late nights with Tammy, her now-gone childhood friend, cramming for exams and splitting vending machine snacks while the rest of campus slept. They used to joke that the library was haunted, but the ghosts were "too self-absorbed" to bother anyone.

Abernathy Library, though? It wasn't pretty. It didn't pretend to be. The study rooms were breeding grounds for hormonal disasters, and the lighting made students look like extras in a zombie flick. But it was real. No ghosts of friendship past, no painful reminders lurking between the shelves. Just students trying—and sometimes failing—to keep their lives together. And maybe that was why she kept coming back. It was messy and awkward, and a little sad sometimes, but it didn't expect anything from her except to find a seat and get on with it.

Thus, Manny and Grant stepped inside Anselm Library through the main floor study area, weaving through rows of dimly lit bookshelves to a secluded computer terminal tucked in a back corner; she couldn't help but find herself looking over her shoulder at the same places they'd sat together—her and Tammy.

Grant logged into the library database so they could access all the resources available, and Manny shook herself internally, refocusing on their task.

"Maybe we can find the full article in here," Grant muttered, as Manny scooted her chair beside him.

There weren't many other students in the library, though there was hardly as much of a need to study. She wasn't sure how concerned students were on-campus—though they'd seen or heard about someone dying in the gymnasium—it seemed the fraternities and sororities had no intention of cancelling their Halloween parties. And she doubted attendance would be sparse.

"No, nothing. I can't find it…" Grant said, trailing off. Then after a few more failed searches. "Wait—here's something."

He clicked on a scan of an old newspaper clipping, the grainy black-and-white image loading slowly.

The headline read:

Campus Tragedy: Third Student Found Dead in Bizarre Circumstances

The article was dated nearly five decades ago, describing the deaths of three students over the first two months of the semester. Their causes of death were vague, but one detail was consistent: each victim was found completely drained of blood.

Grant leaned in closer, his breath warm against her ear. "Well, that's not creepy at all."

"It can't get any worse," Manny said.

"Let's see," Grant said, scrolling further.

Further down, the article mentioned bystanders' rumors of people seen near the crime scenes, but the MPD had dismissed them as "baseless town gossip."

Grant clicked a hyperlink to a blog from an ex-student dated within the same week of the article. The writing was rambling but unmistakably panicked:

They walk among us. Creatures of the night…no one believes me, but they're out there. Everyone knows. I swear. I tried reporting to professors and my Big, but everyone thinks I'm going insane. It all ties back to the founder, Abernathy and his Wardens of the Gate. But I don't know where they meet. We don't matter to them.

The lower paragraphs dove into an "eat the rich" diatribe, which was concerning to say the least.

"The Wardens of the Gate," she repeated. "Isn't that Abernathy's society?"

"Well, that can't be a coincidence. Town founder who was driven by a Black temptress—I swear I've heard the story before. And I've never liked the ending," Grant said, but his nervous laugh didn't mask the tension in his voice.

* * *

When they left the library, the air outside was frigid, and shaking the leaves off the trees. Manny rubbed her arms, wishing she'd worn a heavier coat.

Halfway down the library steps, she froze. Something in her, told her, someone was looking at her. She turned and her eyes locked onto a silhouette standing at the edge of the courtyard, barely visible, just out of reach of the lamppost's light.

"Grant," she whispered, grabbing his arm.

He turned, following her line of sight, but the figure was gone. The lamppost flickered faintly, but they were gone. It was just an empty patch of grass.

"You okay?" he asked, looking down at her.

Manny forced a nod, but her pulse pounded in her ears. "Yeah," she lied, her eyes lingering on the spot. "I thought I saw something."

Though she watched the shadows as they walked away from the building, daring something to jump out at them—she couldn't shake the feeling that they were still out there, somewhere, someone was still watching.

Chapter 16
Tuesday, September 24th

Manny slowly pushed open Professor Moreau's office door, clutching her binder as she stepped inside.

Today, the smell of pine filled the air from the candle lit in the corner. Beau looked up from his papers, and smiled.

"Happy Tuesday, Manny," he said, leaning back in his chair. "I'd say I'm shocked you're here, but I can only assume you must really want that A."

Manny smiled, unsure whether it was his words or her poorly thought out lies that were making her nauseous. She sat down, opening her notebook to show him her many, many pages of research—and her outline, which was only a few days late.

"I wanted to run a few ideas by you," she began, flipping to a page filled with scribbled notes on folklore and vampire myths. "There's something *off* about the old tragedies on campus—they seem like the workings of a serial killer. But they've never been researched as such. Have you ever heard of any connection between the town curse and the…*unusual* tragedies here?"

Beau smiled, as he brought a hand to rest on his chin. "*Unusual tragedies*?" he repeated, perhaps piquing his interest. "Millfield University has its share of myths and well—ghost stories, secret societies, urban legends. But that's true of any institution over a hundred years old, don't you think?"

Manny straightened. "Yes, but have you heard about Abernathy's society, the..." she paused, pretending to check her notes for it. "*Wardens of the Gate*. They were rumored to be frightened of occult beings—witches, werewolves, vampires. Do you know anything about them?"

He let out a laugh; it was soft but sharp, like a blade sliding back into its sheath. "If I did, they wouldn't be very secret, now, would they?" He steepled his fingers, his smile widening. "What made you interested in secret societies? I thought you were focusing on the Abernathy Witch for your paper."

She nodded. Manny knew how she sounded—trailing off to talk about Abernathy's secret society was a little more than off topic. But who else could she ask about Abernathy and his potential interest in Enochian magic and rituals, if not her professor that runs the course on the occult?

As much as she wanted to stick her hand back in the sand, or write it off as her dealing with paranoia or grief—even now her thoughts were racing and fragments of vampire lore popping into her head:

> *The true danger of the occult lies not in their otherness, but in their ability to reflect us so perfectly. Vampires, in particular, are masters of mimicry, capable of adopting the customs, speech, and demeanor of their surroundings. This skill is not merely for survival—it is predation. To deflect suspicion, they craft roles for themselves that allow them to become invisible by appearing ordinary. In doing so, they challenge our perception of safety, forcing us to question whether the true monsters are hidden among us, unseen yet omnipresent.*

She found herself silently thanking Eliza Harrow—she'd written a lot on the occult. In a way that it managed to stick in her head. Particularly on vampires, numerous lines about how well-versed and well-practiced occult beings can be in their interactions with humans.

She stared at her professor, and noticed his lips moved, forming words. But she hadn't heard him. She internally shook herself and refocused on their conversation.

"Forgive me, I've been a little distracted lately."

"It's all right. I was just saying you've been thorough," he remarked, his voice taking on a tone of approval. "Tell me, what did you make of the vampire myth? Why do you think it persists across cultures and centuries?"

His question surprised her, and she hesitated. "Maybe because...they embody something primal. Our fear of death and of predators that don't look like predators."

His smile widened slightly. "*Interesting*. I've always connected it to the allure of power, immortality, the thought of an omnipresent danger." His voice lowered almost imperceptibly. "After all, what's scarier than a monster you can't see coming?"

A shiver ran down her spine, and for a moment, she swore his eyes flickered in the dim light—but then convinced herself otherwise.

It's just the light. She shook her head at herself.

"Will that be all?" Beau asked with a warm smile.

Manny nodded and Beau handed back her notes.

"Good work," he said, his tone warm. "Keep digging—it seems you have a knack for unearthing things."

Walking out of his office, her mind wandered. Something about how he probed her felt…strange. She tried to ignore it, but as she replayed the conversation in her head. He'd been engaging, insightful, and—she couldn't deny it—quite charming. But her question about MillU's secret societies lingered, unacknowledged, as though he'd purposefully sidestepped it. He'd joked about their secrecy, but what if it wasn't a joke? What if it was misdirection? He'd deflected, leaning into clever wordplay and dry humor. She could guess he was one of those professors that didn't like to acknowledge not knowing something. But usually she would catch on the moment they'd evaded the question—no, it was how smoothly he'd done it that puzzled her. For him it was effortless to the point she hadn't noticed it until she was already out of the room.

Her steps faltered, and a shiver prickled her skin. If he knew something, why wouldn't he tell her? And if he didn't...why did it feel like he did? Or was she just being paranoid?

Then she considered the unthinkable. What if Professor Moreau wasn't just interested in her questions—what if he was the answer to them?

* * *

"I think…I think Professor Moreau might be involved." Manny barely recognized her own voice as the words leapt from her mouth.

She couldn't believe she'd said it aloud. In the moment of silence that followed, she considered booking an appointment with Dr. Carter, until that silence was disturbed by the printer whirring to life. A4 sheets of paper helplessly discarding themselves onto the floor, no paper stopper in sight.

Manny had managed to make it back in time to meet with the others in Dean and Grant's apartment. The only space she'd ever been in that was equally lived-in but not quite cluttered, like it was holding onto all their memories without spilling over. It was also uniquely spacious—larger than the cramped two-bedroom apartment Manny called home—all thanks to the two brothers who shared it. They'd managed to snag up a cheaper on-campus apartment on account it didn't undergo the latest dorm renovations.

One side of the living room was neat, *too neat,* really—furniture positioned just so, with a coffee table that looked like it might be an inch off from perfect symmetry. The walls were painted a warm taupe, with framed comic books, or featuring One Piece character art, others more obscure indie designs that Dean had picked out.

Their shelves were adorned with a few quirky items—old concert tickets, rainbow-themed trinkets, and an impressive vinyl collection that could've easily filled the space with an indie vibe—though their current research didn't quite call for it. They had bright orange couches with fuzzy throw blankets and a kitchen a couple yards away that had funky patterns on the walls, and the typical kitchen appliances.

And then, there were the cats. Dean's cat, Shanks—an orange tabby was fluffy and playful—and Grant's cat, Mihawk—black Norwegian forest cat, equally fluffy but generally aloof.

Both were emotional support animals, though Mihawk was, at times, closer to a small tyrant, gracing the apartment with his presence like he owned it. They were often perched in places where they had no business being. The first time Manny had seen Mihawk, he was perched on the railing outside their apartments at the top of the steps, staring down at her with an expression that could only be described as *mildly inconvenienced.* He did seem to warm to Manny when she was hysterically crying over Tammy's death. In less a *'there, there'* sort of way, and more a *'here, pet me, dammit,'* kind of way. Though the jury was still out on whether Shanks was a more comforting companion. When he did choose to cuddle, it was like being smothered by a warm, purring mass—until he suddenly decided he'd had enough, and would dart off, leaving behind only the faint smell of fur and betrayal—as Dean often described it.

Dean raised an eyebrow at her. "You mean you think Moreau's connected to the murders? Like you think he's a serial killer."

"I don't know," Manny said, biting her lip. Her backpedaling was met with more confusion. "It's just—there's something *off* about him. It's like he knows exactly what to say whenever I ask about something..." she trailed off. Silently preparing herself for the *'of course he does, he's the occult professor,'* and wanting to sink into the floor and disappear.

Isla held up a finger as if she'd made a discovery. "Well, he is *unnaturally attractive*," she said with a soft giggle. "But if that's our only criteria, we've got at least *three* other professors at MillU we can make suspects."

Grant snorted. "Okay, *yes,* he's *handsome*. But he is our *occult* professor—we can't just make everyone that knows something about the occult a suspect or a *vampire*."

"We need to focus on the facts," Shantelle said, drawing everyone's attention.

She pulled out Eliza Harrow's book on vampires, *Blood and Bloodlines*, they had been reading it late last night.

Manny had dog-eared pages, and Shantelle slowly flipped to the section on vampire distinctions. *Phobior*; vampires that fed on fear—or more so fed on terrified victims. They would stalk their victims until they were paranoid, and only after they were at the crossroads of sanity and insanity, did the phobior finally feed on them. But phobiors were mostly loners and didn't join vampire covens.

"So, you're proposing what exactly?" Wade asked, as he helped Dean stack papers. "Moreau's a vampire, and he's been hunting students on campus?"

Manny shrugged. "Or he's at least… *involved.* Maybe he's a member of a coven. But everything that I find leads back to Abernathy's secret society—and I swear it felt like he knew something. And if vampires are behind this, they would know how to blend in. And Beau…" she trailed off, her stomach churning. She didn't have any proof, only a gut feeling that he was hiding something. "He just seemed—"

A *ping* came from her phone. Her new notification ringtone. It was only sundown, but the news headline she read when she unlocked it was delivered with grim finality.

Another body.

This time, the victim was a Mexican-American student named Carlos Medina, found in similarly suspicious circumstances. The police were calling it a '*random act of violence*,' though similar to the other students' murders. And if the pattern weren't broken before, it was with him—Carlos wasn't Black, he wasn't queer, but maybe, he was connected to activism on or off campus.

What do you have in common with Donny C, she wondered as she backed out of the news and scrolled through the SafeCircle's 'missing students' channel's chatter with one question in mind: *what if it wasn't about race?*

But about marginalization—focusing on students who challenged the system in ways that made those in power uncomfortable. According to the chatlog, Carlos had been outspoken about his experiences with discrimination in class, and like the others, he had drawn attention to flaws in, specifically, Millfield University's school system. Then she scrolled and found more information on Donny C. Donny—quiet, seemingly average, and *white*—had been funding Winona's legal fees. But he wasn't just offering financial support; he was helping her find a way to make her case against MillU public. And the more Manny read, the more she realized that Donny had dedicated a significant amount of his resources—money, mostly—to give Winona a chance at justice.

Her stomach tightened. His involvement in Winona's case—his desire to help expose the truth—had made him a target.

The more Manny thought about it, the clearer it was.

That's it. Marginalization. Whoever was behind it must've already been stalking them—hunting them. A phobior would take pleasure in doing so...but she still had questions—and she knew exactly who she could ask about them.

* * *

A few hours later, she was walking into Professor Moreau's office—she was ready to hear, *'twice in one day,'* or some other witty comment upon her arrival. Unfortunately, whatever he had said, she didn't quite hear it over her heart hammering in her chest.

Beau's lips quirked into a smile. "You must really like my lectures," he said.

He was teasing her, but she caught an almost predatory glint in his eyes, and she wondered if it had always been there.

Manny laughed nervously, sitting down at the desk. *Relax, Manny, relax.*

"Something on your mind, Miss Webb?"

His eyes searched her face, and she wondered what he hoped to find. "You seem a little…*distracted*."

"Umm…no, I'm just worried some of my research may have hit a dead end—"

But before she could finish, Beau picked up a book from his desk, and began searching for something. His fingers tracing the length of each page before he flipped them.

Manny tried to internally shake off her unease, and stared down at the desk. She couldn't risk staring at him. If he was a vampire, and was using a glamour, maybe that was how he'd been catching her in it. But as he began to speak, she looked up and noticed his reflection in a mirror on his bookshelf, and froze. For a few horrifying seconds, he seemed to distort—his skin liquefied as if trying to escape the glass, as if the mirror couldn't quite hold his image. But when she looked at him directly, he was the same—still one of the most handsome men she'd ever seen. Still, it frightened her.

She blinked, trying to shake off the feeling, but she wasn't sure she could manage it. Especially, considering she wasn't sure when she'd be leaving the office.

Beau looked amused. "Are you feeling well? I know Abernathy's history can overwhelm most scholars…I trust you're not getting too caught up into small town folklore, are you?"

Manny tried to recover, forcing a smile. "No, of course not."

She stood up to leave, deciding their conversation needed to be over. She hadn't even managed a goodbye or *'thank you'* before turning to leave when Beau's voice stopped her.

"Be careful wandering around alone at night," he said softly, his tone oddly protective.

She turned and his eyes locked onto hers. He continued, "It can be dangerous out there…and some things are best left *undisturbed.*"

Manny stared at him blankly, and forced herself to hold his gaze. For a moment, she thought he might be *warning* her—either that or he was hinting at something—but she wasn't going to stick around to find out.

Chapter 17
Friday, September 27th

Some days she wished she moved around as easily as the cigarette smoke wafting in the air inside the pub. Lingering when she need not linger, soaking up laughter and smiles, dancing like no one is watching—like she used to. Instead, she's sitting in The Black Stag's private room, sectioned off by glass doors, surrounded by dim yellow lighting, opening her eyes wider to stare down at her brightly colored fall-themed cocktail.

Tonight, The Black Stag was filled with hundreds of conversations, from crowds of younger, newer Mill U students who in a few months' time won't go anywhere near this place after they find more *'aesthetically pleasing'* options. It didn't matter how polished the wood floors were when they barely absorbed the noise, or didn't exude anything more than a cozy nature. But it was their pub. It didn't scream youthful, but it.

Manny sat at a long wooden table with her friends, a pile of notebooks, A4 printed pages, and a borrowed folklore book spread out like evidence. To their right, the faint hum of music was muffled by the glass doors, save the occasional laugh or shout from other patrons.

"I'm telling you, this whole thing screams ritual," Dean said, gesturing to a page in the book. "It's the same symbol over and over—

it's the only one that appears more than the warden's sigil. I've watched enough newsreels—literally five hours' worth yesterday—tell me I'm wrong." He pushed the book toward Manny, and she studied the symbol—a jagged star, drawn in what looked like charcoal or ash, maybe blood. "What if it's some sort of sacrifice?"

Manny frowned and sighed—thinking back to her and Grant's night in the cemetery. "It's blood magic," she muttered. She tapped her pen against the table. "These symbols were also in a text on magical theory. The wardens' sigil is, of course, connected to Abernathy's secret society…"

Shantelle sipped her drink, her brow furrowed. "The Wardens of the Gate? You mean those rich old creeps from the 1800s who started this school?"

"Exactly," Grant chimed in, showing his tablet to the group. It was an old forum post. "I found this in a forum about campus urban legends. Supposedly, the Wardens of the Gate were known to perform rituals to 'secure the university's future.' There's plenty of rumors about what might've been part of it."

He used his cursor to highlight a line in the post: *'To gain power, one must offer power—perhaps taken from another.'*

Manny's stomach churned. "Do you think these murders are —*sacrifices*?" she asked.

Grant nodded. "Blood rituals require blood. If this theory holds, they're choosing people who could impact the university's standing in some way—and their lives could be payment for whatever spell they're doing."

"Wait, so you think someone is doing a seance or something, and the curse just wakes up?" Isla asked, looking between Manny and Grant. "Dude that's so fucked up!"

Grant nodded. "Yeah, it is, but that's one theory. And I can't figure out who's choosing them…"

Dean's face contorted in disgust, and he adjusted his cardigan. "So, you think they're sacrificing marginalized students to stop bad press?" He looked at the glass doors as if checking if someone were coming, and dropped his voice to a whisper. "How the hell do we stop something like that?"

No one answered.

Outside, the Mill U women's volleyball team laughed as they headed toward the main bar—life still moving on oblivious to the potential horrors threatening their university.

Wade sighed. "Why the hell doesn't this place have blinds," he groaned, shaking his head. "I have to join the call with Dr. Brooks soon."

"Well, the noise could be worse," Dean said, trying to look on the bright side.

Wade shrugged and pulled his laptop out of his bag. He logged in quickly and opened a link in his email.

The video call connected with a stutter of pixels, and then there she was—Dr. Nia Brooks, on-screen, on a laptop propped between half-empty pint glasses and a shared plate of limp fries. Her expression was mildly disapproving, though whether it's directed at the pub's dim lighting or Grant's unapologetic swig of beer remained unclear.

Dr. Brooks is striking in a way that makes people sit up straighter, even through a screen. Her skin is a deep mahogany, so flawless it could double as a makeup commercial's ideal, and her dreads are pulled into an immaculate bun that defies gravity and laziness alike. She has the kind of face you can't help but trust and a knack for helping her students succeed. Her blood-red lipstick is the only sign she doesn't spend every waking moment buried in a book or a grading pile. A well-regarded scholar in esoteric studies that Manny had yet to have the privilege to take a course with at Mill U, but this semester she was on a research leave.

"Let me get this straight," Dr. Brooks begins, her voice smooth, like the first sip of a whiskey you're not sure you can afford. "You're attending my office hours...from a *pub*?"

Wade leans closer to the screen, an equally apologetic and charming smile on his face. "It was the only place we could find with good Wi-Fi—and good *fries*."

Dr. Brooks arched one immaculately groomed eyebrow, a single movement that said she's reserving judgment but not ruling it out entirely. "If this is a prank, I assure you, Mr. Greene, I have better ways to spend my time. Start talking."

Manny cleared her throat and dove into the spiel they'd rehearsed earlier. She explained the sigils and her thoughts about Abernathy's society. Not remotely hinting she thinks any of it is—real. Or mentioning her and Grant's late night trip to the Millfield Cemetery. Grant helpfully held up images of the sigils on his tablet in view of the screen.

Dr. Brooks squinted at them, leaning closer to inspect them. "*Hmmm...*those sigils...aren't entirely unfamiliar. They remind me of sigils used in ritualistic practices—protection spells, *mostly*."

Wade perked up, his face lighting up like a kid on Christmas morning. "So, Abernathy's society might've been into that?"

Dr. Brooks snorted softly, shaking her head. "Abernathy and his cronies were into many things, most of which revolved around self-preservation and maintaining their stronghold in Millfield. If they dabbled in the occult, it was likely more for theatrics than being true believers. They were politicians and performers, not practitioners. But those sigils? They could've been for decoration." She leaned back in her desk chair, her expression contemplative. "Abernathy had a documented fascination with Enochian magic—an *obsession*, some might say. He believed sacrifices, whether symbolic or literal, could shield his legacy and the university from harm."

"You mean *literal* sacrifices? Like *people*," Manny asked. For a moment, she was worried her tone may have sounded a little too eager.

But if so, Dr. Brooks was too polite to take note of it. Instead she shrugged elegantly—even the woman's shoulders were regal. "Hard to say. The records are sparse and heavily redacted, which in itself, most scholars find telling. But what you're considering wouldn't surprise me. Millfield's ugliest truths are wrapped up in secrecy and tradition."

Manny shifted in her seat. "So, any advice on how to stop a ritual? Where sacrifices may or may not be involved?"

Dr. Brooks smiles faintly, a touch of warmth creeping into her otherwise stoic demeanor. "Yes. Go back to basics. Meaning go to the source. Don't trust anyone too charming, and for the love of God—Mr. Greene, stay out of pubs during my or anyone else's office hours."

The call ended with a soft click, leaving the group staring at the blank screen, their fries somehow colder, and no closer to a resolve.

"Well, I guess that means, Professor Beau Moreau remains in play," Shantelle said, her phone balanced precariously between her fingers, scrolling through old photographs, and stopping on one. "Look at this," she said, passing the phone to Manny. "You were right. Abernathy's secret society wasn't just a rumor. It was the society for Millfield's elite—academics, authors, even a few politicians. And get this—a couple of them were alumnis who went on to win Nobel prizes."

Manny rubbed her temples. She could feel a headache coming on. At the moment, she wasn't sure she was ready to absorb any more information.

"Great," she mutters, leaning back against the worn leather seat. "Even more to look into."

"Yeah, it doesn't explain why *ritualistic murder* would be on their event calendar. But it isn't like Abernathy was above it—otherwise the witch wouldn't exist," Shantelle said, shrugging.

"I need a drink," Manny muttered, pushing herself out of the booth. Her thoughts were muddled by layers of academic jargon, urban legends and folklore. She wanted another autumn ember—hoping its notes of cinnamon, apple cider, and bourbon, garnished with a caramel-dipped apple slice would drown out the little voice inside her head.

"I'll come with you," Grant offered, slipping out of his seat.

Together, they weaved through the crowded pub, the air thick with the sour tang of spilled beer and burgers lingering.

Unfortunately, when they stopped at the bar, Manny felt a sudden, unwanted press into her rear. She stiffened, her stomach churning, shifting from discomfort to anger in the span of a second. Manny spun around, she locked eyes with the culprit—a drunken male student with a lopsided grin, his beer sloshing dangerously close to her shoes.

"Back off," Manny snapped.

The guy raised his hands in mock surrender, swaying slightly. “Relax, sweetheart. It’s crowded.”

“Not crowded enough for you to not keep your hands—or *anything else*—to *yourself?*” she retorts, glaring up at him.

Grant stepped between them. “Move along, man,” he said.

The guy mumbled something incoherent then stumbled away, disappearing into the throng of bodies to their right. Manny took a deep breath and released it, her pulse still racing.

“You okay?” Grant asked, his brow furrowed.

“Fine,” Manny muttered, but her nerves were still on edge.

But as they turned back to the bar, a snippet of conversation caught her attention.

“…Founders’ gathering next Friday,” a blonde frat boy said, his voice loud enough to cut through the other pubgoers. “Legacies, only. Not that it matters—dad secured my invite over summer.”

The other guy laughed, clinking his glass against the first’s. “Yeah, but don’t screw it up. The wardens don’t just let anyone in.”

Manny and Grant exchanged a look.

Manny angled herself to hear more, but the conversation veered into jokes about keg stands and future *‘initiation pranks’* for spring.

“Did you hear that?” Manny asked under her breath, the pieces clicking into place. “The wardens. How much do you want to bet they’re talking about Abernathy’s society…”

Grant scratched his head. “Well I know it would be a good way to find out the truth.”

Manny nodded. “So, I guess we’re crashing their little party.”

“I don’t see why not.”

It was their best chance to tie the murders to the society—or it would be their most dangerous move yet. Either way, she would risk it.

Chapter 18
Friday, October 4th

"He's been writing non-stop for thirty minutes. Maybe he's just working on a paper," Manny muttered, stirring the dregs of her tea.

"Doubt it. Look at him—he keeps looking over his shoulder," Grant said under his breath, barely moving his lips. He tapped his pen against the edge of his laptop screen, mimicking boredom.

Grant leaned back in his chair, casually stretching but sneaking a glance in Tanner's direction. "Okay, fair point. But if we're here until midnight and he doesn't move, we're going to need more caffeine."

"Okay, explain it to me again," Manny whispered, looking over her shoulder in case someone was listening—even though they were already tucked away in the world's most depressing study nook.

She'd spent half their time in Anselm library idly flipping through her book, her eyes scanning pages but never really reading. Every once and a while a few students would wander inside, leaving behind a scent trail of burnt coffee when they passed, because they didn't know that Archer's Coffee was better than the liquid toxin that was MillU's student cafe's coffee. And she's half-convinced her chair hasn't been cleaned since the Reagan administration. At this point, she'd rather go back to her apartment, or actually study rather than continue pretending she was.

Grant turned his laptop toward her, the screen's blue glow illuminating his annoyingly smug expression. "I borrowed Tanner's—"

"Stole."

"—*borrowed* Tanner Wentworth's login credentials. Classic legacy behavior; he wrote his password on a Post-it and stuck it on his laptop. 'RowingChamp123,' by the way. Very original."

Manny rolled her eyes. "And?"

"*And*," he said, dragging the word out like he was auditioning for a daytime soap, "his login gave me access to this beauty." He clicked a window, and an email popped up on the screen. There isn't a subject line, and the sender is a string of numbers. But there is a link that he subsequently clicks, making Manny's stomach drop.

"Is that—"

"Yes." Grant smirked. "Encrypted invite. But I didn't even have to really try—Tanner sent himself the passcode for it in another email."

The invitation was short: a date, a time, and a location. Friday, October 4th. Midnight. Langston House/Secondary Humanities Building. Basement. Stoker.

Manny let out a slow breath. "And you're sure he'll lead us there?"

"Positive." He leaned back, crossing his arms. "He's meeting up with some sorority girl that's also going to their little soirée. This stuff is basically foreplay for guys like him."

Manny smacked his arm. "*Gross*. Don't make me regret doing this."

His smugness faded, immediately replaced with something else. "You're not backing out, are you?"

"No," Manny crossed her arms. "But, Grant…what if we're wrong? What if this isn't some vampire cult thing and we're just walking into a half-baked hazing ritual? Or worse, some party for the filthy rich?"

Grant's lips twitched. "Then we'll leave. But if it is what we think it is—if they're behind the murders—we can't just sit on our hands, can we?"

Manny didn't answer. Instead, she looked over at Tanner scratching his neck as he glared at his computer screen. "Fine. But if I die, I'm haunting you first."

"Aww, you'd give me that honor," he quipped, already stuffing his laptop into his bag.

"And you think they'll just let us waltz in there?"

Grant shook his head. "No…but they didn't require RSVP. So, who's to say they'll know? I doubt they're checking IDs."

"And if they catch us?"

He grins. "Then I'll—" he stopped suddenly and gestured in Tanner's direction.

Manny looked at the library's clock. It was 11:45. Tanner was packing up and spritzing on some cologne.

"Showtime," Grant whispered.

Manny didn't laugh. She knew it was meant to make her laugh. But she didn't even smile, because the truth was, she didn't know how much danger they were walking into—or if they would make it back out.

But just as Grant nudged her with his elbow, Tanner threw his bag over his shoulder and strode out the library doors.

* * *

They followed Tanner as he sauntered across the quad, in what was beginning to feel like something out of a bad spy movie. He'd put on a black trench coat, his collar popped so high he looks like a low-budget Dracula, and he kept glancing around like he was expecting paparazzi.

"He's about as subtle as a fireworks display," Manny muttered, huddling closer to Grant as they trailed him.

"At least he's predictable."

Tanner only took a slight detour to makeout with a brunette girl in a brown coat for about fifteen minutes before leading them straight to Langston House.

A slightly pretentious, slightly *punnily named* building, and after five years of attending Millfield University, she still couldn't decide if she admired the audacity or wanted to roll her eyes so far back in her head she could see last week. Named after Langston Hughes—though they couldn't bother to properly tend to the bust they'd made of him. But then, it also feels just ironic enough to be the product of some stuffy old board of trustees trying to look progressive. Or like someone on the naming committee thought they were terribly clever. Like they were saying, *"See? We get the culture."* But maybe, she would like it more if it wasn't a gothic monstrosity designed to flex the university's wealth while housing a bunch of wannabe academics who think they are God's gift to scholarship. To make matters worse, gothic architecture held a truly undeniable beauty, but Langston House wasn't that. It was nothing more than a pat on the back while winking at students, like, *Get it? Langston Hughes? Arts and Humanities Building? Ha ha.* Or maybe not. It was a secondary building—not even a primary. Primary buildings had required courses. But Secondary? Students could attend a few workshops and maybe a few elective classes inside, but there wasn't a single required course inside—even the Engineering colleges' secondary building had required courses. But Langston House could pretty much be avoided. Even the gargoyles grimaced down at her overhead, as if her presence was disturbing them. Though every room was numbered or named, hence why a lecture hall aptly named 'Stoker Hall' would be easy to find.

Their walk to the Stoker Hall was the world's most boring ghost tour, minus the nervous giggles and fist bumping students. She had to weave around a few guys snapping a few selfies together. Inside, Langston House, needed tending to, the fluorescent hallway lights buzzed like angry bees, flickering just enough to make Manny wonder if they'd stepped into a low budget horror film.

Grant led the way, which was fine by Manny because he was taller, broader, and statistically more likely to trip over something first. Even if she never saw any of these students again, she didn't want to embarrass herself tonight. Manny trailed behind him, gripping the stairwell railing, hanging on for dear life taking each steep creaking step in stride. The air grew unusually thick for a Millfield University building, but she didn't make a habit of wandering down to the basements. But when they reached the bottom, it was exactly what she expected: grim, gray, and miserable. A corridor where mold would thrive and where cell signal went to die. Pipes ran along the ceiling, banging and groaning, and every door they passed had this sad little frosted window, the numbers on them barely clinging on, and she swore she heard scuttling when they walked past it.

Probably a rat.

She hated rats. Then there it was, the lecture hall, nestled at the very end. Or rather, the entrance to what she might consider calling *Hell's waiting room* in a short story. The double doors are ajar, spilling out an ominous amber glow into the hallway, and there's a faint murmur—low and steady, like a wasp's nest that had just about enough. Grant looks back at her, and Manny nods because what else was she going to do? Turn back and pretend nothing's going on? She hadn't seen strange sigils popping up everywhere. She hadn't done a blood ritual with Grant in a cemetery. *Yeah, right.* Instead, she moves closer to Grant, her stomach doing somersaults and her teeth on edge, as every nerve in her body screamed at her to turn back. But there they were, walking toward potential danger like a pair of idiots who forgot how horror films end.

When they entered the secret society's soiree, she didn't know what she'd been expecting, but it looked nothing like a lecture hall at the moment. The entire room was illuminated by torches, casting long, jittery shadows across the walls. There were symbols—painted in crimson and gold—etched into every surface: doors, walls, even the floor. Manny didn't recognize most of them, but they made her skin crawl.

Grant nudged her. "Here, take one."

Manny glanced down at three folded garments stuffed in Grant's bag, and she was sure she recognized one of them.

"Did you go through my things?"

"Is this really the time?" Grant asked, pulling out a suit jacket.

Manny sighed. He was right. There were two dresses, both she guessed were scavenged from her undergrad days. She pulled out the burgundy velvet dress, hoping to blend in with the eight other women she'd seen dressed in red.

She ducked behind a column near what used to be a theatre stage to change while Grant kept watch. "So, everyone's dressed like they're auditioning for *Eyes Wide Shut*, and we're just supposed to what—hope we blend in? Whose bright idea—"

"This is your plan. I'm just doing my part," Grant said, shrugging on his suit jacket. He looked good in it, like someone who would actually belong there.

When Manny stepped out in the dress, his jaw dropped. "Wow. If this whole amateur detective thing doesn't work out, you've got a backup career as a femme fatale."

Manny rolled her eyes. "*Thanks*."

They slipped in between two groups of well-dressed students, giddy to be 'entering the circle,' though they maintained their position in the back of the room, staying close to an exit. Around them, attendees were whispering to each other in low, feverish tones. They were dressed like them—formal, polished, but not flashy. Their *'escort,'* Tanner, however, looked like he just stepped off a yacht. Apparently not wanting to blend in with the others in his green velvet suit set, that somehow looked like it was freshly ironed. He'd also gotten bored of his earlier company and was now flirting with a redhead in a yellow dress. Which were all irrelevant details in the grand scheme of things.

In fact, Manny couldn't care less, because the longer she stood there, taking in the room, the more her stomach churned. There was something in the air—melted wax and a more metallic smell—blood?

Or is it that the air feels alive, and not in a good way. It was like being under the full moon in the cemetery all over again, the same charged sensation crawling over her skin. Like static from an old TV, but inside her, the sensation seemed to be building, humming over the students rushing in. It was strange and she wanted to believe her imagination was running wild, but the memory of her warm blood wetting her fingers made it impossible to ignore. This was magic. Real, tangible magic, the kind she had only just began to understand.

But it doesn't feel good. It's not like the warm, welcoming magic people read about in fairy tales. No, this is something else entirely—sharp, invasive, and worming its way into her senses. But why was she smelling blood? Was it her mind playing tricks on her?

Manny looked at Grant, but he didn't seem to notice it—or he was better at pretending he doesn't.

"Do you feel that?" Manny whispered to Grant.

"Yeah." His voice is strained. "It's like when we were in the cemetery…"

They could run. But they can't. Whatever's in here, whatever's giving off this energy, is exactly what they'd come here to find.

It felt like the magic was aware of them, and whispering, You're not supposed to be here. And for the first time since they'd started this insane plan, she was starting to think it was right.

She felt scattered, and she began to look around. Her eyes eventually landed back on Tanner as if he were a marker, or source of comfort. She'd hoped he would look as confused as she was. Instead, he was walking across the room with a cloaked figure, approaching the center of the hall, where a raised platform held a podium draped in black fabric. It seemed other students noticed this as well, and their murmuring died down—and Manny's nails suddenly were biting into her palms.

"This is wrong," Manny whispers.

"No shit." Grant said.

She wanted to tell him *'we should go,'* but couldn't manage it. Because they needed to know the truth—and because leaving now might be just as dangerous as staying.

Tanner helped the hooded figure step onto the platform—their movements somehow oddly graceful. Torches around the hall began to flicker wildly, the flames seeming to bend toward the figure as if in deference. Then, with one quick movement, the hood is pulled back, revealing their face.

"Dr. Whitaker?" Manny said in shock, barely managing to keep her voice low.

Grant froze beside her, his eyes wide. "Isn't that your old history professor?"

"Greek Literature Professor," Manny corrected, her words barely a whisper. Though she wasn't sure that mattered. "He's been at Millfield University for decades—he's on one of the boards, I think."

And now he was standing there, framed by a tableau of blood-red symbols and dripping candles, as if he's stepped out of a nightmare. He looked the same as he always did—soft and scholarly, his thinning gray hair combed neatly, his wire-rimmed glasses perched low on his nose. But tonight, as he cleaned the lenses with a practiced swipe of a monogrammed handkerchief, knots began to form in Manny's stomach. His gentle, sweet-old-man demeanor that reassured floundering undergraduates was lost—even as he cleaned his glasses in an ordinary, almost comical way, it only made the moment more surreal.

"Dearest students," he began, his voice steady, carrying an almost hypnotic cadence. "Tonight, we reaffirm the pact that has preserved our institution for generations."

A murmur of agreement ripples through the crowd.

"The balance must be maintained," Whitaker continued, his gaze sweeping over the attendees. "For power is never free. It demands a price, and only by paying it can we ensure that the Abernathys' legacy is preserved."

Manny swallowed. Grant leaned in closer, his breath warm against my ear. "Maintaining balance? Sounds like a ritual if I've ever heard one." He straightened then. "Magic always has a price."

"*Shh*," Manny shushed, though she couldn't tear her eyes away from Whitaker.

Her old professor stepped closer to the edge of the platform, clasping his hands together in an almost prayer-like gesture. "We are the stewards of this institution's power. The world outside would seek to dismantle us, to strip away what makes us great. But through our unity, our vigilance, and our sacrifices, we remain unbroken."

Sacrifices. The word rings in her ears.

Whitaker pauses, his eyes scanning the room. For one moment, Manny thought his gaze lingered on her, but then it slid past, allowing her to let out a long sigh.

"Tonight, we honor those who came before us," Whitaker continued, his tone softening into something almost reverent. "And we prepare for what lies ahead."

Grant's hand brushed hers, a silent signal: *We need to leave.*

Manny nodded, but she didn't move, it was as if Whitaker's words had frozen her in place.

She couldn't stop staring at him as he leaned forward, his hands clasped in front of him like a preacher delivering a sermon.

"As you know, our continued prosperity is not mere happenstance," he intones, delivering the message slowly. "It is the result of a sacred pact, one forged in the earliest days of Abernathy's founding."

Manny exchanged a look with Grant, whose jaw was clenched so tight she thought it might crack. Her pulse pounds in her ears, almost loud enough to drown out Whitaker's next words. *Almost.*

"Our benefactor ensures this institution's safety and supremacy, protecting it from the decay that plagues lesser universities," Whitaker continues. "But such protection requires...*sacrifices*."

A chill went down her spine. There was that word again. *Sacrifices*. But not metaphorical ones, not the kind you make when you skip dessert to fit into a dress before a first date, or pull an all-nighter for a final. No, *sacrifice* as in—older, darker, bloodier, and teeming with magic.

Whitaker paused, perhaps for dramatic effect. Then he added, "These offerings bind us to their power, which shields us, strengthening the wards that keep Abernathy's chosen *untouchable*."

A few attendees shifted uneasily, perhaps not having learned this part from their parents or finding general discomfort in the idea.

Grant leaned in closer to her, his voice so faint it barely registers. "He's talking about—"

"I know," Manny manages.

The murders. Her throat was dry and tight, and she swore the room was getting smaller.

Whitaker's expression hardened. "The next offering will take place soon—during the Founders' Gala in town. It is a necessary step, one that will ensure another twenty years of prosperity and stability for us all."

Grant stiffened beside her, his hand brushing hers in a silent bid to keep her calm. But her mind had other ideas.

The Founders' Gala. That's only two weeks from now.

She stared up at Whitaker blankly.

"The next chosen has been identified," he continued, his voice stern. "As your parents may have told you, this balance is imperative. These deaths must not be in vain. And if you want your families to prosper, you must take a proactive approach…"

Chosen. A proactive approach? That's how they justify it, Manny thought, bile rising in her throat. And to make matters worse—where the hell would she even begin to stop it? She thought they'd stopped it in the cemetery, but clearly they hadn't. She could see Whitaker's mouth moving, but she couldn't hear him. Though most students were nodding, their movements were stiff and robotic.

Grant squeezed her hand, pulling her back to the present. "We need to get out of here. *Now.*"

Manny managed to nod. Slowly they inched toward the door. All of her instincts told her to run out of this room without looking back. But one question was stopping her—who was the next victim? Their next sacrificial lamb?

They had made it halfway to the door before she had the most disconcerting feeling—they were being watched. Her skin crawled and she turned to her right, locking eyes with the guy from the bar—the one who thought his crotch deserved a VIP seat on her backside.

"Hey!" His voice cut through the silence of the room, too loud, too direct. Heads turn.

Shit.

"Grant," she whispers, grabbing his arm. "Move."

They ran, weaving through the throng of confused attendees. Someone shouted after them, but she didn't dare look back. Her shoes clicked loudly on the stone floor, echoing in the cavernous hallway as they raced through the maze-like corridors of the basement.

"Stop them!" another voice shouted, followed by the sound of hurried footsteps.

"Fantastic," Grant muttered as they rounded a corner. "Nothing like a chase to end the evening."

A shadow exited from a door, at least ten feet ahead of them. Manny grabbed Grant's sleeve and yanked him toward a side door marked "STAIRS."

"Seriously?" he huffed as they ran up them.

"Unless you've got a better idea, yes!"

They pushed open another door, this one led out onto university grounds and near a stoplight. Which meant they had two paths—jaywalking or running through campus. And despite the past hour and a few minutes, Manny liked those odds.

Manny saw the pedestrian signal sign at the intersection switch to the green walking figure at the corner, she considered making a run for it—but just as she intended to, she nearly crashed into Shantelle and Isla. Shantelle was holding a soda and a half-empty popcorn bucket, her brows lifted in surprise.

"What the hell—"

"Sorry!" Manny said instinctively.

But before she could explain, a loud bang came from behind her. Shantelle didn't miss a beat. She thrusts the popcorn bucket into Grant's hands and throws an arm around Manny.

"Didn't you just love the ending?" Isla asks, her voice a little too loud and extremely chipper. "A little different from the others, but still the best movie I've seen in a while!"

They turned back toward campus, and Manny noticed the two men in black instantly.

Shit. Shit. Shit.

"Yeah, the part where the woman leaves behind her career isn't ever my favorite. Would love to watch the whole plot line backward," Shantelle continued, her voice breaking through her panic. "Maybe her parents don't need their Inn saved, maybe they deserve a nice retirement—"

Manny looked over at Grant. He was staring down at the popcorn bucket like it was a live grenade, but he managed to flash a tight smile. "Yep. Classic rom-com. Dependable. We should do this more often."

It was the first time Manny had ever seen Grant struggle to play along. But given their situation, she couldn't say that she was surprised.

The two men hesitated by the door, perhaps weighing whether or not they were worth the effort—if they'd realized they were who they were searching for. Finally, they muttered something to each other and retreated back the way they came.

As soon as they were out of sight, Shantelle dropped her fake grin and glared at Manny. "You two. Explain. *Now*. You already owe me at least three drinks for that performance."

"Three drinks?" Grant repeated.

"Yes, *three*! Now spit it out," Shantelle snapped.

"Drinks. That's fine," Manny said, still trying to catch her breath. "How about we head back to mine then? Somewhere where it's safe."

Instead of questioning what she meant by her latter statement, Shantelle nodded, and they headed to the on-campus apartments. By the time they were safely inside, Manny had internally thanked God several times, they were huddled into her apartment and Isla was wrapping a blanket around her.

"Jesus, what the hell are you wearing?" Isla tutted. "It's barely 20 degrees outside."

Shantelle stared at Manny, blinking a few times before saying anything. "Is that the dress you thrifted for 'slutty storybook' in junior year?" Her voice was much higher than usual. Probably from shock.

"Yes," Manny said.

Honestly, she hadn't realized she was shivering until now. But she wasn't blaming her dress. She blamed the Wardens of the Gate. Her dress barely qualified for entry as Slutty Red Riding Hood for Omega's Halloween party theme—she'd had problems entering at the door—but, in her opinion, slutty costumes were a recipe for pneumonia when you're walking through campus at 3 a.m, and your vodka blanket had all but evaporated especially in Millfield. So, she'd opted for the Barbie-approved version of 'Little Red.' More *'innocent coed meets Pinterest'* than *'lost in the woods and looking for a good time.'* Tammy had rolled her eyes at her but relented after Manny had pointed out that her thigh-high boots for 'her Tiana' wouldn't survive the uphill trek to the fraternity.

Now, sitting in their apartment in the same dress, she couldn't decide if she'd chosen it out of some nostalgic inkling of a 'simpler time,' or simply hadn't thought about it being wildly inappropriate for infiltrating a murderous secret society, borderline cult, given the circumstances.

"Never mind that," Grant said, cutting in. "The Wardens of the Gate are behind the murders. I don't know how, but I think it's safe to assume they're using magic given that they're sacrificing them."

Isla paled, and wrapped her arms tightly around herself. "Sacrifices? What?"

"To who?" Shantelle asked.

Manny stared at her hands, they were trembling slightly as she recounted what she heard. "Some *benefactor*. Professor Whitaker said their next sacrifice is going to happen at the Founders' Gala."

"Maybe we should go to the police," Isla suggested softly, rubbing her arms.

Grant cocked a brow. "And tell them what? Our university's secret society is sacrificing students to some God or entity to keep the rich rich? Does that even sound sane to you?"

"Well someone has to stop them, right?" Isla retorted, her voice shaking. "For everyone's sake. We don't know who could be next. It could be one of our friends for all we know. Why it could be—"

"We will," Manny said, her voice firm. She had stopped shivering, but her heart was still racing. Perhaps from exhaustion or fear, but she couldn't shake the thought that she was missing something. There was something she couldn't quite put her finger on: what did vampires have to do with all this?

Chapter 19
Fall Break
Saturday, October 5th

R*itual resonance*—a fancy academic term for "You've been through something traumatic, but hey, now you can sniff out magic like a bloodhound and might even think meddling with it is fun next time." Apparently, when someone, ergo *her*, is part of a *magical woo woo*—especially sacrificial lambs—they don't walk away empty-handed. They can get a few magical side effects, ranging from moderate to severe symptoms. Like suddenly being able to sense when magic, or if there were any magical, occultish creatures, because their soul now has a VIP pass to *Magicland*—home of wizardcraft and witchery.

Worse…a bond can form between caster and lamb. Like magical Stockholm syndrome but with an extra kick. A victim might start feeling grateful to the person who nearly turned them into a ritual barbecue, even to the point where they're begging for round two if the ritual was repeatable. That is, if they weren't dead. It was sick—it made Manny consider whether or not fairy godmothers would actually be evil. Of course, she'd been hoping something in her childhood would remain untouched by this. And the academics described it all like it was a fascinating phenomenon rather than the existential nightmare it clearly is. Though Manny didn't feel any closer to Grant—at least not that she'd noticed. They were best friends after all.

In fact, she was hoping it would turn off, because it meant she was a metal detector for vampires, witches, and whatever else might be waltzing around Millfield without a care in the world.

Does that mean Whitaker is a vampire? Or warlock? Wizard?

She groaned at the thought. She wasn't sure she could handle another vampire right now. Or accidentally sniffing out a coven. So this week, her first week off of Thanksgiving break, she decided she would try and identify the next victim from the comfort of her living room inside her apartment on Abernathy Row. Attempting to determine any and all possible attendees from the university, which she wanted to pretend was possible. Meaning while most students were headed home to hug their parents and argue over what they are or *aren't* doing with their lives, she'd chosen to stay put. After all, flights home were outrageous, and she wasn't about to drain her savings to eat overpriced snack food at 30,000 feet.

Dean and Grant would be around for the first half of the week, arguing over who would clean what and packing up. But they were bringing Mihawk over to get him acclimatized to a Tammy-less environment, as he had a tendency to bite their younger cousin. So, he couldn't be present at Thanksgiving. Though Grant would argue any and all children needed not to grab Mihawk's tail, and everything would be fine. That didn't sit well with his little cousin's mother, but Grant didn't want him left outside. So, Manny had volunteered to watch Mihawk, hoping to give herself something else to do while waiting for the Founders' Gala and the Abernathy Christmas Market to start.

This evening's adventure was 'get the food from the delivery person,' because cooking required energy she didn't currently possess. She had already skipped two meals today, she couldn't skip a third. When she poked her head out to grab the bag from the delivery guy, she found herself staring past him, just over his shoulder, where Mihawk was silently judging her.

Of course, he's escaped. Again.

He never scratched at Grant and Dean's door, or meowed like any normal, needy feline. No, Mihawk would perch himself on top of the stairway railing, side-eying anyone who dared to exist within his eyeline, as though he hadn't left the apartment on his own accord.

Why wouldn't he stare Manny down as she retrieved her chicken nuggets and fries, making her feel like a lesser human for even thinking about eating fast food. His gaze barely shifted as if he was already thinking about being forced to stay with her. But then he gave an even more judgmental once-over of the delivery guy. He shifted awkwardly, clearly unsettled by the feline's unblinking gaze. Even her downstairs neighbor, Nicole, wasn't spared. The poor freshman struggling to carry her groceries looked like she was rethinking her entire life as Mihawk tracked her movements all the way to her front door.

Manny sighed. "Mihawk," she called, holding the door open, bag of fast food in one hand. "You want in?"

He flicked his tail, staring at her like she'd just asked him to do her taxes. For a moment, Manny thought he was going to stay outside, but then he hopped down and sauntered toward her, in a way that made it clear he didn't need her—he just wanted to let her know she'd been weighed, measured, and found wanting.

"Thanks," Manny told the delivery guy quickly.

"Yeah, sure," he said, before rushing down the stairs.

Manny closed the door and turned back to her feline guest. "Sure, make yourself at home."

Mihawk had leaped onto the sofa and sat in a tight loaf, eyes half-lidded but still watching her.

She took her food out of the bag and put it onto a plate and sighed.

"You can stay," Manny said, pointing a fry at him, "but no commentary, got it?"

He blinked slowly, as if to say, *No promises.*

* * *

Lucky for Mihawk, he hadn't had to tolerate her for too long. After a few hours watching Christmas movies together, him eventually purring loud enough to rival most car motors, Grant had come by to retrieve him. Though he'd be back on Friday, the feline seemed rather pleased with that information after their quiet evening together.

Unlike Mihawk, Manny was starting to disapprove of herself—as she'd come to think they were complete idiots for leaving the society's little soiree early. Maybe Professor Whitaker would've dropped a name, or maybe he'd have mentioned something—anything—helpful. But they were nearly caught. All she knew now was that it would be some student, perhaps involved in activism, perhaps involved in helping someone else—perhaps hoping to be an ally.

But, no, they had to run out like they were in a heist movie. Now here she was, trying to determine which student of color would be the Wardens of the Gate's perfect sacrificial lamb. Unless she planned on rounding up every student of color on campus like a bizarrely overzealous R.A.—yet another thing she was sure she couldn't pull off —so she had nothing.

What little she did know was that the sacrifice was planned on the same day as the Founder's Gala, which meant it would be right when the Abernathy Christmas Market kicks off. Shantelle and Isla were already going to the actual gala—good for them, not so great for her. So, maybe they could scope it out. And while she could probably drag Grant, Wade, and Dean into combing the fairgrounds with her, she had to be realistic: she was about as likely to find the victim as she was to spot Bigfoot selling churros at the cider stand.

And what was she supposed to do if they did find them? It's not like she can stop a vampire. She can barely stop herself from impulse-ordering fast food at 10 p.m. She didn't own a crucifix—where would she even get one? The Bewitchery? This whole situation felt like trying to put out a forest fire with a can of LaCroix, and honestly, she was questioning her life choices at the moment. She had half a mind to book an appointment with Dr. Carter. She hadn't attended one in a while—she should have, but she'd just been too busy.

Manny sat with her head in her hands and considered what she wanted to do.

If I had the attendees list to the Founder's Gala...but, maybe not.

She was stuck inside her head, overthinking. Being her, and someone like her, whose brain tends to work like a blender missing its lid. She couldn't muster up anything, not a single '*aha moment*,' and she cursed herself for not being as brilliant as Nancy Drew. But then, sitting there, staring at her notes, she had something resembling a thought pop into her head.

What if the sacrificial lamb wasn't just a random student? Manny thought, twirling her pen. *What if they're someone who would be at both the gala and the Abernathy Christmas Market? Someone at the gala by default, because they're a necessity.*

And if she were a cartoon character, a light bulb would've lit up over her head: *orchestra.*

Or maybe one of those other student groups the university trots out whenever they need to make the university look inclusive.

She scribbled down "orchestra/performers?" in her notebook and underlined it twice, then sat back, staring at the word like it might transform into a list of names if she stared at it hard enough.

If they're involved in the event, they'll probably be at the gala and wandering around the market after.

It's not perfect, but it was better than nothing. At least it narrowed the field from "students of color and BIPOC allies on campus" to "anyone holding a violin or wearing a tux."

Now all she had to do was find a list of the current students in the orchestra, and cross-reference them with activism on and off campus. Easy enough. It wasn't like she had anything else to do.

Chapter 20
Friday, October 18th

Fall break had gone on long enough, it had been going on for a short eternity—or at least the version of eternity where she was cold, tired, and perpetually running on caffeine fumes. The Founders' Gala, glittering and ominous, was finally here, just a few days after Thanksgiving, and here she was trudging through crispy autumn leaves, arms crossed as they walked down Main Street. Grant joined her with Mihawk on a leash. The feline trotted along the sidewalks, climbing over fire hydrants since he'd decided today's weather was decent enough to bless the masses with his presence. Dean and Wade had agreed to meet them there.

"You sure about this?" Grant asked, as he handed the tickets over to the gate attendant, who stared curiously at Mihawk.

Mihawk licked his jowls at him, as if threatening him with some underlying ancestral instinct to eat people, that still lived inside him.

"As sure as I can be," Manny said, as they walked inside beneath a large tarp sign overhead read 'Abernathy Christmas Market' in big bold letters.

Millfield's Main Street was the town's pride and joy this time of year, transformed from its usual small-town charm into a glittering

Christmas postcard. The Abernathy Christmas Market itself was like stepping into a snow globe, the kind that didn't skimp on the glitter. Fairy lights crisscrossed overhead illuminating their path and wrapping everything in a warm glow. A jumbled row of wooden stalls, each one like a miniature log cabin, with decorations mostly of reds and greens lining the walkways, bursting with seasonal treasures—hand-knit scarves, carved wooden ornaments, and enough peppermint-scented candles to make Santa's workshop smell like a candy cane factory exploded. Local artisans were everywhere, selling their wintery creations.

Manny caught a whiff of a sweet tangy mulled cider as they passed one stall, and somewhere, a brass band was playing *Frosty the Snowman* with an enthusiasm that made her grin despite herself.

At the center of it all stood the Christmas tree, tall and proud, glittering with ornaments and a star that shone like it was made of real starlight. It was ridiculous and over the top, and she loved it. There were families crowded around the tree snapping pictures with their kids, some of which were clutching candy canes as if their lives depended on it. She saw a few classmates and waved a few awkward 'hellos' though she didn't bother with small talk.

"Really?" Grant asked incredulously. "Because 'secluded spots' and 'magical instincts' sound exactly like the sort of thing you'd want to avoid—given the circumstances."

He wasn't wrong, but Manny didn't have the bandwidth to explain how the buzzing in her chest—the same one she'd felt in the cemetery, in the Langston House's basement, and during her nightmares—had become almost unbearable. It was like being tuned to a frequency only she could hear. "Look, the sooner we find wherever the caster is, the sooner we can save the lamb."

It was easier said than done. The cobblestone paths were mostly cleared of snow, but she was still worried about the rare patch of ice she couldn't see, and the last thing she needed was to slip. She noticed a few wooden stalls with wreaths tied over them and the buttery aroma of kettle corn.

Then the buzzing sensation started again, prickling every nerve underneath her skin. It was like she was one of those metal detectors adults waved around at the beach, hoping to find some hidden treasure though mostly finding bottle caps instead. Not at all glamorous, but reliable. Now that she was paying attention to her newfound affliction, there was this pull, like an invisible thread wound tightly around her, dragging her forward whether she wanted it to or not. So, they continued walking in silence, pulled along by her invisible tether, which was drawing her to the far end of Main Street, just past the bustle of the market, where a chapel stood. Its whitewashed walls and tall steeple almost disappeared in the glow of the festive lights. She would've written it off as nerves, but her insides were jangling like a string of badly tuned sleigh bells.

The chapel, small and unassuming, with stained glass windows that glinted slightly under the twinkly lights. Mihawk let out a low, grumbly, *meow*, which reeked of disapproval.

"All right, then, this it?" Grant muttered.

Manny nodded, and pushed open the door, which let out a godawful creak. Inside, the air was thick, dusty and still, carrying that faint, metallic tang she'd smelled in Stoker Hall.

They moved through the pews, floorboards groaning with every step. Mihawk had hopped into Grant's arms, and probably would've made a break for it, if it weren't for his harness. As they neared the altar, the sensation intensified, clawing at her senses. Manny leaned around the chapel, her eyes catching on a small, warped trapdoor tucked behind the pulpit, half-hidden by a statue's shadow.

"Please tell me that's not what I think it is," Grant said.

"It is," Manny replied, already reaching for the latch.

The hinges shrieked in protest, revealing a staircase, with most of its stairs hidden by the darkness. Grant shot her a look—his said, *"I don't like this."* Manny shrugged—because what choice did they have? Then they started down. She rubbed her arms in her cardigan, as it seemed to get colder with each step, and she brought up her arm as the unpleasant odor of burnt herbs breached her senses.

When they reached what she believed was a room, she attempted to fumble around in search of a light. When she didn't find one, she took out her cellphone, and turned on its flashlight.

Dear God.

It was a chamber. Symbols etched into the stone walls, candles melted into pools of wax, and a low stone altar stained with what she couldn't nor wanted to confirm was dried blood. A silver dagger lay abandoned nearby, its blade glinting for a moment before she shined it at the narrow grate above.

"Okay, this is officially worse than I imagined," Grant said, his voice low and shining his phone flashlight around.

Manny didn't say anything. She was too busy looking at the walls.

I know these sigils.

She turned on her camera app and snapped a few photos of them. Then she compared them to a few she had on her phone.

They're the same.

The Wardens of the Gates' sigil was the most obvious. The others —she'd seen during their little soiree. She wondered if they were still feeding off the remaining energy in the chamber. She would wonder if the sacrifice had already happened, but one thing was missing—the sacrifice. They hadn't killed the lamb yet.

There's still time.

"They did something here," Manny whispered. "I don't know what."

"Yeah," Grant muttered. "I can feel it too, but no one's here anymore, Manny. There's no lamb to rescue. What now?"

Damn, she thought.

He was right. They'd found evidence of a blood ritual, yes, but nothing actionable. If she had momentarily considered handing this over to police as Isla suggested, they would need a hell of a lot more.

They're a step ahead.

And she couldn't help but wonder if they hadn't been caught at that meeting, maybe the Wardens of the Gate wouldn't be. That meant they couldn't do the ritual here. So, what was done here? It didn't make any sense.

She touched the Warden's sigil on the wall—it was wet.

She shined the flashlight on her fingers. There was blood on them.

Then it dawned on her.

"Is there anything in that book Trish gave you saying blood rituals and sacrifices having to take place at the same time or location?" Manny said, the words rushing out of her.

"What? What do you mean?" Grant asked.

"*Anything*. Like do they have to happen at the same time?" Manny said. "Anything, anything at all?"

Grant thought it over for a moment. "I mean if they were sacrificing it to a god or…" Grant stopped, and his mouth dropped open. "*Something else*."

"Shit," Manny said, suddenly turning and bolting up the stairs.

It hit her like a slap in the face.

Vampires. Of course. Blood rituals, sacrificial lambs, maintaining power—it all lines up.

The Wardens of the Gate weren't just offering up students for some abstract, mystical power. They were ringing the dinner bell for vampires, luring them in to feast on the "offerings." That's why the victims were always drained of blood completely, and why that sigil was damn near everywhere. These weren't just murders; they were catered banquets for the undead. But what kind of vampire could pack that kind of punch? The kind that could keep the flow of wealth to anyone within the Founders' fold.

Was Dracula real? It made sense, in a sick, twisted way. Their hunger, their presence, it strengthened whatever ward or barrier the society wanted to protect their precious wealth and prosperity for the worthy. Millfield University, really was an elitist, ivy-covered hellhole screaming, *"We eat the weak to shield the powerful!"*

Manny felt like throwing up, and her feet could hardly keep up with her. Grant was barely able to. All this time, they'd been looking for the wrong connections, asking the wrong questions. It wasn't just about who was next—it was about *why*—and *who* they were being fed to. And now, knowing the truth, she wasn't sure if that made it easier or a hundred times worse.

She stopped to catch her breath, and Grant caught up.

“Text everyone,” Manny said, nearly breathless as she tugged her scarf loose. “We need to regroup, fast. Meet at the cider stall.”

Grant looked at her, setting Mihawk on the ground, and pulling out his phone. But as he glanced down at his phone, his brow furrowed. “Uh—hang on.”

Manny stood up straight. “What is it?”

Grant’s face went pale as he scrolled through his texts. “Uh, so the orchestra was let out for a quick break. A few of them are already heading over to the food stalls." He wiped his brow, eyes scanning each text. “Wade says they’re all over the place. And we’ve got a problem.”

Manny blinked. "What do you mean? We have to keep track of the students before they spread out. Where’s Isla and Shantelle?”

He pulled up another text and glanced at it, his fingers typing quickly. “Isla lost track of the violinist."

Manny froze. “The violinist?”

Grant nodded. “Yeah, she’s a Black girl with long braids. She’s gone.”

"We need to find her. Fast."

Grant was already tapping out the next message when Manny pulled out her phone from her pocket and dialed Dean’s number.

It rang twice before he answered. “Hi, my love. What's up?"

"Hey, have you seen Isla? She's lost track of—”

"Yeah," he interrupted. "I know. I just talked to her. She said the violinist’s gone somewhere."

Manny could feel bile rising in her throat. “Has anyone in the orchestra seen her?”

He sighed. “She’s not gone-gone. But...she’s definitely nowhere near me. I don’t like it. Isla was too afraid to follow her, and now no one can find the violinist."

“Does she know which way she went?”

Dean paused for a second. “She went past the giant Christmas tree. I imagine she’s more your way now. I’ll try and coordinate with Wade and we can regroup.”

“Okay, on it.” Manny told him, looking around.

“Baby, if you’re right about this, be careful,” Dean said.

“I will.” Then she hung up without another word.

Grant cocked a brow at her. "What’s the plan?"

"Follow me," Manny said, already moving. Her heart was thudding in my chest, and her legs worked instinctively, moving through the crowd as quickly as she could without bumping into anyone.

Manny wove around another set of people, keeping her eyes peeled, hoping it wasn’t too late. And then, as if the universe had decided to add insult to injury, she ran into something hard.

“Ow!” Manny yelped, stumbling backward. Someone caught her wrist as if it were nothing, holding her steady. It was like she’d run into a wall.

"Oh, apologies, Manny,” a deep male voice said. His other hand held a half-eaten Bavarian pretzel. "Busy day?"

Manny blinked, trying to regain her composure, but she didn’t have time for small talk. “Professor Moreau—uh, it’s fine.” She tried to step around him, but he didn’t let go. His gaze fixed on her, and she felt a strange pull toward him.

He must be one of them.

"How is your paper going?" he asked, taking a bite from his pretzel, savoring it as if the world could wait.

She shifted on her feet. "It’s—uh, it’s going well. Almost finished."

Where the hell is Grant?

Usually he’d cut in at a time like this.

"Good," he said, though it was unclear if he actually cared. Was he stalling? He let go of her wrist and gestured vaguely. “You should enjoy the Christmas market…it's cheery. Don’t you think?”

Manny was about to give him a polite nod and rush off when she caught movement at the corner of my eye. And a secondary tether pulling her away from her handsome, likely *vampire*, professor.

There you are, Manny thought.

The violinist. She was walking past a food stall, her long braids swishing as she moved toward a darkened path in the opposite direction. Her pulse quickened, and Manny pulled out her phone, sending a text to her group chat:

> Found her. She's heading toward a path toward the chapel. Meet there.

"I hope you have a good night, professor," she told him.

Beau nodded and she sidestepped him, power walking through the crowd. Her breath slowly shifted from normal to shallow bursts. She knew she had to be closing in on her—no matter what magic might be working on her. She, Manny Webb, was close—so close.

But as she rounded a corner, she froze.

There, lying discarded in the middle of the path, was a lone shoe. But no violinist.

Manny looked around frantically, but she could barely hear anything over her heartbeat. She stood there, her hand hovering over her heart. Willing it to be still.

She was here. I know she was here.

Manny pulled out her phone and was about to send another text when a blood-curdling scream came from somewhere far away—a shriek that sounded like it had come from the deepest pit of hell. Her heartbeat faded into the background. She didn't even hear when her phone clattered to the ground. Her gut twisted as she realized just how badly she'd miscalculated.

She stood there, staring at the empty path where the violinist had been. Her mind muddled with "what ifs"—if they'd just stayed by the chapel, maybe she would've caught up to her before the violinist went down the path. If she had read more about blood rituals. If, if, if. But was that true? Could she have stopped a sacrificial lamb under the influence of a spell?

Eliza Harrow had described being *enspelled* as being in a state of profound disorientation, akin to the effects of intoxication. Cognitive processes would be practically non-existent. Physical movements became detached from conscious control. A body operating independently of the individual's will. Could she have stopped the violinist? Even though the violinist would've wanted Manny to stop her—

wanted to be saved. But hell, Manny would've at least liked the chance to try.

She could feel her chest tightening, and the buzzing sensation rattling around inside her like a beehive. There was magic everywhere. And a year ago, none of this would have remotely seemed real. But she couldn't fight the guilt she felt, not when her limbs felt so heavy, and her tongue was thick with words she couldn't quite say.

Chapter 21
October 19th

By the time the sunlight seeped through the blinds, she'd already submitted a request for a therapy session at noon. Like, actual therapy. She'd cancelled too many sessions over the past two months. In truth, she hadn't realized how many weeks she'd skipped until she counted them—it was 10 weeks to be exact. At first it was just a canceled session here or a quick emergency check-in there to tell Dr. Carter, *Hey, I'm alive, still a mess, in case you were wondering*. No, she'd made an actual appointment this time. Considering how she'd skipped more sessions than she'd attended lately, it felt like the least she could do for her mental health.

And though she felt guilty, she wasn't technically responsible for anyone's death. Unfortunately, her brain insisted on running its highlight reel of *what-ifs* and *if-onlys*. And truthfully, Millfield News was grossly inconsiderate on how they'd covered the violinist in an article titled:

Local Violin Prodigy Found Decapitated

Really? Could they have tried harder to make it sound like a true crime podcast teaser?

The TV coverage hadn't been much better. A news anchor announced the death of one, Sissell Amara Tucker, the prodigal violinist, by decapitation—and a notable mention of her head being found hanging by a thread of muscle in the news ticker, as well as the later retracted article. Which they then corrected—and heavily apologized for said insensitivity and followed up with a promise to "do better."

A more surprising development, Mihawk *was* a good emotional support cat. Dean had insisted he stay with her for the night, and Mihawk had stayed curled beside her on her bed, purring like a generator, as she drifted off to sleep last night. Mostly because Shanks had taken residence underneath the couch the moment Grant pulled out the vacuum cleaner in one of his deep cleaning sessions, though he'd promised to get the feline to come out. Though there'd been no update on Shanks v. Grant since midnight.

And now, over breakfast, Mihawk had graduated from warm-foot duty to her lap, stealing bites of her scrambled eggs like a furry bandit. It was a quarter to noon, and though he had his own food, he still preferred hers. Leaving her to only award him the middling "good" and not "exemplary" emotional support cat title to him.

"Not your food," Manny muttered, nudging him lightly, but he just gave her a smug, *I do what I want,* look.

But he seemed to like her more now—or at least liked the convenience of her when she was sad. Maybe she wasn't Grant, his rightful owner, but she was a good stand-in with decent snacks.

She only had a few more minutes before her appointment, and it was eating her alive. For some reason, she was nervous. Though she needed to lighten the metaphorical load she was carrying—even if she couldn't say the *whole* truth. Some of that truth meant bringing up Tammy.

Her best friend. Gone.

Manny was sitting there scratching behind Mihawk's ears, thinking about that night for the millionth time, turning it over in her head. Tammy had asked her to come with her to the Hub & Haven.

Just a quick trip, Tammy had said. But Manny had been tired, and honestly, she didn't feel like going out. So, she stayed in, thinking they'd have plenty of time to talk later. Only there wasn't a later.

She could still remember the police knocking at their door. Tammy was dead—no, been murdered—in a horrific way. And now Manny knew who—or *what* and *how*.

The violinist, Tammy—perhaps *all* the MillU Murders. Different nights, different circumstances, but probably the same ritual. She couldn't prove it, not yet, but she didn't need proof. She *knew*.

Manny looked at the clock on her laptop screen: *11:55 AM.* She shifted her weight on the couch, Mihawk gave her a disapproving chirp for disturbing his perfect loaf.

"Sorry," Manny muttered, but he didn't move, just snuggled closer to her like it hadn't bothered him as much as he'd let on.

She was suddenly glad Dr. Carter allowed sessions online. Though she imagined for some therapist, online was better and more convenient for them. But when the video call's *brrr-rump-pum-bum* tune started going, she immediately wanted to chicken out. Somehow her couch suddenly felt harder than usual. But still, she accepted the call, and her therapist, Dr. Carter came into view.

Manny imagined Dr. Carter had a notepad app open and her fingers poised, ready to type up whatever tangled mess Manny was about to spill.

Manny cleared her throat. "It's... been a lot lately," she started, her voice barely above a whisper. "I can't stop thinking about Tammy."

Oh, goody, my first lie. At the top of the hour.

But she couldn't say the Abernathy's Witch or the curse—which probably was never created by the witch—because she didn't trust Abernathy or any accounts from the committee he'd run.

"Yes, I imagine this year must be particularly difficult," Dr. Carter said softly.

Manny nodded, stroking Mihawk's fur, eliciting a small sputtering engine-like purr.

"I just keep replaying that night…her asking me to go to the Hub & Haven with her, and not going. Because it felt…*easier.* And then, given *recent events*…it feels like it's happening all over again."

It is happening all over again.

Dr. Carter waited a beat, nodding slowly. “You feel responsible for her death.”

“Yeah.” The word felt like it had been ripped from her throat. “If I’d gone with her, maybe it wouldn’t have happened. If I’d...” Manny trailed off, knowing how ridiculous it sounded but unable to stop herself.

“You’re holding yourself responsible for things completely outside of your control, Manny” Dr. Carter said. “There’s no way to know what might’ve happened if you’d been there.”

“But what if it’s not just that?” Manny pressed. “What if I’m just...*cursed*. What if I’m destined to screw things up? To let people down?”

Dr. Carter tilted her head slightly. “Do you really believe that? Or is that your guilt telling you that?”

Manny swallowed. “I don’t know. I mean, what am I supposed to think? I keep finding myself in situations that I can’t figure out, like—” she paused, catching herself before she said something she shouldn’t. “Like some creep thought it’d be funny to... to press his *crotch* against me in the pub, and I froze for a second. Then I snapped at him. I mean what kind of person does that?”

Fucking jackass, Manny thought.

She didn’t know the guy, but felt it was safe to think he was one.

“Grant stepped in to help though,” Manny added. “He never lets me down.”

“That must’ve been distressing,” Dr. Carter said without missing a beat. “But freezing isn’t failure—neither is *snapping* at him for it. You were responding and you survived that moment. That’s enough. I’m glad that Grant was there to interfere.”

Manny looked down at Mihawk in her lap, he was fast asleep. “I am too…he’s been there through some tough times. Especially when it came to Tammy. He doesn’t pretend everything’s fine. He hasn’t been telling me to get over it.” Manny brushed her knuckles over Mihawk’s fur again. “But how do I stop feeling guilty about it? What’s the point of pretending everything's okay—when it's so clearly not? It's exhausting. I can't do it. Sometimes I wish I could."

"Why do you think people do?"

"Appearances…I guess. Not wanting to burden anyone else with their problems. And having so few people that you can actually talk to. That would actually understand. Sometimes it's like…I don't know where to even start to talk about it. To fix the way I am."

Dr. Carter adjusted in her seat. "You've already taken the first step by recognizing what's holding you back. That's not easy, and it's something a lot of people never manage. You have the tools you need to move forward—you've always had them. It's about learning to use them in ways that work for you."

Manny blinked at her. She didn't know whether or not she believed her. "So, what? Do I just...start hammering away at my problems like I'm fixing a leaky faucet?"

Dr. Carter gave her a small smile. "Something like that. But it's okay to go at your own pace. And it's okay to ask for help when you need it. You're not alone in this, even if it feels that way sometimes."

Manny nodded slowly. She could accept that. She wasn't fixed. She wasn't magically okay after this one session. But for the first time in a long time, she felt like maybe—just maybe—she could get there.

* * *

Mihawk was nestled on her couch like he paid rent. He stretched lazily, tail flicking as if he wasn't the least bit concerned with the overlapping conversations in the room.

Grant sat cross-legged beside Manny, his laptop balanced on his knees as he showed her the PDF of the Millfield News article, the "Local Violin Prodigy…", which he'd managed to save pre-redaction and editing. The more sanitized version was still proudly displayed on the news site.

"This is the mark they mentioned before," he said, zooming in on the photograph of the victim's wrist. "Well, before they edited it."

Shantelle leaned in, squinting at the screen. "That's the sacrificial mark I was telling you about. When someone's marked to be an offering—to a god, a demon, or in this case, *a vampire*."

"Wonderful," Manny said, sinking further into the couch. "I think we can assume they'd all have one like it—because I'm not breaking into the morgue."

"Yeah, it ties back to the ritual," Grant explained, showing her three pages of information on blood rituals. "The mark is a sort of claim. But for any curse to keep working, especially for this long, there has to be something anchoring it—a vessel…and it certainly wasn't the skeleton of the witch's unborn child. The university itself is too large to be the vessel. I looked over the campus map, and there's nothing in the layout that resembles a witch's circle. Not in the main campus or around any hangouts."

"Did you see anything underground? Tunnels, or anything?" Dean asked. "If there was a chamber in the chapel, who's to say there isn't more somewhere else? Maybe the vessel would be there somewhere?"

Manny nodded slowly. "I felt residual magic in the chamber, but I don't think that knife was the vessel, otherwise they wouldn't have left it behind."

Grant tapped his chin. "If a curse requires periodic sacrifices to keep it going, there has to be an object acting as the conduit for the magic. So, if we destroy it—that should, in theory, stop the ritual."

"But we have no idea what it is," Wade said, rubbing his temples. "*Cool*. We're looking for a needle in a haystack of creepy shit. *Fantastic*."

Shantelle sighed and went to the kitchen. She gestured at the coffee to see if anyone wanted any. She counted how many people wanted some—Isla certainly needed some. The poor redhead looked ill.

"I'd guess an ancient relic, something tied to the ritual's origins. Maybe something of Abernathy's—we just have to figure out what it is," Grant suggested.

Mihawk stared up at Manny and yawned, clearly unimpressed by their theorizing. He stretched back and forth before padding over to her lap and rubbing himself against her hand, requesting to be pet.

"Okay," Manny said, petting the feline. "So, find the vessel, destroy it, and hope it stops the curse. Wasn't that our plan the first time?"

Grant laughed. "Yeah, I guess so…but this time we know it has something to do with vampires. And who's to say the vampires don't have it."

"And if they do?" Manny asked, biting her lip.

Shantelle shrugged, mid-coffee pour. "We figure out the next step."

That was easier said than done.

Chapter 22
November 1st

Manny knew her lips were probably already chapping in this weather. They had only just stepped outside, and Dean's cheeks were already rosy, and their breath was visible. It was already November, and they weren't any closer to figuring out what their curse's vessel was. She fussed with her scarf, burying her face in it as she stared ahead at the rest of the group. She wanted to argue, because she didn't think it was right. Or more simply put they weren't supposed to be here—not at the rink, not laughing, not acting like normal college students who didn't have vampires or curses to worry about. But Shantelle had insisted.

"We need to unwind before we overwhelm ourselves," she'd said, dragging them down the road with more force than her small frame suggested possible.

A makeshift ice rink over the lake nestled at the east-end of the market. The fairy lights above were off, and likely wouldn't turn on until sundown. It was only afternoon now, and little kids wobbled on the ice, gripping their parents with mitten-clad hands. A few couples skated past, laughing and holding hands, clearly enjoying the early Christmas cheer.

Grant was walking beside her, and they were halfway to the skate rental lodge when she grabbed his arm.

"She can't be serious, right?" Manny said, looking around. "What if we're being watched?"

"We probably are," he said with a shrug. "But if we sit around waiting for something to happen, we'll lose our minds. Besides, if a vampire does think we're onto them, they'd expect us to be scared. Not, well…I don't know, getting our fill of holiday cheer?"

Shantelle grinned, already lacing up her skates. "Stop overthinking it, Manny. A little ice skating never killed anyone."

"That's what you think," Manny muttered under her breath, eyeing the ice with the same enthusiasm she reserved for public speaking and dental appointments.

Grant put a pair of skates in her hands. "C'mon, Manny. We're here. Might as well try to have fun."

Reluctantly, Manny sat on the bench, pulling on the skates and fumbling with the laces. She hated tying shoes with gloves on, but she didn't want to take hers off—it was too cold. Her stomach churned at the thought of stepping onto that slick, unforgiving frozen surface and falling in front of a crowd of people.

Minutes later, despite herself, Manny was out there, hand-in-hand with Dean, wobbling like a newborn giraffe. Every time she moved, her legs attempted to go in opposite directions. Everyone else was gliding effortlessly, and Shantelle and Isla were ahead, doing little spins like they were auditioning for *The Nutcracker on Ice.*

"Why are we doing this again," Manny grumbled at Dean as he steadied her.

"Because sometimes the best way to clear your head is to fall on your ass," Dean said with a grin.

Manny pouted. "Good pep talk."

Dean gave her a kiss on the forehead. Probably trying to comfort her, and it did, *some*. In fact, she was just starting to think she might survive this winter activity when a strange prickling sensation ran along the base of her neck. Manny tried to scan the crowd around her. But wasn't exactly sure who she was looking for, because *what* was pretty clear—there was magic or at least, something magical around them. But she had no idea where it or *they* were.

"What's wrong?" Dean asked, his eyebrows furrowed as he stared down at her.

"I don't know," she whispered. "Maybe it's nothing…"

Dean frowned. "Is it that ritual *thingy* again?"

Manny internally shook herself, trying to place what she was feeling. It was a weaker buzzing sensation, but maybe that was due to distance—like when she was in the chapel. But this was even weaker than that.

Where is it?

Dean tugged on her. "C'mon," he said with a warm smile. "You're doing great so far. Just a little farther."

Before she could share her thoughts, Dean was already tugging her further along, where the clear ice turned an ominous shade of dark blue.

"I'm not even *decent*," Manny muttered, holding his hand like her life depended on it. Which it might, given her poor skating skills. "Besides, I'm pretty sure we could drown out here."

"You're overthinking again," he said, slowing down just enough for her to catch her breath. "It's just ice. You've got me. Nothing's gonna happen."

Manny felt somewhat reassured. Even if her ankles wobbled beneath her and her heart threatened to burst out of her chest every time she dared to look down, Dean's grip kept her upright.

They reached the middle of the lake, the deepest part, where the ice was even darker—dark, shifting, creaking under the weight of so many skaters.

Dean pulled her close, his eyes crinkling at the corners as he smiled. "See? Not so bad."

Manny smiled. "Okay, but if I *do* die out here, I'm haunting you."

"You'd make a terrible ghost."

Before she could respond to his playful jab, his expression made her pause. Something was wrong. Not in the way where someone realized they'd forgotten something at home, or questioned if they left the stove on—but the kind where every muscle locks up. Then his eyes widened, dilating, staring past her, at something far away.

"Dean?" Manny tugged his hand, but he didn't react. "Baby, what's wrong?"

Nothing. His grip on her hand loosened, and arm went limp to his side.

"Dean, *seriously*. This isn't funny." Her voice came out strained, as the prickling sensation rose on her neck again, and she instinctively followed his gaze. But there was nothing there—just a crowd of skaters, distant and blurry.

And yet, she knew. She knew because of the way his breath hitched, the slight tremor in his legs, like his body was fighting to stay upright. This wasn't normal. This wasn't like Dean. He wasn't in shock. He wasn't having a panic attack. Something was wrong.

She had the faintest memory of the stupid "Don't Do Drugs" presentation at the orientation assembly her freshman year. That slideshow had so many slack-jawed faces and vacant eyes in it. But Dean wasn't high. Which left only one explanation.

She turned and scanned the crowd again, her pulse pounding in her ears. Somewhere, among the festive throng—a vampire was watching them.

A vampire's glamour, sometimes called vampiric compulsion…God, what was the rest?

"Dean," she tried shaking him, though she knew it wouldn't work. She'd thought they had to be close to do something like this.

Dean moved a few steps away from her, his body moving like a marionette on strings. He slowly knelt down on the ice, his breath misting in uneven puffs as his fist rose into the air.

"Dean, what are you doing?" Manny shouted, reaching for him, but it was like he couldn't hear her. Like the words didn't even register.

His knuckles came down hard against the ice, once, twice, echoing like gunshots in the cold air. The ice groaned. Thin cracks splintered out beneath him, veins of destruction crawling toward the inky blue depths below.

"Stop it!" Manny bellowed, grabbing his arm, but he shook her off with what seemed like adrenaline-induced strength. She doubled-backward and fell on her rear end.

Dean pounded against the ice again.

"Dean, *please*!" Her voice broke, panic rising in her chest as the ice shattered. He stood then, unusually steady, as if he weren't wearing ice skates at all, and stepped forward and stomped on the ice until his skate crashed through the weakened surface—and he slipped under the water.

"Dean!" Manny screamed, lunging at him. She wrapped her arms around his chest and pulled with all her strength. "Please, stop! You're going to drown!"

But he wasn't listening, he struggled against her, threatening to drag them both underneath the freezing depths. She hated ice skating—probably because she knew, deep down, that if she fell through, no amount of yelling *"Help!"* would stop her from freezing solid before anyone could fish her out.

Dean kept struggling, the ice beneath her buckled, making her stomach churn.

Suddenly, someone grabbed her from behind, locking their arms around her and pulling her away from him. "Stop!" Manny screamed, thrashing against whoever it was. "I have to—he's going to—"

She couldn't finish her sentence. Dean was chest-deep in the water now, his movements mechanical, his bloodied fists swaying under the surface.

"Dean, *fight it!*" Manny sobbed, trying and failing to reach out to him again, but whoever had her wouldn't let go.

Suddenly, a familiar voice cut through the chaos. "Dean! Stop, damn it!"

Grant. Thank God, thank God.

Manny twisted to see Grant sprinting across the ice, his skates clattering, his eyes wide. He dove the last few feet, breaking into the water with only a moment's hesitation. The lake seemed to swallow them both as Dean thrashed violently, trying to shove his brother away and push himself deeper into the freezing dark.

Manny scanned the crowd, desperate for a clue, a face, *anything*—

but she could hardly see anything through her tears. It was all blurred figures, splashing and thrashing water, with muffled chatter and shouting, and her racing heartbeat.

But she could feel it. The buzzing inside her was growing. But without a clear head it was useless.

A vampire was out there. Watching. Waiting for Dean to drown.

Manny turned back to Grant and Dean. Grant's grip on his brother didn't falter, but the struggle was too much. The ice around them groaned, threatening to give way completely.

"Come on, Dean! Please!" Manny shouted, her voice hoarse from screaming.

Then she turned back to the ice skaters crowding around them, and just past them, a familiar face—Wade. He was moving—fast, faster than she'd ever seen him move. It was as if he was running on the track once more, completely unphased by his change in footwear and terrain. His eyes were locked onto someone far away, someone Manny couldn't see between the multitude of legs around her. He was skating like a missile toward the edge of the rink. He leapt over the barrier, tackling someone, and Manny blinked.

What the hell—but then the buzzing became too strong to ignore. She adjusted her angle to get a better view.

Whomever Wade had tackled wasn't panicked, though they did seem surprised. But within moments they overcame their shock. Then they moved, unnaturally, twisting Wade's arm behind his back in a move that looked like it might snap it.

Wade managed to sweep his leg beneath them, sending them both backward, and Manny turned back to Grant.

"Pull him out!" She demanded.

Grant gave one final heave, pulling Dean's limp body onto the ice just as Isla reached them. "Shantelle called for help!" Isla said, her voice shaking.

"Dean," Manny said, ignoring Isla, crawling over to him on her hands and knees. "Stay with me," she begged, pulling him to her, letting his head rest on her chest. His skin was ashen and his lips were turning blue. But he was breathing. “You’re okay. Everything’s going to be okay.”

His eyelids fluttered, but he didn’t say anything.

“Isla, help me! He’s freezing!” Manny couldn’t stop her hands from trembling as Isla crouched down. “Stay with me, Dean. Stay with me.”

Chapter 23
Evening, November 1st

Ice and her have never mixed, and now Dean was lying in a goddamn hospital bed, pale as a ghost and hooked up to every machine they could find to keep him alive but sedated, while she was sitting in a chair that might be further impacting her scoliosis.

She was glad it was quiet, apart from the occasional beep from the machines and Wade still muttering to Shantelle about *'how strong the guy was.'*

"That guy—he was *too* strong," Wade repeated, clutching his arm. "I swear, he was going to break it if I didn't let go. He has to be one of them."

In other words—he was a vampire.

Manny would tune Wade out. At least for a little while. She didn't care how strong the vampire was or that she knew Wade finally, truly believed there were vampires in the world. She knew what the man was. She felt what he was. But that wasn't going to help her or Dean now.

Dean stirred slightly, his fingers twitching against the thin hospital blanket. Manny leaned forward, hoping—praying—that he'd open his eyes, say something, *anything*. But he doesn't. He's so still and quiet.

Her throat was tight, and she blinked back tears.

I should have done something. I should have figured it out faster, should have stopped him before he—no. I can't go down that road.

She needed to focus on something else. So, she chose the more annoying details of the hospital room that made me want to scream. The mismatched chairs, one of which Grant was currently slumped in, texting he and Dean's mother. The scratchy, industrial-strength toilet paper in the bathroom, she swore had scratched her labia as she wiped backward. They were all nitpicky things, she had no reason to turn over and over in her head. But it was better than sitting there, doing nothing. She had bitten her lip until she tasted blood, and wished she could go back to yesterday morning before any of this had happened.

Manny stood up from her seat, interrupting Wade's monologue, and pulling an, "Are you all right, Manny? Do you want something to eat?" from Shantelle.

"No, I'm fine thanks," Manny told her.

She wasn't fine. But she didn't want to talk about it.

"I'm just going to get something from the vending machine," Manny explained.

Shantelle's face contorted. "Do you really think it's a good idea for any of us to go off alone?"

Manny knew she meant. Was it really a good idea for *her* to go off alone, because it was *her* boyfriend in the hospital. She and Grant had meddled with the curse, and it only made sense that Dean had gotten caught in the crossfire. Not her. Not Wade. Not Isla. *Dean.* He was a clear connection to both of them. His brother, her boyfriend. She should've seen it coming.

No. No. No. Dr. Carter said—but what if... Manny shook away the thought.

Blaming herself wouldn't do her any good. Instead she tried to remember what exactly Dr. Carter said—*you have all the tools you need*—though that tidbit wasn't going to help her. Did she really have all the tools she needed? Did she need a few more?

"I'll go with you," Grant said, suddenly.

Shantelle jumped. "Grant, are you sure? Don't you think that maybe you should get some rest?"

Grant grumbled and stretched. "Later, it's hard to sleep with Wade going on and on about fighting a vampire."

Wade glared at Grant.

"Vending machine, right," Grant said, rubbing his eyes and looking at Manny.

Manny nodded her head, and he stood up, striding past her and gesturing for her to follow him. She was glad that he didn't ask anything else of her at the moment. She wasn't sure she could manage anything else.

She'd never liked hospitals—they were too bright, too sterile, too loud with machines that beeped and they were always overcrowded. But she was here, and eventually they'd found the vending machine.

"We should've known they'd go after Dean," Grant muttered, looking between the vending machine and her.

Grant clenched his jaw.

"We couldn't have known," Manny said, matter-of-factly, even though she didn't believe that herself.

He shook his head like she'd suggested they throw in the towel entirely. "Doesn't matter. The violinist's dead and Dean's in the hospital."

That was true. The violinist was dead. Blood drained, head hanging on by a thread of muscle.

Thank you, Millfied News for that lovely visual to go with the screaming highlight reel in my head.

She couldn't think of anything to say to comfort him. Hell, she could hardly comfort herself.

She'd barely scratched the surface on the whole ritual resonance thing, but understood enough to know it affected casters differently. Clearly Grant was unaffected when he plunged into the freezing water to pull Dean out—no brain fog, no medically induced coma. Meanwhile, her bones were vibrating every time she got too close to a hint magic.

"Grant," Manny started, glancing at him out of the corner of her eye, "does ritual resonance not...affect you? Like, at all?"

He raised an eyebrow but didn't stop staring at the ceiling. "It might be why the water didn't bother me when I went in. Honestly, I barely felt anything. At first, I thought it was adrenaline, but, *realistically*, I shouldn't have been able to be in there that long."

"So, what, I get magical metal detector and you get *regeneration*?" Manny said. She felt like she was whining, but in some way, she felt cheated, and she didn't feel like stopping herself from saying so. "Fucking magic," she muttered to herself, because by some cruel twist of fate, this was her life, and that was the answer.

So, she turned back to the vending machine, trying to decide if chips or something sweeter would make the day suck less. When she'd decided, she punched in the numbers, happily waiting for it to fall, hungrily watching the whirring, winding metal coil. Then it stopped. The stupid coil *stopped*. Her snack of choice—a sinfully delicious, potentially *unholy* combination of chocolate with triple the amount of peanut butter it was meant to have inside of it—was dangling from the edge of the coil, mocking her. She cursed under her breath and began glaring at it like it had insulted her mother.

"Dammit!" Manny cried out, rubbing her temples. "I hate today."

Grant didn't say anything. Instead, he gave the machine a once-over, and then—*bang!*—he kicked it. Hard. Right in the corner. The kind of kick greasers did to jukeboxes in 90s TV reruns, followed by everyone singing when *Sweet Caroline* started playing.

She could practically hear the *bum, bum, bum* in the song, as the machine groaned, and spat her candy bar out with a pleasant *thunk!* Manny grabbed it from the pick-up box, and it was almost beginning to feel like a Christmas miracle when a *slam* at the other end of the hall made her almost drop it.

The flurry of footsteps and overlapping voices made them step to the side, hugging the wall as a gurney hurtled past.

"Male, mid-twenties—severe lacerations across the chest," a paramedic called out, his voice somehow steady amongst the chaos.

Manny's breath caught in her throat as she looked at the student on the gurney. His eyes half-open and glassy, like he'd been caught mid-sentence and never finished his thought. Blood streaked his shirt, spreading into dark colored patches.

“What else?” someone said.

Behind him, more voices rang out. “One dead on scene. Another’s heart gave out during transport—they’re trying to revive him now.”

Her stomach twisted. *Three victims. Three attacks. So soon after... after Dean.*

The gurney disappeared around a corner, taking the medical crew with it.

Manny felt like she was standing underwater, every sound muffled, every movement slowed. “W-where?” Manny asked, not having meant to say it aloud.

Grant answered, showing her his phone, “The Globe—lower floors. Too dark for them to tell.”

Manny blinked. “Sundown was only two hours ago.” It didn’t make sense. All the attacks had happened at night so far.

But Dean’s attack was in broad daylight.

“They’re escalating,” Grant said grimly. “Or they're running out of time for the ritual.”

Manny nodded. “We need to know more about this ritual.”

“But we don’t know where to start researching,” Grant shrugged. “There’s a ridiculous number of blood rituals out there Manny.”

“Then we need to be able to protect ourselves until we do.”

Chapter 24
November 12th

It had been over a week since they'd left the hospital—with Dean showing no sign of recovery and with little know-how of what to do next—they were back at the *Bewitchery*. Because, of course, the moment her life turned into a low-budget horror movie, the only logical thing to do was consult the woman who smelled like incense and passive aggression—though Trish had killer fashion sense. Grant was already talking about hex-breaking powders, and charms that can ward off vampires like they were items on a grocery list as they walked there. But Manny wouldn't argue. How could she? After the past two weeks—after *everything*—they've had to do, if someone told her tap-dancing while reciting the alphabet backward would keep them alive, she'd start rehearsing.

At this point, Manny would buy a can of vampire mace or a stake-on-a-keychain if Trish had them. Hell, she'd take a garlic diffuser if it meant a good night's sleep. And honestly? The *Bewitchery* was starting to feel safer than her own apartment.

How's that for a plot twist?

Grant opens the door, it creaks ominously, because of course it does, and as soon as they step inside, Manny could feel that strange hum again, like the air itself was buzzing with anticipation.

Grant marches in like he's ready to barter his soul, while she trailed in behind him. Manny couldn't say she trusted Trish, like Grant did, but the witch knows her stuff—or at least she sells it with enough confidence that Manny wanted to believe she did. The spell book certainly seemed to work given their separate-but-unequal side effects from ritual resonance. And right now, believing she could manage to kill vampires, or channel her inner Van Helsing was the only thing keeping her upright. She was still worried sick about Dean.

Luckily, Trish was listening to a podcast at the cashier's till, and Grant was already going through his notebook asking her questions. Meanwhile, Manny wandered toward a shelf of candles with brightly colored labels with words like "Courage" and "Cord Cutting"—the latter was part of a line that was on sale. But she was pretty sure neither of them would help her.

A miracle would be better.

She read a few more labels, knowing she wouldn't be buying anything, but more than willing to read them. *Manifest Your Dreams, Banishing Monitoring Spirits*, and her favorite so far, *Bad Bitch Energy*. She grabbed that one off the shelf—and according to the description label—apparently *Bad Bitch Energy* smelt like pomegranate, rose petals and amber musk.

"Manny," Grant called, dragging her out of her trance.

Manny went over to the till to join Grant and Trish—*witch extraordinaire*. Today she was truly committing to a cool millennial witch vibe, in the best way, and it made Manny wonder if she'd drummed up more business as of late—given the ongoing, rampant murders.

"This," Trish said, holding up a necklace with a tiny vial hanging from a delicate-looking metal chain, "is what you want. It's got nightshade, clove, and a few other ingredients sealed inside that'll ward off werewolves and vampires…"

Grant nods, already reaching for his wallet. "We'll take six of them."

Trish proceeded to pluck multiple necklaces off the wall hooks behind her. Then she began ringing them up and bagging them in little velvet pouches. But Manny was still uneasy.

What if it breaks? What if she forgets to put it on in the morning?

"Is there anything else you can give me?" Manny asked abruptly.

Trish tilted her head, like she was sizing Manny up. "Something else? Like what?"

"Well, if the necklace breaks…" Manny trailed off, trying not to sound too paranoid. Or unexpectedly offend the woman helping them lest she be cursed for the rest of her days. "Like a *backup plan*."

Trish didn't argue. Instead, she turned around and pulled out a perfume bottle, that at most was 2.5 ounces. It was filled with a pale liquid, flecks of gold glitter suspended inside.

"Perfume?" Manny asked, hoping she sounded more confused than dumbfounded.

"It's not just perfume," Trish said, passing it to Manny. "It's infused with protective oils and a few other spiritual additives that will ward off just about anything *unholy*." She said as Manny weighed the bottle in her hand. "It won't stop them outright—think of it as more pepper spray against the supernatural."

Manny eyed the little bottle curiously. For all she knew, it could be a garlic perfume—and she wasn't sure she wanted to walk around smelling like leftover pizza. She twisted off the cap, brought the nozzle up to her nose and tried to smell it.

It doesn't smell like garlic. Maybe cloves or cedarwood, or something earthy?

"Go ahead," Trish said, causing Manny to nearly jump out of her skin. "Spray it. See what it smells like."

Curiosity wins, and she puts a cautious spritz on her wrist. She rubbed the liquid into her skin and raised it to her nose. The scent isn't overwhelming—thankfully—and it's surprisingly pleasant. Warm and slightly smoky, a little like amber musk. It reminded her a little of *Bad Bitch Energy*—so it might be amber musk.

That must be Trish's signature scent, Manny thought.

It left behind a faint shimmer on her skin.

"It's holy water with a few things layered in," Trish explained with a smile on her face.

Holy water?

She hadn't expected that. She would have half-expected it to be labeled with a giant crucifix, though the faint tingle on her skin was different. And if it were any normal day, she would think it was an allergic reaction, if it weren't for the buzzing sensation inside her.

So, she's not lying about the magic.

Manny stared at the shimmer on her wrist.

Definitely a witch.

She had half a mind to spray some of this around Dean's hospital room, though she's sure that would be more than a little frowned upon in a hospital of all places. But she keeps that thought to herself, pressing her wrist to her nose one more time.

Definitely amber musk.

Manny had enough perfumes with that scent to recognize it. She had to admit, Trish had good taste.

Holy water in a scent that could pass for boutique luxury—who knew that was a thing?

"So I just spray it on myself?" Manny asked, her face half-way hidden with her nose still buried in her wrist.

"Or in their face," Trish said with a smirk.

Grant gave her a look that's equal parts amused and exasperated. "You're seriously going to buy that?"

"Yes," Manny said firmly, sliding the bottle back over to Trish. "You can never be too careful."

Trish laughs. "You two are funny," she said, fanning herself. "Tell you what. You can have it for free—since Grant is my most loyal customer."

And with that, Trish rang them up, handed them their purchases, and they left the store, armed with their new vampire repellents. Unfortunately, Manny still felt woefully unprepared.

* * *

Manny had barely shaken the slush off her boots from earlier, and now she was grabbing her coat again. Because, apparently, she wasn't capable of staying indoors like a normal person. But sitting still felt like an admission of defeat, and she wasn't in the mood. They'd armed themselves with Trish's best artillery against the supernatural—or at least, Manny wanted to believe her best. She had to look down to check the necklace was still on—she could barely feel the cool metal against her collarbone. But she didn't want to go back inside. Instead she was going to brave this freezing tundra, hoping that the weather would stop her brain from replaying the moment Dean plunged into the lake.

Snowflakes clung to her lashes as she trudged down the street, and all she could think of was how she was too stubborn to admit she'd rather be binge-watching Christmas movies and eating chocolates or comfort food. But there was something she needed more —*confirmation.*

The walk itself was becoming a test of endurance. Her apartment wasn't too far from Whitlock Hall—two blocks, maybe three on the sidewalk—but when those blocks are buried under a foot of snow and with boots that weren't weatherproofed, it might as well be a trek to the North Pole. Every step forward was a task in itself, and she was beginning to reconsider for perhaps the third time. About halfway there, she started wondering if she should've just emailed him instead. But no, she needed to confirm whether he was a vampire, and that meant she had to stop complaining and get on with it.

She'd already come up with a half-baked excuse: she needed him to review her draft for the research paper that wasn't due for another month to two months. She hadn't titled it yet either. In reality, she had only reworked it a few hours ago. In fact, her coursework was in shambles, a disaster zone of half-baked ideas and abandoned outlines, and her motivation had been buried somewhere under the same snowdrift she was currently slogging through.

Thankfully, all of her professors had pushed deadlines closer to when grades were due in January. January 18th, to be precise—and she had inputted it into her calendar because she was counting down the days. Given the circumstances on campus—or more precisely *the murders*, grieving, loss and fear hanging over students. Finals for other programs were postponed, potentially getting projected grading. Being a creative writing student helped; all of her assignments, big and small, were part of a portfolio. One portfolio per class which was usually due at the end of each semester. But now those deadlines landed on January 10th or 16th. Still, she wasn't winning any awards for time management, unless there was a category for "Most Stress-Induced Staring at Blank Documents." She was falling behind.

Whitlock Hall came into view, and she sighed in relief. The moment she stepped inside, she shook the snow from her scarf. But she didn't have time to worry about bad grades—at least at the moment. This meeting was reconnaissance, plain and simple. If Professor Moreau was a vampire, she'd know soon enough. If he wasn't… well, she'd still get credit for looking like she cared about her academic future.

Win-win, she told herself as she sought out his office.

She hoped there wasn't any lingering snow in her curls, but doubted it. She'd just have to hope some leftover product in her hair would kick in and prevent any frizz.

"Manny, what a surprise," Beau said when she entered the office. "Please, shut the door behind you. There's a terrible draft, but I've got the heater going."

He gestured toward the heater, it was humming lowly, and she did as he asked. Manny hoped she wasn't moving stiffly, and hoped, if anything, Beau would attribute it to the cold. If he asked, she would say, *I just need a moment to defrost*—then giggle a little like anyone would with a bad joke.

"I was just wondering if you could look over my paper," Manny said, opening her messenger bag before he could answer.

Slow down. Slow down. She chastised herself, but that was easier said than done. Though she wanted to give herself the benefit of the doubt; convince herself she could pull this off.

It'll just look like I can't remember where it is in my bag, Manny told herself.

"All right, let's see it," Beau said with a warm smile that made her stomach do a flip.

She couldn't sense any magic emanating from him, but it was equally possible she couldn't make it out through her anxiety.

There you are. Manny pulled her binder out of her bag, as she found the paper.

"Here it is," she said aloud, hoping it sounded convincing.

Beau laughed and smiled. "Well, let's see it."

Am I really doing this?

Manny looked at him, and God…she really hoped he wasn't one of *them.* He was slowly becoming her favorite professor, and she had another class with him next semester. She reached across the desk to pass him the paper, her hand trembling slightly.

She'd drenched her wrist and palm in that perfume, practically bathing them in it before leaving her apartment. Trish said it would work, but Manny needed to be sure. Needed to see for herself. Since their local 'historian' hadn't really explained *what* it did. But as his fingers wrapped around the edge of the paper, his wrist brushed against hers for the briefest moment.

The sound was faint, like bacon hitting a hot skillet, but his reaction was immediate. He pulled back quickly, his expression unchanged but his eyes flicked to his wrist—just for a second. That second was enough. Smoke wafted from his wrist. The skin where they'd touched reddened, angry and raw one second, gone the next, like he'd accidentally leaned against a stovetop, though he healed almost immediately. Their eyes met in recognition, and she wasn't stupid.

Fucking do something you idiot.

Every instinct screamed at her to *get to the damn door.*

Can I even make it?

Probably not. Vampires were faster than humans—that was basic lore, basic *vampire*—but the door was close. She might have a chance. A slim chance, but slim was better than no chance. He didn't say anything, hadn't called her out, which meant he either didn't care or didn't want her to know that *he knew that she knew.*

She looked at the door then at him. Then the door and then at him again.

Great. A standoff in an office with a vampire whose wrist just sizzled like fajitas. Just my luck. Just another Tuesday...

She knocked over the chair, hoping it would block his path, and bolted for the door. Manny went for the knob, clinging to it like a lifeline, hoping to turn it, yank it open and run. Freedom was right there, just outside the door. But before she could even pull it, a hand appeared above her head—it was just *there*—and forced the door shut with a solid *clunk*.

Her stomach dropped. *Shit. Shit. Shit. What do I do now? Beg for my life?*

Slowly, she looked up, and there he was. Standing so close she could feel the heat radiating off of him—or maybe that was just her—or the current from the heater whirring around him and onto her. Could vampires be warm? But that didn't matter. His hand rested on the door, just inches from her face, long fingers splayed out, blocking her escape. Keeping her in *here* with *him*. His expression was unreadable, but his eyes—those dark, piercing eyes—bore into her with an intensity that made her knees wobble.

He wasn't just *looking* at her; he was *studying* her, his eyes searching her face like he was trying to figure her out.

And damn it all, he was still handsome. Ridiculously, *unfairly* handsome. He had the kind of face artists meant when they said *'a face that could make you forget your own name'*—and she stood there, wordlessly, fearfully unable to move, or to think. But right now, his surreal beauty felt sharp, dangerous. *Predatory*. Like the moment in a nature documentary just before a lion pounced on some poor, unsuspecting gazelle.

Her chest tightened, and it started again. That strange, electric hum inside her—it felt stronger now, thrumming through her veins like static, making her hyperaware of *everything*. The slightest flare of his nostrils. The way his lips curved—not into a smile, but into something that felt almost *calculated*. Calling it a smirk wouldn't quite do it justice, but it said, *so you've figured it out*. And maybe, just maybe she was more of a star pupil than she thought.

Then he spoke, "I'm not going to hurt you, Manny," his voice was smooth, like velvet wrapped around a knife.

She didn't believe him. She *couldn't* believe him. At least one vampire was killing students on campus. It was a blood ritual that called to *them*. Why the hell should she trust him? Not after everything she'd seen. Not after what they did to Tammy.

Please don't kill me. Please don't kill me. Manny shook her head.

"I'm not going to kill you," he said, tilting his head. "And, as you may recall, I did try to steer you away from this situation—*and* I haven't harmed you thus far."

"That was before," Manny retorted. "And maybe you aren't killing me now, because you can't."

She was wearing the necklace, though she wasn't sure what it was supposed to do. Maybe it was letting her look at him with fresh eyes. Maybe she was finally paying attention.

Manny's breath hitched when she felt air brush against her neck. It was so subtle she might have thought she imagined it—if not for the object now dangling in front of her face. Manny stared at it blankly. Her necklace. He was holding her necklace a few inches from her face.

What...when did he—fucking vampires.

One second, it was there, her last line of defense, and the next...gone.

Manny looked past it and back at him.

He wasn't smirking. He wasn't gloating like some cartoon villain. His expression was neutral, he almost looked *bored* as if she'd been droning on and on about some particularly uninteresting argument about something she knew nothing about.

"This isn't going to do you any good, anyway," he said, his tone smooth and disarmingly calm. "You haven't had it *blessed*. That makes it useless against me—or *anything else* for that matter."

Manny gulped. *Blessed?* Trish hadn't mentioned that. Her face must have betrayed her confusion because one corner of his mouth twitched into what was definitely a *smirk*.

"I've not *killed* anyone if that's what you're worried about," he said, his voice softer now, but no less intimidating. "Or at least not here and...*not students*..." he trailed off for a moment. "I've been trying to find the coven responsible. They're *dangerous*—more dangerous than you realize. But you wouldn't heed my warning."

Heed his warning? When had he tried to warn her—and who the hell used the word *heed* nowadays? Manny's mind scrambled to piece together every cryptic comment, every reading he'd given her in the last few weeks. Could he have been trying—given in a warped, unusual way—to protect her? She didn't know whether to feel relieved, angry, or confused. She'd heard him say *'anything else,'* which meant there were obviously more *monsters* out there. But she could at least commend herself for realizing there might be a coven in the first place. The more pressing matter was that there was a coven—albeit she also had other questions for her professor.

"Now," Beau said suddenly, his voice dipping lower, "you've put yourself in the middle of something you're unprepared for. And please, for the love of God, trust me, you're *unprepared...*"

"What do you kill—or *hunt?*" Manny asked abruptly.

She wasn't letting him get off that easy. If he was one of the good ones, he needed to prove it.

His expression was unreadable as he leaned against the door, arms folded loosely. "I don't kill indiscriminately," he began, his tone clinical, as if delivering a lecture. "Only those who deserve it—the truly vile. Rapists. Serial killers." He paused, his lips quirking faintly. "*Occasionally*, the odd werewolf, but only if they give me a reason. They tend to taste...*too gamey* for my palate." That seemed to amuse him. "But I'm not some...*feral* monster. I do know how to conduct myself with dignity."

Manny blinked. *Taste*. She was surprised, she managed to keep her face neutral. She wasn't sure how she felt knowing werewolves taste *gamey*.

"You don't have to worry about werewolves around here though," he added with a small shrug. "The last one left Millfield decades ago. Which is why I settled here in the first place."

Manny tried to process everything at once—predators, werewolves, "gamey" meat—but he kept going, his voice taking on a slightly sardonic edge.

"And then I suppose there are those rumors about sunlight…" He gestured vaguely toward the window, where pale daylight filtered through the blinds. "That's a well-crafted lie, one that suits us quite well. It makes it easier to hide in plain sight."

Her head reeled as he continued, and she sat back down in the chair.

"So, everything we know about vampires is a lie?"

Back to the drawing board then?

Beau laughed. "Humans don't know most things about us. For instance, I come from a pure line, directly descended from Dracula himself. I was born a dhampir, and with my father's assistance, I became a full vampire in my thirties, though the logistics are...*complicated.* And I'd rather not overwhelm you with information."

Manny's breath caught in her throat, but before she could question him further, he cut her off.

"What matters now is that you stay away from this. You're not equipped to deal with it. Walk away now, before you dig yourself in any deeper, and—"

"No."

The word tumbled out of her mouth before he'd even finished speaking.

His eyes narrowed. "I beg your pardon? You can't begin to understand what you're up against."

"Maybe not," she shot back, the trembling in her hands at odds with the steel in her voice. "But I've seen enough to know I can't just step aside. Students are dying, and if you think I'm going to sit on the sidelines while this keeps happening, you're wrong."

His jaw clenched. He stared at her. She stared at him. They were in yet another standoff. And after a few minutes that way, he sighed, he studied her again as if trying to decide whether she was brave, stupid, or some maddening combination of both.

"I think you'll come to regret this."

"Maybe," Manny said. "But I can't stop. Not now that I know that I'm right."

For a moment, she thought he was going to argue, to keep pushing her to back down.

"Fine," he said, straightening to his full height. The sudden movement surprised her, her instincts screamed for her to *be careful.* He passed her and went to his coffee machine. "If you're that determined to get yourself killed, we'll work together."

Her eyebrows shot up. "What?"

"You heard me," he said, his voice clipped. "We'll work together. I'll share what I know, *but*"—he raised a finger, his tone darkening—"there are conditions."

She sighed but nodded, bracing herself. "What kind of conditions?"

His eyes bored into hers, searching for any hint of hesitation. Finally, Beau nodded, as if satisfied with whatever he found. "No more recklessness. No more putting yourself in dangerous situations, because you don't know what you're up against."

"Who's to say that I—"

"Who do you think sent someone to pull you out of that lake?" he said sharply, cutting her off.

Her heart panged with guilt. She hadn't even thought about who it was—only that Dean had gone under.

"You—"

"Compelled someone to go and grab you—but luckily for you, MillU's favorite track star was talking to me about extra credit at the time," Beau said sternly, and Manny hesitated. "You and your friends' scheming has nearly gotten you killed *twice* now. And it's become painfully obvious that you haven't realized it until recently."

"Why didn't you stop the *other vampire* then?"

He shot her a look that made her flinch. "What do you think I was doing there?" He said pointedly, waving his hand in the air. "I was tailing them, but I didn't get a good look at them. You should ask your friend what they look like. That'd be useful information."

Manny didn't answer. She nodded, her mouth suddenly dry. She hadn't thought to ask Wade anything about the vampire. She didn't want to hear him talk about the lake anymore, but he was the only one of them that saw them up close.

"Third condition, your friends," he said, stepping closer to the chair. "They can't know what I am. Understand?"

Manny nodded. She knew she had to be fine with it. She'd have to keep this part of the investigation to herself, at least for now. As much as it was unnerving to be so close to someone so...*otherworldly*, she couldn't deny the edge it gave her. She would get further now, she was certain of it.

"Fourth. If you're going to be in the middle of it, then I need to know what you're doing and what you're planning. No more surprises. All plans go through me. Understand?"

"I understand," she said quickly, surprising even herself.

She bit back a potential retort. *Isn't that the point of all this?* But then again, she could answer her own question. No. It wasn't. Not for him. He was trying to keep her out of harm's way, or—more than likely—keep *her* out of *his* way.

Then he smiled, and she decided it was a smirk of approval.

She sighed, and she hated to admit it, but she couldn't help but feel a sense of satisfaction—she'd been right all along.

Chapter 25
November 13th

Author's Recommendation: There is much unexplored material for novels, screenplays and films in, "The State of the Unliving and Undying," by Anastasia Wei. I suspect it would lend itself nicely to all future scholars with concerns on vampires or other immortal occult entities.

— *From the author's note in the fictional work, "Valley of Blood" by Eliza Harrow*

She hadn't been back to the hospital since the afternoon where everything went to hell. Too many crying babies, too much of that hospital smell—like bleach and boiled cabbage with just a dash of helplessness.

But here she was, feet on the same gray linoleum, pretending she could focus on being the concerned girlfriend instead of someone who's recently realized Millfield is probably neck-deep in bloodsuckers. Manny was trying to ignore the buzzing in her chest as she passed a different hospital room before she reached Dean's.

His mother was there, perched on the edge of the world's most uncomfortable chair at his bedside, one hand holding Dean's limp right-hand, her other clutching her handbag tightly like someone might run off with it. Grant was sitting in another chair, scrolling on his phone, mumbling to himself.

"How's he doing?" Manny asked, knowing the answer before the words even left Mrs. Altman's mouth.

"No change," his mother said, her voice tight. "But the doctors say that's not necessarily a bad thing."

Manny nodded.

But it's not necessarily a good thing either, is it?

In many ways, she blamed herself, and she wished Grant would admit he blamed her too instead of texting her back with one-word replies. But instead of hanging around, she said something noncommittal and promised to come back later, even though she had no idea when "later" might be.

Manny rushed out of there, and went to the front desk, where a nurse stared at her curiously. Probably because she was jogging in a hospital.

"Can I help you," the nurse said.

"Yes, actually," Manny answered, trying for sweet but probably landing somewhere between suspicious and anxious. "I was wondering if I could visit someone. A friend of mine was admitted the other day—Dantrell Williamson. He's a track star, really tall—he saved my life not too long ago?" Manny tacked on a little laugh, hoping it sounded like a perfectly normal request.

The nurse frowned at her, typed something into the computer. "Room 214," she said, jerking her head toward the elevator.

Manny thanked her and made her way there, and she did her best not to make eye contact with anyone else on the floor. Though she was sure that only made her look suspicious.

When she made it to 214, it was relatively quiet, save the faint beep of machines and whoosh of the heater. Dantrell "Danny" Williamson was out cold, sprawled on the bed like he's finished the longest marathon and fought tooth and nail for first place.

Maybe I should leave.

But then his eyes fluttered open.

"Uh…hi," Manny said, stepping closer. "How are you?"

Dantrell blinked at her, after a few seconds, his eyes widened. "You're the lake girl."

"Yeah," Manny said, because she couldn't think of anything else to say.

He slowly sat himself up, wincing as he did so. Dantrell Williamson still had the same natural, easy athleticism as the other stand outs on the track team—she had taken some time scrolling his athletics page, reading his stats. Though she couldn't make sense of them, she could appreciate hard work.

Dantrell had long, powerful legs that had carried him to more than one medal—and she was surprised the hospital bed could fit him. His skin was a rich, deep brown, smooth except for a small scar on his chin, perhaps a souvenir from some long-forgotten tumble. His hair was short and neatly cropped, though he looked tired. Understandably so.

"Sorry, I've been feeling…*weird.* All day, really," Dantrell said, putting a hand on his head for a moment. "Like off and on, it feels like there's something under my skin. And you…" his eyes narrow. "It's kind of like you're setting it off…"

Nausea riled her stomach.

Is he experiencing ritual resonance? But he wasn't part of a ritual. Was he? Oh no, no, no.

It wasn't like she could ask him. If he was part of some ritual, she couldn't imagine him telling her outright. But if this was something else, she wanted to know what. But it was the same way she felt standing in this room—the electric hum under her skin, like she was a live wire waiting to short-circuit.

Manny was trying to maintain her poker face, nodding and *mm-hmming* like the perfect listener, but inside, she was doing laps around her brain.

Danny's face was a mixture of exhaustion and confusion. "Honestly…I don't even know how I got to you that fast," he said, his voice hoarse. He coughed and reached for the water beside his bed and drank it. "It was like my body just... moved on its own. And ever since then, I've felt *off.* Like I was talking about it with my team, but they thought

I just needed some rest, and we were going to take a trip to the pub." He scratched his stubble. "It's all been a bit overwhelming. I don't really think of myself as a hero. I don't even know why I ran to help you—it's not that I wouldn't have," he said that part quickly, as though he's worried of what she'll think of him. "Sorry…it just…what happened doesn't make sense."

She didn't know how to explain it to him—nor did she think she should. The last thing she wanted was to involve yet another person in her *mess*.

Manny smiled and nodded again. "That is weird, haha."

She hoped her laugh sounded like a sweet giggle, though she wasn't so sure. But Dantrell wasn't paying attention to her. His eyes had drifted to his arm. He had a bandage wrapped around it, just below the elbow.

It was stained, dark and ugly. She wondered when the last time someone had changed it. Her stomach twisted, but she tried to keep her face neutral.

"What happened to your arm?" Manny asked, casually.

Dantrell shrugged, now acting as if he'd forgotten it was there. "Oh, *this*? I don't know. Antoine, Quentin, and I were headed back home—then I don't really know what happened after that. It's no big deal."

Antoine Reese and Quentin Hayes—the other victims.

Manny had read about them in the news. Antoine Reese was dead on-scene; he'd been dismembered—severed limbs, blood splattered everywhere—an awful way to go. Quentin Hayes' heart was punctured by something sharp—he had quite a few puncture wounds, but none of them were described as teeth-like. But it was becoming more apparent, Dantrell was the only one left alive, because it was more than clear that whoever attacked them was more than capable of killing him. So, why was Dantrell left alive?

And as for his bandage. That was *no big deal*. Was only *no big deal* until she noticed his veins above it were…*wrong*. Darker than they should've been, with a black streak creeping along them like poison, climbing up his arm.

And slowly the pieces clicked into place. The ritual resonance coming off him was probably an effect of the glamour. But, as for his arm, according to everything she'd read—Dantrell had been bitten.

"Oh, uh-huh," Manny muttered, because she had no idea what to say to someone who might be turning into a vampire. "You should probably get that checked again. It looks…like they've not changed it."

"Yeah, they gave me antibiotics," he said, rubbing his neck.

Manny nodded, trying not to stare at him too long. A quote from *A Beginner's Guide to Understanding Immortals* popped into her head:

Newborn vampires are highly volatile and unpredictable. Approach with extreme caution.

Her brain was screaming at her to leave, to get out of the room before he suddenly sprouted fangs and was driven to test out his new diet plan on her.

"You know what? I'm just gonna grab a coffee or something, really quickly" she said, already halfway to the door.

He frowned, confused. "You just got here."

And Manny would normally feel guilty, because she didn't imagine it was great being bedridden or slowly dying, or becoming immortal—she'd only seen it in movies. But she didn't need to see it in real life. In fact, this was the one thing she was willing to keep fictional. If she never had to see someone change into a vampire, it would be too soon.

"I'll be back!" Manny called over her shoulder, flinging the door open like it was the emergency exit to a burning building.

Her heart was pounding as she stepped into the hallway, her hand gripping the strap of her purse so tightly she was pretty sure she'd bruised her palm. But she could finally breathe a sigh of relief.

Out of danger, she thought, *for now.*

She took a few more deep breaths, leaning against the wall outside Dantrelle's room, letting the hospital smell of disinfectant and despair flood her nostrils.

Breathe in, breathe out.

But her heart was still drumming in her ears.

Breathe in, breathe out.

She shut her eyes and tried to focus on her breathing.

Breathe in, breathe out.

She was convinced that would be her mantra for the next hour.

Breathe in, breathe out.

The buzzing was taking on a new intensity. It had gone from buzzing bees to horses galloping through her veins and toward her heart.

Jesus Christ.

She fished her cellphone out of her pocket, and found herself searching for Professor Beau's faculty page. She found his office phone number, and dialed. The line rang twice before he picked up.

"Hello, Dr. Moreau speaking," he said, his voice smooth and infuriatingly unbothered, like he wasn't spending his evening drinking tea and dodging sunlight.

But he doesn't have to avoid sunlight. Does he? A voice inside her tutted.

"It's me," Manny said, nearly breathless. "Look, there's…a *situation* here at the hospital. If you could come, I'd really appreciate it."

She heard him sigh on the other end, which she hoped meant, he didn't want to, but he would come anyway. "I'll be there shortly," Beau said.

Before Manny could thank him or hang up, something slammed her against the wall. Her cellphone slipped from her fingers, clattering to the floor as the air left her lungs.

Whoever it was had a strong enough hold on her neck, because her feet were floating, and she was positioned in a way to completely prevent her from hurting them. She couldn't kick. She couldn't scream.

Their grip slackened slightly, and it took a few seconds before the stars clouding her vision cleared. Replaced by an otherworldly face framed by black hair with a silver sheen and Manny tried again to kick at him.

And, though it took a moment—she recognized him. The man from the bar. The one she couldn't leave. Who she'd assumed had triggered her anxiety, and now, outside of Dantrell's hospital room, she had an unpleasant thought: *it wasn't her anxiety at all…it was her instincts.*

Her ritual resonance hadn't fully kicked in yet. She'd only experience a small twinge inside her brain—*painful*, but not enough for her to think anything of it. Why would she? She'd thought they'd stopped the curse then. But all of it added up. His otherworldly good looks. The disgusting smell of burning flesh—given her *eau de Holy Water*—though he wasn't letting go. Suddenly it all made sense.

He's a fucking a vampire.

He watched her face, a wolfish grin on his mouth, as if he'd heard what she was thinking, or he was relishing in the power he had over her.

"Have you not read anything about shielding your mind?" He asked, slowly, studying her face. "That's disappointing, Manny."

She found her eyes drawn to his mouth and gulped. *Where did those come from?*

"Let me go," Manny managed, her voice shaky but loud enough to echo down the hall. She wasn't sure if she was threatening him or begging him, but either way, she wasn't going down without a fight. And since she couldn't physically fight at the moment, an argument would have to do.

He laughed. Her stomach knotted.

"Are you trying to threaten me?" He asked, leering over her, silvery eyes boring into her own. "Really, *sweetheart?* You're no more frightening than the cat that hangs around your apartment."

What? Manny felt her heart jolt in her chest. *Mihawk. He's been watching me?*

And, to make matters worse, she hadn't noticed.

"I'm not a cat killer though, I find them quite *adorable*," he said, staring at her. "But, really *darling*, why would I be frightened of you?"

"I think you should be," Manny said, trying to sound braver than she felt. Her mind raced, trying to figure out her options. Scream? Pray? All of the above? But his grip tightened, and his face was close enough now that she could see the glint of something dangerous in his eyes. Manny swallowed, the fear bubbling up inside her as she realized just how little control she had over what was happening.

"Relax, I'm not going to rape you," he told her. "Though if you make any sudden movements, I may change my mind."

Any sudden movements? Is he going to let me go, Manny thought, hopefully.

"Are you frightened, love?" his lips were close to hers, and a wicked smile spread across his face. "You should be."

His grin widened, and suddenly, she heard his voice, not through her ears but inside her head.

Panicking, are we? his voice taunted. It was like he was sifting through her thoughts. *What a mess you are.*

She gasped, her body jolting as if she could physically throw him out of her head. "Stop it," Manny snapped, though her voice cracked.

Her stomach twisted. And she tried to think of something —*anything*—but her current situation.

Desperate to redirect the conversation, she blurted, "What did you do to Dantrell?"

"Dantrell?"

That did the trick.

"The boy in this room," she gestured toward the '214' on the wall.

Then he laughed, a low, guttural sound that shook his chest and sent chills down her spine. "Oh, *him.* That wasn't me."

"Then who?"

His smile widened, fangs flashing. "Ah, you're angry now. *Good.* And if you must know, it was someone else."

She didn't say anything. *How many more of you are there?* She wanted him to answer the question, hoping to get him to tell her, or to let him know she wouldn't play his little game.

"Margery."

Is she part of your coven? She noticed the vampire's grin faltered, just for a second, and she smirked. His grip tightened in retaliation, and though he was choking her again, she had her answer. She was part of his coven.

She needed to tell her professor. But she had to get out of this first.

"Professor? What professor?"

Crap.

His grip on her throat slackened, perhaps hoping she would speak. Instead she tried to shove all thoughts of her professor into some mental closet, slamming the door shut and pretending she wasn't terrified the vampire would pry it open. She had no idea what shielding was, but she sure as hell didn't want him inside her head.

"You're trying, how *sweet.*"

Condescending, bloodsucking bastard.

"You needn't be upset. Shielding one's mind isn't easy."

Manny gritted her teeth. She couldn't tell if he was mocking her or comforting her, but it didn't matter. She wasn't any closer to escaping him.

What the hell do I do?

She was scared, but she didn't want him to know how scared she was.

"Now," he said softly, his breath brushing her lips. "Stay still, my darling, this may hurt a little."

But instead of kissing her, in one swift movement, he turns her head and bites her. The moment his fangs sank into her neck, it was as if someone had driven searing hot pokers straight into her flesh. A scream clawed up her throat, but it'd turned into a pathetic, choked gasp. Her body jerked violently, she managed to pull an arm free, and began pushing at his arm in a frantic, useless attempt to shove him away. This wasn't normal pain—it was something ancient and wrong.

Heat surged through her veins.

Is this what hell feels like?

Or was this hell itself, a cruel promise of what was to come? Every wave of torment was met with another.

She thrashed, but her strength was being drained away. Her mind leapt from one thought to the next looking for something—*anything*—to hold onto. A passage of text, even a single word to steady her. But all she could hear was the sickening sucking, slurping sound of his feeding.

No, please, no.

But she was too weak to keep fighting. Then something changed—it was like ice was flooding her bloodstream, chasing the fire with a chilling numbness that crept down her limbs. She was lightheaded again, like she was floating—or maybe falling.

Is this how it ends?

She wanted to scream for help, but couldn't, even as darkness curled around the edges of her vision.

Then, just as abruptly as it started, it stopped. His teeth withdrew, and the sudden absence of pain left her gasping, raw and hollow.

He let her go, and her knees gave out. Manny crumpled against the wall, the cool surface pressing against her cheek. Blood trickled down her neck, soaking into her sweater.

Manny wondered how long it would take her to lose consciousness—to just slip away into death's waiting arms. She looked up at him, her body trembling, and he looked down at her.

"The pain will pass in a few hours," he said softly, wiping his lips with a handkerchief he'd pulled from his pocket. "I'll make sure they find you before then."

She stared at him wordlessly. Then finally found the strength to say. "Am I going to die?"

The vampire smiled, and kneeled down in front of her. "No."

He reached out and touched her face, stroking her cheek.

"You needn't be afraid of me, Manny," he told her, brushing his thumb over her lips. "At least…*not anymore.*"

She didn't want to let him touch her. She'd rather be burned alive than let this vampire touch her. He was part of the coven that was murdering students—students like her.

The vampire looked amused. "Things will be different the next time we meet."

"Different how?" Manny asked, breathlessly.

He stood up to his full height and smirked. Then, without another word, he turned and vanished into the shadows.

Different how, she wondered. But before she could mull it over, her head lolled against the wall as her vision turned dark as a warm gush of blood rushed down her neck.

Chapter 26
November 14th

Manny's eyelids felt like they were glued shut, but she pried them open, wincing as the harsh fluorescent lights made everything around her swim for a moment.

A hospital bed.

Scratchy white sheets and a thin blanket covering her.

What the hell happened?

Her brain sputtered like an old car engine, then the memories slammed into her like a freight train: the vampire, his fangs, the pain —*her blood.* Her fingers instinctively flew to her neck, feeling for the puncture wounds, but all she found was a bandage.

"Don't touch it," a voice said, and she nearly jumped out of her skin.

She turned her head. A bad idea, because it sent pain shooting straight through her skull.

"You scared me," Manny said, holding her chest.

"Scared, you?" Grant said, scoffing. "They found you passed out in the hall, *bleeding*. What the hell happened?"

Manny blinked at him. The last thing she remembered seeing was the vampire—and feeling her blood trailing down her neck.

Her hand hovered over the bandage again, and her stomach twisted. *Am I...am I turning?*

She hadn't read any accounts about that. Or none that immediately came to mind.

"Seriously, what happened to you?" Grant pressed, leaning forward now, his brows knitting together. "Manny, I need to know."

But she didn't know where to start.

Then, if her vision hadn't cleared, she probably wouldn't have noticed him as he swept into the room. For a man with such presence, he moved unnervingly quiet, the low hum of the hospital machines doing enough to mask his arrival.

"Ah, awake at last," he murmured, his tone so calm it sent an involuntary shiver down her spine.

Grant turned, clearly startled by his sudden appearance. "Uh, why are you here?" he asked, glaring at him.

Beau didn't so much as blink. Instead, he stepped closer, a small smile curling on his lips. "Manny contacted me," he said smoothly, his eyes locking onto Grant's with unnerving intensity.

But before Manny could interject, Grant's expression softened. His shoulders relaxed, the tension gone. His eyes glazed over, that now-familiar faraway look she'd seen before—in Dean's eyes.

"Why don't you step out for a bit?" Beau said gently, though there was a sudden vibration flowing throughout her body. "The doctor's come to see, Manny. She's in good hands, and you could use some coffee, maybe a bite to eat too."

"Yeah...that sounds nice," Grant murmured, his tone strange. He walked over to a chair, grabbed his jacket and left the room without further argument, the door clicking shut behind him.

Manny's heart sank. "You can't do that," Manny said, her heart racing. "You can't just glamour my friends, besides, he's right, it looks strange—"

Beau inclined his head slightly, making her stop in her tracks. "*Compel*—not glamour—and he won't remember I was here," he said matter-of-factly.

He studied the room as if he were looking for something in particular.

"So, he'll just forget?"

"He'll think the doctor came—*not* me."

His voice was clipped. He was done talking about it.

"What happened?" he asked, stepping closer to the bed. Then he sniffed and leaned closer to look at the bandage on her neck. "You were bitten."

Manny hesitated, removing her fingers from the bandage. "I don't remember much," she admitted. "Just...the bite. And the pain."

Beau nodded slowly, his eyes darkening. "That's not surprising."

She could feel his breath on her throat and then he pulled back. "A vampire's venom has a way of hampering memory—especially when it's meant to subjugate."

"*Subjugate*?"

He nodded again. "I suspect Mr. Williamson was made subservient to someone. A more powerful vampire."

A memory of the vampire who'd bitten her flashed inside her head. And with it, a name. "Does the name Margery mean anything to you?"

Beau's brow furrowed. "No, I'm afraid not. Can you tell me anything about the vampire that bit you?"

Manny nodded and described him as best as she could. His long dark hair, his sharp, fox-like features, the way his silver eyes bore into her like a predator. And of course, his mention of someone named *Margery* who'd attacked Dantrell and possibly his friends.

When she finished, he didn't say anything. Instead, he pulled out his phone, thumb tracing his screen until he found what he was looking for. He turned it around and held it out to her—a photo of a group of people, their clothes decades out of date, all of them smiling.

"Him," he said, pointing at one man.

Her heart lurched as she spotted him immediately. The man in the photo had the same wolfish grin on his face, his hand resting lightly on the shoulder of another man, who was laughing. And beside him, to Manny's shock, was Beau himself.

Manny nodded.

"Vlane Cicero," he answered. "He is nomadic—or more *parasitic* and latches onto whatever coven is willing to host him. I suspect that Margery must be a member of that coven. They must've decided to *collect* the track star."

"Why?" Manny asked, her throat dry.

Beau seemed to think over the question for a few moments. "Some covens have a particular taste for people," he explained. "They don't just target anyone—they prioritize the rare and beautiful. Seeking unique abilities—or creativity. They prize the arts over all else. And also, unfortunately for Dantrell, he knew what I looked like—which means it won't be long until Vlane's coven knows I'm here."

Manny swallowed. "And me?"

He didn't answer right away, but there was a flicker of something in his eyes—regret, possibly—and it told her enough.

"We'll have to wait for the side effects." Beau explained.

Side effects. That was just what she needed. Something else to contend with after already dealing with ritual resonance for weeks.

Because why stop at magical metal detector, Manny, she chastised herself. *You really had to go for the gold. Didn't you?*

"I beg your pardon?" Manny asked.

He sighed, running a hand over his face. "The type of bite you received determines the outcome," he said, studying her with that same unnervingly calm expression. "And, well, there are three possibilities."

"Possibilities?" She asked, her voice coming out higher than she'd meant to. "As in, different kinds of vampire bites?"

You've got to be shitting me.

He pulled up a seat at her bedside, and leaned back in it. "Yes, and unfortunately, we'll have to wait."

"Well that's reassuring," she muttered, the sarcasm doing little to mask the tremble in her voice. "And what are these '*types*'?"

"The first," he began, "is meant to poison. We refer to it as *infection,* because it imitates human infections. The venom spreads like a sickness, weakening you until..." He gestured toward her and trailed off. "Let's just say, it's not a pleasant way to go."

Manny swallowed. "Um…*we*?"

"My fellow academics…" he said. His lips twitched, but it wasn't a smile—more like a reflex. "*Vampires*. Though some of them are academics, artisans, and—"

"Okay, got it. What else?" Manny asked, interrupting him.

"The second is *affliction*," he continued. "It transforms you—changes you into a vampire. Which I'm sure is much easier to understand—"

"And the third?" Manny said.

His eyes darkened, and for a moment she wasn't sure if it was because she kept interrupting him, or because of whatever the third 'possibility' was.

"The third is...*conception*. It binds you to the vampire who bit you. It's rare, but when done, it's usually for a purpose—to be a familiar—whether for platonic purposes or to *breed*."

Manny had the distinct feeling he had chosen his words carefully. But that didn't stop her skin from prickling at the implications.

"*Breed*," she repeated.

The word made her sick. She knew vampires reproduced, but she still hadn't pieced everything together.

He nodded. "It creates a bond that's difficult—but not impossible—to break. It would mean he claimed you—*for life*."

Manny stared at him, her breath shallow. "But how long does it take—"

"Some of them share a few side effects, but you'll know the difference. Each of them has a distinct initial symptom."

"Which are what exactly?"

"For infection and affliction, the first symptom is chest pain," he said. "A sharp, searing pain right here." He tapped his sternum lightly. "You may feel like your bones are breaking—both will feel like a heart attack—but only infection will make you vomit pus."

Her stomach turned. "And affliction?"

"You'll feel like you're having a heart attack—and your heart will stop—but you'll still be alive."

Well, I don't like the sound of that either.

"And conception?" Manny asked hesitantly, almost afraid to hear the answer.

He paused, studying her, as if checking if she were about to faint. "A *soul-stirring* sensation. Like a deep, primal pull inside your body."

Her stomach turned. "But how will I know?"

Infection and *affliction*—those two seemed easy enough. Chest pain? Great, she has a lifetime's worth of anxiety attacks to compare them to.

But *conception*—what the hell did he mean a *primal pull* inside her body? Was she going to wake up one morning, staring out the window like some lovesick princess, thinking about the vampire who bit her? Because if that's the case, she'd rather have the chest pain. At least she could take ibuprofen for it.

"You'll know," Beau said sternly. "I promise you, you will."

Well, that's comforting.

And he must've seen it on her face—or overheard her thoughts—because he followed up with. "Either way—I'll help you," Beau said. "Infection and Affliction are the easiest of the two to manage, but conception...well, we'll cross that bridge if we come to it."

Manny didn't press further. He didn't seem interested in elaborating further. Instead Beau picked her cellphone up off the side table and, without asking, turns it around to scan her face, and goes to her contact list. "When you notice something...*call me,*" he said, handing it back. She didn't even get a chance to thank him—or argue, for that matter—before he adds, "Now, get some rest."

As if it was that simple. Like she could just lie back and not spiral thinking about what kind of ticking time bomb she might be. But either way, he was leaving.

Chapter 27
November 15th

By the time they discharged her, it was nearly 3 am, and they sent her off with antibiotics that she already knew wouldn't do anything against whatever was inside her.

But sure, let's pretend a few little white pills can cure vampire venom like it's a sinus infection.

Manny shook her head at herself. She'd get a medical bill in her email eventually, which was worse because it meant she needed to calculate how many months of instant noodles it would take to pay it off. By the time she reached her apartment, she had a headache from just thinking about it. She'd considered asking her family, calling her mother, but reconsidered it. She didn't want them to worry.

And ultimately, she wanted to worry about one thing at a time.

Instead she headed up to her apartment, as she normally would—not calling anyone. She left her purse by the door and made a beeline for her bed. For a few hours, nothing happened, she couldn't sleep. She knew she was tired, but couldn't manage to do anything other than toss and turn. Luckily, after a while, her exhaustion took hold.

At first, it was a nice dream—but that didn't last.

There were fangs, blood, flesh between someone's teeth, silvery eyes boring into her soul, his breath on her neck. His laughter. Him, feeding. That horrifying squelching sounds in her ears, buzzing in her chest, rattling around her head until she woke up gasping, the sheets tangled around her legs.

Oh my God, she thought, clutching her chest.

Her heart felt like it was trying to burst out of her chest, and her neck…well, that had just started throbbing. Her face was tight, clenched—*was I grinding my teeth last night?*

Her jaw muscles said 'yes,' and she sighed. *Ibuprofen then.*

Manny swung her feet over the edge of the bed, slid on her slippers, and staggered into the bathroom. She peeled off her sweat-soaked clothes, and turned on the shower. Quickly taking an ibuprofen from her medicine cabinet and swallowed it.

Am I coming down with a fever?

Her cheeks were flushed and sweat beaded on her forehead. She was uncomfortably hot, but she didn't have any other symptoms that aligned with any of Beau's proposed *possibilities*. There was no pain in her chest. She wasn't nauseous and her heart rate was normal—or at least, normal after a nightmare.

Manny got into the shower, and sighed as the water washed down her body. She let her head lull back as she tried to relax. But as she did, there was another throb, a pulsating throb, not in her neck or her head…somewhere else. She jerked her head up, and she looked down. Her eyes widened as the throbbing persisted, becoming slightly painful.

Holy shit. Holy shit. Oh my—what the fuck!

She put a hand against the wall and let out an uneven breath. Instinctively, she turned up the water, perhaps to the point it could potentially scald her skin—but she didn't care. Manny grabbed her loofa, putting body soap on it and let out a long sigh. The word *primal* was making a lot more sense. But the word *pull* was an understatement.

She was scrubbing herself like Lady Macbeth, trying to erase any remnants of *him*—Vlane Cicero—the feeling of his hands, his teeth, the venom. Clearly conception did more than bind her to him—it gave her *urges*. Or what Beau had called *soul-stirrings*. She couldn't believe it.

Well at least I'm not dead...or undead.

But this wasn't any better. She was turning into some...*feral thing?* She pressed her forehead against the cool tile and groaned. Steam was slowly clouding the bathroom, but it was nothing compared to the sudden heat rushing through her.

This can't be happening. There's no way I'm going to be some vampire's mindless little...breeder.

The word *'breeder'* was enough to make her gag.

Unfortunately, the thought of it, caused a vivid image flash into her mind—him. On his knees in front of her, his hands gripping her hips, his tongue on her—

God, no.

Manny balled her hand into a fist, squeezing her eyes shut as if she could physically push the image out of her mind. But it's there, vivid and unrelenting, and she isn't sure if she's more horrified by what she's not feeling than what she should be. Three words: Disgust, revulsion, fear. All of them were missing. Instead her nether regions warmed at the thought of him, and that terrifies her.

She banged her fist against the shower wall, hard enough that pain shot up her arm, snapping her back to reality. Manny cursed under her breath.

It's the venom. Pull yourself together, she told herself.

She raked her hands through her wet hair, trying to ground herself. Then she shut her eyes, trying to imagine the image evaporating, hoping she can push it away, force it into the darkest corner of her mind where it can rot.

You are not going to let this thing control you. But as she turned off the water and stepped out of the shower, and wrapped herself in a towel, another thought pops into her head: *What if it already is?*

Manny internally shook herself. *No. Fuck him.*

She still had control over herself, and she wasn't planning on giving up any time soon.

So, she went to her room, changed into a pair of pajamas, and looked at the clock. *Noon.* It had only been eight hours since she'd gotten home—and she didn't have any idea how long it'd been since she'd been bitten. But she refused to sit there and do nothing. Instead, she grabbed her phone and made a note of it in her notes app—she could at least keep track of her symptoms. Maybe they'd be of some use to Beau. Then she opened her food delivery app, scrolling through it, staring blankly at the options. *Chicken nuggets? No. Ramen? Not now. Pho? Maybe.* She could barely focus, and she wasn't entirely sure if the hunger gnawing at her was for food or… *him.* The memory of Vlane's teeth on her neck sent an involuntary shiver down her spine.

Bile rose in her throat. *It's food. It has to be food. I haven't eaten in hours, and no amount of vampire venom flowing through my body is going to change that.*

Chapter 28
November 15th

She eventually settled on chicken nuggets—something filling and loaded with trans fats, because to her nuggets were safe. Nuggets don't remind her of a vampire pinning her to a wall and sinking his teeth into her neck. She orders a combo with large fries, because apparently, she was going to stress-eat her way through this. She wanted comfort—at times that meant *comfort food* and the meal her six-year-old self loved was the closest she could get at this hour.

After placing the order, she stretched out on the couch. Her body was still screaming for something more, but she didn't want to think about or acknowledge what that "more" meant.

When the food finally arrived, she tipped the delivery guy and tore into the food like a starving animal—no time for etiquette. Shoveling fry after fry into her mouth before she's even closed it again. She must've been quite the sight given the look on the delivery guy's face. The well-salted fries and the comforting spicy chicken nuggets pulled her back to normalcy, as if she was just a regular girl winding down after a bad day. But the hunger—the *real* hunger—didn't go away. It sits there in her chest, waxing and waning, reminding her of how hungrily he looked at her. It was as if he wanted to know how her blood would taste. She dipped another nugget into barbecue sauce and bit down with more force than necessary, as if chewing it hard enough would make it easier to ignore the sensation. But she knew it didn't matter. It was all just a sad distraction from the fact that she was turning into someone—or *something*—she didn't recognize.

Finally, she reached the bottom of the bag, where beneath the crumpled napkins and stray ketchup packets, she spotted something—a piece of paper folded neatly into a small square. She wiped her face with a napkin, taking out the note and half-thought it might have been something accidentally placed in there. But when she unfolds it, sure enough, the elegant script scrawled across the page makes her blood run cold.

My Dearest Manny,

Imagine my disappointment when I arrived at your hospital room and found it empty. Such a shame—I was hoping for a proper reunion. You'll find me at the Argenté Luxe, suite 1602. It's quite a charming hotel, though I imagine you'd prefer to come on your own terms. At least, that's what I'd prefer. We don't want you getting too ravenous, my darling.

Also, tell my brother, Damiel, I said hello, won't you?

Yours in anticipation,

Vlane Cicero

The note slipped from her fingers and landed on the table.

He had come back to *the hospital*. After she'd left. He'd been looking for her. She stared at the words as if they might disappear as if this were all some drug-induced nightmare she'd wake up from—could antibiotics make her hallucinate? And Damiel?

Who the hell is Damiel?

But at the moment, that didn't matter. Vlane knew where she was. And worse—he was waiting for her. At the most expensive hotel in the wealthiest part of town. About a mile or two away from her—in a suite.

If I get a hold of him—she shook her head at herself. She wasn't sure what she'd do. Kill him? No, she wasn't sure she could do that or in her current state. Fuck him? She couldn't risk going near him—if that was the case.

Manny's hands fumbled as she unlocked her cellphone, her hands were shaking. She was glad no one could see her inside her apartment. Her breathing was shallow so she couldn't call. She wouldn't—her voice would crack too much. She didn't need to feel more embarrassed.

A text. Short. Direct. She types it quickly, her hands still shaking.

Need to meet. Urgent. Are you free tonight?

Manny hit send before she could overthink it. She didn't have time to mull over every possible scenario in her head where he didn't reply, and she was left to deal with it alone—he had promised to help her. And as the minutes ticked by, she began to hear her pulse in her ears. But if Vlane was waiting for her, he'd be waiting for the rest of his immortal life. She wasn't going anywhere near that suite. If he thought that, he certainly couldn't have ever heard of the axiom *'the indomitable nature of the human spirit'*—revering how humans managed to endure. She would endure before she endured sex with him. It didn't matter how much her mind raised the same question over and over: *is it really worth torturing yourself?*

It came from a part of herself she didn't recognize. But then, three little dots appear in her message app, and Beau's response appears.

Beau
I'm free now. Where do you want to meet?

Manny lets out a breath, and her thumbs hover over her phone for a few seconds before she replies.

Your office. I'll be there soon.

His next reply gets there faster.

Beau
I'll be waiting.

She locked her phone and pressed a hand to her chest. She looked at the note. She wants to light it on fire. But decides balling it into her pocket will have to do until she can show Beau. And as for Damiel—whoever the hell he is—she was going to get answers.

* * *

Beau looks up from a leather notebook in his hand, studying her as if trying to piece things together from the look on her face.

"Sit," he said, gesturing to the chair in front of her. "You look…*uncomfortable*."

Disturbed. Manny internally corrected.

She sat down in the chair, her hands gripping the chair arms like it'll steady her.

"I think I've...uh..." Manny cleared her throat, her face burning. "I think I've been having what you called...*soul-stirrings*."

Beau sets down the book carefully. "Go on."

"Well, if *soul-stirrings* means feeling like an animal in heat, then yeah. *That's happening*."

For a second, he just stares at her, his expression unreadable. Then he leans back in his chair.

"*That*," he said finally, looking somewhat amused, "would qualify."

She wanted to bury her face in her hands. Beau is smirking slightly, the kind of smirk that would be insufferable if it weren't paired with his annoyingly handsome face. His dark hair is slightly tousled like he's just come from some heroic, academic battle—probably against a particularly stubborn library archive.

God. She was starting to hate him. Not because he was attractive, but because she would bet anything, as a vampire, he knows he's attractive, and worse, *he knows that she thinks it*.

"What's so funny?" Manny snapped, crossing her arms over her chest.

"Nothing," he said, clearly lying. His smirk widens a fraction. "Just appreciating your candor."

"Yeah, well," Manny muttered, looking anywhere but at him, "don't appreciate it *too much*."

But his smirk was slowly turning into a grin.

"And in the spirit of candor," he started, drawing her attention to his face. "I think you should know, I can hear your thoughts—I'd assumed you hadn't picked up on that—and you can correct me if I'm wrong," he said, as casually as someone might announce they've switched to oat milk in their coffee. Like it's *no big deal*. Like it's *completely normal* to drop that bombshell in the middle of a conversation.

Her heart sank. *Sweet mother of God.*

Every single embarrassing, fleeting, completely inappropriate thought she had ever had about him—*in this very office*—comes rushing back in horrible technicolor.

"Oh God," she mumbled, her hands flying to cover her mouth. "Oh *no*. You can't be serious."

"Yes," he said, his voice far too calm for someone who just shattered the illusion of privacy she'd been clinging onto like a life raft.

Why the hell am I surprised?

She knew she shouldn't be. If Vlane could hear her thoughts, it wasn't impossible that Beau could as well.

"But—" she stammered, trying to find the words that would claw her way out of this slowly growing humiliation vortex. "But I—I'm so, so—"

Shit. Shit. Shit.

Manny dropped her hands and glared at him. "You *knew*?"

"Of course," he replied smoothly, leaning back in his chair, completely composed.

"So, the whole time, every time I've come into your office—"

"Yes."

"And I've thought *things*—"

"Yes."

He wasn't remotely intimidated by how angry she looked—and God, was she angry at him. That meant he knew everything. He'd known she was lying about her paper. He'd known why she'd been researching in the first place.

What doesn't he know?

"I didn't know about the perfume," he answered, as if to prove his point.

"Oh my God," Manny groaned, sinking into the chair, hoping she would melt into the floor if she tried hard enough. "This is mortifying. I knew someone that used that word once during class and thought they sounded pretentious, but if there was ever a time to use that word it's now because—*I'm mortified*. Jesus Christ. This is at least number three in my top five worst things that have happened to me."

He smirked, the infuriating, chiseled devil.

"Well," he said, folding his hands together in an insufferably calm way, "if it makes you feel any better, I'm flattered."

She wanted to throw his stapler at him.

"But, as for more *important* matters—you'll have worse days ahead of you, *if* we don't deal with your *predicament*."

Manny glared at him. "No, *shit*."

He leaned forward slightly, resting his elbows on his desk, and for a moment, the glimmer of amusement faded from his expression. His eyes lock onto hers, and he said, "You're handling this better than most would."

Manny snorts. "If by 'handling it,' you mean 'running straight to my professor like a three-year-old in ballet class running to their parent,' then sure, I'm doing great."

The corner of his mouth twitches, like he's trying not to laugh *again*. "I'm glad you've been able to keep your sense of humor. You'll need it."

She didn't say anything. She was too busy trying to figure out if she wanted to punch him—or if she just hated how nice his smile was.

But rather than embarrass herself further, she decided to change the subject.

"How about you tell me about how this whole thing works," Manny said, pointedly. Though she wasn't sure entirely which thing she was referring to—*vampires*, or the *bites*, or whatever else he might be willing to tell her.

"Well, you were made a *familiar*—which I'm sure you've learned about it in your research," he explained suddenly.

Her stomach twisted. "Yeah, I guess—but nothing I've read has gone that in depth…but I'm guessing it's nothing like a cat to a witch."

"Not remotely."

She hated when he was vague. Or when he acted like every explanation needed to be some long drawn-out lecture. Familiars made her think of creatures bound by some unseen thread, doing the bidding of their master. Was that what she was now? A puppet on invisible strings? The thought made her stomach churn. Did it ultimately mean the vampire owned her—Beau had said Vlane had bound her to him? So maybe he controlled her now?

"I doubt he could control you, *Manny*," he said with a smirk, answering her unspoken thoughts.

"Don't do that!" she snapped.

"Sorry," he said, feigning innocence. "Your thoughts are always rather *loud*."

"Well, try to tune me out."

That was something she never thought she'd say—and to make matters worse, it made him laugh.

"And to be clear, Manny, there are three types of familiars," he said. "Familiars are either enslaved, platonic or *sensual*."

She blinked at him. "I'm sorry, what?"

"The enslaved," he repeated, voice clipped like he was clicking through slides from a lecture she hadn't attended. "The most common. Those familiars are used to lure victims to their masters or mistresses so they can feed. Essentially, they become both a bloodhound and bait." he continued, "*Platonic* are for vampires who want companionship—a lifelong friend. Or, in this case, an immortal life shared with someone. They might roam the world together, enjoying their prolonged existence as equals."

"And the last one?" she asked, as if she could forget the word *'sensual'* having left his lips.

"*Sensual* is a bond rooted in lust. In those cases, the familiar is consumed with desire so intense it overrides all basic needs. They can't sleep, eat, or drink without first *pleasing* their master."

Her mouth went dry. "And I'm guessing that means I'm probably—"

"Sensual—yes," he said softly, and there was a flicker of something in his eyes—*pity*, maybe.

She folded her arms defensively, as if to say, *'don't you dare pity me,'* though she also considered pity might be the only thing making him help her.

"You seem to know a lot about familiars."

"I've been alive for hundreds of years—I make it my business to know," he said sternly. "And while I've met many who keep enslaved or platonic familiars. I've often avoided those who choose to enslave humans, be that by enslavement or sensual means—because they *disgust me*."

"Why?" it wasn't that she didn't understand why, slavery in all its forms was inhumane, but she needed to keep him talking. She didn't know when he would be willing to share this much about his kind with her again.

He tilted his head, as if he were baffled by her question. "Because it's *unethical*. Being the reason someone's entire body becomes consumed with lust so they're nothing more than a slave to their master's whims…it's *abhorrent*. It strips away their autonomy and turns a human being into a slave to sex—and I refuse to associate with vampires who do. *Ever*."

Her stomach churned. "So…considering that's what he did to me, then what? I'll just...stop caring about everything else?"

Beau's gaze locked onto hers, unflinching. "You won't hunger for anything more than pleasing him."

She wanted to throw up. She stared down at her hands in her lap. The idea of being reduced to...*that*—it was worse than anything she'd imagined. Worse than death. Worse than becoming a vampire.

Her emotions had gone from one extreme to another and she would be exhausted if it weren't for—*that*.

"Manny."

She heard his voice from somewhere far away. When she finally looked at him, his expression had softened. "We'll figure it out," he said. "You aren't alone in this."

Her throat felt tight, and she nodded, though she wasn't sure if she believed him.

"It just means Vlane sees you as a threat…which despite what you may think now—is a good thing. It means you're much closer to finding the coven than I was," Beau continued. "If I had known they would go after Dantrell, I would have told you to avoid him at the hospital—but now that we know—we can plan better in the future."

Is that supposed to make me feel better?

Manny wasn't sure she wanted to be a threat to a vampire—especially now that she was dealing with the consequences of it. To make matters worse, all the people she'd managed to drag into it. All because she couldn't leave well enough alone. Dantrell's life was going to be changed forever because of her—whoever had bitten him hadn't killed him. So, clearly, whatever type of bite he was given would eventually rear its ugly head, and she was responsible.

But at the same time, it was hard to feel the full weight of her guilt when her body was practically rebelling against her. Considering she felt like a cat in heat. Every brush of fabric against her skin—especially *down there*—was heightened, every fleeting thought of Vlane sent an unwelcome shiver down her spine. She hated it—this loss of control, this absurd, primal need that seemed to permeate through her body.

Beau sat down a mug in front of her, steam wafting into her face and breaking her spiral of self-loathing.

"It's a tea I found the ingredients for decades ago," he explained. "I was helping a friend—but it should help you *resist* the effects. It should regulate…your new *impulses*."

Manny eyed the mug, its contents a murky shade of brown that looked more like dirty water than tea. "And this works?" she asked, her tone laced with skepticism.

"It's better than nothing," he replied dryly, opening the mini fridge beside his desk and pulling out a cheese and cracker plate. "You'll be hungry afterward. Happens with most teas like this."

He placed the plate in front of her, and as she glanced at the open mini fridge, her stomach twisted. Among the neatly stacked containers inside, a pitcher caught her eye. Inside it was a thick, dark liquid, and was unmistakably—blood.

He shut the door, her eyes snapped back up to her professor, who was now leaning casually against his desk as if a pitcher of blood in a mini fridge was the most normal thing in the world.

Manny wanted to ignore it, which, though she hated to admit it, wasn't hard—given her current physical state.

She picked up the mug and took a sip. The taste hit her immediately—bitter and earthy, like steeped ashes with a hint of asphalt. It wasn't like any tea she'd ever had, and stomaching it was going to be a challenge. Still, she forced herself to drink it all.

Disgusting. Absolutely disgusting.

She shivered. She waited, and she felt nothing. Then a strange weight settled in her stomach, sinking into her limbs, dulling the frantic energy that had been coursing through her nether regions all day. But as the weight settled, another sensation took over—an aching hunger that clawed at her insides. She turned to the cheese and cracker platter, and before she knew it, she was reaching for it.

Out of the corner of her eye, she could see Beau's lips were moving, but his words didn't register. All she could focus on was filling the emptiness inside her. She grabbed a cracker, piled it high with cheese, and shoved it into her mouth. Not caring how she looked. But slowly, as the food began to fill the void, the sound of his voice came back into focus, like a radio tuning into the right frequency.

She chewed mechanically, and suddenly realized he'd been watching her the entire time, a faint smirk tugging at the corners of his mouth.

"Feel better?" He said, the smirk turned into a smile.

She gave him a sheepish grin. "I may have missed what you said," she admitted, gesturing to the empty plate. "I was...*distracted*."

His smile widened. "I gathered as much."

"Well, given the situation," she began hesitantly, surprising even herself with a sudden thought. "Technically, I could use myself as bait—"

"No." His tone was sharp, cutting through her sentence like a blade. "Absolutely not. You're inexperienced, and in your current state, you'd be a liability."

Manny bristled at his words but didn't argue—he was right. He knew it, she knew it.

He reached into his desk drawer and pulled out a sleek canister, placing it in front of her. "You should keep this. It's the tea I just gave you. Inside, you'll find compressed tea leaves. It smells more pleasant than it tastes—as you now know."

She unscrewed the lid and leaned in for a sniff. The scent was surprisingly pleasant—floral with a hint of something earthy—but she already knew better than to trust how it smelled.

He pointed to the canister. "Drink it three times a day. Once every eight hours. Don't wait until your 'soul-stirrings' start; the whole point is to prevent them, not chase after the effects when they hit."

She nodded, slipping the canister into her messenger bag, but her mind was already racing. *Don't wait until I'm out of my mind horny. Simple enough, right?* She let out a nervous laugh.

Beau tapped his phone and added, "I'll text you when it's time for us to meet again. In the meantime, stick to drinking it on a schedule, and try not to do anything reckless."

"Reckless?" she repeated, raising an eyebrow. "Ohhhh, you mean like walking into a vampire's lair."

"Exactly," he said with a faint smile. "Though I have to admit, your wit would make a decent distraction."

She rolled her eyes but couldn't help the small smile tugging at her lips. "No, not a chance. I'll follow your lead," she said, nodding her head. "After all, I wouldn't want your tea to go to waste."

He smiled at her.

God—that smile.

She swore his smile held a million secrets, and that it could overpower any draught, no matter how potent.

Don't think about that, she scolded herself, gripping the strap of her messenger bag tightly. *No sexy thoughts about your professor. Just tea, his rules, and resisting primal urges.*

Because anything else was like playing with fire—and she was already feeling dangerously hot.

"Oh and, does the name Damiel mean anything to you?" She asked, and Beau's smile faltered. "Vlane had told me to tell *Damiel* hello, but I don't think I've come in contact with anyone by that name."

Her professor looked less relaxed now, as if a weight had suddenly settled on his shoulders. "Why didn't you mention that?"

"Well, it was pretty recent—he sent me a note…" Manny trailed off, not wanting to admit she'd found it in the midst of her comfort eating stint.

Beau leaned back in his chair, and his gaze dropped for a moment before meeting hers, his voice quieter than before. "The name he mentioned—he was talking about me," he admitted, reluctantly.

Her breath caught in her throat.

What.

"Vlane and I are half-brothers. We share the same father, but different mothers."

Manny didn't even try to mask her shock. How could Beau and *him* be related? They barely looked like each other. Vlane almost looked more vampire than him, more otherworldly, though Beau—*Damiel,* whoever this vampire across from her was, was definitely the more handsome of the two. She could barely reconcile the two in her mind, but before she could say anything—anything at all—he continued.

"Our father…didn't exactly show restraint when it came to continuing his bloodline," he continued, his tone laced with bitterness. "He impregnated multiple familiars—women bitten and bound to serve him, specifically chosen to be breeders. After conception, they're called *seedbearers*…and they're protected under vampiric law. Especially between allied covens—if a seed bearer is pregnant, no harm can come to her. It's an unspoken law between covens. Anyone who breaks it risks starting a war."

Manny's stomach churned as he explained, her mind conjuring up images she'd rather not have.

Seedbearers. Enslavement.

She'd had just about enough of vampires for the day. No—she needed a break for at least a month. She had only just begun to grasp the simplest concepts—now here she was realizing she'd barely scratched the surface.

"Of course," he said, grimacing, "vampires don't create immortal children. That's...*unethical*, even by our standards. The point of breeding is to create a *dhampir*. When they reach maturity, as in their frontal lobe is fully developed, the vampire who sired them turns them into a vampire...*purifying* their blood. My coven prioritizes maturity, but, other covens..." He trailed off, shaking his head. "They may turn children or teens, creating immature vampires—they're unruly, unpredictable, and *dangerous*. It's a disgrace...and most of them end up dead within their first year."

The disgust in his voice was palpable, and for the first time since meeting him, she saw something more raw beneath his usually composed demeanor. She didn't know what unsettled her more—the new information about vampires or the fact that he had ties to Vlane. He wasn't just another vampire to her professor. He was blood. His blood.

Manny felt nauseous.

"That's... a lot to take in," she admitted, her voice shaky. "I mean, *a lot*."

His expression softened, a hint of understanding in his dark eyes. "I know it's overwhelming, but you can trust me. I can assure you I hold no allegiance to him or his coven."

She snorted, and let out a dry laugh. "You're telling me I might be some vampire's breeder-slash-bonded familiar. And on top of that, you're his brother? You have to give me a moment to process it."

"I know," he said gently. "But my goal hasn't changed. I have promised to keep you safe—and I intend to."

Manny stood abruptly, the chair scraping against the floor. "Look, I

—I just need some air—maybe some time. This is way too much for one day."

He didn't stop her. "Even if you don't believe it yet, I need you to try. For your own safety, Manny."

he hesitated at the door, one hand resting on the doorknob, as she looked back at him. "Trust is a lot to ask right now, Beau—Dem —*professor*." And for some reason, seeing the look of hurt in his eyes made her say. "I'll try—*try* being the operative word."

With that, she stepped out of the office, the door clicking shut behind her. And she hoped that after a nap, maybe she could begin to think over everything.

Chapter 29
November 16th

She had gotten out of there like a bat out of hell. Once back at her apartment, she had practically flung herself onto the couch, shoes still on, before passing out in exhaustion. Then she woke with a start, heart pounding against her ribcage, shirt clinging to damp skin as she gasped for air. It took a moment to gather her senses, but as she saw the clock on her phone's lock screen, she groaned.

Almost 8 hours.

And unfortunately, an uncomfortable warmth was starting to bloom low in her nether regions.

Damn it. She dragged herself off the couch, shuffled into the kitchen. She unscrewed the tea canister on the counter, and turned on the electric kettle. After a few minutes of staring at the kettle, she unlocked her phone and started scrolling through social media to distract herself. But the moment she opened it, her heart skipped a beat.

Five missed calls.

Her professor's name or his *alias*, stared back at her. She tapped the call log and was surprised all of them had been made in the last hour. Then there was another notification—a text from him:

Beau
Answer your phone. It's important.

He couldn't even manage a please?

Manny downed her tea quickly, and swore she could feel it sloshing around in her stomach, making her feel queasy.

Manny walked to her bathroom to get the taste out of her mouth.

She fired a quick text back:

> What's going on.

Her phone pinged almost immediately.

> **Beau**
> I have a lead. We need to meet tonight.

She was beginning to wonder when she'd gone from being the girl who binge watched horror movies to the girl lurking around in the dark grave robbing and vampire hunting. Manny stared at herself, her toothbrush hanging limply from her mouth. She remembered daydreaming about being the hero of her own story, and yet here she was a *sidekick*.

She wasn't even the *lead* in her own life at the moment. Just an unlucky supporting cast member to a dashing vampire professor—and she wanted to be recast.

She spat toothpaste into the sink and rinsed her mouth, muttering under her breath, "What's next? Matching costume and a theme song?"

She grabbed her phone again, firing off another reply:

> Fine.

He responded almost immediately:

> **Beau**
> Parking Lot F. Midnight. Don't be late.

It wasn't like she wanted to go crawling around abandoned warehouses at night like a wannabe Nancy Drew. But…she sighed, wiping her mouth with a towel. He wasn't exactly the villain here, was he? Sure, he was related to *her* villain, but family drama wasn't a crime. If it was, everyone would be in jail.

So, Manny pulled on a hoodie over her head. Tugged it down and looked back at the mirror, and sighed.

If Beau or Damiel said there was something worth investigating, then maybe there was. And if she didn't go, she'd just end up lying in bed wondering if her *'savior'* was getting himself killed somewhere. Just the average night of someone who used to think her biggest problem was affording rent. But she wasn't sure she could fully trust him—not yet—but she did trust him *enough* to go with him.

Her first few steps down the stairs were fine, unfortunately, at the bottom, she slipped on ice and landed on her butt. But, luckily, no one was around to see it—*unfortunately*, it was also foggy outside.

Her trek to the parking lot was boring, predictable even—which was nice. Manny didn't mind a boring walk across campus without thinking a vampire was going to pop out at her. Or that she was the next student on the human sacrifice list. Instead, she made her way there, cool, calm and collected—until she approached Parking Lot F, where the flickering lamps and cracked asphalt made her skin crawl. She could hardly believe it was part of Millfield University's campus.

A few parked cars looked like they'd been abandoned years ago—dusty windows, flat tires, the works. Then, somewhere in the dark, a cat yowled, and Manny jumped, clutching her bag a little tighter. She half-expected her professor to materialize out of thin air—but no such luck.

But then a pair of headlights flashed at her, cutting through the darkness like twin searchlights. She squinted, shielding her eyes, and slowly she was able to make out: a sleek, black 1967 Chevy Impala purring like a tomcat.

She stopped dead in her tracks. "Seriously?" she muttered to herself.

A vampire in a muscle car? She wanted to laugh. It couldn't be a beat-up Corolla like Dean's. No, of course, it had to be a classic. Nothing else would suit Damiel.

The driver's side door opened, and there he was, waltzing over to the other side of the car to open the passenger door—like a gentleman. Though his tone via text still left something to be desired. But she wondered what time he was from—clearly a chivalrous enough era—though she didn't feel like dissecting every word he'd ever-spoken to figure it out.

"Glad you could make it," he said. He sounded slightly annoyed, which made her roll her eyes.

'Yeah, *I made it*. Without as much as a *please*," she replied. "Nice car?"

He raised an eyebrow, clearly amused. "Will you *please* get in the car?"

"Very funny," she shot back, sliding into the passenger seat.

He chuckled and shut her door. Then before she knew it he was starting the car and steering them out the parking lot.

To make matters worse, their ride was quieter than she'd expected. Manny had thought maybe he'd at least lecture her about how dangerous whatever situation they were walking into was, but he seemed especially focused—or he was giving her space. His hands were steady on the wheel, eyes watching the road as he drove. The Impala's engine growled, vibrating through her seat. Manny stared out the window, trying not to think about what might happen next—or why her stomach fluttered every time she looked at him. When the car pulled up to their destination, her jaw nearly dropped.

"You can't be serious," she said, leaning forward to get a better look.

Manny had only seen it in passing—and every time she'd passed it she was with Tammy. The hotel was massive—it had polished marble steps out front with gold accents climbing up the staircase, and a valet station manned by attendants in green uniforms. And a gold 3D sign in a cursive font, reading: *Argenté Luxe*

She turned to him. "Why the hell are we here?"

He didn't answer right away, shifting the car into park and cutting the engine. Then, he turned to her. "When I was inside your head, I looked through your memories, and decided to walk by the area a few hours ago—"

"And."

"And I noticed a few *inhuman scents* that might have left us a clue or two."

Manny glared at him. "Excuse me?"

"Other vampires—I can smell their scent. It's a *vampire thing*," he said as if he were teasing her for her *humanness*.

She groaned in frustration, trying to decide if she was offended or irritated. "And that's just normal? Going through people's memories like they're photo albums?" Manny snapped. "You had no right."

He raised a brow, clearly unbothered. "Maybe I didn't, but I did anyway, because you were *withholding* information—which you agreed *not* to do."

"Don't try to pin the blame on me," Manny snapped. "This is a *privacy issue* which is also a *respect issue*—because you could've asked to look through my memories."

"You would've said no," he pointed out with a shrug. "This was faster and you'll thank me later."

She doubted that.

The Impala's door shut with a thud behind her as she followed him into the hotel. Inside, the lobby was even more luxurious—marble floors with gold inlay, crystal chandeliers, and staff that looked ready to faint at the sight of her less-than-pristine combat boots. She stuffed her hands in her winter coat's pockets, letting him do the talking at the front desk while she tried not to look out of place.

When he turned, holding a key card between his fingers, his expression was unreadable. "Let's go."

She wanted to ask how he'd gotten it, but decided it didn't matter.

They stepped inside the elevator and stood in silence. She desperately tried not to fidget but couldn't stop looking over at him. He was calm, too calm, like he'd done this a hundred times. Meanwhile, her heart drummed in her ears, and her palms were sweaty. She watched the floor number tick up and up.

Then the elevator dinged, he stepped out and she followed him down the hall to suite 1602 like a lost puppy. But what else was she supposed to do? He hadn't explained the plan. He slid the key card into the door and pushed it open, stepping inside with her close behind.

Inside, the suite was massive, all high ceilings and velvet furniture, but she barely had time to take it in.

He froze mid-step.

"Don't move," he whispered.

She would have argued, if he didn't look so alert. And for a moment, she cursed her humanness, because being human put her at a strategic disadvantage when it came to inhuman creatures.

But then she heard something, and before she could react, he turned and shoved her backward. Then she was hurtling through the air, weightless—as though the room itself had stopped obeying the laws of physics—until she collided with a velvet couch.

She heard glass shatter on the other side of the room.

Manny scrambled upright just in time to see Beau locked in a fight with someone else—a man with wild eyes and dark, bulging veins, crawling up his neck and hands. The professor dodged a swing that might've knocked him across the room, his movements fluid and precise, completely unphased by the attacker.

The other man lunged again, but his body moved strangely, in a jerky and uncoordinated way, as though it wasn't under his control.

Poison, maybe. Manny thought, as she stared at his veins again.

The professor sidestepped, delivering a sharp blow to the man's stomach that doubled him over. Following it up by snapping the other man's arm in two, and throwing him down onto the floor. The other man grunted, then Beau stared down at him—in a way she'd never seen before. It wasn't quite anger, or determination, in fact she couldn't begin to place the emotion.

Beau held the other man down by the neck with one hand, and she wondered what he'd do next. But then a sickening *crack* echoed through the suite and her heart skipped a beat—and the man went limp.

"What do you say, truce? Before things can get any worse," Beau said, his voice cutting through her shock.

But she knew he wasn't talking to her. He couldn't be. But then she followed his gaze to an open door.

"I don't want anyone else to get hurt."

Who the hell is he goading?

Whoever it was, didn't take it lightly. Three men strode out of the door—all three dressed in suits, but their eyes—their *red* eyes darkened with hunger and malice.

Manny's stomach churned. *Holy shit.*

But before she could blink, they launched themselves at Beau like a pack of feral dogs.

He was ready, meeting them head-on with that eerie, unnatural grace he always had, and the suite erupted into chaos. Furniture splintered as bodies hit them, a lamp shattered, and after one vampire was hurled through a wall that she saw the other room.

For a moment, she thought about helping—grabbing something, throwing it at them—but then something moved in her peripheral vision.

"*Shit*," Manny hissed, ducking just as a woman lunged at her, brandishing a knife.

But this woman wasn't a vampire—she was human, though her appearance was grotesque: those same sickly black veins snaking up her neck, her eyes bloodshot, pupils dilated, and her movements rigid, almost rabid. Her breathing ragged as she slashed the knife left and right—Manny bobbed and weaved around it. But the woman was ridiculously fast as if she were drugged or glamoured, and Manny arced, but rolled her ankle and fell. She gasped, then rolled under the table before the woman could crawl on top of her. Her heart pounding as the woman stabbed the spot where her head had been a moment ago. Manny scrambled on all fours, crawling toward the opposite end of the table, but the woman's hand shot out and grabbed her sprained ankle.

"Come here," the woman snarled.

Manny kicked instinctively, hitting the woman in the face. She let go with a yelp, and Manny scrambled to her feet, bolting to an overturned velvet chair, and not looking back to see if the woman had regained her balance.

"Stay still," the woman snapped, stalking toward her with a manic grin.

"No thanks," Manny shouted back, her voice trembling as she

grabbed a chair and flung it toward her attacker. It hit the woman's shoulder, making her stumble, but it didn't stop her.

Shit.

Manny could faintly hear Beau still fighting—given the grunts of exertion and snarling echoing from the other room. She didn't care to look—she wanted to stay alive. She would've thanked her newfound adrenaline if the chair had worked, but it hadn't and she was running out of ideas.

"What the hell is wrong with you," Manny shouted at the woman, as she creeped toward her.

"Master will be so pleased to have a fresh meal," she said, rasping as she walked. "I won't hurt you. I just have to tie you up for him."

She's a fucking familiar. What the hell.

The woman lunged again, and this time, she managed to tackle Manny to the ground. They hit the floor hard, knocking the breath out of Manny's lungs as her back collided with the cold floor.

Dammit.

Before Manny could find her barings, the woman was on top of her, her knife poised inches from her face, trembling in the familiar's shaky, dark veined hands, with a twisted grin on her face that stirred something within Manny. A sudden surge of adrenaline and perhaps sheer, *animalistic instinct*.

Manny screamed, driving her knee into the woman's ribs. The familiar hissed in pain but didn't get off, leaning closer, her bloodshot eyes wild with determination to prove herself to some creature—some *vampire* that the woman likely served.

Manny's fingers scrambled across the floor, searching for something, *anything* she could use to defend herself. Her hand brushed against a splintered piece of wood, and without thinking, she grabbed onto it.

"Get off me!" Manny shouted, thrusting the jagged end upward with all her strength.

The familiar froze, her mouth opening in a silent gasp, and Manny stared back at her blankly as she realized what she'd done—as she saw a chair leg lodged inside the woman's chest. Blood gushed from the wound, the woman's eyes filled with shock and…perhaps *relief*. She slumped forward, gravity claiming her as she rolled limply to the side.

Manny stared at the empty spot where the woman had been for a moment, chest heaving. She turned and looked at the dead body, then her hands—trembling and wetted with blood.

"Well done, Ms. Webb" Beau's voice came from behind her, calm and utterly out of place.

Manny turned to him as he strolled out of the room, dusting off his suit jacket, which all things considered was relatively clean. There was a streak of blood along his cheek, but other than that, he looked composed.

He took one look at the scene—Manny on the floor, the dead familiar beside her, and the destroyed hotel room—and raised an eyebrow. "You okay?"

Manny stared at him, her hands still shaking as she wiped them on her pants as if it would undo what she had done.

Physically—maybe. She wasn't sure how bad her sprain was at the moment. She was still high on adrenaline. *Mentally—ask me tomorrow*.

He had her change into a fresh pair of pants—probably the dead woman's pants—since she doubted any of the male vampires could fit them. And Beau left the room for a while, and returned with a few hotel staff —*glamoured* hotel staff—and they started pulling out plastic sheeting and gloves like Beau was hosting some impromptu macabre arts and crafts session.

Manny sat on the couch, her hands shaking, watching as they rolled the familiar's body onto the plastic with surprising care. But no amount of blood seemed to disturb their trance. And perhaps this was the difference between Beau the professor and Damiel the vampire. Which would make it much easier for her to think of him as *Damiel*, and not *Beau*.

"Is this a...regular night for you?" she asked, her voice trembling.

"Not always," he replied with a small smirk. "But it's not my first time. You did well tonight, by the way."

Manny blinked. *Did what well?*

"You held your own, kept a level head—relatively speaking—and you *survived.* That's more than most would've managed," he said, answering her question. Once again, violating her mind-reading rule—one she hadn't spoken though didn't think it should be necessary to.

She laughed dryly, in some ways hoping to stave off any oncoming insanity. "Yeah, because stabbing someone with a chair leg is a transferable skill."

"You'll need those instincts. And trust me, the first time is the hardest for everyone."

"Comforting," she muttered, watching as the staff packed the tarp-wrapped bodies into the duffels and loaded them onto luggage carts.

Once the room was clean—spotless, thanks to him—Beau, or *Damiel* straightened—then he handed her a long black coat and gestured toward the door. "Come on. Let's head back. They'll handle the rest."

Manny put on the coat without argument. Perhaps because she was still in shock or because she wanted to hide the blood on her pants. Though she was thankful no one was in the lobby—outside of the night staff, who Damiel told to delete footage of the past three hours once they left. And they nodded with goofy grins on their faces—*thrilled* to please him. The valet wore the same expression when he'd brought the car back, and promised to delete parking lot footage.

And even as she slid into the passenger seat, knowing they'd get away with it—she couldn't manage to say anything to him. She didn't know what to say. Instead, she stared out the window, watching as Christmas lights blurred past them as her mind churned. When they pulled into the parking lot near her on-campus apartment, Damiel turned to her, and rested his hand on her arm.

"You did well—I mean it. You didn't freeze. That's what is important. That woman was already gone—there was nothing left of whoever she was *before*."

She didn't know what to say so she nodded, and weakly whispered. "Thanks…"

Damiel smiled and took his hand away. "Get some rest. And remember—tea every eight hours."

Manny nodded, slipping out of the car and heading toward her building. As she climbed the stairs to her apartment, she couldn't help but replay his words in her head. *You did well*—she didn't feel like she had—she was guilty and *nauseous*.

Her legs somehow felt heavier as she climbed the stairs up to her apartment. When she reached the top, she spotted Mihawk, in all his glory, perched on the railing in his usual judgmental gargoyle fashion, his eyes fixed on her like he knew exactly where she'd been and what she'd done, which, oddly—pleased him. As if he was happy that they now shared something that made them kindred spirits—though his bloodshed was mainly birds, mice, squirrels, or any other small creature unlucky enough to cross his path. Whereas hers was a human—or a *familiar*. But that didn't make them less human to her. Hell, she'd been turned into a familiar. She was still human.

"Mihawk," she muttered, stepping closer to him.

Mihawk flicked his tail in response, and gave a small *brrr*.

"Yeah, same," she said, scooping him up. He let out a small *meow* as if questioning what she was doing, but ultimately melted into her arms.

Manny carried him into her apartment, making sure to lock the door behind her, reassured by the bolt locking into place. As if she could lock everything that happened out.

She crept over to the couch, cradling Mihawk like a plush toy. He squirmed for a moment, but when she scratched behind his ears, he settled, his *purring* filling the living room.

"It's you and me tonight," she murmured, laying down on the couch, and he curled up against her, seeming to agree with her.

She ean her fingers through his soft fur, hoping to ground herself, as if trying to remember that not everything in the world was either human or supernatural and evil.

Her pain had stopped, and bone-deep exhaustion was slowly settling in. She held Mihawk closer, burying her face in his head, the steady rhythm of his purring relaxing her.

But in the end, she couldn't hide from the truth.

A familiar. She'd fought another *familiar*. Not a vampire, not a full-blown immortal monster with fangs and a blood addiction, but a *lackey*. Someone who—like her—didn't even get emergency coverage in their evil vampire health plan. And it had taken everything she had not to get killed—or at least, cut enough to be viable for whomever the familiar aimed to please.

How the hell am I supposed to fight a vampire if I can barely handle their underpaid intern?

Her fingers were beginning to ache from how tightly she'd gripped the chair leg—she probably needed to dig splinters out of her palms. But she hadn't thought about any of that in the moment. There'd been no plan—just sheer, desperate, *please-don't-kill-me* terror.

I could have died.

Of course, then there was Beau, who was actually Damiel. Calm, collected, shoving her out of the way and killing vampires like he'd done it a hundred times before. Which, for all she knew, he had, given his unknown age and origins. Meanwhile, she was one bad decision away from being a vampire's midnight snack.

I'm screwed.

Mihawk, in all his judgmental glory, yawned and stretched, maneuvering his head to rub against her chin like the concept of existential dread was beneath him. As if to say: *It's okay Manny, I still love you.*

Chapter 30
Day, November 17th

The morning sun was blinding. Manny squinted, groaning as she sat up and flexed her fingers. That was her first mistake.

A sharp sting shot through her palm, and she hissed, glaring down at the angry red spots peppered on her skin.

Splinters. Tiny, evil reminders of my little chair-leg-stabbing escapade. Hooray.

Manny rolled her eyes at herself, and shuffled to the bathroom. Mihawk trailed after her, plodding along as content as a cat could be. She sat down on the edge of her bathtub, armed with a pair of tweezers and a magnifying mirror she'd borrowed from Grant ages ago.

The first splinter came out easily enough. Unfortunately, the rest were lodged deeper, like they'd set up camp with no intention of leaving.

As she tugged at another one, she couldn't help but replay the fight in her head. The familiar's face covered in black veins. How fast everything had happened—the chair leg. For a moment, she wondered why she didn't have black veins, but then wrote it off as, either having to do with the type of familiar she was or because she hadn't given into to Vlane yet. And then there was Damiel, walking out of that room like a model in a horror-themed cologne ad, dusting himself off—waiting for his close up.

She yanked harder than she intended to and winced. “Jesus! I fucking hate him!”

Mihawk hopped onto the sink, perhaps trying to get in her eyeline, watching her with what she swore was amusement.

“Okay, maybe I *don’t* hate him,” she grumbled, pulling out another splinter. “But you weren’t there. You don’t know what happened.” She held up her hand, showing how it was dotted with tiny pink pinpricks. “Exhibit A,” she said, waggling her fingers at Mihawk.

Mihawk flicked his tail, *unimpressed.*

“Yeah, well, I’m not usually out hunting things,” she told him. “Not like you.”

Mihawk meowed, which she chose to interpret as agreement.

By the time she’d gotten the last splinter out, her hand was inflamed, but she’d convinced herself the worst was over. She rinsed it under cold water, and sighed.

Her phone buzzed on the counter just as she finished bandaging her hand. She grabbed it, expecting another text from Damiel or maybe a scam call. Instead, Grant holding up a peace sign lit up her screen.

“Hey,” Manny answered, pressing the phone to her ear as Mihawk jumped down from the sink. “What’s up?”

There was a pause, and she could already tell something was off. When he finally spoke, his voice was quieter than usual. “Remember that guy who saved you at the lake—Dantrell.”

Her stomach dropped. “Yeah, what about him?”

“He died,” he said bluntly. The words made the hairs on her skin prickle as if every nerve inside of her was screaming—*you’re next.*

“How?”

“Sepsis, apparently. His body was taken to the morgue.”

Sepsis. But that wouldn’t make sense—that wouldn’t line up with what Damiel had suggested but whether he was dead or turned remained to be seen.

“And I overheard some nurses talking…” Grant said. He sounded uneasy. “They were talking about his veins…that they were unusually dark…but I didn't catch all of it. They seemed pretty freaked out though."

Her grip on her cell tightened. She went through her mental checklist. The strange veins, her ritual resonance reacting to him. Between the two possibilities she wasn't banking on him being dead, and if he wasn't, when would the vampires come to collect him?

"Listen," Manny said, her voice stern. "Stay away from the morgue, Grant. Don't go anywhere near that room, or Dantrell's body, *okay*?"

There was a pause. "Why? What's going on?"

She gritted her teeth. He deserved an explanation, but she couldn't give him one—not now, that everything had become more complicated. "Just trust me on this," she said firmly.

Another pause, longer this time. "Okay," he finally said, though he sounded irritated. "But if you know something—"

"I'll explain later," she cut him off. "Just promise me you won't go near Dantrell."

She hated shutting him out, but she could deal with any hurt feelings later. She didn't want to him potentially going up against a newborn vampire.

"Fine," Grant said reluctantly. "But whatever you're not saying, better be worth it."

She hung up, her stomach churning. Mihawk brushed against her leg, and she scratched his head.

If the nurses saw something strange, then it was already too late. But what the hell would I even do about it?

She couldn't handle a familiar, much less a *newborn.*

Manny took a deep breath, her hands were shaking. Dantrell's blood was on her hands, no matter how unintentional. She had sought out vampires and they'd found her. There was no taking it back. These were the consequences of her actions, and she had to come to terms with that.

She internally shook herself and typed out a message to Damiel.

Track star. Dead. Sepsis. Need to see you.

It was as coherent as she could manage at the moment, but as she stared at the screen, her thumb hovering over the send button—she wasn't sure she gave a shit if she sounded coherent. When she finally tapped it, she rolled her eyes at herself and put her phone into her pocket. Manny dragged herself back to her bedroom, Mihawk padding behind her.

Her bed was still a mess, but she didn't care. Mihawk happily claimed a spot at the foot of the bed, and curled up under her blanket. Her legs tangled in the sheets like they were trying to trap her there.

Probably for the best.

She needed the time-out. Because at this rate, she was going to become one of those twitchy, frazzled messes running around in movies that people immediately said, *gee wonder what happened to her?* She couldn't be like them—always looking over her shoulder, mumbling to herself, hair sticking out at odd angles. A *fucking* nervous wreck.

It was impressive she'd made it this far *without* that happening.

She was already a vampire's familiar—and she'd fought *another* familiar last night and somehow survived. And now Dantrell…what the hell happened to him?

Poisoned? Turned into a newborn? Turned *into* a familiar? None of the above? God, she didn't know. All she knew was that her stomach was doing somersaults, her head was pounding, and her body was screaming bloody murder—because, of course, the draught was losing its effectiveness. But what else could she expect? That was just her luck. How was she supposed to sleep when her brain wouldn't shut up?

Still, as her head hit the pillow and her body sank into the mattress, slowly her eyes shut against her will.

Fine.

She could nap. Just a quick one. Long enough to stop the world from spinning, and maybe long enough to stop herself from spiraling.

* * *

In the dream, one moment there were shadows wafting around her like smoke, wrapping around her waist, ushering her further into the darkness. She was wearing a white nightgown and searching for—*something*, but couldn't put a finger on what, and then *he* was there—*Vlane*. His lips quirked up into a smile, his fangs sharper and more predatory than she remembered and everything else about him: dangerous, teasing, and utterly infuriating. He was aristocratically handsome, regal in the same way period dramas made lords and viscounts. To say she was mesmerized would be accurate, though that didn't quite capture how relieved she felt seeing him, and alarmingly, she knew it was mostly because of the bite, but it didn't change the fact that her attraction had nothing to do with the curse. Vlane was attractive, and she was positive it was genetic, which made her wonder what he and Damiel's father looked like.

Vlane cocked a brow and walked toward her. She tried to back away but her back collided with a wall—and it was only then she decided to question—where they were. The obvious answer was inside her head. She had gone to sleep and didn't remember leaving her bedroom so that meant she was still in her apartment—and that meant she was dreaming.

Well if this is a dream. I can stop him.

"Stop," she told him, and he did stop—less than a foot away from her.

Her back was against a wall, but she just had to get it to disappear.

It's not really there.

She smacked her hand against the wall.

Ouch.

"I'm afraid you don't have control here, my darling," Vlane told her, taking another step forward. "Or at least…not anymore."

She flinched when the back of his hand ran down her cheek.

Vlane chuckled lowly. "How long has it been? A few weeks? I'm amazed you've lasted this long. Most women would have come to me by now," Vlane said, taking in her person, eyes raking over her.

The look in his eyes sent a warm rush through her body, and it took all she had not to lean into Vlane. He moved closer to her, bending down to let his lips brush her ear.

"But you did visit my suite—didn't you?"

Then he pulled back and stared down at her with a predatory look in his crimson eyes—as if to say *nowhere to run.*

"Go to Hell."

"I'm sure sweet Tinsley will be glad to see me there—all things considered." He smiled sheepishly and then smirked. "I quite liked her…she was so *eager to please*."

"I won't let you turn me into *that*."

"You won't allow me to pleasure you beyond your wildest dreams," he whispered, his voice a low purr that sent an unwelcome shiver down her spine. "You already belong to me. Why fight it?" Those words should've disgusted her. She should've reached out and slapped him, but his breath ghosting her lips only made her gasp.

She tried to will away the warmth rising in her cheeks. She hated it —hated him—but she couldn't conjure up the strength to push him away.

"I don't fantasize about people or vampires *raping* me."

He ignored her, letting his cold fingers trail along her jaw lightly, and her breath hitched against her will.

"It wouldn't be rape—rape is *non-consensual.* Hence why I'm waiting for your answer."

"No," she hissed, her voice trembling but firm. Manny hit her hand against the wall again, trying to break free from whatever hold he had on her, but the wall wouldn't move. "My answer is *no*…and I don't know how you got inside my head. But you're getting the hell out —*right now.*"

His laugh was soft but cruel, and he tilted her chin up, forcing her to meet his eyes. They seemed to glow. "I can find you whenever I like my dear—your dreams were just the easiest route. Luckily, for me and you, you've failed to ward off your dwelling, which would make it so easy for me to walk to your front door if you'd like, *right now.*"

"Fuck. Off."

He moved closer to her and his hand trailed down to rest on her hips, and she told her hands to move, to do something, *anything* to stop him.

"Submit to me," he breathed, lowering his lips to hers, and her mind and body screamed.

Every muscle in her body cried out—to reach for him, take off his clothes and let him have her, right then and there—and her mind rebelled. She wouldn't lose herself to him.

When he broke the kiss he looked down at her.

"No," she repeated.

Vlane gazed down at her, and he changed the position of his right hand before gripping her nightgown, and pulling up the fabric and gazing down at her. "I can see how close you are in your eyes..." his voice trailed off, her body was trembling as Vlane's hand pinched the soft skin of the uppermost portion of her inner thigh. "I can wait, my darling, but I'd rather you didn't test my patience."

'My darling'—those words alone start a slow, simmering pain that quickly spreads, down her stomach and into her groin. Her knees felt weak, her hands trembling as she fought to stay upright, but it's like her body was working against her, begging for something she refused to give him. Every movement like a spark to dry kindling, and standing in front of him—his scent, his crimson eyes glinting with dangerous curiosity, as if wondering how much more she can take—and it all only makes it worse.

It's mortifying.

"Still fighting it," he said softly, almost amused. She doesn't have the strength to answer—she was too consumed by the pain ricocheting through her body, setting her on fire from the inside out.

His right hand moves again—this time to cup his palm around the most intimate part of her body.

God, no. no. no.

She wanted to headbutt him, but couldn't find the strength—and she was worried her *familiarity* might take over and she might kiss him. Then she would be done for. But her body was still screaming for orgasmic release and pleasure at Vlane's hands.

Then he laughed. The asshole laughed. He grabbed Manny's chin, forcing her to meet his eyes. "You can fight me all you want, little one, but it won't change anything. *You're mine*."

And just like that, she headbutted him—to his surprise and her own. He gripped his nose and lurched for her. She jolted awake, sitting upright, suddenly back in her bedroom, holding the front of her shirt. Her skin was clammy, her hands trembling as she stared down at them.

It was a dream. She told herself. *It was only a dream.*

But she could still hear Vlane's voice in her head, feel his hands touching her skin. Her body ached, and her skin was consumed with a frustrating, all-consuming heat. Tears pricked her eyes.

Manny's phone vibrated on the nightstand, and she snatched it up, desperate for a distraction. A text from Damiel lit up the screen:

Damiel
I'm home now. Here's the address.

Manny read it three times, her thumb hovering over the reply button. He'd been her anchor these past few days, keeping her from spiraling completely. But showing up at his house, after that dream? What the hell was she supposed to say?

Manny groaned, rolled onto her back and stared up at the ceiling. She couldn't do this on her own. She needed his help, his stupid draught, his stupid calm demeanor that somehow made everything seem less insane. He'd know what to do. He had to.

She typed a quick reply:

On my way.

She changed into a black, long-sleeve dress and winter fleece tights. But not before she grabbed a cup of the leftover cat food, and placed it in a bowl for Mihawk and set it down on the floor. Petting him quickly before she grabbed her jacket and keys, and left her apartment.

It's fine. Everything is fine.

Leaving Mihawk alone was normal. Completely normal. And seeking a professor's guidance—was normal. No ulterior motives. No inappropriate thoughts. She just had to make it through their interaction without humiliating herself. She *had* to.

Chapter 31
Night, November 17th

She got to his house faster than she would like to admit. It wasn't far—just across town—but far enough that rideshares were more than happy to pick her up, give her time to stew in her thoughts and try to convince herself this wasn't weird.

Not weird at all—just visiting my professor at his house—after a nightmare that made her skin crawl. Totally normal.

Surprisingly, his neighborhood looked like something out of a period drama. Big, old-fashioned houses with perfect lawns. His, somehow, was nicer than the others, and it was well decorated.

The shuttered windows had red and green candles glowing in perfect symmetry. There was a little snowman family out front and lights wrapped around the trees accenting all the glossy windows. Even the porch railing was wrapped in thick strands of garland, tied off with big velvet bows that probably cost more than her outfit. And as if that weren't enough, the entire roof was lined with enough lights to blind the neighbors—warm whites, all of them—even the strands on the pine trees in the front yard. The lights also made an appearance on the pillars surrounding the wraparound porch, which probably hadn't ever seen a single speck of dirt on its pristine white exterior.

But the *pièce de résistance?* The massive glowing reindeer, its head mechanically nodding up and down like a lunatic in the front yard, complete with a scarf, and a suspiciously jaunty lean.

It didn't scream vampire. Hell, it didn't even whisper it. There were no gargoyles, no eerie ivy crawling up the walls, not even a hint of gothic flair. If she didn't know any better, she would've thought it looked like the sort of place where a well-dressed widow would invite her bridge club over for gossip and scones.

Wealthy, obsessive about symmetry, and a clear love of Christmas.

Because surely this was too many decorations for trying to pass as human. But still, not at all what she expected.

Hell, the sight of it made her wonder how he kept his finances in order. Did he have an investment portfolio? A trust fund? How did he even open a bank account without raising any eyebrows every few decades? Did he give it to himself as an inheritance? Did he switch banks often? She had so many questions.

But she wasn't sure she'd ever ask them—she was staring at the door knocker that was almost hindered by a wreath the size of a tractor tire, complete with little twinkling fairy lights that blinked like they were powered by Christmas cheer itself—because in the end it didn't matter. She was here for help, not to audit his finances.

Manny lifted the door knocker and gave three solid knocks, the sound echoing in the frosty night air. But before she could take a step back, the door swung open, and there he was—Damiel standing in a dark turtleneck and slacks, looking every bit the polished, ageless vampire he was.

"Come in," he said, stepping aside. His voice was calm, but she swore his eyes flicked over her like he was assessing her for damage.

And in some ways, she found that oddly comforting.

But that feeling went away the moment she stepped inside and had to keep herself from gaping like a fish. It was like she'd stepped into a magazine spread. The entryway had pristine marble floors, a grand staircase made from rich mahogany, leading up to a second floor, and soft lighting that gave everything a warm glow. She noticed the faint scent of pine and cinnamon. But his house didn't just look perfect; it smelled like Christmas threw up.

Does he normally have guests? Or is all this decorating for himself.

And maybe he did. Maybe he would invite all his vampire friends over and they'd dance the night away drinking blood from whatever or whomever they wished.

Manny swore, he said something about being careful not to *track in snow*, but she barely registered it because her attention was elsewhere as they walked through the house. She was struck by how *non-vampire* it all was.

There was a Christmas tree in one room, a glittering masterpiece with ornaments that looked like they came straight out of a designer catalog. Another room was cracked ajar, revealing a sliver of a study, no doubt, lined with bookshelves. Manny thought she glimpsed an old globe in the corner, but they moved too quickly for her to be sure.

Manny nodded occasionally as he spoke, though her brain was only catching half of anything he said. Something about the history of the house, maybe? Or how it had been restored? She couldn't focus. It was all too much. The decorations. The wealth. The sheer contradiction of a vampire living in a Millfield home decorated like he was running for "World's Most Festive Bachelor."

But then, they reached the living room, and he gestured for her to sit.

God, it's ridiculously comfortable.

Manny sank into it as he sat across from her, waiting for her to speak. She'd almost forgotten she was the one that had asked to see him.

"You needed my help with something?" Damiel said, dragging her back to reality.

"Well, for starters—Dantrell is dead," Manny stated, her nails digging into her palms. "And I'm not sure if he's dead or *immortal* now."

Damiel nodded. "That's to be expected—and I suppose, it remains to be seen."

"*Also*...I don't know how much longer I can keep ignoring these...*soul stirrings*," Manny said, her voice barely above a whisper.

"Toward Vlane…" his name did unsettling things to her stomach, but she pushed on. "The tea isn't working as well anymore. And—" Manny hesitated, grabbing a pillow off the couch to steady herself. "He showed up in my dream. It was a very vivid nightmare—it was like it was real. And I-I don't know how to block him out."

Damiel leaned back in his armchair, one hand resting against his chin as he stared off into the distance like a brooding philosopher.

"That isn't *ideal*," he said finally. "The draught's failure was always a possibility, but I had hoped we'd have more time before—"

"Before? You knew this would happen?" Manny snapped before letting out a dry laugh. He didn't argue, which was… concerning.

God, just when I was starting to trust him.

"You *can* trust me," Damiel said, leaning forward in his seat, elbows resting on his knees. "We'll figure something out. There are other methods we can try to reinforce your willpower. Perhaps rituals to—"

"Could you change who I'm a familiar to?"

He froze, his brow furrowing. "What are you suggesting?"

"*You*," she said, the word coming out faster than she intended, "you said a more powerful vampire's will can take over a weaker one's hold. Would you say you're stronger than Vlane?"

His expression darkened. "In theory, *yes*. But—"

"Then why not?" Manny interrupted. "You could take me on as your familiar. I'd still be tethered to someone, but at least it'd be to someone who doesn't want to toy with me or… or *break* me." Her voice cracked.

Damiel leaned back again, his eyes narrowing as he considered her suggestion. "It's not a simple process," he said slowly. "It's invasive, and possibly more painful."

"I'm in pain now!"

"There are risks."

"Risks?"

"The bond would be stronger than the one you have now," he explained. "You'd feel my presence constantly, more than you've felt his. But unlike him, I wouldn't invade your dreams. Or manipulate you for personal gain."

"Then do it," Manny said, surprising herself with her resolve. "I can't keep living like this, and I'd rather it be you than him."

He didn't answer immediately. Instead, he studied her in that unnervingly calm way of his, like he was searching for another option.

Then, Damiel sighed and said, "This isn't something you should rush into. You need to think it through—"

"I *have* thought it through," Manny shot back. "It's all I thought about on the way over. And unless you've got a better idea, I don't see any other option—and it *distracts* from our mutual goal of finding the coven—doesn't it?"

His jaw tightened, but he didn't argue.

Instead he stayed perfectly still, his hand on his chin and his gaze fixed on the floor, as though the Persian rug's pattern beneath them held the answer. Finally, he let out a deep breath and said, "I can't."

"Why not?" Manny asked, but she didn't know whether she felt angry or betrayed. "You just *admitted* it's possible."

"Yes, but that doesn't make it the *right solution.*" He repeated, but it only felt like he was twisting the knife deeper. "There are too many factors to consider—"

"What else is there?" Manny demanded, sounding more desperate than she'd intended. "I'm already a walking *come hither* for him as his familiar. I've got a target on my back the size of Jupiter for a damned vampire coven. What's one more risk, Damiel?"

Damiel sighed and massaged his temples. "Well, for starters, there's the power dynamic to consider. I'm your professor. You're my student. Even though this bond wouldn't be...*romantic*, the lines could blur. Jeopardizing your future and my own. The optics alone—"

"Do I look like I give a damn about *optics*," Manny interrupted, but he held up a hand, stopping her.

"You should," he said firmly. "Because the rest of *your* world does. If anyone were to find out—students, staff, the administration—it wouldn't just cost me my job. It would ruin *your* future. Your name would be dragged through the mud, and in today's world, scandals like that don't just go away. They follow you for years—or for the rest of your life, Manny. It would cast doubt on everything you do, everything you achieve. Every opportunity you pursue could be hindered by one little mistake."

Manny opened her mouth to argue, but he wasn't finished.

"Then there's Vlane," he continued, his voice quieter now but no less serious. "Seeing as he has already noticed my scent on you, he already suspects I'm involved with you in some way. And doing *this* would confirm it. And trust me when I say that would make you an even *bigger target*. He wouldn't just be toying with you then—he'd be coming after you. With his coven. And he wouldn't stop with just having you *submit* to him."

Manny swallowed hard.

"And thirdly," he said, leaning forward again, "there's the bond itself. It's not something to take lightly. It would tie us together in ways you can't fully understand. You'd be opening yourself up to a level of vulnerability that most humans wouldn't willingly choose. And once it's done, there's no turning back." His eyes were darker then, and his expression unreadable. "It's not a light switch, Manny, you can't just *turn it off*."

Manny looked away, her eyes studying the rug's pattern. "Then what am I supposed to do?" She asked finally, her voice barely above a whisper. "Just keep drinking tea until it completely stops working? Hope Vlane gets bored—what?"

He didn't answer.

Her eyes prickled with tears. She hated crying in front of people—but she was at her wits end. And now, with no real way out, no real solution, she couldn't hold them back.

Tears burned hot down her cheeks as she swallowed back a sob. "I don't know what to do," she admitted, her voice shaking.

Again, he didn't say anything. And then, before she could catch her breath, before she could try to pull herself together, a sharp, searing pain ripped through her body.

It was sudden—*violent*. Like something had reached inside her and ran its claws down her spine. Those claw marks turned into heat—until it felt like her blood was boiling. She gasped, but it came out as more of a strangled cry as she crumpled against the couch.

No. No, no, no. Not here.

More tears ran down her cheeks.

Not in front of him.

She tried to sit up, but when she leaned forward, gravity pulled her down. She hit the floor hard, curling in on herself, clutching her legs. It felt like someone was calling to her—pulling at her insides, demanding her submission. Her breathing turned ragged.

"Shit," Damiel muttered from somewhere far away.

Then, suddenly, there were hands on her. Strong, steady hands. One cradling the back of her head, the other turning her head to look at him.

"Focus on me," he said.

She tried, but she couldn't. Instead she shut her eyes, trying to block out the pain.

"Open your eyes, Manny, and focus on me," he told her, this time his voice seemed to echo in her ears.

She forced her eyes open, blinking through the haze of pain, and when she finally met his gaze, she sucked in a breath. Her vision wavered, blurring at the edges, but his face was clear in the haze. But something strange was happening.

His pupils—shrinking, flickering smaller, then back to normal, like a pulse. A reaction too precise and for a moment she thought she was seeing things. But just as she realized what she was slowly forming the thought through the pain.

Is he glamouring—

He was glamouring her.

"Focus," he ordered.

His gaze pinned her in place, and suddenly she was lighter—weightless even. Her body seemed to respond to it—like a moth drawn to a flame, knowing it would burn but unable to resist.

Then, his voice dropped lower.

"*Sleep.*"

The command sliced through the weightlessness and cut through the heat and the haze. Her body obeyed before her mind could resist—then everything went dark.

Chapter 32
Day, November 18th

Manny woke up warm and sinking into the softest mattress she'd ever laid in. For a moment, she didn't move—just let herself exist in that perfect in-between state, where sleep still clung to her like a second skin. Her skin wasn't on fire, no aches or pains, no unbearable burning sensation clawing at her insides. Just…peace.

Then her mind caught up to her.

This wasn't her bed.

Her eyes snapped open.

The ceiling above her was dark wood, high and carved with intricate details she was sure she'd appreciate more if she weren't trying to piece together what the hell had happened. Slowly, she turned her head.

Oh, wow.

Dark red curtains draped the windows—thick enough that light couldn't creep in. The bed she was in was enormous, the comforter a rich, expensive black that she wanted to assume had never seen a single wrinkle until she'd ruined it by sleeping there. Satin sheets, satin pillows. In one corner, a heavy, antique wardrobe that looked like it weighed a thousand pounds. In the other, a chaise lounge.

The whole room was stunning.

Manny let out a breath, sinking back into the pillows for just a second longer. Okay. She was still alive. She felt…*better* than she had in days.

Now, she just had to figure out what came next.

Then a shadow moved from the chaise lounge and she nearly jumped out of her skin.

"Jesus Christ."

"It's me."

"*Damiel*, you scared the hell out of me," she said, holding her chest as he stepped out of the shadows. "Did you glamour me last night?"

"*Compel.* But yes, and I've also come to a decision."

"What?"

"I'm willing to…" he hesitated. "To change who your *familiarity* is attached to—"

"What changed your mind?" Manny asked, sitting up and rubbing the sleep from her eyes.

He sat on the bed and shrugged. "I'd forgotten how sadistic my half-brother is."

"So, you'll fix it."

"Yes," he said, and Manny sighed in relief. "But Manny, if I do this—"

"*When*," Manny corrected. She refused to let him use '*if,*' when he'd already committed to it.

Damiel nodded. "*When*...I need you to know that there may be a reaction between my venom and Vlane's venom inside, and if the pain becomes too much. Just think it—and I'll stop."

"Damiel, I don't care how much it hurts…I need the stirrings to stop."

Damiel sighed. "But just in case—"

"Damiel, *do it*."

He let out a long sigh, and leaned toward her, his expression unreadable as she brushed her hair away from her neck in the same place Vlane had bitten her.

And her heart leapt as she saw his fangs extend—they were longer than she'd imagined—and looked sharper than Vlane's. She thought she would be more afraid—she *was* afraid—but there was something else there, too. An awful curiosity, one she didn't want to admit to.

With a faint click, his fangs extended fully, and her breath hitched. They were beautiful in a way they absolutely shouldn't have been, gleaming like ivory blades in his mouth.

"This will hurt," he murmured, his voice a low rasp. "But it will pass."

Before Manny could respond, his hand came up to her neck, his thumb brushing over an artery. His eyes fixed on her neck, and she blushed as his breath ghosted over her skin.

And then he bit her.

The pain was immediate—the same hot poker-like sensation under her skin through the new puncture wounds in her neck. A choked gasp left her mouth, tears stinging her eyes as the pressure increased. She thought she might scream, but instead she held onto his shoulders.

But just as suddenly as the pain came, it began to fade. What felt like cold water had washed over her skin, and she was relieved. She let her head fall to the side, and realized she was lying on her back now. His hands held her: one hand against the satin sheets, the other held her ribcage beneath her breast, keeping her still, but it was enough to make her forget how to breathe.

Then came a hunger. Raw, feral, and possibly *carnal*. Her head swam, her skin tingling, and she wanted to move—to writhe, to press herself closer to him—knowing even as he injected her with his venom, this attraction wasn't entirely driven by it. They both knew that. He'd heard her thoughts time and time again.

Is it the bite or just me?

Her blood was on his lips—her heart hammered at the thought. Then there was the pull, something of pure instinct, like her very existence now revolved around the man—no, the *vampire*—latched onto her neck.

Her breath hitched, her body trembling as if it could barely contain the heat surging through her. She wanted him—needed him in a way she couldn't explain, couldn't control.

But he wasn't finished. His fangs were still embedded in her neck, a steady pull that sent waves of a pleasure-pain coursing through her body. She could feel *everything*—and she had never felt more alive—but then there was the unbearable, all-consuming need building up inside her.

Somehow, they shifted, limbs tangling, the smooth brush of satin against her knees. Manny didn't know who moved first, only that she was straddling him now, her knees pressing into the mattress with her legs on either side of his lap. He shifted them again, and her back hit the headboard, trapping her between him and the wood. One hand was in her hair, holding her still, but she wasn't sure she could move her neck if she wanted to. And she didn't want to—she liked being exactly where she was.

But she couldn't stop herself. Her hips moved on their own, rolling against him in a desperate, frantic rhythm. Every motion sent a shudder through her, intensifying the need wetting her core.

The headboard creaked as she ground down harder, grabbing onto his shoulders, his shirt, his hair—anything she could hold onto as she lost herself. She couldn't think, couldn't breathe, every nerve in her body focused on the agonizing, *intoxicating* friction.

He didn't stop her.

His other hand held her hip, steadying her movements but not controlling them. His lips remained at her neck, fangs buried in her neck, his tongue lapping up any escaping blood as she moved.

Oh God, yes.

Her body trembled violently as the hunger overtook her completely. And then it happened—her nails digging into his shoulders, her hips stuttering against him as moans escaped her lips. It built and built until her entire body went rigid, as she cried out. When it was over, she sagged against him, her forehead resting on his shoulder as she tried to catch her breath.

Then he pulled away, his lips brushing her skin one last time before his fangs retracted.

She felt his hand come up to her chin, tilting her face to meet his gaze. His eyes were dark, unreadable, but his expression was calm. He was completely composed, as if she wasn't still straddling him. As if she hadn't just orgasmed.

"There, now you're bonded to me," he said softly.

He said it in a low, soothing, almost tender voice which sounded more like something whispered between lovers in the dark, rather than what they were now.

Chapter 33
Afternoon, November 18th

Oh, God.

She had dry-humped her professor. Beau Moreau to everyone else. Damiel to everyone that knew he was a vampire. But Manny had done it willingly. She had let go—for a moment. Like some desperate, *mindless animal,* rutting against him while he drank from her. Her hunger had taken over completely, and she hadn't even tried to stop it. Hadn't *wanted to* stop it.

She squeezed her eyes shut, pressing her lips together, hoping if she stayed quiet long enough, she'd cease to exist.

But no, she was still here. In bed. In his arms.

And he was still staring at her.

She hesitated before looking at him again. *God, what the hell did I just do? What was I thinking—what is he thinking?*

Manny wasn't sure she wanted to ask him. Not now that she had —*Jesus*.

She shook her head at herself, and looked at him. His expression was unreadable. Not smug, not disgusted, just…completely unfazed.

Of course, she wanted to disappear. This wasn't supposed to happen. None of this was supposed to happen. She had asked him for help, and instead, she had—she had—she wanted to bury her face in a pillow and scream.

What the hell was she supposed to say? *'Sorry for grinding on you while you were trying to undo another vampire's claim on me,'* or would that be inappropriate?

Jesus Christ. Nice job, Manny. Way to go from regular student to hot for teacher roleplay in a matter of minutes.

She swallowed hard, her throat dry. "I—"

Damiel sighed, his hand slipping from her chin, and she dared to hope—pray—he would just let it go. That they could pretend this never happened.

Because if he acknowledged it, if he said one thing about what she'd done, she wasn't sure she'd survive it.

"It's completely natural," he said.

Manny's mouth almost dropped open. That was his response? To go into professor-mode and turn this into a lecture about *'the birds and the bees'* vampire edition?

"*Natural?*"

"I told you it would be more intense—though there are things I hadn't *predicted*." Damiel said.

Manny could guess what those *things* were, but she wanted to think about *anything else*. The sheets beneath them were rumpled, evidence of what had just transpired, his hands holding her in place, and the soul stirring sensation of his fangs in her neck. The worst part? A small part of her wanted him to do it again.

God, no. No.

She couldn't think about that. Manny cleared her throat, sitting up a little straighter, even as her body still hummed with the aftermath and moved off of him. He straightened as well, even running a hand through his hair.

Then she had a thought.

"Um…so how do you manage it?"

He titled his head. "Manage what?"

She gestured vaguely at him, and the room around them—hoping to change the subject. "You. Looking like that…" she trailed off, feeling herself blush. "No one ever asks about your age. You've practically got a mansion—and a job, bank accounts—a real life. How do you make it work? You know…as a *vampire*."

There. A safe topic. Or at least, safer than *Why did I just grind on you like a desperate virgin and can we do it again?*

His lips twitched slightly.

God did he hear that? Damiel, are you listening?

Damiel leaned back, and had that same calm, collected look on his face as he considered her question. "*Carefully*," he answered. "Paper trails have to be managed. Identities rotated every few decades—a tragic accident here or there to account for my disappearance—but it's easier *now*, with technology. *Harder*, in some ways, too."

Manny narrowed her eyes. "But what about pictures and facial recognition?"

Are you really asking him about his digital footprint, she chided herself.

Damiel nodded. "A long time ago, all I needed was a well-forged birth certificate and the right connections. Now, I have to be a bit more…*creative*."

She wondered what that creativity entailed. After all she'd seen how he'd handled the bodies in the hotel suite—and she was beginning to wonder if glamouring people was second nature to him. Maybe it was an if-needed thing or something that was convenient for him. But she could push past that—the same way she would tuck away this morning's events.

Just a normal Sunday. Manny exhaled slowly.

She wouldn't dare let herself think otherwise. Or she might think how her newfound instincts took over, and how she'd melted into his touch so easily.

God she needed to talk to someone, but definitely not Dr. Carter. She certainly couldn't imagine an emergency therapy session talking about how she accidentally dry-humped someone—it was hardly a crisis. Though it was unlike her, either way she didn't imagine it would go over well. But she could worry about that later. And after giving herself an internal shake that brought her back to reality—it also came with the revelation that Damiel was watching her. His expression was completely unreadable—and she was getting tired of that.

"Well, now that you're free of Vlane—what would you like to do?"

She hesitated, hands gripping the satin sheets. What she wanted was to rewind time and pretend the last hour hadn't happened. But since that wasn't an option…

"I need to talk to a friend."

He nodded slowly. "Well, I certainly wouldn't advise against having close confidantes. The world would get lonely otherwise."

Manny swallowed. "Yes, but…" she hesitated, knowing he probably wouldn't like what she said next. "About…*this*. About what's been going on with Vlane—his link to the murders around Millfield."

Damien's jaw tightened. "That's not a good idea."

She bristled. "I don't like keeping my friends in the dark. If I could tell just one of them—"

"You would be putting them at risk." His voice was calm, but firm. "If any of them know too much—Vlane could go after them."

Manny's stomach twisted. "So, what? I just distance myself from them?"

He sighed, and shook his head. "No, I'd say be selective with how much of the truth you tell them."

Manny frowned. "So, lying—with extra steps?"

His lips twitched, just slightly. "You can tell them that things are *complicated.* But you can't tell them *everything*. Not about me. And very little about Vlane—and if they're anything like you, they'll want to know more. And his coven already went after you in broad daylight."

Technically they went after Dean—Oh God, Dean.

Her boyfriend was in a coma. *Because of her.* Because she hadn't been able to convince him that going to the lake was a bad idea. Because she couldn't pull him out of the water. Because she had let herself get dragged further and further into this world of witches, vampires, familiars—and God knew what else was lurking in the shadows.

And now, as if that wasn't enough, she'd gone and dry-humped

Damiel. Didn't that count as cheating? Or did the whole vampire-familiar relationship supersede that through some otherworldly loophole? But the way her body had *responded* to him. She had never given in to something so primal and *hungry*.

Dear God, the hunger.

She had dry-humped Damiel. And he had let her. He held her. He had bitten her, and she had liked it. And her boyfriend was lying in a hospital bed, in a coma she wasn't sure he'd ever wake up from. She wanted to scream. Or cry. She should want to slap Damiel for not warning her.

She hated knowing it was her decisions that led her here. She hated the idea of keeping things from her friends. But she hated the idea of them getting hurt because of her more.

"Selective truths?" She muttered.

He took her hand, and looked at her. "It's the best option," he assured her, and she believed him. "Some things, but not *everything*."

* * *

The rideshare ride home was quiet, save for the occasional hum of the driver's music playing low through the speakers.

She had slowly come to establish what she could tell someone—and who'd she'd tell it to.

She could say she was attacked by a vampire—Grant knew that she was attacked—she would have to fill in the rest of the details. Manny could tell him that a vampire had forced her to be his familiar, and that she'd found a way out of it—by becoming someone else's familiar. Obviously, redacting that someone was their professor. All of those things were true. But she didn't know how much she *wanted* to tell him—so she decided there was a better option—Shantelle. Knowing Shantelle she would've read up on familiars and their familiarity when they were researching—hopefully.

But she needed it to be Shantelle. They were the most alike. They were both on the asexual spectrum, and Shantelle was the first friend she'd made in her freshman year at Millfield University. If there was anyone she could trust with this, it was her. Shantelle would understand —at least, Manny hoped so.

And she needed to talk to someone. She needed comfort. Reassurance.

She *couldn't* go to Grant—not with this. He couldn't know what she'd done with Damiel. Dean was his brother, and when it came down to it, he couldn't know right now. If she could ever tell him at all.

And after a quick text, Shantelle sat cross-legged on the couch in Manny's apartment, watching as Manny paced back and forth. Though Shantelle had listened to all Manny could disclose intently: the vampire attack, her becoming an unwilling familiar to her becoming a willing familiar, to her dry-humping said other vampire. Without disclosing said vampire's name.

Manny had even made sure to mention that she wasn't sure how much control she had over herself anymore to top it all off with a bright red bow—or red flag, depending. And then, because apparently self-sabotage was her new favorite hobby, she had admitted the worst part—

"The thing is," Manny explained, voice hoarse. She needed water. "It's not just the familiarity that's making me attracted to the vampire —I was already attracted to him…it'd be simpler if it was just because of the bite."

Shantelle took a deep breath and sighed. "Okay," she said, dragging the word out. "That's…a lot."

Yeah. No kidding.

"I get it if you think I'm a terrible person," Manny forced out a laugh, which made her throat ache. "I feel horrible. Like, Dean's in a coma for christsake, and here I am—"

"You're not a terrible person, Manny," Shantelle cut in a little too quickly. Her fingers tapped against her knee, the only outward sign of her thinking. "It's just…*complicated*."

That was exactly how Damiel had put it.

Shantelle sighed. "Okay, so—what do you want to do?"

Manny didn't have an answer. She wasn't sure what she wanted to do. She wasn't sure if she was looking for advice—or just needed someone's support.

"Well, what do you think I should do?"

"I think you should relax—I mean Dean's in a coma—but things are going to be okay…*eventually*," Shantelle said, sounding confident. "And I think the priority would be finding a way to stop—what's his name, Vlad—"

"Vlane."

Shantelle rolled her eyes. "*Vlane's* coven," she said with a shrug. "Besides, in case you haven't noticed there's still plenty of people dying and we still don't know why the coven is helping the rich in the first place. I mean if vampires live forever—it's not like they need the money. I'm sure they've found some way to survive all this time. It seems very unlikely that this would be about money."

Manny thought about it, and did think it was strange. But wasn't any closer to figuring out what the curse was or how to stop it. And now that she didn't feel like a cat in heat—maybe she could focus on that.

"Well, we need to figure out what ritual it is—it clearly has something to do with blood and vampires," Manny said, thinking it over, and something struck her. "Can vampires do magic?"

Shantelle shrugged. "I'm sure if they can that we can find something on it."

"Okay—and *maybe* we can find something to wake up Dean while we're at it too," Manny suggested.

And whether it was love or guilt driving her—she decided it didn't matter.

Chapter 34
November 22nd

Manny managed to avoid thinking about the hospital too hard, because every time she did, her guilt gnawed at her. Instead, she threw herself into research. If she wasn't going to visit Dean, then she could at least try to *save* him.

She spent hours hunched over her laptop, scrolling through folklore and rituals. Mostly obscure, half-forgotten spells on witch's forums. Some users claimed comas were the product of a trapped soul—and someone would have to pull them out of it. Others claimed the right combination of herbs and incantations would pull anyone out of a coma. But most of them sounded more like desperate prayers than actual solutions.

She hadn't found anything viable—at least not yet.

Manny sat back, rubbing her temples, and sighed.

If there was a way to wake him up, she wasn't finding it. And worse, part of her wondered if she even *deserved* to.

God—ow. She hadn't even realized she was gripping her hair until a sharp ache bloomed on the left side of her scalp.

There has to be something, she thought, there has to be—

"Stop."

Manny leapt up and looked around the room.

Great, I've finally lost it.

Because she knew for certain—that voice in her head? Definitely wasn't hers. But also not unfamiliar.

"No you're not," the disembodied voice said, and she swallowed. *"But you are trying to meddle with things that could cause irreversible damage."*

It was just her and Mihawk, here, because Shanks is with Dean's mom at their hotel, and Grant is staying at the hotel with her. Manny had offered to watch Mihawk—that and she didn't want Grant to worry about taking care of the judgmental feline, which would allow him to wait by his brother's bedside—and also make him feel better about her being alone in her apartment. But her apartment should be silent, well, aside from the distant hum of her refrigerator.

But that wasn't her voice, or her thoughts.

Am I finally sleep-deprived enough to hallucinate?

She rubbed her temples, trying to recognize the voice—the low, measured cadence, and already seeming prepared to give her a presentation on *what-not-to-do* in regards to witchcraft and the occult. And then it clicks.

You can't be fucking serious—Damiel? Is that you?

But she didn't need an answer. It *had* to be him—inside *her head.*

Her mouth goes dry. *Oh, that's just fantastic.*

First, she humiliates herself in his bed, now he's wormed his way into her brain like a damned pop-up ad.

Her breath shudders out. *Okay, so not a stress-induced psychotic break. Just Damiel popping into my head. It could be worse, maybe?*

You're in my head again, she thought, feeling oddly exposed. Though they'd shared an intimate moment, where she had lost control —she wasn't interested in reliving that moment at present.

"How is this even possible?" she asked instead. *"Are you near my apartment or something?"*

"No, I'm at home," he said as if it were the most obvious thing in the world. *"And while it takes time and focus to master telepathy—as you know I've had plenty of both. It's also much easier to reach you given you are my familiar."*

Great—she hadn't thought of that. Though she had looked into more information on familiarity earlier, in an article about mentally shielding yourself from vampires in a chapter from Eliza Harrow's book, *The Bloodbound Codex,* called 'Familiars and Their Master/Mistress':

A vampire's call is absolute, drawing their familiar to them with an irresistible pull. However, a familiar, when overwhelmed by heightened emotions (example: fear, pain, or desire), may also summon their master or mistress in return. Calls aren't usually a conscious request but an instinctive cry woven into the bond itself. A familiar who calls too often risks deepening their dependence, making it harder to resist their master's influence. Likewise, a vampire who answers too eagerly may become possessive—territorial over what is now, by blood and bond, theirs.

In other words, he could just *pop* into her brain whenever he wanted. No privacy, no warning. Just a vampire in her head. But it also means she had inadvertently *called* him—and he was doing his vampiric duty.

"I understand that you love him," Damiel continued, his voice softer now. *"But tampering with a coma patient is dangerous. The wrong move could trap him there forever—or worse, pull you in with him."*

Manny's stomach turned.

"You need to let him heal on his own time," he finished. *"For both your sakes."*

Manny considered it for a moment, thinking over the lack of progress she had made in the past few hours. And the fact that she hadn't called Shantelle to ask if she'd found anything in the library—though Manny now realized, she should've gone with her.

Dammit, she thought, shaking her head at herself. *Fine. You're right—but don't expect me to be happy about it.*

"Good, and if you continue to pursue this course of action—I'll know, and I will stop you."

And just like that, his presence in her mind faded, leaving behind only the silence—and she hated that he was right. Hated that every logical point he made stacked against her like a rigged game of Jenga, and if she so much as looked at a block wrong, the whole thing would come crashing down.

It would be selfish to risk it. And on top of that, risk being stuck in a hospital bed, brain swimming in whatever limbo comas kept people in. The coven would finish what they started, and she'd have failed, and maybe she would try again—if she even woke up before the next ritual took place. But that was only if she wasn't hunted first or killed in her hospital bed.

So, she did the mature thing. The reasonable thing. She closed her laptop with a little more force than necessary and tried not to overthink about whether or not Dean would ever wake up again.

Chapter 35
December 4th

Vampires are duty-bound to protect and sustain their familiars, to ensure mutually beneficial bonds. A well-fed, healthy familiar strengthens their vampire, providing a stable connection for telepathic and magical resonance. However, history has shown that not all vampires honor their duties. Some, particularly those with more sadistic tendencies, use the bond to starve, weaken, or manipulate their familiars for amusement or control. These cases, though less common, serve as a grim reminder that a familiar's well-being is entirely dependent on the nature of their master or mistress.

— ***From the article, 'Familiars and Their Master/Mistress' in the occult non-fiction book, The Bloodbound Codex by Eliza Harrow***

Manny arrived at Damiel's gated community, already having gone over the opening statement for her argument, twice. She didn't give the driver the gate code. Instead, she thanked the driver, hopped out of the car, and waited on the sidewalk until some unsuspecting dog walker came by.

The man was bundled up in a puffer jacket, and so was his Italian greyhound—a lithe, shivering dog in a red puffer vest with a matching hat. Which she would've normally found adorable, if she weren't repeating her argument over and over in her head.

Manny followed them through the side gate pretending she lived in the community. The greyhound barked at her, probably calling her out for trespassing, but its owner shushed it and kept walking.

She stuffed her mittens in her pockets as she walked through the pristine, cookie-cutter neighborhood. Passing by a home decorated like a gingerbread house, where the elderly owners were handing out candy canes to passing families.

Manny had no clue how they were standing outside in the snow. But at the moment, the neighborhood looked even more like a Christmas card in daylight—the freshly shoveled driveways, snow-suited children, and the occasional person swearing under their breath as they fought with their snowblower.

But she didn't care. Everything could be picture-perfect. She fully intended to ruin *someone's* peaceful evening for trespassing inside her head.

When she had reached Damiel's home, she had intended to knock but the door was unlocked—so she shoved the door open and kicked off her shoes by the door.

"Damiel," she called at the door, hanging up her coat on the coat rack, and balling her mittens into the coat's pocket. "Damiel!" She repeated, locking the front door.

Manny walked down the hall to the living room, and glared at him. There he was. Standing in the middle of his obscenely tasteful living room, looking like something out of an old Hollywood film. Perfectly put together. Hair in place. Shirt unwrinkled. Like he hadn't spent a few minutes, a few days ago inside her head like some smug, *omnipotent bastard*.

She wanted to scream at him for violating her privacy, *again,* but also—God help her—he looked good. Damned good.

Her cheeks were growing hotter by the second, but she narrowed her eyes at him, which seemed to amuse him.

"You can't just pop into my head whenever you feel like it!" she said, pointing a finger at him. "We've talked about this—*privacy*. I need some! I should be able to think without you popping in like some omniscient creep."

Damiel cocks a brow looking between her finger and her face. But he remained perfectly composed, completely unfazed by her anger.

"I *intervened* to prevent you from doing something stupid," he retorted.

She laughed, her hands flying up in exasperation. "Oh, *right.* Because I'm just some reckless little human who needs a big, strong vampire to keep her in check?" Manny glared at him to make her point. "What century are you from, because in *this one*, women have rights."

She crossed her arms and considered turning her back on him, but wasn't sure if that would come off as childish, or theatrical.

He sighed, and pinched the bridge of his nose. "That's not what I'm saying."

"But that's exactly what it is, isn't it?" She asked, taking a step closer to him. "You get to do whatever you want. Pop inside my head, dictate my choices, make these grand, *moral* decisions for me. And I —" She presses a hand to her chest, voice rising. "I have no say. *No control. Nothing.*"

Some emotion flickered across his face. A break in his composed demeanor. He expression softened. "I'm trying to protect you, Manny."

Clearly he meant it. She could tell he did, and she knew it was in his nature to protect her—given everything he was, and everything she was to him now. It wasn't just a promise. Vampires were duty bound to care for their familiars to *an extent.*

Her heart fluttered the longer she looked at him, but, instead she took a step back.

Manny shook her head and scoffed. "Yeah? Well, it doesn't always feel like protection. In fact, I honestly feel like a supporting character in my own life. Do you know how that feels?"

Her voice cracked, and all the frustration, all the exhaustion, everything she'd felt the past few days came up.

"I don't know what I'm doing," she admitted, wrapping her arms around herself as if that would somehow hold her together. "It's like I barely have a grasp on *anything* some days, and I can't control what's happening. Not my body, not my mind—I have no idea where the coven is. I can't even sort out my life."

For once, he didn't argue. He didn't tell her she was overreacting. He just looked at her, those dark piercing eyes pulling her in, closing the space between them, and suddenly—warmth. His chest, his strong arms wrapped around her, holding her close, but not too tight.

He smelled good—like expensive cologne, with something richer underneath—something undeniably him. She hated how easy it was to lean into it, how the tension in her shoulders eased as he held her. But God, it had been so long since someone held her like this. Since she felt anything but scared or alone.

Then, finally, he said, "You're not alone, Manny—not anymore."

And maybe she wanted to hold onto her anger toward him. But she couldn't. Maybe the words should've felt like the kind of thing people said just to be nice. But they didn't. Because the way he said it—the way he looked at her when he did—made her think maybe, just maybe, he was being genuine in his vampiric duty bound way.

Chapter 36
December 5th

For a moment, she didn't know where she was when she woke up. She squinted up at the ceiling, buried under blankets and yawned. On her left, she noticed light peaking through the blackout curtains. She sighed and stretched, letting the blankets pool at her waist as she sat up and let out a long yawn. The room was warm, and somewhere a heater hummed. But even though she didn't quite know where she was, she felt completely safe.

Then she realized why. It was *him*.

Damiel wasn't physically in the room, but she could feel his presence in his home. The safety of having him nearby was placating her anxiety. She knew she needed to be careful with that, being completely dependent on someone wasn't ideal in any relationship.

With a groan, she looked down at the nightstand, and her mood dropped almost instantly. There was a royal blue sweater, and a black skirt neatly folded on top of it with a note.

She stared at it, and her stomach twisted. *For Manny,* it read.

Because it wasn't just *there*. It was *for her*.

He can't be serious.

Manny threw back the duvet and got out of the bed, fully intending to give him a piece of her mind when she found him. Slowly she made her way downstairs, following the smell of coffee and something toasted.

She was still groggy, but then her stomach growled. And it was as if the gentle hum of domesticity sunk into her bones, pulling her in.

When she finally found the smell's source, she found Damiel sitting at a dining table, a wine glass filled with something thick—that she could safely assume was blood—and a plate set out for her. On it: french toast and eggs.

When their eyes met, he studied her for a moment, and then gestured toward the empty seat with the plate in front of it. Manny nodded in return and sat down cautiously. Her stomach growled again, and she almost completely forgot her argument. Instead, she picked up her fork and began poking at the eggs. The eggs were nearly as warm as she was. Warm. Safe. And, well...cared for? For the first time in weeks, she didn't feel like she was drowning.

But she shouldn't feel this way. She didn't deserve to.

For not visiting her boyfriend. For waking up in another man's bed. For how comfortable she was in his presence.

She stabbed at her eggs, trying to suppress her guilt.

At the very least, she should have the decency to be *uncomfortable*. But no, her traitorous body was all *ooh, he made you breakfast, how sweet*.

"I want to introduce you to someone," Damiel said, suddenly, breaking her trance.

She glanced up, chewing slowly. "Who?"

"Eliza Harrow," he said, sipping from his glass. "I believe you've been using her research."

She blinked.

Eliza Harrow? *The* Eliza Harrow? The academic whose papers she had devoured, whose articles on witches, werewolves, and *especially* vampires, which had given her some grasp on what was happening in Millfield?

"You *know* Eliza Harrow?" she asked, setting her fork down.

Damiel nodded. "There's a conference we'll be attending this evening. *The Occult and the Modern World*—Eliza Harrow will be a speaker there."

She swallowed. *A conference with Eliza Harrow?*

Warmth bloomed in her chest, perhaps from excitement or from something else. She glared at him.

This was *his* doing. Their bond. Making her feel all warm and fuzzy, making her *grateful*. Making her want to be near him. Making her—

She aggressively took another bite of toast, trying to ignore how much she was looking forward to the conference.

Eliza Harrow wasn't just some academic writing dry, theoretical nonsense from the safety of a university office. She was a woman of color who actually *knew* things—*real* things—about vampires, about werewolves, about the supernatural underpinnings of the world that people like Manny had spent their lives unaware of.

Manny had read her papers, and highlighted passages at three in the morning like they were mana from heaven. And now, she had the chance to *talk* to her. To ask questions. To get answers from someone who wasn't just a smug, handsome professor who now held a *prominent* position in her life.

This was a rare opportunity. *A woman like her*, someone who understood what it was like to exist in spaces where people underestimated you, who had learned and thrived despite it, was willing to share her knowledge.

She could learn so much. Maybe even how to navigate this new reality without losing herself. Or at least she could hope so.

* * *

Manny wasn't *fully* ready, but she made do. Using a few handfuls of water, a dollop of travel-sized leave-in conditioner, and a bit of styling gel—from her emergency hair care kit she always kept in her bag because Millfield's weather had *zero* respect for curly hair. Though she hadn't planned to stay the night, here she was, smoothing flyaways with the kind of precision that only came from years of dealing with mother nature's mood swings.

Manny barely had time to do a final once-over before Damiel shuffled her out to the car, barely managing to click her seatbelt into place before they pulled out onto the road. It was early evening, but the ride was quiet except for the hum of the engine or the occasional click of the turn signal.

Damiel, of course, looked perfect. Crisp, composed, *annoyingly unbothered*, like he hadn't spent most of his night awake and comforting her. But, of course, vampires didn't *need* sleep. Though she was beginning to wonder what he did with his time, if he wasn't sleeping—she imagined he could be studying, or grading papers.

God, I'm behind, she scolded herself. But she was only behind with her coursework, because she had been preoccupied. Though she kept reminding herself that grades weren't due yet and neither were her assignments. Unfortunately, that didn't mean she wouldn't be pulling a few all-nighters during winter break.

She crossed her arms and watched other cars blur past. The conference was at the Aldwych Center for Historical Studies—which she'd never been inside—and was a relatively long drive since it was practically on the edge of campus. Meaning there was plenty of time to pretend she wasn't hyperaware of the man sitting next to her.

She could practically hear the never-ending mocking voices in her head—the sorority girls from undergrad, partial to lip gloss and judgment, side-eying her over their overpriced lattes:

"Didn't you say you were asexual? Guess that was just a phase."

"Professor Moreau? You and half the campus, babe."

She scowled at her reflection in the car window. In fact she could still hear when she'd explained it to one person—a close friend that quickly became an ex-friend after that interaction: "You gave up on sex, because of one bad experience? I could never."

But she hadn't given up on sex—and it hadn't even been about what he'd done to her—she'd been like this her whole life.

If they were here now, she'd have told them to go to hell. Because yes, she was asexual. Or *gray asexual*, to be specific. Just because she wasn't dead inside like half the heavily stereotyped asexuals on television were. Hell, if they even existed in shows, they were either the weird loner with no social skills, or the rude genius who thought emotions were beneath them, or the smug, *holier-than-thou* type who looked down on anyone with a sex drive. Apparently, if you weren't horny 24/7, you had to be a robot or an asshole.

And here she was—gray asexual, perfectly capable of attraction, *when it actually happened,* but still knowing that she didn't experience the same way other people did.

She could effectively count on both hands the people she'd actually been attracted to. Her boyfriend, obviously. And as of late, a few...*vampires*. Apparently, blood-sucking immortals had snuck their way onto the list, meaning it now surpassed two hands—which was both alarming and incredibly inconvenient.

If a TV writer got a hold of her life, they'd probably turn her into some repressed ice queen who just needed the right man to "fix" her.

Gross.

She clenched her jaw. Just because she was *occasionally* susceptible to the effect of a vampire's glamour—didn't mean she wasn't still herself.

Suddenly, the car turned into the Aldwych Center's parking lot, the headlights bouncing off its old brick exterior. A grand, gothic-style building with towering columns and stained glass windows depicting gods, demons, and whatever else the architects thought would combine academia and the occult. It was definitely the kind of place where students in tweed blazers and wire-rimmed glasses debated existential dread over triple shot espressos.

Manny swallowed.

Meeting Eliza Harrow was exciting. But also terrifying. Because what if Manny asked the wrong questions? What if Eliza Harrow saw right through her and realized how out of her depth she really was?

Damiel pulled into a parking space, and turned off the engine.

"Ready?" he asked, his voice calm, steady.

No, she wasn't—but she nodded anyway.

* * *

The lecture hall was lit by a dim golden glow, with rows and rows of plush red seats that had probably seen more half-asleep grad students than actual intellectuals. The stage was more well-lit, with a long table where the speakers had been seated earlier, and now, as the conference wound down, people were milling about, chatting, some chattering more enthused than others.

Manny sat rigidly, fingers curled around the program brochure, skimming over the four featured presentations again:

Albert Halloway, PhD – *The Mythology of the Undead Across Cultures*: A deep dive into how different civilizations have interpreted vampiric figures, from Slavic folklore to the Jiangshi of China.

Mariana Telford, MA – *Hexes, Hauntings, and Hysteria*: A historical examination of witch trials, focusing on how paranoia and superstition shaped centuries of persecution.

Eliza Harrow, PhD – *Blood, Magic and the Like; the Intertwined Histories of Vampires and the Gifted*: A look at how witches and vampires have shared alliances, rivalries, and an ongoing struggle for power throughout history.

Gavin Cole, MMST – *Occultism in the Modern Age*: A discussion on contemporary magical practices and whether those histories are doctored.

Manny had scribbled notes so aggressively her pen had nearly torn through her journal's paper. Dr. Harrow had explained how vampires and witches had historically crossed paths, from magical pacts to conflicts over power—and Manny knew what she wanted to ask. But wasn't sure how to phrase it, and she hoped she'd find the words before they met face to face.

But even looking at her from a distance was nerve-wracking.

Brown skinned, shoulder length natural curls, and a black dress—she looked polished but not pretentious. And when she smiled at Damiel in greeting, it wasn't the kind of fake, polite smile most academics did. It actually looked genuine.

They spoke for a few minutes, and then he walked back over to her. Meanwhile, Manny's stomach was tying itself into a thousand little knots, while she rehearsed her questions.

"We'll meet her at Calloway's around the corner," Damiel said, as soon as he reached her.

Calloway's—Millfield's cheapest, grungiest pub. Right. Because nothing said *serious discussion on supernatural goings-ons* like sticky tables and the lingering odor of last night's spilled beer.

But Manny was also thankful—she really didn't think she could sit there any longer. She was tired of pretending she also could rattle off ancient texts like she was discussing last week's reality TV drama. When two grad students had turned to her to talk about myths in literature, she'd managed to weasel her way out of that situation by discussing Shakespeare—which was *basic* in certain pretentious circles at Millfield University, but it was the fastest route out of whatever lengthy dribble she would've been dragged into.

Manny sighed, "Okay. Lead the way."

* * *

Their drive was short, but necessary, because it was raining—and she to walk on a crowded, rainy sidewalk. Especially when she was more likely to be jam-packed like a sardine.

Still she'd watched shops blur past, trying to think of intelligent things to say, or at the very least, that wouldn't completely embarrass her in front of *the* Eliza Harrow—a woman whose research she'd devoured like some starved creature that needed knowledge for sustenance.

When Damiel pulled up to the curb to park, she grimaced—Calloway's was exactly how she remembered it: poorly lit, humidity fogging the windows, and smokers overflowing off the sidewalk.

They get out of the car, and quickly pass through a cloud of cigarette smoke, and enter the moist, warm pub that was filled with conversation and booming music, and the occasional celebratory clink of glasses.

Manny scanned each table as they passed, until they finally saw her —Eliza Harrow, sitting at a corner table, a notebook and a half-full wine glass in front of her. She was scribbling something in the notebook, and had three silver rings on her right hand.

Damiel went up to the hostess stand while Manny steadied herself.

Don't overthink it, Manny. Act like a normal, functioning human.

The hostess gestured toward Damiel, who in turn, gestured to Manny, and they followed her to the table.

"Eliza," Damiel said, smoothly giving her a quick hug. "I'd like you to meet, Manny."

Eliza looked at Manny and gave her a soft smile. "So, you're the one with all the questions."

Manny swallowed. "That's me."

She slid into the booth and settled in beside Damiel. Damiel draped one arm over the backrest, as if he were perfectly at ease. "As I mentioned on the phone, I've filled her in on some things."

Eliza nods, taking a slow sip of her drink. "*Good.* That'll save us some time."

Manny looked between them, wondering what had been said—especially given that the real discussion—the important part—had happened without her knowledge.

Damiel's expression shifted and his eyes grew darker. "I thought it best she know *something*, but not *necessarily everything.*"

Eliza hums, tilting her head slightly at him.

Wait, are they— Manny thought, and she looked between them. *They are.*

She was sitting there like an idiot, listening to them, thinking she was part of the conversation. When in reality, she'd been sitting right there while a whole second conversation happened between them. The pauses, the looks, the way Eliza's expression continued to shift before Damiel even opened his mouth—*their eyes*. Eliza's brown eyes looked almost auburn, leaning more into its reddish hues with gold flecks in them.

That isn't human…and that means.

Eliza Harrow wasn't just some academic. She wasn't a scholar with a niche interest in the occult or even—*vampires*. She was one of them.

Oh. My. God.

Eliza turned to Manny, expectant. "And what do *you* think about *things*?"

Manny cleared her throat. "I don't think I have the full picture yet."

She smiled, slowly, *knowingly*. "No, you don't."

Manny was suddenly more nervous than she could explain. How could Damiel have forgotten to mention that? But, of course, he wouldn't. How could she be surprised? Of course, two vampires would have a whole damn telepathic chat right in front of her.

Fine, I'll play your game, she thought, though it was mostly to herself.

Manny leaned forward, hands on the table. "So, what made you so interested in the occult?"

Eliza sat her glass down with a *clink*. "I didn't have much of a choice."

That got her attention. Eliza didn't sound pretentious or bitter—just matter-of-fact.

"I was a familiar once," she continues, eyes flicking to Damiel before settling back on Manny. "Against my will—then *voluntarily*."

Manny's blood ran cold for a moment.

Eliza gave her a knowing look, like she could hear every thought running through her head. Every piece of the puzzle falling into place—and maybe she could. "I sought out help, did my own research, and eventually met someone in our coven." She gestured toward Damiel. "A man who decided to help me."

Manny turned to him, but his face remained impassive. No confirmation, no denial.

Is that why you're introducing us?

Damiel didn't face her, but Manny knew he could hear her. But didn't seem interested in answering her.

"So, you're like me?" Manny asked turning back to Eliza.

They'd both ended up tangled in the world of vampires, though under different circumstances. And while she wouldn't see herself as studious—not compared to an actual academic—but they shared a common truth. Being a familiar, or having dealt with familiarity, and now, clearly, Eliza was a full-fledged vampire.

Eliza let out a long sigh, and leaned back in her chair. "*No*," she said, shaking her head. "I *was* like you, darling—about a *hundred* years ago now."

A hundred years—Jesus Christ.

"Demetri didn't think it would be *proper* that I remain his familiar, seeing as we've become so much more over the years," Eliza explained softly. "The man prior to him was *cruel*, but after many identities, I was able to escape him, but enough about me—*your questions*."

"Um…" Manny hesitated. "Well, based off your presentation, I was wondering if vampires could actually use magic?"

Eliza nods. "Yes," she answered. "I mean some of them were human once, and some practiced magic before they turned. Others might pick it up later, usually for a darker, or *macabre* purpose."

"But not all of them?"

"No," she answered. "Just like how only some of us choose to master our abilities—telepathy, compulsion, our newfound *heightened* senses—others are too *lazy*. Magic comes with a cost—most don't want to pay it. Some may dabble, or dedicate their entire existence to learning everything there is, while others avoid it entirely."

Manny glanced at Damiel, wondering which category he fell into. But as usual, his expression gave nothing away. For the moment, Manny wished he would say something to her—maybe something comforting. Instead of allowing her to sit there in a state of *'what the hell do I do with this now.'* Eliza had turned her predicament into a career, while Manny was still in the *'staring at the ceiling at 3 AM wondering if I'm losing my mind'* phase.

Eliza wrote academic texts and quickly highlighted what she'd deemed the *need-to-know* information about vampires and their magic usage. Meanwhile, Manny was googling things like *how to wake someone from a vampire-induced coma at stupid o'clock.* And of course, nothing about vampires could ever be normal. Just various shades of dark and bleak.

"Don't worry, you'll adapt," Eliza told her with a small smile. "It takes time, and now that you're a familiar, you have *more* of it." Then she glanced at Damiel. "And Damiel is a good man—unfortunately, his brothers are *lacking*."

Manny smiled and nodded. She found it odd, but she was comforted by Eliza telling her Damiel was a good man. Maybe because she was a woman. Maybe because she needed an opinion outside of herself. But then something about what Eliza said struck her as odd.

"Wait—what do you mean I have *more time?*" Manny asked Eliza.

Eliza smirked at Damiel. "Now Damiel, don't tell me you didn't let your little familiar know that she lives as long as you do?"

Manny's heart sank. "W-what? Does that make me—"

"You aren't immortal—*not really*—you still need food, water, and you still *bleed*," Damiel said, making a point of it. "You just won't age, or at least, not the way humans do."

Manny nodded in response, but she felt nauseous. Her head was spinning.

What the hell. No. No..

"Strange thing not to mention given that if he dies, you certainly will—" Eliza said calmly, swirling her drink. "But your death…it would feel a bit like a *pinch* to Damiel—very *little* pain."

She wasn't immortal. But she wasn't mortal either. Her life was linked to his by an invisible thread.

This is bullshit! If he dies, I die. Just like that. No grand moment, no final stand. That would be it—Manny Webb, gone.

But if he *didn't* die? Then what? Would she just…keep living like this? Not aging *normally*? Living but not really *living?* She wasn't a vampire. She wasn't fully human either. Just *stuck.*

Her stomach turned again. *God, I'm going to throw up.*

She didn't want to be immortal. But she wanted to be something. Not this weird, half-formed existence where her body didn't belong to her anymore, where she was bound to someone else's survival.

It was no wonder familiars could easily become dependent on their vampires. Their survival was *entirely dependent* on them.

And what if he decided she wasn't worth keeping around? Would he just abandon her? Would she even know it was coming? The *not-knowing* was the worst part. The fact that every breath she took was borrowed, and she had no idea when the loan was due.

"Manny," Damiel said, softly, pulling her back to reality.

"I need some air," Manny said, standing up from the table, and accidentally knocking over Eliza's drink, to the scholar's amusement.

Eliza laughed. "Oh, now you've done it, Damiel."

"Be quiet, Eliza," Damiel snapped at her, moving to stand.

Manny raised her hand, palm facing him—a clear, undeniable gesture to '*stay back.*' "I just need a moment."

A part of her wished she'd never met Eliza.

She felt terrible for thinking that, but it was how she felt. If she had only allowed herself to live in blissful ignorance, worrying about things that actually mattered to normal students—like assignments and rent and whether she had enough conditioner to last the next two weeks. She wouldn't have wound up a familiar—unwillingly or willingly—she had gone too far and couldn't take it back.

Now, she knew too much.

Ignorance was bliss—and a privilege, *apparently*.

Manny had pulled back the curtain just enough that it couldn't be closed. To make matters worse, she was responsible for taking that first step. For dragging her friends and *boyfriend* into it. Now she was reaping what she sowed. Given a half-life, an existence that wasn't fully hers anymore. And where would she go from here?

Chapter 37
December 6th

Manny wasn't looking for trouble. Not *really*. She was just mindlessly scrolling while Mihawk purred in her lap, her tea growing colder on the end table beside her. It had started with her researching familiars, and ended with her scrolling on the MillU subreddit, crossposted by some random local, who had a history of claiming celebrities were being replaced by clones.

The post read:

Did Millfield University's Track Star Have a Twin?

Saw this guy with some woman last night, but it couldn't be him…unless he came back from the dead.

The poster had included a link to a picture of Dantrell Williamson, and then another picture with a young man of a similar stature beside a beautiful red-haired woman smiling at a bartender.

Manny's stomach twisted. *Shit. Is he a familiar now?*

She guessed so, because making him a newborn vampire, straight out the gate wouldn't necessarily benefit them. But then again, she wasn't an expert on vampires. She'd considered calling Damiel—but after she'd stormed out last night, she didn't think it was a good idea.

His last text to her was:

Damiel
I'm sorry about Eliza. Please, let me know when you get home safely.

It was sweet, and she knew Damiel was kind—she didn't hate him. She had asked him to take her on as his familiar, though she hadn't remotely considered the consequences. Of course, some might say*, to err is human*, but every time she was beginning to reach a point of acceptance; she found herself backtracking.

Every time she was out, she was pulled right back in—and the comments in this post were a mess:

"Dude, that's messed up. His family doesn't need this bullshit."

"It's either Photoshop or you're seeing things. Delete this."

"Have some respect, man."

Some were more vulgar, calling the poster names; others bought into the conspiracy theories. Manny couldn't care less about the reason, she was too busy staring at the photo. Because she knew exactly what she was looking at.

It was Dantrell—who had died from *sepsis*, who should have been still in the morgue or six feet under—but he'd been turned. Maybe just a familiar, maybe a newborn vampire. But either way, he wasn't dead. Not *really*.

Manny closed the tab, leaned back, and sighed.

I should call Damiel—or at least text him.

She shook her head at herself, and instead went looking for answers. Eventually she found herself on a forum about witchcraft, scrolling through old threads about Millfield until she found something interesting—according to the user, *selfawarewitch*, Millfield was one of twenty known magic hubs that were centered around a curse of wrongdoing that dated back centuries.

A few other users like *Sophwiththemost* pointed out it wasn't the curse that made Millfield a hub, but something the founder did. Something *truly evil.* But, at least for those on this forum, at the time, there were no known evil actions the founder committed.

Last Manny checked, a ritual designed to target marginalized people and feed them to vampires would qualify as *evil*—especially if those vampires were doing magic. And who were they? Why marginalized people?

Who are you? She thought, though she wasn't sure what she was looking for at first. But then she found it.

The old photo of Damiel and his brother. There had to be more pictures. She started with the university's digital archives—because they had a collection dedicated to Millfield's town history. But, unsurprisingly, the school's database was a nightmare to navigate. Half the documents were mislabeled, and the search function was laughably useless unless you knew exactly what you were searching for. She didn't.

So, she clicked through historical records, old faculty directories, and grainy photos of students from past decades. Most of it was boring—fundraising events, the occasional scandal that was barely a scandal. With nothing in any way that resembled the room Damiel and his brother had been standing in.

Frustrated, she switched tactics. The town archives were next, some things were accessible through a clunky government website that seemed like it hadn't been updated since the early 2000s. She hoped to find something there.

First there were only records of land ownership, obituaries, old newspapers digitized with varying degrees of success. It was a mess, but at least it had potential. And then, when those turned up nothing but dead ends, she thought of the open-access archives. She knew those were a mess—she'd gone through them for a history assignment as an undergrad. But still, she typed the town's name and founder.

Scrolled.

Scrolled some more.

And then—*finally*. A photograph, faded and yellowed with age. Two figures stood out to her—Damiel and Vlane.

Thank God.

She'd found it. Or found *something*. She save the photo and then selected a few faces from the image and began plugging them into a tool she'd found online. She ran multiple reverse image searches. Cross-referencing names from old records, archived newspapers, and it was slow—tedious work. Then she used an AI-photo matching search tool that would scour the web to find similar faces. It took a long time, but eventually it came back with four men who consistently showed up in images all the way back to the conception of the heliograph itself.

There are four figures, men who hadn't aged a day between the large group photo with Damiel and his brother, and who she was able to find together in other photos.

She found one image that was just the four of them—in it they could easily pass as ordinary aristocrats in their time—dressed in outfits wreaking of wealth.

Their names were listed from left to right:

Alistair Chrisanti, front and center, had a cold, calculating stare, his black-gloved hands resting neatly over a silver-tipped cane. Beside him, Victor Moreau whose piercing eyes stared at the camera, his expression unreadable. Elias Duvall looked pale and spectral, his hair seemed to reflect whatever light they'd been in. Then there was Laurent Devereux, thick-armed and smirking like he's already won whatever game they're playing.

Manny took a screenshot of the photo, pulled up a document and highlighted their names, pasting them in there determined to make good use of them. And down the rabbit hole she went. Their names dropping off and resurfacing in different decades, like stones skipping across water, vanishing before rising again. They were careful, but they clearly weren't afraid of getting caught with the same name or identity. Sometimes there was a *second*, or *third* tacked on the end of their name. But she didn't doubt it was them. She traced their "ancestry":

Laurent Devereaux disappeared from the records in 1897, only to reappear in 1923 with a nearly identical signature on a land deed. Elias Duvall II was listed as the owner of a Millfield textile warehouse in 1834, but then there's nothing—no record of a death, no transfer of property—until a man with his same name and same face shows up in a business registry for a shipping company in 1905—and in 1968, another photo of him and his wife an African American woman after she'd won a prize for her strawberries at the Millfield Strawberry Festival. Their names, plain as day, listed beneath it. Victor Moreau was the hardest to track—he mostly showed up in legal disputes that seemed to resolve themselves without a clear verdict.

But Alistair Chrisanti and Victor Moreau—both of them—appeared on a manifest back in the 1600s.

They came to America *on* the Mayflower. But it didn't make sense to her. The Mayflower was filled with Puritans and colonists searching for a new life, not vampires. But their names were there, plain as day—at least on one copy of the manifest.

A chill ran down her spine.

They've really always been here.

And the more she stared at the picture of Victor, the more she could see Damiel and Vlane's faces—and she was more than certain they were related. Victor was either their father or an ancestor.

Manny's fingers hovered over the trackpad.

How many lives have they shaped, controlled—ended?

Manny swallowed, her pulse loud in her ears. *What are they planning?*

They'd lived in Millfield for centuries, and these vampires could be responsible for everything. Wouldn't Vlane follow in his father's footsteps? What if all of this was for him? And now that her connection with him was severed—what would the coven do to her? And worse, did Damiel know everything already?

Her laptop screen flickered for a moment before a low battery screen popped up, and she sighed. She searched the room for her charger to no avail. Her thoughts were racing as she thought of worst-case scenarios.

Then, her cellphone rang and she jumped. Her heart hammering in her chest as she grabbed it from the coffee table, and Mihawk makes a displeased *brrreow* at her sudden movement.

Unknown number.

Manny shook her head at herself but still answered.

"Hello?"

A pause.

"Finally…" a woman on the other end of the line said softly. "We need to talk."

Manny tightened her grip on her phone. "How the hell did you get this number?"

The woman scoffed. "I took it from Damiel's phone," Eliza replied. "I imagine you're feeling a bit… *unsettled.* Given everything you've learned."

Manny scoffed. "*Unsettled*," she muttered. "*Sure*. Let's go with that —maybe a bit *angry* too."

There's a brief silence, and then Eliza yawned before saying, "I'm calling because I've realized I may have…*meddled* with your trust in Damiel. Though I assure you it wasn't my intention to *harm* your relationship."

Was that meant to be an apology?

Manny internally shook herself. "There is *no* relationship—he's a vampire and I'm his familiar."

Eliza sighed. "I imagine you're questioning things. *Him*. Your place in all of this. I may have added to that doubt, but I need you to understand—Damiel is the only one standing between you and far worse beings. Whatever you may feel toward me due to my behavior—should not affect your relationship with Damiel."

Manny rolled her eyes. "Again, there's *no* relationship," she stressed. "Besides, why do you care? Why are you so adamant that I trust him?"

Eliza didn't answer for a few seconds.

"*Because*," Eliza finally said, "I know what happens when you don't trust the one person keeping you alive…and I have been in your shoes, so I know what you are afraid of."

"You don't know me, Eliza."

Eliza laughs.

Are you fucking kidding me.

When Eliza finally stopped, she said, "You do not have to make my word for it, Manny. You are his familiar. You know whether or not you can trust him, deep within your bones—all familiars instinctively know if they can trust their—"

"Don't you dare call him my *master*."

"I was going to say *fate* actually. It sounds more—*romantic*." Eliza paused as if she were deciding what to say next. "I can vouch for him," she repeated, firmer this time. "Because he left the Chrisantis to form a coven with my Dimitri…and a bit later he began his little Sherlock shtick."

Chrisanti—like Alistair Chrisanti?

Manny put her phone on speaker and sat it on the coffee table. "So? People leave different crowds all the time. Doesn't mean they're good people."

Eliza laughed in a way that sounded somewhere between amusement and exasperation. "He left because of *their ways*. Because he doesn't see humans as beneath him. You do not know it yet, but *that is rare*. Vampires—especially the *older ones*—don't change their views easily," Eliza explained, matter-of-factly. "Our sweet Damiel has never had a familiar. He always worried about tying someone to him for life —if he were *worthy* of them—and given his father…I am surprised he didn't turn out more arrogant."

His father. She knows his father?

Manny hesitated, wanting to ask about Damiel's father, but in some ways worried that if she did, she wouldn't learn anything else from Eliza. So instead, she asked a less important question, "He's really never had a familiar?"

"*Yes*," Eliza confirmed. "And yet, here you are…causing *trouble*. Dimitri always talks about how interesting Damiel finds humans, of course, Dimitri didn't understand until he met me. But now…Damiel has you, and you are angry with him, because of me, and that simply won't do."

Manny sighed. That statement opens up a dozen more questions, but there's one she needs answered first. "Do you know anyone named Victor Moreau?"

"Hmph, very good" Eliza said, sounding pleased. "What about him?"

"Is he Damiel's father—I know Damiel was a dhampir before—"

"Yes, he is—Victor lives in Louisiana."

"Is he part of that coven—"

"The Chrisantis—*no*."

"Why? Alistair looks rather chummy with Victor in a few pictures I've found."

"Deal gone wrong."

"What deal?"

"That is something for you to ask your f—"

"Don't call him *my fate*. Fate has nothing to do with this," Manny snapped at her. "Besides, between the two of you—you've been more forthcoming with information. And if you think—"

"If you want that to change, you need to speak to Damiel," Eliza said sternly. "State your terms to him, and do not compromise."

"Okay," Manny said softly.

"And Manny…" Eliza said, her voice softening. "Do drop this little act of yours of knowing less than you let on. It's unbecoming of a young lady."

"I—" a click came from the other end of the line before Manny could finish her sentence.

Manny sighed and slumped forward, hiding her face in her arms. She knew Eliza Harrow was clever—how could she have thought, she'd be able to trick her? Maybe Eliza had a point about making up with Damiel. Maybe she should stop being so stubborn about it. But then there was what Eliza had referred to him as—*fate*.

Manny didn't used to believe in it. She used to think people made their own choices, shaped their own lives. But now? It's getting harder to tell where her decisions end and where something else—something *out there*—started pulling the strings.

Was she always going to wind up learning about vampires, witches, and magic? Was there some iteration of her in the multiverse that didn't? Or was it all just coincidence, a chain of bad luck and terrible decision-making?

And if fate is real...what does that mean for her future?

Her phone rang again.

Manny groaned aloud—she didn't want to answer it. Then she felt a soft thump against her arm. Then another, more insistent this time. She sits up just enough to see two wide, golden eyes staring at her, pupils blown like twin full moons. Mihawk tilts his head, ears flicking forward as if he were trying to find reception. And for a moment, Manny wonders why she couldn't have gotten the ability to communicate with animals from this whole experience.

She lowered her head back into her arms.

A sharp, impatient *mrrp* follows. Then a heavier thump as a warm, fluffy body lands squarely on her back. She sighs, feeling the gentle weight settle as he kneads into her shoulder, claws barely unsheathed.

"I'm fine," Manny mutters.

Mihawk doesn't seem to believe her. He hops back onto the table. Another *mrrp*—this one dangerously close to sounding like his normal judgmental self.

Manny lifts her head, resting her chin on her arms. "You're worse than Dr. Carter, you know that?"

Mihawk flicks his tail, as if to say *Obviously*. Then, satisfied that she's at least marginally more upright, he worms his way in between her head and the table, purring.

Her phone rang again.

She answered it, putting it on speaker and petting Mihawk's head at the same time to the feline's pleasure.

"Why the hell didn't you answer the first time?" Grant snapped, voice tense. No jokes, no usual snark. That alone was concerning.

"What's wrong?" Manny asked, sitting up, and Mihawk lets out a disgruntled *mrreow*.

"I thought something had happened to you—it's—" Grant exhaled sharply. "It's about Isla."

Manny sat back on the couch. "What about Isla?"

"She's missing."

Manny's heart sank. "What? How?"

"She went to a concert with some other students a few days ago, and no one has heard from them. A few of them would've been… perfect *chosen ones*." The way he said it makes her pulse spikes immediately. "She never made it back to her and Shantelle's apartment. Shantelle tried calling her five times."

Manny swallows. "And you think—"

"I know, Manny. Something is wrong, and Shantelle found something too. About the ritual."

Her heart hammered against her ribs. *The Chrisantis. The Moreaus —and now this.*

"We're going to meet up when the weather warning clears," Grant told her. "Can you come?"

"Yes, of course, I can come," Manny told him. "I'd be grabbing my jacket right now if I could."

Grant sighed. "Yeah, you and me both."

Stupid fucking snowstorm.

Like she didn't already have enough to deal with. Her weather app had been blaring about it all day—warnings slapped across her screen every time she so much as glanced at her phone:

Heavy snowfall. Whiteout conditions.

Stay inside unless absolutely necessary.

If she were braver, she would be lacing up her boots, about to trudge out into the night because Isla was *missing*, and Shantelle had found something on the ritual. But it was good to hear from him, though—Grant, her closest guy friend.

"It's good to hear from you, Grant."

He doesn't say anything for a few moments.

"It's good to hear from you too," Grant said finally. "You should come visit the hospital. The doctor thinks Dean will wake up in a few months."

"That's good to hear," Manny said softly.

Meaning she had a few months to figure out how to explain everything that's happened—hopefully in a way that wouldn't lead to Dean breaking up with her. But more than that, there was hope he would wake up, and enough hope to go around. Given Shantelle had found something—and if she'd figured out what the ritual was—then maybe, just *maybe*, they could do something to stop it. She just hoped they weren't already too late.

Chapter 38
Night, December 12th

Vampiric familiars exist in a liminal state between mortality and immortality, bound irrevocably to the vampire who turned them. While all familiars experience an extended lifespan—tied directly to the survival of their maker—their abilities vary depending on the strength and nature of the vampire who sired them. Some inherit heightened senses, others minor regenerative properties, and a rare few develop unique traits reflective of their master's power. However, this aspect is inherently one-sided; should the familiar perish, the vampire would be unaffected. But if the vampire is destroyed, so too is the familiar—erased from existence as though they had never been.

— *From the chapter, 'An Un-Familiar Life' in the occult non-fiction book, The Bloodbound Codex by Eliza Harrow*

Snow had been piling up for days—snowflakes turned into slush, slush turned into ice, roads turned into death traps—and the entire town, in a rare moment of unity, collectively decided to hunker down. Her friends have been out of commission since Monday—feverish, sniffly, texting the group chat in various states of delirium about how they might be able to meet the next day.

Leaving her to reply:

Drink some water and rest, Shantelle.

Meanwhile, she was fine. Better than fine. She could probably go for a jog, or take an online cooking class—and she'd done the latter twice. And of course, this was only a perk of being bound to a vampire *way* higher up the vampiric food chain than she ever would be. No flu, no chills, not even a sniffle—which was yet another reminder she wasn't exactly *human* anymore.

Manny had only just woken up, and been laying in bed thinking about that for a few minutes. She wasn't sick, but something was off. Something had woken her up.

She's curled up in bed, Mihawk a warm, heavy weight against her side, purring like an engine. Her bedroom is dark, but that's normal—she had turned off the light before going to bed.

Still, there was a strange, disquieting sensation in her stomach telling her something was *wrong,* but not *what.* Manny reached for her bedside lamp. Pulled on the pull string. Nothing.

Lightbulb must be dead.

She sat up, shrugging off the duvet, and earning a *bbrrreow* from Mihawk. Then she walked to the hallway. Tried the light switch there. Nothing.

Her phone on her nightstand buzzes. She walks back into the room, grabs her phone—an alert:

Widespread power outage reported in your area.

Crews are working to resolve the issue

Manny sat back on the bed, and clicked the link to open up the Millfield News site. Reports were coming in, timestamps stacking over the past few hours—outages rolling through town in patches, no clear reason.

Her stomach twisted.

Some instinct—the same one that's been keeping her alive this long—tells her to text Damiel. She hesitates—it had been a little over a week since she'd last texted him. She shakes her head at herself. Sends a quick, simple message:

Power's out. I feel strange. Are you all right?

She waits. Five minutes go by. Ten. Then Fifteen.

No response.

She looks down at Mihawk, who's staring at her like she's just personally offended him by existing at this hour. His big, golden eyes are half-lidded, his ears flicking lazily, as if to say *why are you awake, you silly little human?*

"I know, I know," Manny mutters, running a hand through his thick fur. "I should just go back to sleep. But I feel sick."

Maybe I am sick.

Mihawk doesn't care. He just stretches out, pushing against her side like he's trying to physically shove her back under the duvet.

Manny sighs, glancing at her phone again. Twenty minutes—no response. Not even a little 'delivered' checkmark.

A knot forms in her stomach.

"Do you think I should check on him?" Manny asked Mihawk. "I mean, I could…I'm sure he wouldn't mind. I *could* just swing by. Make sure he's okay. Just to be sure."

Mihawk's tail flicks.

Manny sighs. *I could send him another text.*

She didn't like double texting people. But the snow wasn't *too bad* outside, though there was frost on her windows. But going out at this hour, alone, when something feels *this* wrong?

Maybe it's a bad idea.

She shook her head at herself. *This is stupid. I'm being stupid.*

Manny looked down at Mihawk, who was already staring at her with a *you're being stupid* expression. But she couldn't ignore what she was feeling—so instead she changed out of her pajamas and into a turtleneck, long skirt and fleece tights.

"I'm going," she tells Mihawk, grabbing his cat food and pouring it into a bowl. "Just to check. I'll be back soon." She promised, pulling her coat off a chair.

Mihawk blinked slowly and craned his head at her.

Manny tugged on her boots, wrapped her scarf around her neck, and shoved her phone in her pocket. Then she hesitated, just for a second, hand hovering over the door handle.

I could be overreacting. Maybe his phone is just dead. Maybe the power is out at his house too.

But the feeling wouldn't go away.

Manny shook her head at herself again, and opened the door. Stepping outside into the cold, and locking the door behind her.

The moment she stepped outside, she was glad the snowfall wasn't too bad. The roads were somewhat clear, so a snowplow had come through, which meant rideshares would be operating. She books one, while she walks down the shoveled pathway, waiting for the app to confirm her driver.

A car pulls up five minutes later, headlights cutting through the dark.

She gets in, rubbing her gloved hands together for warmth, and stares down at her phone. Still no reply from Damiel.

She tries calling him—once, twice—it rings both times, but it goes straight to voicemail.

Manny clears her throat. "Damiel, it's me. I'm heading over to yours. Call me back."

She hung up just as they reached the gate, and she stepped out onto the sidewalk. Lucky for her—but bad for neighborhood security—someone had left the side gate cracked, so she walked inside, and shut it behind her.

When she finally reached his house, the windows were frosty, but there was a faint glow in them.

So, he's awake.

Manny knocked on the front door.

Waited. *Nothing?*

She knocked again. "Damiel?"

No answer.

The knots in her stomach tightened.

Something is wrong.

She stepped off the porch, boots crunching in the snow, and made her way around the back. Her breath turned into smoke in the cold air, and she pulled her coat tighter around herself.

Jesus, what the hell happened here?

What might have been a generator was a mess of mangled metal and exposed wiring. Its once-sturdy casing now peeled back in jagged, uneven strips. It looked like it was clawed apart.

The wires inside dangled like severed veins, some of them snapped clean while others fray at the edges, their copper guts spilling out. Snow had started to gather in the openings, melting slightly where the engine still held onto the last traces of residual heat. Wires torn, casing mangled—the nagging thought that *maybe* a wild animal had gotten to it.

Manny felt her pulse quicken, because maybe she shouldn't be questioning '*what happened?*' Maybe the better question would've been '*who happened?*'

But she couldn't worry about that now. She needed to get inside. He wasn't dead, she knew that much, because *she* would be, if that were the case.

Manny checked under the mat. Nothing.

Damnit, she thought, rolling her eyes at herself.

She knocks twice. Then, the door clicks.

Her heart skips a beat as it creaks open, nothing but pure darkness inside the room beyond it. No one on the other side. No footsteps. Just the wind howling behind her and an open unlocked door.

Manny stepped inside, and shut the door behind her. She took a step forward, and bumped into something metal. She smooths her hand over it—the Impala. It gleams under the dim light coming through the window. Beside it, two other cars. She imagined were fast, sleek, and equally expensive.

She pushed away from the Impala, and fumbled around in the darkness until she reached a cracked door with light behind it, and nearly landed face first in the kitchen.

He has to be here—somewhere.

But it was still too quiet. Too *still.*

And she still hadn't seen him.

But as she stepped further into the kitchen, she finally did.

It's a silhouette, but she's certain it's him. There's a sliver of light on his face as if the moon itself had taken pity on her. Damiel is standing, but hunched over the kitchen island, his shoulders rising and falling in deep, uneven breaths. His usually neat clothes are disheveled, his dark hair an unruly mess.

"D-Damiel," she said weakly.

His fingers pressed into the island, knuckles white, as if he's holding himself together by sheer will. She doesn't have to ask—she knows what's wrong. The overturned chair, the half-spoiled blood bags discarded near the sink, the faint but unmistakable scent of rot in the air.

The destroyed generator. No power. No way to keep his supply fresh.

He's fiending.

She'd read about in the *Bloodbound Codex's* glossary:

> ***Fiending***: *a critical state of extreme blood deprivation observed in vampires, marked by a rapid decline in cognitive function, heightened aggression, and an overwhelming physiological compulsion to feed.*

Manny stood there, unable to think. She just stared at him. Eliza's account of vampires in this state—*razor-thin control, minds reduced to hunger, bodies running on nothing but thirst*—she had only understood in theory. But it all made sense. The uneasy feeling she'd had all night—it had been him.

He lifted his head just enough for her to see his eyes. They were darker, more sunken in, rimmed by almost bruise-like markings. But the way he looked at her that made her breath catch. Not like someone she knows, or who knows her.

Like a predator.

"*Leave.*"

His voice came out raw, guttural.

Manny didn't move.

He gripped the counter. "I said—"

"I *heard you*," Manny interrupted, stepping closer despite the alarm bells going off in her head. "But you need to feed…"

His jaw locked.

"I'm *fine*."

"*You're not*."

"I won't—" He exhaled sharply, like he was fighting something inside himself, like the words tasted wrong in his mouth. "I won't *drink* from you."

Her heart wrenched, though she didn't understand why, but his refusal felt like a slap in the face.

"Given the state of things—you're generator, your *voice*, you—" she was hesitant to say it. Not sure how far gone he was. Unsure how much longer he would be able to distinguish between her being an ally and prey. "You *called* to me. *Summoned* me—"

"Unintentionally."

She took another step closer, he growled.

"You'll die if you don't…" she said, trailing off and trying to decide if she should take another step forward. "And *I'll* die if you don't."

"I've survived *worse*."

Manny didn't answer. Instead she reached out, not physically but *mentally*, pressing into the space where she knows their connection exists. She could *feel* his hunger radiating off him, the sheer force of his need pressing against her like a second pulse.

"*Get out*."

He emphasized his demand with an animalistic *huff*.

Manny didn't move. Instead she looked around the kitchen, at first not sure what she's searching for, until she found it. A knife block. She took a step toward it, glancing between it and Damiel, until she bumped into the counter. She pulled herself onto the counter, trying to steel her nerves.

She knew what she needed to do, but not where. She figured if the cut or the bite were visible she might end up in the hospital or worse a psych ward which might lead to a police investigation after seeing the bite. She couldn't have that.

Meaning it couldn't be her neck, or wrist, but it could be *somewhere else.* So she pulled a knife from the block and lifted her skirt—fully aware that he was still watching her.

This is stupid.

She knew it, and yet, she still lowered the knife to her leg, running the blade over the soft, sensitive skin close to her pubis. It split easily, and the pain was immediate—and she hissed. It was a brief sensation, but blood bloomed quickly from the open wound.

Before she could even register the movement, he was there—in front of her—so fast, so quiet, that for a moment, she thought it was her imagination. Damiel stood over her, staring down at her, the hairs on her neck prickled as he stood so close, his breath ghosting her lips. Her pulse quickened, blood still warm and flowing from her wound, she felt much more vulnerable now with the fresh cut on her thigh.

Her breath hitched involuntarily—because even in his disheveled state, he was still handsome. A low, guttural growl reverberated through his chest. His hands pressed into the counter, one on either side of her thighs. Their close proximity made her pulse jump in ways that had nothing to do with fear.

She raised a hand to his face, tracing his jawline with her fingers, and brought her hand up into his hair. The strands silky between her fingers as she guided his head and mouth toward the wound she'd made. Then, in one swift motion, his fangs punctured the tender flesh of her thigh.

A pinch, pressure, a jolt through her entire body. But there wasn't any pain. Instead, a sensual hunger roared through her, humming inside her veins as he fed. His fangs sank deeper, and the sensation shifted from discomfort to something else entirely. The pressure of his lips and tongue against her skin sent waves of pleasure rushing through her, igniting something primal, or *untamed.*

Manny felt drawn to him in ways she didn't want to admit. He drank slowly, as though he were savoring every drop he took. And with every pull, she felt her body responding in ways that defied logic—her breath came faster, her legs trembling as something hot but pure coiled low in her abdomen.

She gripped his hair tighter, as though trying to anchor herself as the overwhelming sensations coursed through her. Her other hand tangled in his hair, as the heat consumed her.

Her chest rose and fell unevenly, his fangs in her flesh had turned into a slow, seductive burn that left her aching for more, and her body betrayed her as a soft moan slipped from her lips, unexpected, breathy, and filled with a mixture of surprise and yearning.

Damiel growled in response—but not in displeasure, in *acknowledgment*. Manny leaned into him, fingers tightening reflexively in his hair, pulling him closer, not wanting him to stop. She didn't resist it, she let it fill her, allowing each pull to draw a deep, involuntary response from her lips. He didn't pull away, and she was practically begging for more—everything was bleary, like a fever she couldn't shake. And if this was a sickness, maybe she didn't want to shake it.

In the haze of her growing desire, her thoughts felt slower, muddled, caught somewhere between the undeniable attraction she had for him and the fear that she might not have enough blood to satiate him. But the more he drank, the less it seemed to matter to her—the feeling was intoxicating.

Why does it feel so good?

Every inch of her body hummed, with one hand in his hair, another cradling his neck, urging him closer. Her back arched instinctively, and moans kept slipping out of her in helpless little gasps, each louder than the last, filled with a lust she couldn't quite contain.

His mouth was affixed to her inner thigh, but she knew physically and *mentally*, she was begging him for more. For some form of release, if any were available.

P-please.

Then slowly, his fangs pulled from her thigh, a slurping, popping noise followed. But he didn't look up at her, perhaps because her fingers were still interlocked in his hair, and for a moment, she was confused, and wondering what was happening. Did he hear something? Was someone coming?

But then, he slowly turned toward her pubis. Inching closer and closer—and her heart leapt.

Wait is he really—

His mouth was so close now, breath brushing against her underwear, the only barrier between the intimate flesh and *him*—and she gasped.

What are you waiting for?

Damiel growled.

Go ahead, I want you to.

He didn't hesitate; his fangs tore through the delicate fabric of her underwear like paper, a *rrrrip* echoed in the room. The violence of it—the sheer force he'd used, the way he spit the fabric onto the floor—sent a shiver of both fear and arousal through her. The heat of his breath passed through the remnants of the fabric, and he moved closer—

Oh, God. Oh, yes.

She gasped as his tongue went over the length of her opening, making her twitch against him. But he dug her fingers into her hips and held her there before taking another long, languid lick eliciting another moan from her. She could hardly believe it—her breathing came faster, her mind finding the same sensual haze as she tried to grasp what she was doing.

Never in a thousand years had she imagined this for herself.

Her underwear torn, the way he held her with such primal need, had her heart racing with a mixture of fear and desire. Fear of what she'd become—of how far she was willing to go with him. She fought to keep her eyes open, gazing down at him, her eyes locking with his. He was watching her, every subtle shift in her expression, every breath she took, every tremble that ran through her body. There was a hunger there, but for the moment, it wasn't for blood—it was *for her.* The fact that he was watching, that he was fully aware of her every reaction, only made the experience more intimate, more all-consuming.

She was tingling, dissolving, being devoured by him, and, oh God, she wanted more...

He obliged her. He kept going, and going, and going until she was moaning and gasping helplessly for him. With every lap of his tongue, she was being wound tighter and tighter, burning, yearning, until finally—something broke through—

"Damiel!" She cried out, shuddering against his mouth, gripping his hair, letting it consume her, blearing the world around her, and she shut her eyes to keep herself upright as she let out another gasp.

Her chest heaving as she loosened her grip on him, and he pulled away. Then she opened her eyes, looking up at him as he rose to his full height, staring down at her. Before she could react, he kissed her and she surrendered to it, letting her head fall back as she pulled him closer by his collar and spread her legs for him.

Keep going.

She didn't say it aloud, but she knew he could hear her. A low, animalistic growl vibrated in his throat. He pulled her closer, and one second, she was on the kitchen counter, kissing him, the next, she felt herself being lifted effortlessly. Her senses overwhelmed by her lust, she barely processed the speed at which he carried her up the stairs, as if time itself had slowed for him, but left a disorienting rush of sensation overcoming her body. Maybe she would have thrown up if she weren't caught in the passion between them.

But her feet didn't touch the ground; he laid her down on the bed, his bed. Her body sinking into the silken sheets, her mind struggling to catch up. She hadn't even realized he had pulled away until she felt the absence of his lips, the loss of his touch. Her heart was pounding her chest as she stared up at him. His face was just above hers, close enough that she could still feel his breath against her flushed skin.

His eyes bore into hers as he undid his button-up shirt, searching, waiting—as if he were still holding himself back despite everything that had just happened between them.

She swallowed, her throat dry, knowing she wouldn't be able to take back what she was about to say. But took a deep breath before she let the words leave her lips.

"Kiss me."

It wasn't a demand. It wasn't even a plea. He stared at her face, as if he were memorizing it, lingering on her parted lips.

Then before she could take another breath, his lips met hers. He claimed her in a way that was raw—*hungry*. Like he had been waiting for her to ask, waiting for permission he hadn't needed but hungered for anyway. All she could was pull him closer, the hard muscles of his chest pressed against hers as her heartbeat drummed in her ears, and suddenly—*warmth*.

Chapter 39
Midnight, December 12th

Damiel kissed her shoulder, fangs grazing her skin as he gathered her skirt up and tugged her hips forward. He pulled away from her only to undo his belt and toss his pants and briefs onto the floor before hovering over her. For a moment she wondered if she should do the same, but then he guide himself against her slick opening. She moaned at the sensation as he aligned his body with hers, and lowered his lips to her neck, lightly nipping, and licking her neck, before growling at her again.

He gradually sat up right, his torso illuminated by the moonlight, and his face was shadowed—in some ways, she wondered if he didn't want her to see his face. She didn't move, and she could feel his gaze on her. His hands trailed down to her hips, framing her as she lay there waiting. And then—he thrust into her, hard and fast, filling her instantly.

Manny let out a breathless, strangled gasp.

He stilled for a moment as if letting her adjust to him. Manny let out a whimper, though Damiel hadn't caused her pain. His body sheathed inside her, longing swelling in her chest, it was all too much to bear.

But he was a vampire—a *fiending* one at that. She faintly registered how his thumbs drew circles on her hips as he waited. Every muscle in his body tensed, caught in a battle between restraint and raw instinct—and his restraint was waning.

His breathing was shallow and rapid, and his body tremored, but he didn't speak. So, Manny tapped into their connection, half-curious, half-concerned what she might find.

Damiel.

"I refuse to hurt you," he told her. The thought was desperate, but beneath it was something else—*"I can't."*

She tilted her head, exposing the curve of her throat. *You don't need to ask. Not tonight.*

His grip tightened on her waist. *"You don't understand what you're offering."*

She did. She really did. *I do and I'm willing.*

He growled, and then, finally, he gave in.

She barely registered the shift in his weight, or the fact his hand was gripping her hair, or the pain of his fangs sinking into her neck—those discomforts were peripheral and inconsequential—he was inside her…and her pulse thrummed in time with his feeding.

She held onto his shoulders, fingers curling involuntarily, needing something to hold onto as a warm sensation settled in her nether regions. A moan escaped her before she could stop it, and she blushed.

His grip on her tightened, and as she held onto him, a word pushed into her thoughts—his voice, growling out: *"Mine."*

Damiel drew back and began to thrust into her, again, and again, and again…and with every movement, the bed creaked beneath them. His hands, firm against her hips, keeping her exactly where he wanted her—pinned and utterly at his mercy. But it didn't hurt her, instead her body trembled with spasms of pleasure that spread through her like liquid fire, every nerve alight with sensation.

Her breath stutters, catches in her throat, as he continued his feverish onslaught inside her body, pleasure surging inside her, spinning upwards into blissful ecstasy.

"Damiel!" she cried out, and he growled in response as she came.

But he didn't. He continued thrusting, continued feeding, his stamina and strength such that she orgasmed two more times, until his fangs left her neck with a sharp pull, and the sudden absence makes her whimper—in relief and frustration.

Before she can fully process it, he flips her with an ease that makes her breath hitch, pressing her front against the silken sheets. He tears through her shirt and bra, and she moved forward, allowing him to pull the fabric away, then his hand scooper her breast, his warm thumbs on her nipples for a moment before he pulled away to reposition himself. He pulled her closer to him, and she glanced back at him just as he leaned over her, heat radiating from his body as his hand found the curve of her hip, and he moved her closer to him, fingers trailing down her throat gently.

And she tilts her head, exposing her throat to him in offering.

A low growl rumbles in his chest, vibrating against her back, but he doesn't immediately take it. Instead one hand finds the curve of her hip, steadying her before he thrust himself into her, and his fangs sink back into her neck. He thrust himself into her faster, harder, faster, harder…eliciting moans and mewls from her in response urging him on.

And then he changed the tempo of his thrusts, surging forward into her until she let out one final release, and Damiel emitted a growl and a low groan. Manny shuddered as Damiel's fangs pulled from neck and his member from her body. He lay down beside her, and looked at her. She moved closer to him, and he gathered her into his chest in a warm embrace.

Manny closed her eyes, breathing in his scent, knowing she wouldn't find a heartbeat in his chest. His fingertips tracing her veins, knowing what they'd done.

Words in Eliza's chapter on familiars…words, she had spent days reading, dedicating them to memory, and yet in this moment, she wondered if she cared what they meant:

For a fiending vampire, drinking from a familiar is not simply about survival—though as the lines between feeding and claiming blur, the act itself is a paradox of dominance and devotion, an unspoken exchange of power.

Tonight, she could lay here in his arms, curled into him, as they had done something that bound them together in ways far beyond venom—or blood.

Chapter 40
December 13th

Manny yawned and stretched, immediately noticing a twinge in her back. The satin sheets beneath her were cool to the touch, and Damiel was notably missing. She opened her eyes, and noticed the blackout curtains were pulled shut, but fingers of sunlight were slipping through the window's edges.

She checked a side table, finds a lamp, and clicks it on.

His bedroom is nothing like she would've imagined, and yet, exactly what she expected. Deep, earthy tones. Dark wood furniture. Bookshelves lined with old books and small statues—perhaps figures of gods and goddesses.

It's…nice. Cozy, even. Her stomach growled at her, with it a craving that swirled in her gut, but the two were uniquely different. It's not all hunger. Not exactly. But it made her restless, makes her think of *him* and their *bond.*

Shit, she thought.

Then the door opened, and he stepped inside, carrying a tray with food.

He looks…normal again.

All physical traces of his fiending gone—it was as if last night had never happened.

She wrapped the satin sheet around herself, covering her breasts, as she looked up at him. Damiel sets the tray on the nightstand before sitting on the edge of the bed, looking at her for a long moment before he finally said. "Thank you for last night."

He brought her hand to his mouth and kissed her knuckles. She noticed a flicker of emotion on his face, and he continued, "But I think… we should try to cut back on that aspect of *our bond.*"

She blinked. "That *aspect*?"

He rolled his eyes. "You *know* what I mean."

"It's called *sex*, Damiel," Manny told him. "Anyone and everyone I know calls it sex. Call it *that*."

"I *know*," he said carefully, "It's not as if I'm opposed to *that* happening again. But I think we should be careful, and we need to be conscious of what we're doing. Considering what we can *become* to each other."

A logical argument, but one that didn't account for the fact that they'd already crossed a line.

Manny let out a scoff, shaking her head at him. "*Now* you want to set boundaries?"

He sighed and gave her a look.

"I don't know what you expect from me," she snapped. "I don't know what the *rules* are. I don't know how I'm supposed to feel, or act, or—" Her breath hitched. "I may not know how to be a *familiar*, but I do know I'm sick of vampires. Sick of *you* hiding things from me."

She figured now was as best of a time as ever to bring it up.

Damiel sighed. "You knew there would be risks."

"And yet, I'm the only one who has to deal with them?" Manny said.

Damiel scoffed. "You think it's just you? Who do you think destroyed my generator?" Damiel gritted his teeth. "I was *locked* inside by some *sigil* burning on the ground outside—it was a *miracle* you were able to get in."

Manny's heart dropped. "I'm sorry, I didn't see…I didn't know…"

"It's okay…" Damiel said, trailing off. "I assume the snow must've put it out, or maybe some animal disturbed it."

"I saw the generator when I came in…I didn't think—"

"About what you might be walking into?"

"Yeah, I have a bad habit of doing that. Maybe I've been a little irrational lately," Manny explained and sighed. "And, well, *my friend*, Isla, is missing. No one knows where she is—and it's been days. And I guess I was angry, because she's out there and I'm in here, having sex and being your personal blood bank while she—"

"I *will* help you get her back," he interrupted, voice firm. "But we have to be careful."

"Careful," she echoed. "*Right*. My friend is out there. God knows what's happening to her, and we're sitting here talking about what we *shouldn't* do instead of figuring what we need to do to get her back!"

"You think I don't care?" Beau said. "You think I don't want to find them? For my coven and I to tear them apart. To turn their bones into *ash* for all they've done to the humans in this town. If their plans are what I believe them to be, and you know where they are—all you need to do is point me in their direction."

"If only..." She breathed, because she wasn't sure she wanted to finish that sentence.

They were too close now. Heat was radiating off his body, and she wanted to—but he kissed her first, and she kissed him back, hard. She didn't know if she wants to fight him or *devour* him. Maybe both.

He grabbed her waist, pulling her against him. Her fingers tangled in his hair, and he pulled away then his fangs scrape against her neck.

One second, she gasped as his fangs entered her neck.

The next, he's on her. She doesn't know if she intends to *fuck* him as his familiar or just *fuck him*, but in that moment, it didn't matter.

She gets lost in it. In *him*. In the way his body moved against hers, the way he pulled her under him, until there's nothing left but heat, desperation, and him thrusting inside her. Over and over—her hands gripping the sheets beneath her, the clinking of plates shifting on the breakfast tray on the bedside table as his heavy breathing and her soft moans filled the room. The tray teetered with the weight of her untouched meal, but it was drowned out by the steady tempo of their bodies—until that inevitable, need to cry out her release.

When it's over, she lay there, breathless, heart pounding.

And though she was still reeling, she couldn't help but think about how he had been imprisoned the night before—by magic. She would have to see the sigil for herself—check if it was Enochian. That would mean the Wardens of the Gate were responsible—and that they knew *what* Damiel was. Or if they weren't the ones who had trapped him—either a vampire or a *witch* was responsible. And she only knew of one witch in Millfield.

Chapter 41
December 20th

Mihawk weaved between Shantelle's legs purring like a jet engine, rubbing his fluffy little face against her boots. He'd been restless the past few days, pacing her apartment like he needed to tidy up before Grant came over. He had been generally unimpressed by Manny's absence, her lateness, her general failure as a live-in human. But now, with her friends finally crammed into her living room, he was content—making his rounds, rubbing against their legs, settling into Grant's lap like he was reclaiming lost time. She half-wished Dean was here too, but she also half-loathed the thought—because where would she begin to explain what she'd been doing?

Her friends kicked off their boots, peeled away their gloves, and settled in her living room. She wished she could be as relaxed as Mihawk. Everyone looked exhausted, but even then Shantelle is the first to speak.

"I found it," Shantelle said, passing her notebook to Manny. She scanned the hastily scrawled notes. "The curse they're using—it's old, but not unheard of. The earliest recorded instance I could find was in Yorkshire, England." She explained, pointing to a section of her notes. "It feeds on societal neglect—which is why it's focused on marginalized students and their allies. Apparently marginalized students generate a distinct form of emotional and spiritual energy—that's what the curse draws power from, and then that power is given to the occult entity to wield and bestow unto others. But it only works if the caster completes the cycle. Which means—"

"We need to kill the caster," Grant finished grimly.

Manny swallows. "Kill a *vampire*," she corrected, turning the words over in her head. "I've fought a familiar—and I was lucky to survive. And you want to *kill* a *vampire*?"

Shantelle nods. "Whoever is casting it is the key. They have to finish the ritual, or the power fades."

"You fought a familiar?" Grant asked, scrunching his brows. "When?"

Shit. Manny swallowed. *Why the hell did I say that out loud?*

"*Focus*. We can't worry about that now. The fact of the matter is we need to stop them before they can start the final stage—" Shantelle said, skimming her notes. "Let's see…number of victims. *Here,* the final victims have to be sacrificed at the same time—on a full moon. And I think that's what they took Isla for." She pointed under a sigil she'd drawn in her notebook.

Manny shook her head. "When is—"

"It'd be next month—so we have *some* time, but not a lot," Grant said.

"Which means we'll need some weapons from your *witch* friend," Wade said, cracking open a beer and taking a swig of it. "So, like stakes, holy water—"

Manny shifted uncomfortably. "But we don't even know where they are."

"True," Wade agreed with a shrug. "But we have time to figure it out."

"Is anyone here thinking rationally?" Manny asked, looking around at them. "I'm telling you, they're going to be *ridiculously* strong. They're *fucking* vampires for christ's sake."

"We'll just have to find a way to weaken them," Grant said.

Wade threw up his hands, "*Again*, holy water!"

"Shantelle—"

Shantelle took Manny's hands and squeezed them. "Manny. Isla is missing and we all know she's going to be a sacrifice. So, *we* don't have time for second guessing."

Manny pulled her hands away. "I'm not *second guessing.* I'm saying we need a better plan than just going in guns blazing. I mean you can't get the jump on a vampire—they're faster, stronger…"

"Well, maybe you can ask your vampire friend for help," Shantelle suggested.

Manny's stomach dropped. *What the hell, Shantelle.*

This wasn't how she wanted to tell Grant. She'd told her that in confidence. Manny had kept him in the dark for his own good, and for her own reasons. But she hadn't trusted him with this because how could she casually drop '*Hey, by the way, I've been working with a vampire'* into conversation? Because she's also been—what? Bound to him? Letting him sink his fangs into her as he gives her never ending toe-curling pleasure.

"Vampire friend?" Grant repeated, leaning closer to her. "Manny, what is she talking about?"

And just like that, the moment she'd been dreading, was here.

"He's more like vampire Sherlock," she said weakly, trying and possibly failing to land a joke.

Grant looks at her for a long moment, and then he nods. "Okay, but can he help us?"

Manny nods. "He can help us—he told me the other day that he and his coven want them dead, because of what they've been doing in Millfield…"

"Great, then we can gather a few things at The Bewitchery, while Wade…" Grant trailed off looking over at Wade. "Can *sober up*."

Wade belched. "Yeah, I'll do that."

Manny nodded feverishly. Noting to herself to thank Wade for his drunken behavior later, because it may have been the only reason Grant wasn't interrogating her with questions right now.

* * *

They shuffled their way through five inches of snow, and made it to the *Bewitchery*. But the moment Manny stepped inside, she knew something wasn't right. It was subtle at first, lingering beneath the usual layered scents of dried herbs, candle wax, and incense. It's like a strange little twinge in her brain, like an itch she can't scratch.

What is that? Burnt sage, dried lavender, beeswax candles melting behind the counter—but there's something else. Something—musky, metallic, something—

"Do you smell that?" Manny whispered to her friends.

Shantelle and Grant don't seem to notice. They walk ahead, talking to each other, looking through jars of crushed herbs and searching shelves for holy water—probably holy wood for stakes, too.

But Manny's stomach is tying itself in knots.

Because she knows that smell.

Shit. Oh my God. Manny turned and looked at Trish behind the counter.

"Everything all right, doll?" Trish asked her.

That smell. She'd noticed it in the hotel suite, when she was face to face with that familiar. But it's more than that—it's a feeling, an instinct, something underneath her skin.

Trish's eyes are perfectly lined with smudged eyeliner, and her black nails tapping rhythmically against the counter.

She's watching us, Manny thought. *No, she's watching me...*

Shantelle is talking about some ingredient Grant insisted they get, but Manny can barely hear her. Because Trish is more than a witch.

She smells like him—and it takes everything in Manny not to react because suddenly everything made sense.

Vlane.

Manny was just about to say something—maybe call her out, maybe pretend she didn't know exactly what she was and play along—when the front door slammed open. The bell above it barely jingled before a blast of cold air rushes in, carrying the cold and *them*. Three men—no three *vampires*. Tall, muscular pupils slit like snakes.

Manny turns to say something to warn her friends, but then the first one moves, flitting past her field of vision. She's not even sure how she's able to see them. Grant barely manages to stagger backward before the vampire's fingers close around his wrist, squeezing hard enough to make him yelp. A tall, dark-skinned vampire with sharp fangs, hissed in Grant's face.

Shantelle is looking through oils that had fallen on the floor. "Get your *dead* hands off him, you corpse-looking piece of sh—" She doesn't finish. A pale vampire with ginger hair is on her before the words are fully out of her mouth, grabbing her by her shirt collar and lifting her like she weighs nothing.

Manny lurched forward, trying to get to them, but the third one, a blonde-haired man with porcelain white skin is suddenly in front of her, a smirk curling his lips back, flashing his fangs.

"Hello *little one*," he purred with an accent, she couldn't quite place.

Then everything happens at once.

Grant kicks the Black vampire in the knee—he roared at him. The Ginger holding Shantelle grins, tightening his grip—until she swings her arm up and splashes something straight into his face. He *howled*, roaring and dropping her like she'd hurt him—and maybe she had, because steam was wafting off his face, his skin sizzling.

Holy water.

"I hope that hurts, asshole," Shantelle hisses, scrambling backward.

But the vampire in front of Manny obscured her view. He doesn't grab her. Doesn't even bother lunging at her. Just steps closer, and she takes a step backward, until her back hits a bundle of dried sage.

Manny tried to move around him, but he's already *too close*, and her body knows it before her brain does.

The vampire's pupils go from snakelike to normal. He paused, titling his head, nostrils flaring.

Then his gaze dropped.

Not to her throat, like she'd expect. Even though her pulse is racing.

Lower.

To her abdomen.

His lips parted slightly, like he was about to say something, but he doesn't. Not at first. He just watched her, like he was figuring *something* out. As if he was fitting the remaining pieces of a puzzle together.

Then he spoke. Low, but stern. The words rolled off his tongue quickly, but his eyes never left her face. He wasn't speaking English. The language—though she couldn't place it exactly—she was sure was Slavic. But the way he said it made her skin crawl.

Damiel, can you hear me?

She had some instinct that he must be able to, and in this moment, she didn't mind if he was eavesdropping.

The Ginger vampire answered in a different language. Harsher. Clipped—perhaps from the pain.

"Sounds Gaelic," Damiel's voice whispered inside her head.

Her stomach knotted. *Thank God...you're here. Can you understand them?*

"It's a bit hard listening through your ears from this far away."

Where are you?

The Slavic vampire said something else—and gestured toward Manny. The Gaelic, ginger-haired vampire shouted something at Trish. Shantelle is looking between them, gripping her mace, shaking.

"I'm on my way," Damiel said.

She sees the Slavic vampire's lips move. Was he speaking to her?

"What?" Manny asked.

"You are *tainted*," the Slavic vampire said in English. "With the *unfinished*."

Tainted. Unfinished. What the hell is he talking about?

He backed away from her slightly and stared down at her as if slowly gathering that she didn't understand him.

"Prey tainted by predator?" The Black vampire asked; he had an English accent, and was still holding Grant's neck.

"I beg your pardon?" Manny asked the Slavic vampire.

The large muscular Slavic vampire grabbed her chin and made her look at him, before saying just above a whisper: "I do not harm *seed-bearers*."

Chapter 42
December 20th

A familiar carrying a dhampir does not endure pregnancy so much as survives it. The child's presence may result in a gnawing sensation deep in the womb, as if the fetus is already testing its instincts. In rare and more sinister cases, still-forming dhampir offspring have been known to pierce the uterine lining with their needle-sharp teeth, drinking from their mother—as a parasitic rite of passage. Familiars may be prone to feverish nights and an insatiable craving for rare meat, though they won't die unless their sire allows it. Other symptoms may include nocturnal restlessness, and an almost preternatural sensitivity to the presence of their vampiric mate, as if the child itself is reaching out for the one who sired it.

— *From the article, 'Parasitic Gestation,' by Eliza Harrow*

Manny had been doing a lot of pacing lately. Here she was, pacing around the *Betwitchery* like a caged animal, arms crossed, her mind racing, jumping from one conclusion to the next. All of which, given recent events, was entirely possible.

Seedbearer. He called me that, so the logical conclusion is—God no.

She couldn't be pregnant. How wasn't his sperm dead? She had spent at least a decade of her life trying to understand that any time dhampirs had come up in novels or movies. It never seemed like vampires got pregnant—or did they? Were there movies with lore about pregnant vampires? Hell, she could probably ask Eliza.

Manny looked over at Trish—because they weren't the ones in hot water, at least, not anymore. The Slavic vampire, Alexandrov, was saying something harsh and in *latin* to her, and it was definitely *latin*. Grant was behind her whispering about that. Callum, the ginger that switched between Gaelic and English, seemed particularly perturbed, and kept pointing at his face. The English vampire with the pleasant accent, had a terrific smile and was quite apologetic when he'd let Grant go—his name was Icarus. Which was definitely the kind of name she'd deem worth repeating, *'I shit you not'* when she told someone about it.

These vampires hadn't turned around and given her an ominous, *we'll be seeing you*—like Vlane. Probably too civilized for that. Alexandrov, who had sniffed her like a bloodhound and muttered something in Latin, had turned on Trish, grabbed her from behind the counter, because—as Grant roughly translated to modern English—she and her master had been playing everyone like a rigged game of blackjack.

To which, Shantelle replied, "Vampires play blackjack?" And Manny had nodded—as if it were need-to-know information. But Manny had to admit, it was nice to see someone else getting the supernatural screw-over for once. Though she wasn't completely off the hook.

Manny rubbed her lower abdomen. She had never been pregnant before—*if* she was—and she couldn't shake the mental image of a dhampir being similar to a chestburster, and violently *bursting* out of her uterus, leaving nothing but blood and guts in its wake.

Alexandrov had *sniffed* her. Had called her *tainted*…and she was beginning to wonder if vampires saw dhampir as abominations. Meaning perhaps he knew something she didn't.

Like what if the reason she was feeling *off* lately was her body playing catch-up with the fact that she was currently being fed on like a prime-cut steak?

What if—no. No spiraling Manny. We will figure this out.

She stopped pacing, and rubbed her face with both hands. She needed answers. And unfortunately, the only person who could possibly give them to her was still on his way.

When the bell *tinkled*, it suddenly stopped the flow of Trish's interrogation, but they all turned toward Damiel.

"Errm...Prince Damiel, I take it?" Callum said. "Sorry we didn't roll out the red carpet for you, but we were here on business—or we *thought* we were."

Trish swallowed. All the blood had drained from her face, and her expression said a lot more than she'd let on. Vlane hadn't come to the aid of his other familiar, but from how frightened she was, Manny didn't think he held the witch in any higher regard. Trish was disposable, just like the panting raving woman that had attacked Manny at the hotel.

"Damiel will do just fine," Damiel answered, he glanced over to Manny, as if assessing her for damage.

She wasn't, though she wished she would've explained more to her friends and worried less about her problems at the moment.

"Hold on, Moreau is a vampire?" Grant whispered to her.

Shantelle's eyes widened. "Oh *shit.*"

She gave Manny a knowing look, and Manny shot her a look that she hoped said, *Thank you, Shantelle, I know.*

"Who sent you?" Damiel asked the three vampires.

Alexandrov straightened and said. "Vlane, but I did not know this was a *family problem,*" he looked between Manny and Damiel. "I'm not in the business of *starting wars*. We were told it was a simple job—we receive half the payment before, the other half *after*. Nothing about *feuding brothers.*"

"Vlane has been led astray," Damiel retorted. "And I think you'll find my father has disowned him and taken his title—so you would be well within your right to kill him without retaliation."

"What's the matter? 'Fraid to get your hands dirty," Callum said, butting in.

Alexandrov put a hand on Callum's shoulder, and said something in latin. Before saying, "Let it go, Callum," then he turned back to Damiel. "We were told we would be killing a *human* that had been quite the troublemaker—not a *seedbearer*—"

"I believe what Alexandrov is implying is that we're more than willing to help make it right. There's no reason we shouldn't be able to reach some form of agreement." Icarus said, interrupting, however somehow in a polite manner. "Your familiar is unharmed, and we volunteer our services in a *one-time repayment*."

Damiel stood there, pretending to think it over.

Stop acting like that—we need to talk. Now. Manny thought, barraging her thoughts at him.

Damiel glanced at her, nodded, and turned to them. "*Fine*, but don't leave, and I still need to question *her*."

He gestured toward Trish, who looked alarmed by the statement.

"We can handle that—free of charge, of course. Our repayment still outstanding," Icarus suggested, holding out his hand in a gesture of good faith.

Damiel shook his hand and nodded in agreement. He walked over to Manny, his expression unreadable, and though she wanted to hug him, she didn't—because what would Grant think?

"Are you all right?" Damiel asked.

Manny nodded. "Just a little shaken."

"Good, and your friends," Damiel asked, looking toward them.

Grant and Shantelle nodded.

"Why are you in this shop in the first place?"

Manny's stomach twisted. *Shit*.

She hadn't thought about how she was going to explain that.

Damiel stared at her, expectant. Manny could practically hear the gears in his head turning.

Manny shifted uncomfortably, suddenly very interested in a loose thread on her sleeve. "We were…just looking for some things."

"What kind of *things*?" Damiel asked.

Shit. Shit. Shit.

But she had to tell him—didn't she? Damiel would know if she was lying. He probably had her heartbeat mapped like a topographical chart. Waiting for it to reveal every lie she told.

Manny sighed, and straightened. "Fine. We were looking for things to hunt vampires."

A beat of silence—then he laughed. *Laughed.*

Not a *haha, you're so funny* laugh. Not even a *what a ridiculous idea* laugh. No, this was a *you silly little humans, do all of you have a death wish* kind of laugh.

Manny glared at him. "Glad you think it so *funny*."

"Oh, I don't." His smile dropped, replaced with something like a grimace. He stepped closer, looking down at her like she was something fragile, something in way over its head. "Tell me, darling, did you think a few vials of holy water and a stake were going to save you?"

She tried not to pout, because it might not have been her idea to go full vampire hunter mode, but she had hoped knowing the horror movie basics would help her a little bit. Because they hadn't thought this far ahead. Because she hadn't really planned for what came after getting the supplies.

"We're not *stupid*," Manny muttered, defensive now. "We just—"

"Don't know what you're doing," he finished for her. "And yet you're still determined to throw all caution to the wind and potentially get yourselves killed?"

Manny lifted her chin, stubbornly. "I understand plenty."

Damiel gave a long look. Then, pinched the bridge of his nose like the sheer weight of her stupidity was giving him a migraine. But finally, he sighed. "We'll talk about that later too."

"Well, we found the ritual they're using," Shantelle piped up, perhaps to make them sound smarter.

Thank God for Shantelle, Manny thought.

Shantelle held up her notebook, and Damiel took it. He was a vampire, but he was also an academic, and academia was a bitch at the best of times, but at the moment, academia was a bitch with fangs.

Damiel flipped through Shantelle's notes and nodded repeatedly, as if he were taking the information in.

"Yes, ritual sacrifice to an occult entity—vampires, witches, or werewolves—usually," Damiel said softly.

Shantelle smirked, which was expected. She was bright and it deserved to be acknowledged. Grant had paled, which was also expected. He was probably still digesting the fact that their professor was a vampire. Manny, however, was waiting for Damiel to get to the inevitable conclusion they'd already reached.

"The spell helps direct influence, and would require *repetition.* So, who better to make a deal with than vampires? Whoever the caster is needs magic to continue to gift others power," Shantelle continued.

"*Yes*, love that for us," Manny muttered. "So, *what* do we do?"

"It isn't just one person making a deal," Damiel said, tapping the notes. "Four points of a compass. Four humans. Thirteen sacrifices—at most, three per person. A spell like this requires balance. If we don't find these four before the *last part* of the ritual—though I assume whoever it was knows *them*."

Grant cocked a brow. "Do you think they're students?"

"Or faculty. Doesn't really matter if we don't find them—I'll get these to Eliza. See if she can make heads or tails of where the coven helping them might be," Damiel said, flipping through the notebook. "You three can come with me."

She was beginning to think she should've looped him in sooner—or at very least the moment her friends had suggested they go to the Bewitchery.

Manny sighed. "And how is she going to track the coven?"

Damiel studied her for a moment, like he was debating how much to tell her. Then he said, "Eliza won't be tracking anyone—*but* I know a tracker. Best one I've ever met."

That was it. No name, no further explanation, just *I know a guy* like he was involved in some kind of supernatural mafia. At this point, she was ready to accept that anything was possible.

Manny scoffed. "And you're not telling me who *because*…?"

"Because it doesn't matter yet."

Manny rolled my eyes. "Right. Of course. Why would I need to know anything?"

He ignored that—shocker—and instead said, "You and your friends should stay with me tonight."

That confused her.

"Stay with you?" Manny echoed.

He nodded. "It's safer than your apartment, especially once Vlane realizes his plan didn't work."

Manny wanted to argue. But she knew he was right—her apartment was a target now, and it wasn't like they had anywhere else to go.

Manny huffed. "Fine."

That was all it took for them to load up into his car, and head to his home. Wade came later—after he'd packed a few things for Manny from her apartment, then did the same for Grant. He even set the automatic feeder in their apartment for their cats.

Damiel had offered them the guest rooms. Though none of them actually wanted to sleep in a guest room.

Instead, they settled in the living room, curled up on the couches and on the floor in sleeping bags, because none of them wanted to be alone tonight. There was a massive flat-screen TV, which helped, and Wade put on a movie.

Manny stared at the screen, barely registering what was playing, her mind still stuck on the tracker—and the war Alexandrov had prevented by just smelling her. And she'd fallen asleep that way.

* * *

By the next morning, there were thirteen of them total in his home—eight vampires, including Damiel, and then her, Shantelle, Grant, Wade, the only *squishy* ones in the group.

Or she was at least 75% sure she still qualified as *squishy*. The jury was still out, given the growing dhampir inside her.

Three vampires from Damiel's coven had arrived, and they were—a mixed bag. A red-haired couple had spent most of their time in the corner by the bookshelf, the woman, Adeline, looked vaguely amused, and her mate, Christopher had a permanent scowl on his face that suggested he wanted to be *anywhere else*. Klaus, a blonde with regally long hair, porcelain skin, and piercing blue eyes was in the kitchen filling up the refrigerator with blood transfer bags.

"You are lucky they did not damage your refrigerator, Damiel," Klaus said with a thick accent. "We don't make snacks out of friends, do we?"

He laughed then. Alexandrov, Callum and Icarus laughed with him —clearly not finding the joke distasteful.

But Damiel's *tracker* hadn't arrived yet—he would arrive with Eliza and Sebastian.

"You can trust everyone here," Damiel told her, leaning against the counter.

Manny rolled her eyes at him. "I can trust that they all want to kill Vlane, at least. But I don't like relying on the 'hope we get him before he gets us' as a strategy."

Damiel nodded. "Agreed."

"Then we need a backup plan."

He frowned. "Which is?"

Manny looked at him, then at the others. "Me."

He hesitated. "While I *love* your enthusiasm, Manny, that is a bad idea."

"Not if you teach me how to fight them, especially now that I'm—" she paused, gesturing to her stomach. "There's plenty of research that says, they won't harm seedbearers?"

Damiel didn't answer.

Klaus let out a long laugh. "I like her, Damiel, she has spunk."

Manny ignored him, keeping her eyes on Damiel. "If worse comes to worse, I'm the one who could get close enough to drive the stake through their heart, right?"

Damiel's jaw tightened. "*Most* won't harm seedbearers. And that's not—"

"I can do it."

He shook his head. "I'm not putting the two of you at risk."

The two of you—so there is a dhampir inside me.

"Maybe not. But it's better than us *losing*."

For a long moment, Damiel just looked at her, as if trying to gauge how serious she was. Then he sighed. "…Fine, but only so you can protect yourself, if someone attacks you. *Not* because you're the backup plan."

He didn't approve. He certainly wasn't agreeing with her. But it was something—and that had to be enough.

Chapter 43
December 25th

Christmas. Of all the times for a student society slash murder cult to be taking a vacation, of course, it *had* to be now. Because apparently, even bloodthirsty bastards who sacrifice people for power still respect the sanctity of a good Christmas dinner. Leaving Manny in Damiel's home office, practically begging him to teach her *something*.

Manny groaned, flapping back against the couch. "I can't believe we're celebrating while the coven is getting away with this."

"They can't finish the ritual until the next full moon," Damiel said, far too calmly for her liking. "So, we wait."

This is bullshit.

Wait while the coven took their sweet time prepping their next move. *Wait* while Isla was an unwilling member in their final performance. *Wait* while Damiel treated her like she was too fragile to be of any real use in their fight.

Manny shot Damiel a look. "You *said* you'd teach me."

"And I will," he said smoothly. "*After* Christmas."

Manny groaned again, letting her head drop back against the couch dramatically.

Because of course that was what he'd decide. Vampires had all the time in the world, and while technically, she had *more of it* as had been established—she was sick of waiting. But of course she was the only one losing her mind over it.

"I agree," a soft feminine voice said, her voice as smooth as a razor blade. "Training her is the most logical solution to our present predicament. It's a good idea, Damiel."

Manny whirred around quickly. *Where did she—*

"Eliza?" Manny said, blinking a few times to make sure she wasn't dreaming. "When did you get here?"

Eliza smirked. "A few moments ago, I had to bring—"

"I didn't say it was a bad idea. I said—not until *after* Christmas." Damiel corrected.

Before anyone else could speak, another set of footsteps echoed from the hall, and a deep male voice along with them called out: "Where is this little familiar—I want to meet her! Damiel, where are you!"

This voice that apparently made Damiel pinch the bridge of his nose, looking one second away from an aneurysm.

"Damiel!"

Eventually, the voice's owner arrived in the doorway. The man was tall—broad-shouldered and dressed in a deep charcoal coat that couldn't quite hide the way his frame filled the space, muscle defined beneath layers of dark, expensive fabric. His skin was pale, but not sickly; more like untouched porcelain, smooth and cold, almost glowing under the dim light of the study. His hair fell in loose waves, just past his collar, slightly longer than in the old photographs Manny had seen.

Unlike the photos, right now, he was smiling, and his eyes frightened her. They were deep-set and dark, like ink spilled across parchment, revealing nothing, but taking everything in.

Does every old vampire look like this?

"...Father," Damiel said, stiffening. "It's good to see you."

Father.

"King Victor, that is the familiar," Eliza said, gesturing toward Manny. "Her name is Manuela—"

"I prefer *Manny*," Manny corrected.

King?

Victor studied her for a moment, then his smile widened—a slow, knowing smile that revealed his fangs and made Manny's stomach twist.

"She's *beautiful*," he said, with a Louisiana accent that managed to sound like velvet lined with steel. "And I must say, I'm rather excited to finally be a grandfather."

Manny swallowed. Her throat was dry. She needed water or to get out of this room.

He's the tracker, she thought, looking between the two of them. *He called his father to track the coven?*

She knew it made sense. Victor was a descendant of Dracula, he had probably lived for centuries, tracing and hunting *things*, probably supernatural, animal and human. Who better to rely on to find the coven. And he was also a *king*.

Damiel—who already looked stressed by his father's presence—sighed, pinching the bridge of his nose like he'd replayed this moment in his head a thousand times before Victor's arrival. "You are already a grandfather, considering Nikolas has three children and Raphael has *five*."

Victor waved his hand, dismissively. "Yes, yes. But your elder brothers are a bit...*uncivilized* for my liking," he explained, waving his hands around as if he could somehow grasp the right word. "They are my inner demons turned loose as your grandfather would say. They are hardly *my* children."

"And who did they learn their behavior from?"

"They are my *past's* children," Victor corrected smoothly, as if that wiped the slate clean. "This one, however—" He gestured at her, or at her *entire existence*, "—is *different*. I can *feel it* in my bones. The bloodline is strong in her. She holds the next Dracula."

Manny had absolutely no idea how to respond to that. So, she settled for staring at Damiel, wide-eyed, hoping he had a better grip on reality than his father did. *Hoping* he'd say something that insisted his father was incorrect.

"We don't know that it's a boy," Damiel muttered. "It could very well be—"

Victor rolled his eyes. "I was not establishing something as boring as *gender*, Damiel. I was speaking of *promise*—the little one will usher in a new era for all vampires. Why my oracle—"

"Here we go with the oracle," Damiel mumbled, letting out a long sigh.

"She told me," Victor continued, talking over him, "that *our* bloodline would produce a strong dhampir—one that would change the world of vampires and humans as we know it." He turned to Manny. "They would merge them before they became a full-fledged vampire."

Manny stared at him blankly. "I'm sorry, *what?*"

Victor nodded, as if this was a completely reasonable thing to drop into casual conversation. "A *new era.* A civilized world where vampires and humans coexist without hunting one another down like rabid dogs."

Damiel groaned, rubbing at his temples like *this* was causing him actual physical pain. "You can't possibly believe this is the moment she was talking about."

Victor arched a brow. "You doubt my oracle?"

"I would like *you* to stop bringing her up every time I see you," Damiel shot back. "Because you *somehow* manage to twist *her* words to fit whatever *bizarre*, self-important prophecy you want to be true at the moment."

Victor scoffed. "That is a *baseless* accusation."

"The last time you did this, you told Nikolas his secondborn was destined to rule the vampire world."

"And?"

"And she was *three years old.*"

Victor shrugged. "Greatness can start young," he said matter-of-factly. "Why, when I was your age, I could take down entire covens myself without anyone's aid. But *your generation* spends too much time worrying and gathering and *avoiding* your natural instincts and habits to make the humans *comfortable*." He shook his head as if the entire concept was ridiculous. "We are *vampires*. We *eat* like everyone else, and if they were willing, we could thin the herd of the *unsavory* of their kind."

Manny bit her lip, trying not to laugh. What he said wasn't *funny*—not even a little bit. What he'd suggested earlier was. Because she was standing in a room with an actual vampire king who was fully convinced, she was going to birth a supernatural messiah.

Damiel looked more than a little agitated. "And you think a child of *mine* will unite vampires and humankind?"

Victor smiled, smugly. "Time will tell."

Eliza cleared her throat, cutting through whatever cosmic destiny nonsense Victor was about to launch into next. "Fascinating as this is," Eliza said. "We need to focus on the task at hand."

Victor sighed, placing a hand over his chest like she'd personally wounded him, and turned to Damiel. "You're always so serious. You get that from your grandfather."

Damiel pinched the bridge of his nose. "And you take after a Victorian drama queen. Can we *please* move on?"

Eliza rolled her eyes. "We need you to track down Vlane. He is with a coven, who are hunting well outside their rights—interfering with human's futures, giving them power and influence, and not truly deciding whether or not they should really have it."

Victor's eyes widened. "Vlane? You are sure he is responsible?"

"Yes," Damiel confirmed. "We know he's involved with the coven, father. He's gone to great lengths to try and protect them—including forcibly turning Manny into a familiar—before she became my familiar," he explained, and Victor looked at her, his eyes softening. "If we can track him down, we can find *them*."

Victor let out a long sigh, studying Damiel, and then he scoffed, "You doubt my abilities?"

"*No*," Damiel muttered. "I wouldn't have requested you to come if I did."

Victor shrugged. "Then consider it done."

In truth, Manny would've expected more of an argument from a father having to hunt his son. But she wasn't going to pretend she understood it.

"I suppose it's my fault he is like that," Victor said, giving Damiel a sad smile. "He is young, and maybe if I had spent less time in his life, he would have turned out more like you. Intelligent, civilized, still a touch—*human*."

Damiel didn't answer for a moment. But even Manny knew that was Victor giving his son a compliment.

"Maybe," Damiel finally said.

Chapter 44
Day, December 29th

Manny had spent most of her days on the couch—while Victor spent his nights hunting and his days hovering. Tracking the coven wasn't an easy task, even for a vampire as experienced as him, and every night, he and her would-be assassins—Alexandrov, Callum, and Icarus—returned empty-handed. Not that Victor seemed particularly bothered by it—he treated every failure like an opportunity for more *quality time* with his son and future, though currently *womb-ridden* grandchild.

She wasn't sure who was more annoyed by it—Damiel, whose patience was slowly thinning, or Eliza, who looked increasingly like she wanted to lock Victor in a coffin and throw away the key. Eliza would give them scouting spots, but the coven wouldn't be there, leaving them with a large map of Millfield with nothing on university grounds or close to it, and the same question as everyone else: Where the hell were the students performing the ritual?

Manny wished she could help in some way. She had tried looking into which students would be the *perfect fit* for the four-points of the compass based on the criteria of:

1. Whose family was desperate enough?

2. Whose parents have a business or career that's currently failing?

But as of recently, she'd stopped. She had slowly begun dealing with a crisis of sorts.

Her body was changing—but not just *changing*—it was *demanding*. Food. Rest. More food. And then, just when she thought she couldn't possibly be hungrier—even more food.

She caught her reflection in the hallway mirror one night and nearly choked. The bump wasn't quite prominent, it definitely curved outward in a way that wasn't just too many *late-night snacks.* It was real. Tangible. Small little bump that said *Manny Webb is expecting.*

She sat her palm on her bump today, and was grateful Grant hadn't taken any note of it. Probably due to him being stressed about being in a home filled with vampires.

"Hungry again?" Victor asked, appearing out of thin air like the vampire menace he was, smirking down at her with something suspiciously close to amusement.

Manny scowled. "I'm *fine*."

He hummed, unconvinced. "Insatiable hunger is natural for dhampir mothers, you know. Especially for someone hosting a *dracula*. Your body's working overtime to nourish someone extraordinary—for two to three months of your life."

"Great," she deadpanned. "Thank you for making me aware that I'm housing a black hole in my uterus."

Victor laughed, clapping her on the shoulder. "You are very funny, Manuela. But do not fret, you are housing our future. Victor will help you."

Manny stared at him in disbelief—and she wasn't sure if it was because he offered his assistance, or because he'd referred to himself in the third person. She hated when people did that. It made her feel like they were about to start monologuing about themselves.

But still, she allowed him to steer her toward the kitchen.

"Sit," he said, hands on her shoulders as he lightly pushed her to sit in a chair, in a commanding tone, as if he was leading her into battle instead of dinner.

Manny didn't argue. Mostly because she was *starving*. Again.

He gathered ingredients, chopped them with alarming speed, and tossed them into a pan without measuring a damn thing. The whole place smelled like heaven within minutes, and Manny had to stop herself from drooling like some feral beast waiting for scraps.

Eventually, Victor plated up warm salmon with a rich sauce, and set it down in front of her, and then…

He pulled out a vial.

The silver vial was beautifully decorated, and the liquid inside was dark and thick. Before she could ask, Victor uncorked it, let a single drop fall onto her food, then tucked it away.

Manny stared at him. Then her plate. Then him *again*.

Victor gave her a fanged smile. "Eat."

And because she was starving, and because somehow the food smelled even better than anything she had ever eaten in her life, she did.

And after she finished, for the first time in days, she actually felt *full*.

She dropped her fork, and took a deep breath, grateful to not feel like a ravenous animal. But then she turned to Victor, eyes narrowed. "What the hell was in that vial?"

Manny half-expected him to tell her it was some potion or other concoction like Damiel had made for her weeks ago.

Victor's grin widened. "A little something to take the edge off."

"What kind of *something*?"

His grin didn't waver. "Something necessary for your growing *child*."

Manny swore under her breath and said, "*What?*"

"A little of the *original blood*," he explained with a shrug. "I brought a vial of some, in case you needed it, I figured Damiel wouldn't have any at home. So, I added some to the sauce and additional afterward. You must be *nourished* not *famished*."

"Original blood," Manny repeated in confusion.

What the hell does that mean? And why is he giving me blood—and then she sighed aloud. *Why wouldn't he be giving me blood?*

She was growing a damn dhampir inside her. Of course, food wouldn't be enough. Why had she ever thought it would be?

"It is the blood of Dracula—vampire blood—all royal families have some," he explained candidly. "It is what made us stronger than the rest. You can't maintain order without strong vampires, and you cannot have strong vampires without the original blood. My blood can only take my children so far—I have a few centuries on me, but nowhere near the potency of Dracula, himself."

Manny wished she was more bothered by the fact that he'd given her blood. She wanted to be grossed out, and maybe she would be—if it was human blood. But it wasn't. And somehow that made it better? Like, if someone had handed her a cup of warm, freshly squeezed person juice, she'd have projectile vomited across the kitchen and then launched herself into the sun for good measure. But this? Vampire blood? Barely an *ick*. Which was insane—and probably something she should discuss with a therapist. If Dr. Carter could get past the whole, *vampires and many, many other creatures are probably real* thing.

But she knows with every fiber of her being she *should* be disgusted. She should be dry heaving. She should be reevaluating every single life choice that has led her to this moment.

But instead, all she can think is: *Huh. That was actually kinda good, and I do feel stronger. Fantastic. Next stop: swirling it in a goblet and wearing a Victorian era ball gown with a corset.*

"You may be confused, but it keeps the baby from sinking their teeth into you," Victor said, matter-of-factly.

And she wasn't sure what was worse—how easily he'd said it, or that she was sure he'd meant it to be comforting. She'd never considered drinking blood before, but now, with this strange new being inside her, she realized that the idea didn't repulse her the way she might have expected it to.

Is it the baby? She wondered, staring down at her stomach.

Could it influence her thoughts? Could her child, even before it was born, be capable of something like compulsion? Of glamouring her, controlling her thoughts the way a full-grown vampire could? The way Damiel could, if he were so inclined, though he wasn't that type of vampire, and every instinct inside her told her that. But still, the thought of it made her uneasy and a little curious—so maybe she did have more than one academic bone in her body. If the baby was this strong now, what would it be like once it was born?

Manny stared blankly at Victor, at not just a vampire, but a vampire king, and not just a vampire king, but the father of her child's father, a man who had answers to questions she had probably never thought of asking. He was standing there, watching her, with the same unreadable expression Damiel used to hide his emotions, but something about how Victor seemed so certain, so comfortable with his nature, so sure his next grandchild was the supernatural messiah—made her want to understand more about him, about the history of the Dracula bloodline she had unwittingly connected herself to.

Who better to ask questions than the vampire standing in front of her, a man who had lived through centuries, who understood the intricacies of vampire life and blood—who was probably waiting for her to ask.

Despite the fact that power seemed to radiate off him, he didn't move to leave, as if he knew what she was thinking. She could sit there studying the hard lines of his face, staring into his cold, ancient eyes. Or she could learn something from him.

If she could just ask the right questions, maybe, just maybe, she could understand what to expect. What was coming. But would she dare to open that door, knowing what it might mean for her, for the baby, for whatever came next?

Chapter 45
Afternoon, December 29th

I *should just ask*. But where to start—does he know Dracula? What was he like? Was he some broody nobleman throwing elaborate balls or running a black market for stolen relics, or something? And what else was real? Wendigos? Werewolves? The Loch Ness Monster? Is Bigfoot just a very unlucky man that was transformed through a half-assed transformation spell leaving him stuck halfway through the process?

Victor's face contorted in amusement, and for a moment, it seemed like he might've been reading her thoughts—and she wasn't sure she wanted to ask him anything.

"Walk with me," he told her, gesturing for her to follow him.

She did. Following him a few steps behind, trying to ignore the fact that her stomach still felt unsettlingly full.

"So," Manny started, because if she didn't say something now, she might have lost her nerve. "On the subject of Dracula. You have what—met him?"

Victor chuckled. "*Met* him? My dear, he's my great-grandfather—he bounced me on his knee when I was three. Damiel has as well, but I guess he hasn't told you..." He trailed off, glancing back at her. "Not surprising. I wouldn't expect him to discuss our family."

Manny blinked. "So, Dracula is…one hundred percent real?"

Victor threw a look over his shoulder, amused. "*Of course* he is real. You think humans just conjured the myth out of thin air? Honestly, humankind isn't *that* creative."

Manny didn't answer, mostly because, yeah, she *did* think that. But now she couldn't stop picturing Victor and a younger Damiel at some extended family gathering, sitting across from *Dracula*, making polite conversation about bloodlust or whatever vampires talked about over dinner—or a bleeding carcass.

Victor continued, unfazed. "Dracula was a complicated man when I was born—as all powerful men tend to be—ruthless, yes, but pragmatic. A visionary, really, in his own way."

"Uh-huh," Manny agreed, watching her step as they moved into a narrower hall. "And by visionary, do you mean 'mass murderer with a cool cape' or 'brooding aristocrat with a never-ending bloodlust'…?"

Victor laughed, the sound bouncing off the walls. "Ah, you are a *delight*. No wonder my son adores you."

Before she could unpack those two statements, they stepped through an arched doorway, and suddenly, she was standing in what looked like a small art gallery. The warm light glowed against dark wood paneled walls, casting shadows over rows of framed paintings. Some were landscapes, others portraits, but all of them were old. Some older than others—with names and years of birth and death—which would have surprised her, if she hadn't known he was a vampire. Each professionally done, which were definitely museum-level quality, and didn't look like they should be casually decorating someone's home.

Victor clasped his hands behind his back, surveying the room with a small smile on his face.

"Tell me, Manny—do you like history?"

Manny had never thought about it. She enjoyed understanding the world around her—so in some ways, *yes*, because the past influenced the present. No matter how much some people might like to ignore that.

"Yes, I guess I do," Manny answered.

Victor nodded. "Good, so my words won't be wasted," he said, slowly walking over to a portrait.

Manny followed, wondering what he intended to tell her. She looked around the room at the different portraits, confused as to why he'd stopped in front of this one.

She looked up at Victor. "So…I've been curious…about *dhampirs*. Like what happens to them? I mean, long term." She paused. "I know you didn't leave your sons behind, but how do they become…full vampires?"

Victor smirked, clearly pleased with her question. "It's a short process…" He gestured for her to follow as he took them deeper into the room, and paused when they reached a large, centuries-old painting of a regal-looking man with dark eyes and an eerily familiar face. "It requires that I, as their father, inject venom—directly into their bloodstream. The transition is not as violent as it is for humans, but it is still…*painful*…as change can be."

Manny shifted uncomfortably, thinking about the little dhampir growing inside her. "What is it like?"

Victor let out a dry laugh. "I do not remember the change. But I have done it many times. Most of my boys were turned in their late twenties—except for my youngest, Vlane. I changed him at twenty-five." He clicks his tongue, shaking his head. "That was a mistake…an *experiment* in timing that didn't work in my favor."

Manny stared at him blankly. "What do you mean?"

Victor turned to face her fully. "I believe Damiel's older age—thirty-two, when I turned him—allowed for a stronger sense of self before he became a vampire. He had lived a full human life, developed discipline, *restraint*. But Vlane? He was a rather…*overzealous* newborn." He sighed, shaking his head again. "In hindsight, twenty-five was too young. He never quite learned moderation—or how to treat his familiars with *dignity*."

Manny swallowed. "So, what you're saying is…if someone became a vampire too young, they might be *worse off*."

Victor gave her a sad smile. "Oh, my dear, you have *no idea*."

Manny nodded slowly, shifting her weight from one foot to the other. She felt like a toddler playing a game of twenty questions, and given their age gap, maybe that's how he saw her. "So, if Dracula's in Europe—what made you come here? To America?"

Victor let out a long sigh, shaking his head again. He said something in another language and then said. "I was banished for a crime—but I do not regret it."

Manny stood there in disbelief. *Banished?*

It wasn't like they had humanity's morals to uphold. Murder? Please. That was just breakfast. Theft? Highly doubtful—what would a vampire need to steal? Blood? Immortality? Some poor bastard's WiFi? No, she imagined whatever the crime was, it had to be something so heinous, making him an unsavory character in their little immortal ecosystem where even his undead peers went, *absolutely the fuck not.*

Which only made her even more curious.

Manny craned her head. "What was the crime?"

"Oh, my dear, if I told you *that*, you might start looking at me differently," he said, all traces of sadness leaving his face.

"Well, I already know you drink blood and turned your children into vampires," she deadpanned. "I don't think anything can top that."

Victor half-smiled, then he leaned against a nearby display case with a vase inside. "Fair enough. I was banished for *treason*."

Manny blinked. "Treason? How?"

"I do not believe in *their* version of preserving the 'natural order,' and *some* disagreed with my beliefs." He waved a dismissive hand. "Vampires, other nobility, the like—and they didn't take too kindly to me speaking out against them, and they had to set an example. So, I am here, still banished, but *alive*."

Manny gaped. "You were exiled for having an opinion?"

Victor chuckled. "Well, I didn't exactly keep my opinions *quiet*."

Manny waited for him to continue, then he smirked at her. "Then I came to America for—what do you kids call it—ah, a *fresh start*. Left behind my older children—grown by then—and built a new life." He gestured vaguely. "My last wife divorced me, of course. She wanted to stay in Dracula's good graces—and she did enjoy a good ball."

Manny was still stuck on *divorce*. "Vampires get divorced?"

Victor laughed as they walked to another portrait. "*Especially* vampires. Immortality does not make marriage easier." He gave her a pointed look. "Imagine spending centuries with someone you slowly grow to despise, and then they give you an easy out."

Manny hummed. She wasn't sure if she was disappointed or not. "It sounds like regular marriage—except some humans actually work on theirs."

"Precisely," Victor said with a shrug. "Humans have less time, it only makes sense that they would try harder to make something so *insufferable* work." Then his expression softened, and he said, "But, of course, Damiel's mother was the *exception.*"

Victor gestured toward the portrait in front of them—it's a portrait of a woman. She's incredibly beautiful, with dark curls, a soft smile, and even softer eyes.

So, he has his mother's eyes.

"Human," Victor continued, his hand waving over the painting. "I came across her in a museum, staring at a painting—she was twenty then—" He stopped, thinking, then chuckled to himself. "She was unlike anyone I'd ever come across—as beautiful as she was brilliant. And she loved me despite what I was...but I'm sure you do not want to hear an old vampire reminisce."

Manny gave him a soft smile. "You loved her."

"More than *anything*," Victor murmured. "I intended to turn her, you know, provide her with forever. But she..." He sighed and shook his head. "She didn't want that."

Manny frowned. "She didn't?"

Victor nodded. "She also believed there was a natural order of things. Life, death—very *human.* But she wasn't afraid of death." A pause. "She died peacefully, in her sleep. I was with her—holding her hand. That was the last time Damiel and I were in the same room. He would contact me *occasionally*—letters here and there—but of course, things were never the same."

Manny didn't know what to say. Didn't know how to comfort him, but she understood loss.

Victor gave her a wry smile. "But you can understand why I was so eager to meet you, my dear." He glanced at her stomach. "It's been a long time since I've had family born into this world rather than turned."

Manny laughed. "Yeah, no pressure."

Victor laughed, the somberness in his expression fading just slightly. "None at all."

And for a moment, she felt so small beside him. But not in a bad way. It was more like standing in a cathedral and realizing how high the ceilings were—and noticing the light refracted through its stained glass windows.

There was something surreal about hearing history from someone who lived it. Someone who didn't just *study* it, but walked through it, shaped it, and left pieces of himself behind in every century. And yet, for all his wisdom, Victor was still just…a man, a vampire, and someone's father.

Chapter 46
December 31st

Normally, she'd be at the pub with her friends, crammed into their usual booth, nursing some overpriced cocktail with a ridiculous name like Night Thriver No. 2—which, today, felt ironic. They'd be making half-hearted resolutions they wouldn't keep, watching the countdown on some blurry TV, and pretending they weren't all debating whether to go home or order another round.

Instead?

Manny was here on New Year's Eve. Her fists met the punching bag again and again, while Damiel held it steady. His entire body was tense, though she knows it doesn't have anything to do with their training session.

But she doesn't need or want to ask what's bothering him. She already knows. It had been days since her conversation with Victor—which was interrupted the moment Damiel had sought her out and rudely interrupted.

"You're distracted," Damiel muttered.

"I *wonder* why," she fired back, rolling her shoulders before throwing another punch. Her knuckles hurt, but if she stops, their training session will be over.

Damiel took a deep breath. "I just don't understand why you

needed to talk to my father—I can understand him giving you the family blood. I hadn't thought about it until the other day...and I have a little in storage."

Manny scoffs. "Good to know, and I didn't know I needed permission to speak to your father. I'm only having his grandchild for fuck's sake."

Damiel glared at her. "That's not what I—" He pause and ran a hand through his hair. "You don't need my permission. I'd just rather he not bother you with his never-ending *nonsense*."

Manny throws another punch, much harder this time. "*Nonsense?* The 'nonsense' about me carrying the vampire messiah? Or your family history?"

"Haha, very funny. My family's history is complicated to say the least. Whereas the vampire messiah nonsense is just that—*nonsense*. He talks to his oracle about everything and then she gives him exactly what he pays for."

Manny stopped, dropping her hands to her sides. "You don't know it's nonsense," Manny crossed her arms and glared at him. "And is it so strange that I want to know more about you—given that I'm both your familiar and the mother of your first child. They are your *first*, right?"

"Oh, you're just full of zingers today, aren't you?" he said, rolling his eyes. "Yes, they will be *my first*, as you're *my first* and *only* familiar. And while I may not know—neither do you nor *my father*. But that's never stopped him from going on and on about prophecies whenever it suits him. I would like to assume that our child will have a relatively normal childhood."

Manny wiped sweat off her brow. "Maybe you're mad because there's something you don't want to talk about. Like the changes our kid will have to go through to become a full-fledged vampire—to not be alone."

Damiel's expression hardened. "You think I *don't* think about that? I've never once considered bringing a dhampir into this world, but now that it's happening, I have. And I want them to be able to make an informed choice on whether or not they want to be a vampire—

whether they want to give up the little things, like enjoying food or sleep."

"Well, maybe I wish you would tell me more—"

"If I felt you'd listen then maybe I would."

Manny didn't argue. He had a point.

"And as for whatever his oracle said. It isn't something we should be worrying about *right now*. They're still growing and aren't a product of a prophecy or some grand design—that's *ours*. Our child—and they should come into this world knowing they're enough."

Manny let out a long sigh. Her hands still hurt, but she knew he was right. She didn't know what to do, only that she wished she could do more for them. Be more prepared for whatever the little one would need from her.

Damiel sighed, clearly done with their previous exercise, and gestured for her to follow him to a different area of the training room. She trailed after him, until he stopped them in front of a long wooden table, where a sleek, modified bow rested—except instead of arrows, it's armed with stakes. Thick, sharpened ones, and she wanted to laugh.

"We're switching things up," he said, picking up the weapon and giving it a once-over. He turns to her, expectant. "This is so you can keep your distance when time allows."

Manny huffed, stepping forward to take it from him. "Wow, you have so much faith in me."

"Well, you need to know how to shoot a stake with precision. Otherwise, you might as well be throwing toothpicks at them," Damiel answered with an all-too dashing smile.

Manny rolled her eyes but lets him position her properly to aim at the target across the room. The wooden cutout had a crude, painted figure on it, a bright red circle marking where a vampire's heart would be. Luckily, it was the same as human anatomy.

"All right," he instructed, stepping back. "Aim."

"I know how a crossbow works."

Manny adjusted her aim, and she could feel his eyes on her.

"Higher," he instructed. "You're aiming too low."

She adjusted. Loosened her grip slightly. Exhales. "Are you still mad?"

"I'm not mad," he muttered.

Manny released. The stake flies, embedding itself into the outer ring of the target.

Dammit.

"They'd certainly feel it in their chest, but if it's not their heart, it won't matter," Damiel said.

Manny huffed out air and lowered the bow. "You're a terrible liar."

He sighed, stepped forward, and adjusted her grip on the bow. His hands were warm, and he was standing close enough for her to feel his breath on her neck—and she had half-a-mind to elbow him in the stomach. "I just think this—" He gestured around the training room. "*All* of this should be secondary. You should be *resting*. Your friends are here—trying to enjoy New Years Eve with vampires—but they are *trying* to enjoy it."

Manny cocked a brow. "And they can enjoy it, but I like to be prepared."

Damiel almost cracked a smile, as she tried and failed to notch a stake.

"Like this," he said, grabbing a stake off the table and slowly loading it for her, and clicking everything into place.

"Why do you have one of these?" Manny asked, looking up at him.

Damiel shrugged. "I didn't. Eliza got it off of some hunter a few years back. She brought it."

"And the hunter is—" Manny hesitated, but she already knew the answer. "Right—so why *did* you come to Millfield?"

Changing the subject right now made sense to her. Especially, since she hadn't won an argument yet.

Damiel's hands dropped to his side. "My intervention was required due to vampiric law."

"*Vampiric law?*" Manny looked up at him. "There's a law that can make you come all the way to Ontario?"

Damiel nodded. "There are certain laws we have to follow—most of them are to keep humans from *noticing* us. My father never cared much for them, but I—" He hesitated, as if he were choosing his words carefully. "The King of the Eastern States requested I meet with him and asked me to come here to make sure things remained *civilized* with out friends up north. So, I used one of my degrees, got a job as a professor—and here I am."

Manny released the second shot. This one hit closer to the heart. *Not perfect,* but better.

"A little higher and more to your left," Damiel instructed.

Manny notched another stake. "And the coven?"

"They aren't following the laws of this jurisdiction, but they are vampiric citizens of New York."

Manny lowered the bow slightly. "And what happens to vampires that break them?"

His eyes darkened. "They get dealt with."

"But won't the king mind that you've brought more vampires into *his domain*?"

Damiel sighed. "You need to aim higher," he whispered into her ear.

Manny groaned. "Are you ignoring my question?"

He stepped behind her, and angled the crossbow. "No, I'm not. And no he won't. He doesn't care how I handle it. As long as certain parties are *executed*, and I help keep the peace."

Manny furrowed her brows. "So, *he* is making you do it?"

"The king sent for me," Damiel clarified, stepping away. "Before I arrived in Canada, we talked over the phone. He told me a coven was drawing attention to the area—I asked why it would concern my coven. And he kindly informed me that my younger brother, Vlane, was suspected of being involved—and you can understand even an *ex*-Prince of Darkness violating another kingdom's laws isn't a good look for any family. And that was that."

Manny drew the string back, and looked toward him. "Did you *know* your brother was working with them?"

"Not at first." Damiel admitted. "I guess I didn't want to believe it. But once I met you, started and read your mind now and then—"

"Still creepy, by the way," Manny muttered.

"—I *pieced it together.*" He said. "It sounded like he was involved, but ultimately it was you that led me to the truth, so *thank you.*"

"For which part exactly?"

"Well, I can say I'm going to enjoy letting the king know that he was bested by a human in finding the coven responsible."

Manny was so surprised to hear the compliment, she loosed the stake. It struck just shy of the target's center.

Fucking seriously.

"Better," Damiel complimented. "But we'll have to work on your form."

"Maybe we should work on your *communication skills* too," she shot back.

Damiel sighed and rolled his eyes.

Manny watched him walk toward the training equipment and fish out more stakes. She didn't know why she was picking fights with him. Maybe she wanted to. Maybe it was strange to think about vampires having laws. Actual, *structured laws*, like any human society.

She supposed it made sense. They had kings, courts, and *Dracula* —who decided what was allowed and what wasn't. But it was still strange to think about. It was one thing to read about vampires in fiction or theory, but hearing it straight from the source? That was downright strange to experience.

Even funnier? The Vampire King of the Eastern States—an ancient, all-powerful ruler of the night, lord of his domain—had a coven causing problems with his Northern allies right under his nose. And it wasn't one of his own kind who'd sniffed it out. Not a vampire from a legendary bloodline. Not Damiel, the dark prince, "Prince of Darkness," who he personally requested to handle it—with all his dashing good looks, intelligence, and centuries of experience—hadn't found them.

No.

It was her.

A human.

A graduate student at Millfield University.

A young woman, barely getting by on caffeine and spite, who stumbled onto a dangerous coven before any of his people did.

A *somewhat* mortal, now *familiar*, very sarcastic woman currently standing in said vampire Prince Damiel's basement, learning how to shoot a stake like she was training for the Undead Olympics.

It was almost enough to make her feel bad for them.

Almost—because honestly, that would definitely be more than a little embarrassing for a vampire.

Chapter 47
January 3rd

I*t's official—I'm carrying the world's most dramatic fetus.* Either that or their so-called vampire messiah was practicing its first attempted murder in vitro. Between the heartburn, the back pain, and the fact that she could smell blood from three blocks away—which she'd only discovered when she'd stepped outside one day to get some air, and found it both *disgusting* and weirdly *appetizing*—and she was starting to wish she'd thought of protection, or at least *her future* before bumping uglies with an immortal.

When she wasn't eating family blood marinated meat or training with Damiel, her vampire companion was forcing her to put her feet up —and relax. Which was easier said than done. After all, she was still unprepared and the full moon was right around the corner.

And of course, the minute they finally got some answers, she was too busy dry-heaving into a potted plant to enjoy the moment.

By some miracle, her would-be assassin, Alexandrov—who, after taking his sweet time—managed to capture one of the culprits last night, and after a night of torture, the vampire was ready to speak. Probably due to Damiel's promise of freedom, and his *benevolence* being the only chance at keeping his head attached.

Not that Manny could stomach most of it.

Because, as it turns out, one whiff of that vampire's blood—*ancient* blood that somehow smelled like decay with not quite the right metallic *tang* in the air—and bile instantly rose in her throat. She barely had time to mumble, *I'm fine* to Damiel, *before* bolting out of the room and emptying her breakfast into the nearest plant.

Pregnancy really is humbling.

By the time she'd staggered back to the makeshift interrogation room, she was lucky the low-level lackey wasn't already dead.

Damiel had them remove the furniture from this particular guest room. No bed, no dresser, no warm touches that might have once made it blend seamlessly into his beautiful home. All that remained were four empty walls, a single blacked out window shut tight, and a wooden floor scuffed from the hasty removal of furniture. They had brought up a tarp and a metal foldable chair out of the closet.

The Chrisanti lackey was bound to that chair, chains coiled around his arms and torso, his ankles locked to the chair's legs with reinforced iron cuffs. His pale skin was bruised, his shirt was torn, and if he could sweat, she was pretty sure he'd be drenched in it—and he still reeked—but the blood pooling at his feet was to blame for that.

Alexandrov crouched in front of him, twirling a dagger between his fingers like he was bored. "I'll ask one more time—*where are they?*"

The Lackey coughed. "And you'll let me go?"

His accent sounded the closest to televised version's of Dracula she'd ever seen.

"Of course, my friend, we've promised the prince." Icarus said, gesturing toward Damiel, who was leaning against the wall, staring straight ahead at them.

Manny didn't need to look at him to know he was lying. She straightened, and nearly leaned against Damiel, but instead leaned against the wall beside him.

"Better?" Damiel asked, looking down at her, brushing her hair out of her face.

Manny sighed. "I wish."

Manny looked back at the lackey, who still seemed hesitant. But after twelve hours of torture, anyone would be desperate to escape, and desperate people do stupid things.

"Warehouse. An old clothing factory near the docks," he muttered. "Chrisanti created tunnels underground in case he returned. That's where they hole up when they rest—I don't know who the humans are though. North is the oldest Warden. The other three are *younger*—about *her age,* I think. I don't know. It's been so long since I've been human."

Well, that covers one direction of the compass, Manny thought, thinking over the other three.

Callum grabbed the lackey by the hair, and made him look at him. "We want numbers, boy."

"Fifteen or *twenty* guards…" the Lackey's eyes landed on Manny —causing just a split-second of hesitation. "You aren't considering bringing the *seedbearer*, are you?"

Callum punched the Lackey in the gut. "That's no concern of yours," he snapped at him, spittle flying from his lips. "Mind your manners, she's right there. Now, how many are in your coven?"

"Twenty—if you don't count the newborns," the Lackey explained, his eyes fixed on Icarus' own. "The guards are mostly familiars. There's five vampires among them, but I'm sure you can tell the difference. Usually there's two on the ground floor. Three inside protecting the entrance to the tunnels. But you won't make it that far—"

Alexandrov grinned. "That so?"

"You're good fighters, but the Chrisantis are *smarter*, and brains beats brawn every time," the Lackey said. "Hunting laws be damned. We have to feed, the King of the Eastern States knows that."

"Not on *innocents*," Icarus snapped with disdain. "If you had any *decency* you would've abided by that."

"Decency?" The Lackey coughed a few times. "You act as if humanity is so decent—an apple falls and they can figure out gravity, but hundreds of thousands of corpses fall at humankind's hands through genocides and war and they can't figure out *empathy*."

Harsh, but she had to give credit where credit was due. Though not all humans *lacked* empathy, and it seemed worse to pigeonhole a whole species based on the actions of a few. Especially considering he too was once part of that species.

But he'd told them what they wanted to know. The coven's location, their movements, their numbers. He'd spilled it all, then insulted his captors and humankind, probably thinking it would buy him time.

But from the look on the men's faces—it wasn't. It had only annoyed them.

Then, before she could argue to keep him alive, before she could even think something to Damiel, or flinch, or even feign shock, they were on the Chrisanti Lackey:

Alexandrov's hands gripped the Lackey's head, while Callum held down his shoulders, and they began to pull. The skin stretched to inhuman proportions between them, as Alexandrov pulled, until the flesh tore, exposing the muscle underneath, blood rushed down his chest, and they kept pulling. Muscles became thinner and thinner, sounding out with little grotesque *snaps* as individual strands gave way —Icarus took a scalpel to his collarbone and dragged it downward. *Snap, snap, snap.* Organs tumbled onto the floor. *Snap, snap, snap.* Icarus separated them into bags. *Snap, snap.* Double-bagged them. *Snap, snap, pop.* Alexandrov dropped the lackey's head onto the tarp, the mouth opening and closing as if he were gasping in disbelief. As if he were wondering how this had happened to him. Why this was the consequence for his disloyalty to his coven. But she didn't need to read a vampire anatomy book to know it was nothing more than nerves still sending signals to his muscles—reflex actions—still running, still working.

Maybe that's why they're bagging him.

Because at the end of the day, vampires are still vampires. And to some degree, he was still alive. They would have to burn every part of him. Turn him into ash—because someone had to pay for breaking their laws.

* * *

Manny made her way downstairs, hoping to rejoin the others after watching the whole macabre ordeal. She was so focused on making her way downstairs, she nearly bumped into Grant.

Grant jumped in surprise. “You all right? Did they find out where they’re hiding?”

Manny stared at him blankly, and nodded. She wanted to answer with words, but she couldn’t. She considered hiding her stomach with her hand, but wasn’t sure there was a point, touching her bump would only draw attention to it.

Grant had his hands shoved in his coat pockets—he seemed to have just come inside. He had a distant look on his face, like he was already three steps ahead of the conversation they were about to have.

Grant sighed. “What’s on your mind?”

Manny hesitated. “I need to tell you something.”

She’d been meaning to tell him—but hadn’t figured out how. Grant’s head tilted slightly, but he didn’t speak. Just waited.

Manny swallowed. "I’m pregnant."

Grant blinked. “…*Okay*.”

“Okay?”

“Yeah,” Grant said, scratching the back of his head. “I mean, I don’t know what else to say. It was getting pretty hard to ignore.”

He gestured toward her medium-sized bump—but in vampire time she was about *14 weeks pregnant*, and with that information, meant the baby was about the size of a lemon, according to a mothers-to-be forum she’d found.

He didn’t say anything for a few seconds. Then, “It’s the professor’s, right? Since you’re his familiar.”

Manny nodded.

Grant hummed. “Right. And you’re…what? Expecting me to tell you how pissed Dean’s gonna be? Or were you worried I’d be pissed?”

“Well, I wouldn’t blame either of you…”

Grant’s jaw tightened, but he didn’t look at her like he hated her—that was nice. “I mean he might get pissed. I don’t know. I’m not—but that’s because I spent a lot of time *reading* about vampires and it’s not like we chose to be a part of all this. It just sort of *happened*.” His eyes search hers. “That doesn’t mean I think it was right for you to—I don’t know—can it even count as cheating since you’re his familiar?”

“Maybe, I don’t know…” Manny muttered, trailing off. “I wasn’t exactly planning on *this*.”

She cradled her stomach, though she hadn’t meant to. Maybe because part of her didn’t want the little one to think she was blaming them. If they could hear her.

“No one plans on shit like this,” he said, shaking his head. “Look… I’m not mad at you. I don’t know what I would’ve done if I were you.” He said lowering his voice. “But when it comes to telling him…that’s on you. I’m not doing it.”

Manny nodded again. “Yeah. I know.”

Grant sighed and scratched his chin.

“All right,” he said. “Well, any good news about the coven?”

Manny thought to bring the subject back up, but decided, she wasn’t sure she wanted to. Because it was her cross to bear at the end of the day. She was the one pregnant with a dhampir.

“Yeah, the coven—”

“Their whereabouts will be checked out by a scouting party before we go near that district,” Eliza said, interrupting them.

It was like she’d materialized out of thin air.

Where did she come from?

“Scouting party?” Manny asked, turning to her.

Eliza nodded. “It seems necessary. We need to make sure his intel is good.”

Wouldn’t it have—

“Wouldn’t it have been better to keep him alive for that?” Grant said, as he looked up to the second floor, where Icarus was carrying a bloody tarp, and Alexandrov was wiping his bloodied hands on a dish rag—saying exactly what Manny had been thinking.

Eliza shrugged. “He is dead now. If it’s a dead end, we’ll just grab another.”

The thought of another decapitation was enough to make her nauseous, and unfortunately—*hungry*. The hunger was definitely the growing dhampir inside her, but the nausea was all her.

"I'm—I'm hungry," Manny said, which received a bewildered look from Grant.

But he was happy to help her to the kitchen, where Victor and a few other vampires were waiting, and more than happy to share their meal. Shantelle was eating a steak at the other end of the table, talking to Icarus, who was swirling around a wine glass filled with blood.

They sat around for a while, waiting. Talking. Not talking. Pretending everything was normal, when absolutely none of it was. And as always, Manny's hunger was not in a cute '*I could go for a snack*' way, it was a blackhole that was sucking everything into it.

She grabbed a plate, loading onto it a feast of turkey, cranberry sauce, and whatever else was available, and focused on eating. The food was warm, but it didn't really taste like anything until Victor added the 'family blood,' and weeks ago she might've cared. Instead, she was just grateful.

The conversation around the table stayed at a low murmur—ranging from frustrated voices to a few terse arguments about what had just happened. She ignored it. She didn't want to argue about ethics. She was disturbed by the Chrisanti Lackey's decapitation. A few weeks ago, she would've screamed or thrown up.

And at the moment, she was more focused on the fact that her appetite had kicked in instead of her conscience when she thought about someone being decapitated. In fact, she licked her lips. Thankfully, she had cranberry sauce in the corners so it didn't look strange. But she wanted blood, and she was still a familiar, still at least partially human.

Fucking disturbing—you're fucking disturbed, Manny, she thought, chastising herself.

Damiel sat down beside her. "I did tell you, you didn't need to be present during it," he whispered in her ear. "If you'd been resting or—"

"No," Manny said.

"Manny," he said, brushing her hair out of her face. "You should be more concerned about yourself rather than *this*."

"I can't just forget about all the students they murdered, Damiel," she told him, shoveling food into her mouth and chewing so hard she bit her cheek. "*Dammit.*"

But Damiel ignored her. Instead, he looked toward the open archway that led to the hallway.

"What is it?" Manny asked.

"They're back," Damiel told her.

Everyone's heads turned toward the archway, all waiting. Then the scouting party walked in, coats damp with freshly fallen snow, and hair clinging to their faces.

"We found them," Klaus said, making eye contact with Damiel as he draped his coat on the back of a chair. "In the district—their numbers are just as he said. It's secluded but definitely not fortified—"

Eliza smirked. "Secluded, but not fortified?" she repeated grimly. "So, they are idiots?"

Manny glanced at her, Eliza sounded disappointed as if it wasn't enough of a fight for her. But the air in the room seemed to shift, as people exchanged looks, because now all they had to do was decide when they would act.

"Now," Alexandrov said. "We should attack *now*. Before they realize their man never made it back."

"That's reckless," someone countered. "If we wait until the full moon, we'll have time to hunt and be stronger."

"And they'll be ready for us," Callum snapped.

"That's reckless," Christopher countered. "If we wait until the full moon, we'll be stronger."

"And they'll be ready for us," another shot back.

Manny chewed her food slowly, listening. She wasn't sure which side of the argument she agreed with. On one hand, waiting meant they'd be at their best. On the other, waiting meant giving the coven time to prepare, or *worse*—to prevent them from stopping the ritual.

"Before is better," Adeline said in a Scottish accent. "Catch them off guard. They'll be resting up for the full moon—probably at their weakest."

"Or at their most paranoid," Grant countered. "We don't know what state they're in—you killed our only lead."

Alexandrov scoffed. "You question my methods, *human?*"

Manny leaned back, hands on her stomach, her hunger sated but her mind restless. She wished they'd stop arguing, but she could only think of one thing to say.

"They won't all be there before the full moon," Manny said.

Everyone turned to her.

"They'll gather *for* the full moon," Manny continued, keeping her voice steady. "But *before*—some of them might still be out, *preparing*. Others might make a run for it, *if* they suspect something, but they've been getting away with this blood ritual for decades. They wouldn't think for a second that anyone was onto them…"

Alexandrov sighed, then muttered something in latin. "So, we wait, then?"

"It's the only way to be sure we get as many as possible," Damiel said. "The only problem is—"

"The ritual itself," Manny said, finishing his sentence for him.

If they performed the ritual—if they finished it before they reached them—then none of this would matter. Isla would die. The casters would get away. The coven would be gone, or underground. And the cycle would keep repeating. But she couldn't let that happen. Not for Isla's sake—or for Tammy's—the coven needed to answer for their crimes, and they were so close.

Manny stared down at her hands, rubbing a thumb over her bump. She didn't want to wait. She wanted to get the bastards responsible. But they had to wait, otherwise they'd fail, and she wasn't failing one of her friends again.

After a long moment, Damiel sighed. "Then we wait."

One by one, the others nodded in agreement—because their prince had decided. For better or worse, everyone here was on board.

Chapter 48
Evening, January 14th

As the sun hovered low on the horizon, coloring the sky with streaks of orange and violet—just enough daylight left to make their approach safer, but not enough to risk exposure for those who couldn't safely walk in sunlight. Their convoy of cars rolled to a slow stop at the rendezvous point—a crumbling, abandoned building near the warehouse, once a cafe, now little more than skeletal remains.

The Duval Warehouse stood as a dark silhouette against the dying light. And for an old warehouse, it didn't look half-bad.

Alexandrov and Callum went inside first to clear the shuttered cafe. Any stragglers unlucky enough to be lingering inside were dealt with swiftly, and Manny avoided watching the whole ordeal. Then they dragged the bodies out of sight. Once everyone had slipped inside, they took down chairs from dusty tables; vampires stretched while the humans unpacked their weapons. A few vampires carried daggers forged from blessed silver, others were sharpening claws with nail files. Icarus was showing Shantelle how to throw the daggers. Grant and Wade were gearing up, and strapping stakes to their person.

Alexandrov was monitoring the warehouse's perimeter from a window with a pair of binoculars, as they all waited for nightfall.

This was it. No more waiting, no more debating. The full moon was closing in, and they were stopping the ritual *tonight.*

"Once we move, we won't be stopping," Damiel murmured behind her. "So, do me a favor and stay close to me."

Manny looked up at him, intending to argue, but noticed how soft his eyes were.

"I can't fight at my best if I'm worrying about you the whole time.

Manny nodded. "Okay."

"Don't forget to say your goodbyes to your friends—and *good luck* wouldn't be a bad idea either—we're all going to need it," Damiel told her.

Manny walked over to Grant first, her throat constricting, she wasn't sure she could find the right words. He was the first to believe her, or at least consider it was plausible there was something supernatural happening on campus.

"Hey, you ready?" Grant asked, smiling down at her.

Manny looked up at him and smiled. "Define ready?"

"Still breathing?" He offered.

"For now," Manny said, wiping away a stray tear.

Don't cry now.

"You two ready," she asked Grant and Wade.

Wade shrugged. "I've already tackled a vampire, and that was pretty stupid. I'm not sure where vampire hunting falls on the dipshit spectrum."

"Well, I'm sure we'll figure it out when we're charging into a nest of bloodthirsty vampires," Manny joked.

"*And* holy water," Wade said, swishing around a metal water bottle. Then he stared at it for a moment. "Do you think if I drink some that it'll fuck up a vampire if they bite me?"

"You could put it on your skin—it'll burn them a little," Manny answered.

Wade nodded, opened it and started applying some to his neck like cologne.

Grant rolled his eyes at him. "We'll be fine. I'll keep him out of trouble."

"And I'll be with Icarus," Shantelle said, sneaking up behind Manny and giving her a hug. "We'll get the jump on them—" she paused. "I didn't hurt the little one, right?"

Manny shook her head and hugged her back. "No, you didn't."

Wade laughed. "It's a vampire, you can't hurt it."

"*Dhampir*," Grant corrected, rolling his eyes, and then he said, "Be careful, okay? Especially you, Manny."

Manny nodded. "I will, and you three do the same, all right?"

She turned to Shantelle and pulled her into a brief but tight hug before stepping back. Manny did the same with Wade and Grant—holding onto Grant just a moment longer.

"Thank you for believing me," Manny whispered, shutting her eyes to hold back the tears.

Grant nodded. "Always, Manuela Bella."

Her heart lurched, and she opened her eyes just as the final sliver of daylight slipped away and dusk turned into night.

"*It's time*," Damiel's voice echoed through her mind, and she let Grant go.

She stepped away from her friends, and went to Damiel's side. Then they slipped out of the decaying building and into the open, closing the distance between them and the warehouse.

Manny stayed beside Damiel and she swore she could feel heat radiating off him.

The night air was filled with the smell of damp concrete and then that disgusting, *horrifyingly wrong*, metallic smell.

Then, a man lunged out of the shadows, moving fast—too fast—but Damiel was faster. He caught the attacker's arm mid-air, twisted, and threw him down with bone-shattering force. A snap echoed through the alley as the man dropped to the ground—his face marked with black veins—only a *familiar*. But more were coming. Two men rushed them, and just as quickly, Eliza and Callum rushed forward to meet them, matching each other blow for blow—

Vampires.

Manny stayed close to Damiel, while shooting stake after stake, at vampire after vampire—most times, only slowing them down long enough for someone else to kill them. Damiel faced the attacker's head-on, deflecting a clawed swipe with his forearm before driving a hand into the attacker's chest, and using his other hand to rip off the man's head. When a second tried to catch him from the side, Manny gasped, but he ducked low, ripping through his opponent's throat in one clean motion.

Manny barely had time to catch her breath as more of them funneled out. She raised her crossbow, fingers steady as she notched a wooden stake. One of the vampires—taller, broader than the others—was a few feet away from her barking orders, then he locked onto her, empty black eyes on her, and he snarled.

Manny fired.

The stake struck his shoulder.

Dammit. She adjusted and fired again. Another miss.

In seconds, he moved through the throng of bodies locked in battle, his hand closing around her throat before she could react. His eyes were pure black and angry. But he didn't squeeze. His nostrils flared. His grip tightening just slightly as a low, guttural growl rumbled from his chest. Recognition flickered in his expression—not of her, but of something else.

"*Interesting*," he murmured in a strange accent. "A *seedbearer*."

Before she could struggle, before she could even call out, others closed in. She caught a glimpse of Damiel, still fighting, still pushing back—

Damiel! Damiel!

She called out to him internally—he turned—locked eyes with her. Then they overwhelmed him, and he, too, was restrained.

"No," Manny managed to squeak out, and the vampire glared at her.

His grip loosened, and he said. "Him. *Prince Damiel?* Shall we join him? Hm?"

He lowered her to the ground, but quickly bound her hands behind her back. Manny managed to look over her shoulder just in time to see her friends in the chaos. They were still fighting—blessed steel slashing off fingers tipped with claws, the sickening metallic blood in the air. She could barely see them, but she saw enough. Shantelle swung her dagger again as Icarus supported her, protecting her left side, and sending a vampire flying in the opposite direction. But Manny couldn't find Grant or Wade anywhere.

No matter which way she turned her head, as she was steered further into the warehouse and the door shut behind them.

Manny twisted in her captor's grip, heart pounding. Damiel was ahead of her being dragged forward by two vampires who were bigger than him—but then he glanced back at her and—one second, he was stumbling forward. The next, he twisted, wrenching himself free. His elbow shot back, connecting with the first vampire's ribs, sending him staggering backward and gasping. Before the second could react, Damiel spun, his hands locking onto the vampire's head—then he snapped it to the side and pulled it off. As the warehouse, and the rest of the vampire's body landed in a heap.

Manny stared at him blankly. Then she struggled, twisting against her restraints—but her captor was too strong. Her bow was gone. She needed a weapon.

Her captor growled, trying to force her forward. She let him. Just enough.

Then she threw her head back forcefully and saw stars.

Pain flared at the base of her skull—like she'd reverse-headbutted a brick wall. And, in a way, she *had*.

The vampire hissed in pain, his grip loosening for a second—but that was all she needed.

She yanked herself free, tumbling forward, and sent a stake skittering across the floor.

Damn.

Manny looked to Damiel, but he was busy fighting the other vampire, so he couldn't free her. So, somehow, she needed to free her hands.

At least her skull was still *intact*. Though it felt like it had cracked open. But she was still in one piece, which was more than she could say for that other vampire's body.

Small victories.

She managed to maneuver her way over to the stake and grab ahold of it. Her hands were still bound, the rough rope digging into her wrists, but she had a stake—and stakes were *multifunctional*.

Manny twisted her wrists, angling the sharp tip against the rope. It wasn't ideal, but she sawed as best she could, the fibers fraying with each pass. Her arms ached, her heartbeat thundered in her ears, but she *refused* to be helpless.

A few more tugs—then *snap*.

But she barely had time to celebrate, as she noticed something move in her periphery. She spun just as a vampire lunged, fangs bared, eyes glowing with hunger.

And for once, she didn't think. She *reacted*.

She lifted the stake and *drove it forward.*

It wasn't clean. Her ex-captor twisted at the last second, and instead of the heart, she got caught in between his ribs. He snarled, grabbing her wrist, trying to wrestle the weapon away. But by some inhuman amount of adrenaline, she wrenched the stake free of his hand, using its momentum, and plunged it in again—and she didn't miss.

He stiffened, a ragged gasp leaving his lips—then his body slumped, growing heavier by the second and she let go of the stake.

She shoved him off, breathing hard. Damiel was already moving toward her, eyes scanning the dark hallway ahead.

Damiel shot her a look, part exasperation, part something else—something bordering on amusement. "Did you just *headbutt* a vampire?"

"I panicked," she muttered, rubbing her head. "And my hands were kinda busy."

She stared down at her fingers.

No blood—that's good.

She hadn't dented her skull either.

Damiel chuckled. "You could've given yourself a concussion."

"I could've died." She gestured toward her now-deceased captor, before wincing again. Even thinking hurt. "So, you know. *Priorities*."

Damiel shook his head, smiling down at her. "You're ridiculous."

He offered her a hand, and she took it. He helped her up, and they began their walk through the corridors, which eventually had some halfway decent lighting. She could see some things around her, but not *everything*.

They moved quickly, navigating the warehouse.

Every now and then, they would hear footsteps or voices, and stop. But then, they trailed two familiars to a large, faded map bolted to the wall, likely a remnant from when it was an actual functioning warehouse.

"Well, that'll help," Manny said, pointing to the map.

Damiel stepped closer, eyes scanning the layout, fingers tracing possible routes. "It looks like there's large room further in. That's probably where they're gathering."

"Then why aren't we moving," Manny said.

"Because I was memorizing the map," Damiel told her, gesturing for her to follow him.

Manny rolled her eyes—of all the times she had to forget her phone. She would've loved to snap a picture of it. She followed Damiel down hallway after hallway, winding deeper into the warehouse. The further they went, the more worried she became that they wouldn't find it in time.

Then there were louder voices.

Damiel pulled her toward the source, and slowly they made their way forward. Peering around the corner, there were a handful of grotesquely veined familiars. Half-life humans dressed in simple clothes, moving quickly, preparing for something. And where they were heading—

Manny's eyes widened. To a room—*the* room. Damiel's instincts had been correct, its entrance was barely cracked open, but a strange blue light was trickling out of the door. And the familiars were—putting on robes. Black robes.

Culty, she thought.

Manny glanced at Damiel as he thought the same thing she did—a *disguise*.

A familiar, a woman separated from the group stayed behind, looking around, as if by some instinct—probably *her* scent. But before the poor soul even realized she was being watched, she was already being yanked into the shadows.

Manny winced. "A bit dramatic don't you think."

Damiel shrugged, taking the robes from the familiar's arms. "We need disguises. She had two."

Manny sighed, taking the other robe from him. "You could've at least given her a *chance*—like *glamoured* her or something."

Damiel rolled his eyes, slipping the robe over his shoulders. "I'm not going to take risks with familiars—on the off chance there's an older vampire here than me."

Manny huffed, but didn't argue. She knew he was right. Instead, she pulled the robe on, shaking out the fabric, trying to ignore the eerie *wrongness* of wearing something that had likely seen its fair share of horrors and blood rituals.

Still, it was a good plan. Now they just had to *play along.*

Manny noticed Damiel kneel down beside the familiar, and for once, she didn't have to question what he was thinking.

He pulled a blessed knife that was strapped to his ankle and dragged it across the dead woman's throat. A fresh, dark line opened, blood welling at the seam.

Manny swallowed hard. "I would like to say—"

Damiel shook his head, dipping his fingers into the fresh blood. "Tilt your head."

She scowled. "You could at least *ask* first."

But she obeyed, tilting her head as he smeared the blood on her skin—along her pulse point, her collarbone. It was warm, thick, the scent strong enough to make her stomach turn—in discomfort and *hunger*. Nausea whirred in her stomach.

"There," Damiel said, stepping back. "They'll be less likely to notice you now. You'll smell like them, but maybe a little off—*dirty*, maybe a little *rancid*."

Manny wanted to wipe it off her neck, but went against her instincts. "*Fantastic*. Thank you so much," she said sarcastically.

"You're welcome—and hold onto this. You might need it," Damiel grinned, smugly, putting the blessed knife in an internal breast pocket on the robe. Then he said, "Shall we?"

They stepped out of the room, trailing after the remaining living familiars. No one questioned them—just two more robed figures in a long procession.

The large chamber they stepped into was different from the rest of the warehouse. While most of the building was abandoned, filled with rusted machinery and dust-covered crates, this space had been *transformed.*

No debris, just smooth concrete. At the center, a massive stone altar stood like a dark monolith, its surface engraved with strange, twisting symbols and sigils. The markings seemed to pulse faintly under the dim lighting.

Two bodies lay on top it.

One—*Isla*. The other—an african american male she didn't recognize in a letterman jacket.

Tall iron candelabras lined the edges of the room between cloaked figures. Beneath the altar, there were rust-colored stains. She wondered what made these last two sacrifices so sacred—why keep them pure and the rest be killed *anywhere?*

When Manny looked up, she noticed there was a glass ceiling—wide and unbroken, stretching above them. The full moon loomed overhead, impossibly large, its silver light spilling into the chamber and bathing everything in an eerie glow.

And then—four people standing near the altar in a glowing blue circle.

Dr. Alan Shepherd, a professor she'd respected throughout her undergrad, who'd just been appointed as associate dean. He'd been a good man. But now, standing near the altar, his presence left her with nothing but resentment. Had he chosen Tammy as a sacrifice? He looked relieved under the moonlight, and the way he looked at the ritual unfolding before him was unnerving. *Reverent.*

And the students beside him?

South, Julian Sinclair. East, Ophelia Mercer—and West, Elizabeth Astor. Fucking seriously?

Julian's family practically *owned* half of Millfield's historic buildings, passed down through generations of old-money aristocrats who had always had their hands in things—his family wasn't on hard times. Ophelia was in her class—she had called her *Manny Manslaughter*, she was Isla's sorority sister—and the daughter of a media mogul, raised in a world where influence was currency and secrets were more valuable than gold. Elizabeth Astor was from California, the daughter of a CEO whose business's stock had recently seen a significant downturn—something she clearly aimed to *change*.

What the hell.

She didn't hate nepo babies. Nepotism was definitely a cryptid of the creative world, a mythical beast they all knew existed but only a few dare to say its name lest they summon the unholy terror. After all, it crops up damn near everywhere. It's not the kids' fault, of course—they were funneled into a life of pre-approved talent. Like, good for nepotism and all its children? Bad for literally everyone else fighting tooth and nail for scraps, trying to build a career from scratch, but that wasn't her problem with nepotism. Sure, they all start somewhere, but if someone is born at the finish line, maybe they call it a race.

More unfortunately, Dr. Shepherd—was an outlier on the compass. No nepotism. He had come from nothing, desperate for a taste of the power that people like Julian, Ophelia, and Elizabeth took for granted. And what better way to secure his place among them than by proving his worth in a ritual meant to maintain that power.

Manny kept her breathing steady, her mind racing as she took stock of her options. She couldn't take on a vampire in hand-to-hand combat—and *win*. She'd gotten lucky with her impromptu head butting maneuver. And though her pregnancy had saved her before, she wasn't about to bet on it saving her *again*.

She had no bow. One stake strapped to her person. And she still had her mind.

Manny looked around—the room was huge. The moon wasn't at its highest yet—the altar was a focal point. The students were *human*.

They just needed a distraction.

A way to get close enough to free Isla and the unconscious student beside her.

Slowly, Dr. Shepherd stepped away as a man moved in front of him, cane tapping as he walked. He was tall, draped in flowing black robes, his pale skin almost luminescent under the moonlight—Alistair Chrisanti. Beside him, *Vlane*, his expression unreadable as Alistair patted Vlane's shoulder.

Alistair smirked. "It's good to see you all," he started, surveying the crowded room. "I know you all must be hungry."

The vampires around them roared.

"Tonight we will feast," Alistair said, his voice carrying over the crowd. "My dearest newborns. Your hunger is still fresh, still *raw*, still aching to be satisfied…I remember my own turning. That unbearable thirst—the way it consumed me. How it burned through every thought, every impulse. No longer will you be famished. You stand on the brink of greatness—of *immortality*—but first, you must embrace it."

The newborns stirred now, eyes darting between each other, their hunger so palpable Manny could feel it pressing against her like a living thing.

"Don't worry," Damiel's words slithered into her mind. *"Newborns are too distracted by their hunger to focus on any one target without assistance."*

How do you know? She shot back, cradling her stomach.

"Because I remember," Damiel answered. *"Because I was like them once. Newly turned. Mindless with thirst. It's the only thing that matters to them—and you aren't their target. That's why the other familiars are safe. And the more mature vampires are in red robes guarding them."*

Manny looked around, noticing the familiars that lined the walls, and their red robed companions.

"If your hunger is not satiated after these little appetizers then we have a buffet surrounding you," Alistair said, gesturing toward the familiars in offering.

Some of the newborns stirred, shifting them back and forth in waves. Instinctively. Hungrily. She forced herself to allow them to move her, forcing herself to breathe normally, as her mind raced.

Then Alistair took a slow breath, as if savoring the atmosphere, then opened his mouth to speak again—but he didn't.

Alistair's gaze swept the room, as his lips curled slightly into a sneer.

"Someone here," he murmured, pausing for a moment, "*does not belong.*"

Manny's heartbeat drummed in her ears.

Shit. Fuck. Fuck.

A sudden crash echoed through the warehouse—something heavy, maybe a door, being torn off its hinges. Then came the unmistakable sounds of a fight having broken out somewhere outside the door. Snarls, cries, a distant *thud* of bodies colliding.

"Deal with that," Alistair ordered, and with the wave of his hand, several vampires left the walls.

And that makes how many newborn versus mature vampires?

Damiel didn't answer.

Please say something.

Manny swallowed hard. She felt bad about what they might have to do—she couldn't guarantee whether or not these newborns had chosen this life, or if they hadn't. But they had no choice. Not when Isla was still unconscious on that slab. Especially if they wanted to stop the Chrisantis from performing it *permanently*.

Isla stirred, and even at this distance, Manny heard her let out a low groan as she shifted against her restraints. Frightened. Helpless—such a small movement, but it was enough.

Enough for the newborns to notice.

Hungry eyes fixed on her as she shifted, and a tremor passed through her body—

Oh no, she's going to—

Isla screamed.

The male sacrifice followed suit. A ragged, terrified wail tore from his throat, echoing off the room's walls. It was high-pitched, desperate —*primal*.

It was like a spark hitting dry kindling. The newborns surged forward.

Manny grabbed onto Damiel, and he held onto her wrist, as the newborns pushed them forward, lips peeling away from their fangs. They started hissing.

"We need to move to the front—now," Damiel told her inside her head.

They moved. Damiel led the way as they slipped through the gaps forming between the frenzied newborns. By the time they reached the front, Alistair was already lifting a hand, attempting to regain control.

But the newborns weren't listening.

"Insolent little brats," Alistair mumbled. "Silence!"

Manny barely had time to react before Damiel's voice echoed in her head. *"Take this."*

He pressed something into her palm—cold, metal, a small glass vial.

She looked down at it. *What is it?*

"Holy oil—I need you to pour it as we walk," Damiel explained. *"It will give us better odds. We'll set it on fire and keep the newborns at bay, then we'll only have to deal with two vampires instead of ten."*

One problem. Both of those men are vampires—and I'm a familiar.

Manny's breath hitched as she looked around the swarming newborns. They were practically vibrating with hunger, drawn forward like moths to a flame.

She internally shook herself.

Okay, fine.

Instead, she held onto his hand and moved. Manny opened the vial, and began to pour a thin, glistening line of oil along the concrete floor. Watching it as they weaved between newborns—the smell was *disgusting*. Worse than vampire's blood. She shook her head at herself, forcing herself to ignore it.

They moved quickly, and Manny silently thanked God that the

newborns were too preoccupied to notice them, their focus shifting between Alistair and the sacrifices, their bodies trembling with anticipation. Manny watched the trail of holy oil.

Do we have to go all the way around?

"My father has the other side covered," Damiel told her. *"He'll close it off."*

Thank God.

Victor was somewhere in the crowd, working to close the perimeter on the other side, which meant they'd meet in the middle. Which meant they would be three against two. She liked those odds.

The male student wouldn't stop screaming, and his panic was sending fresh waves of excitement rippling through the newborns.

Almost there.

She poured the last of the oil in place and stepped back, gripping Damiel's sleeve as she whispered, "Done."

His eyes flicked toward her, then down at the line.

But then Manny had the most disquieting sensation that she was being watched—and she turned in the direction of the source, and her eyes met Vlane's.

Vlane snarled. "There!"

The word reverberated throughout the crowd—none of the newborns reacted, but Damiel certainly did. He pushed a zippo lighter into her hand.

"Light it," Damiel told her, while glaring at his brother.

Manny opened the zippo lighter just as Vlane shot toward them. Damiel grabbed him, and then were locked together, throwing punches, brother hitting brother.

And she flicked the lighter. But it didn't light.

Flicked again. Nothing.

Dammit. Come on.

She flicked it again, getting knocked backward by another surge. It clattered to the ground, and she got ahold of it before it could be kicked away.

Come on, please. She flicked the lighter again, and it lit.

Manny touched it to the oil and suddenly—it grew, hungry and wild.

The holy oil caught on fire, racing around the incomplete perimeter like a serpent uncoiling, spitting sparks into the air. Screams followed —as the newborns caught in the blaze twisted and thrashed, their bodies igniting.

She looked up just as Victor twisted away from the creeping flames just in time, barely avoiding a newborn's outstretched hand, reaching for help.

Manny saw Alistair's eyes narrow as he hissed, "Victor—you bastard! What have you done?"

Manny covered her nose. The stench of their burning flesh made her eyes water.

Vlane tackled Damiel, and they skidded across the floor, toward the flames, narrowly missing them. Damiel got up, pulled Vlane, and leaned his brother against the wall of fire and he wailed. Vlane headbutted him to free himself. Then they hit each other again, and again, and again.

"They're here to stop the ritual!" Vlane shouted between strikes.

Manny barely had a moment to jump over the flames, as more newborns were caught in the fire's path. Some shrieked and ran, their movements clumsy in their frenzy, while others turned on each other in blind panic. The heat pressed against Manny's skin, sweat beading on her forehead.

"No! My children!" Alistair shouted, glaring at Victor. "Victor, you will pay!"

Alistair's eyes darkened to pure black as he growled. He launched himself at Victor, his coat billowing behind him, the firelight catching on the sharp planes of his face. There was no hesitation. No thought—just unbridled rage.

His claws were long and curved—ready to tear through flesh and aimed at Victor's throat. His fangs bared. The impact sent both of them crashing into the concrete floor, rolling through the debris of burning bodies. Ash flew as Victor caught Chrisanti's wrist mid-swipe, stopping the strike just inches from his jugular. Perhaps they locked eyes for a split second, but then Chrisanti twisted, wrenching himself free, and drove his knee into Victor's ribs with a sickening *crack*.

Victor was seething—and Manny was frozen in fear.

And then Dr. Shepherd started chanting—in latin.

Oh, God it's starting.

Her hands clenched around what little she had left: a single stake that had been trapped to her person and a small bottle of holy water. Then there was the blessed knife in her pocket—but would that be enough? It wasn't exactly an ideal arsenal for fighting vampires. She had two options:

1. Stop Alistair from attacking Victor
2. Stop Vlane from killing Damiel, the very immortal, very attractive *vampire father* of her unborn child.

The decision was easy enough. But then—

Wait. No—I'm asking the wrong question, she thought, and looked around.

The better question was: Who was capable of casting the spell?

The first rule of magic was *all magic followed rules*—and of course, it always came with a price. But those rules were often built on symbolism, and if there's one thing she knew, it was *symbolism*. That was middle school English—and if this spell was built on requiring the points of a compass, then *North* was the key—it's the most important point on a compass. The primary reference point for every other direction.

Manny's mind raced, trying to remember something from the ritual, something from Shantelle's notes:

Casters are only a vessel, but can't be of mortal flesh. Power is granted by the dominant entity that acts as a vessel for this power. Their body may be witch, may be vampire, may be were-wolf—but all sacrifices must be human.

She stood there, blinking in disbelief. The words rearranged themselves in her head, fitting together plain as day, until the final piece of a puzzle clicked.

They didn't have to be a vampire. The spell had to be cast by a dominant member—but needed an occult entity's power.

Then why the hell was Dr. Shepherd still chanting?

Her breath caught in her throat. The entire fight—the chaos, the attacks—she had assumed Alistair or Vlane was necessary for the ritual to succeed.

But what if—what if Dr. Shepherd doesn't need either of them to finish the spell. What if...

A memory flashed into her mind, over the chaos around her—the scorching flames behind her, the newborn's screams, the vampires fighting, the chanting—inside her head, it was quiet.

There was only a *photograph.* A little faded at the edges, but clear enough. An image of a vampire named Elias Duval III with sharp features, his wife at his side, laughing, her arms wrapped around a basket overflowing with strawberries. In 1968, at the Millfield Strawberry Festival, an African American woman won, her name recorded *incorrectly* on the award plaque—using her maiden name. She had been the wife of Elias Duval III. And in that same image, with her overflowing strawberry basket, she had been pregnant.

Her name was improperly recorded as *Marabeth Shepherd.*

A piece of history that had been staring her in the face the entire time that she'd written off. This building had never left the family's ownership—Elias Duval constantly returned here. But what if he died? Wouldn't it go to their child, their very *dhampir* child?

North is the most important point on the compass.

Alan Shepherd was North. His name wasn't a coincidence—it was his mother's surname. He wasn't just part of the compass. He was the *caster.*

It didn't matter if he was a full vampire or a dhampir—both were occult entities. Everything about him made sense now—he hadn't aged, the way he had sent her away when she had come to him for answers about how alike Tammy and Yasmine Brewer's deaths were.

He always knew the truth, because he was a part of it—all of it, Manny stared at him. *He was responsible.*

And she didn't give a damn what coven he was a part of—he'd killed Tammy and was trying to kill Isla now. But in order to finish the ritual, he'd have to stay in the circle, that was Witchcraft 101.

Manny's grip tightened on her stake, her pulse pounding.

He can't finish the spell if he leaves the circle.

Her body moved before she could second-guess herself. She sprinted forward, ignoring the horrified screams behind her, sweat beading on her forehead as her feet carried her over the blood-slicked floor.

Chrisanti's arm nearly snatched her mid-stride, but she ducked low, rolling past his reach, feet skidding as she sprang back up.

And then she jumped and landed on Dr. Shepherd's back, her arm locking around his throat as he snarled in surprise. He twisted, but she clung tighter, her free hand raising the stake.

He turned his head and his eyes locked on to hers.

She gulped—they were pure black, decrying something *deeply* wrong. His lips peeled back in a feral hiss, fangs bared, sounding more *beast* than man.

He bucked, exhibiting animalistic strength trying to throw her off *again*, but she held on. But she couldn't angle her stake right—his chest was massive, but she couldn't keep her both out of his reach and drive the stake through his heart from her current position.

So, she sank it into whatever she could reach.

The sharp tip plunged into his shoulder first.

A furious snarl ripped from him. "You little bitch!"

He twisted again, and her grip slipped—but she regained it and stabbed into his side. A shallow wound between his ribs.

Not deep enough. Not *killing* blows. But she had *hurt him.*

Shepherd's muscles coiled like a predator ready to strike. His hands shot up, gripping her arms in a vice, and before she could drive the stake in again, he threw her.

For a time, she was weightless, flying backward toward the fire—humid wind rushing by her, pushing her curls, blinding her even, everything gone, then the ground came up to meet her. She slammed into the blood-slick concrete. Heat roaring at her back, flames licking closer. A few inches more, and she would've been part of the inferno.

Pain bloomed in her side, and she gasped.

Dammit.

Everything hurt.

Shit, I better not have broken anything.

She gritted her teeth and forced herself up—her ribs screaming at her in protest as she did so, and she wasn't sure why she even bothered. She just knew she couldn't stay down.

Manny glared at Dr. Shepherd, her eyes burning. "*Why*?" She demanded, her voice raw. "Why did you kill Tammy?"

Dr. Shepherd arched a brow. He straightened, rolling his injured shoulder, his black eyes reflecting the firelight. He didn't look remotely remorseful. He looked *irritated.* Annoyed as though they were back in class, and she was asking something *obvious*.

Then he sighed and said, "I needed an effective first offering."

Her heart lurched. *An offering.*

His expression didn't waver. "She had *limitless potential.* A mind that could have reshaped the world. That kind of brilliance? It's rare. A perfect sacrifice to sustain power for the next generation—I couldn't pass up such an opportunity."

Tears blurred her vision. Tammy was brilliant, kind, full of life—she was her best friend—but to Alan Shepherd, or *Alan Duval*, Tammy was nothing more than a resource to be spent.

"My father started this ritual to make sure the right people *prospered.* Tamara's life was put to better use—human's constantly waste their potential—so why not repurpose them? My mother knew her greatest act as a familiar was to bring me into this life. To continue on my father's legacy."

"Why here? You could have gone *anywhere* to harvest sacrifices?" Manny asked desperately. She didn't know if she was buying herself time or trying to run out the clock—outlast the full moon. "You could have set up your little scheme anywhere—why here?"

"No, this is my placement—*my burden.*" Shepherd laughed bitterly.

"We switch out every once and while. My siblings and I collect offerings from everywhere, HBCUs and Ivies alike, finding talent, searching for *potential*. After all, excelling anywhere too long can put a target on your back. We rotate placements every few decades. Our ritual allows others to prosper—it was merely Millfield's time for collection. This year was yet another great request."

Manny was shaking. *It was just their time for collection.*

And he'd led them like lambs to the slaughter. They were being harvested. He'd taken the exceptional. The exemplary. He had praised Tammy while setting the stage for her sacrifice. Let her climb, let her reach, just high enough that when he cut her down, he could say it was for something bigger. That it had meant something.

He didn't want to collect her like the Chrisantis collected humans —she wasn't worth anything to him *alive*.

Manny got to her feet, hoping her adrenaline would overtake the pain, and straightened. There was a small twinge in her back, but she forced herself to ignore it. She stared at Dr. Shepherd.

He rolled his head. He wasn't gasping, wasn't bleeding like he should have been. He just stood there, fully composed, and then he laughed.

"Energy transference, Manny," Shepherd said, cracking his knuckles. "Did you not learn about it in Moreau's class?"

Manny noticed the student's wincing—their bodies trembling, but not seeming capable of falling over.

She could use context clues well enough to know that he'd passed it off. Taken his pain and shifted it onto them. Their hands clenched or teeth gritted as the pain of wounds they didn't have took hold.

Sick twisted bastard.

Manny wiped the tears from her eyes.

They were suffering for *him*.

Something inside her snapped. He was standing there like some untouchable god, dealing in deaths like he was the grim reaper himself.

"Come on, Manny, *pay attention*," Shepherd said, sounding bored.

Manny clenched her fists. She wanted to drive her stake into his heart, but she needed him to leave the circle. She just had to figure out how.

"What's wrong?" Manny shouted at him. "Can't handle a little pain?"

He scoffed. "Is that your feeble little attempt to provoke me?"

"No—I was wondering why you've been hiding behind the Chrisantis?" Manny asked him. "I mean it has to be fear, right?"

If she was lucky, he'd feel insulted.

"*Hiding?*" He repeated, taking the bait. "I offered to give their newborns a taste of blood charged with ritual resonance—to push them out of the newborn stage. A win, win for both of us." He said with a shrug. "They'll not have to deal with their feverish adolescence and Chrisanti doesn't have to worry about any laws being broken. It's so important to maintain control of one's coven in this country. I should know—and you should learn given the *devilish* bun in your oven."

Dammit.

Manny wiped the blood from her lips and straightened. She took a step closer to the circle. "So, you're supposed to be what their *business partner*." She forced out a laugh, shaking her head. "No wonder you're hiding. After all, if someone like me—*a human*—can find you. Then why wouldn't you?" She shrugged. "You clearly can't manage on your own. I mean, what kind of self-respecting vampire shoves his pain off onto a bunch of *students*? You're pathetic. *Weak*."

His expression didn't shift, but she caught the flicker of something in his dark eyes. *Annoyance*, maybe?

Good.

She was just going to have to push harder. "You know, for someone who built this whole performance around *power*, what happens when *your coven* realizes you're not as powerful as you *pretend* to be?" She tilted her head, feigning curiosity. "Will they still follow you then? Or do you think they'll overthrow you—tear you apart limb by limb, burn you, and dance on your ashes?"

His jaw tensed.

Bingo—and she knew exactly what to say. "You needed *her*—needed Tammy's *limitless potential*—because you don't have any of your own. You're just a coward hiding behind other, more powerful vampires, stealing power because you could never *earn it*."

His expression cracked; his lips curled into a snarl. He moved—stepped out of the circle—and the magic pulsated, rippling through the circle's lines, flashing blue. The magic pulsating but wavering without him.

"All right, Manuela," snarled Shepherd, and Manny could see his fangs extend. "I don't give a damn that you're a seedbearer. I'm going to tear you apart."

Manny didn't even have time to turn around before he grabbed hold of the front of her robe and slammed her back onto the floor. She gasped, as the air left her lungs, stake skittering just out of reach. She tried to reach for it, but he grabbed her ankle, and pulled her back.

"You and your cursed seed!" Shepherd hissed, kicking her abdomen.

Manny tried to pull away, but Shepherd climbed on top of her. He extended his claws, and raised one hand.

"Say hello to Tammy for me," Shepherd said with a laugh, giving her the second she needed to find the wound in between his ribs, and she dug two fingers into the wound and twisted it.

Blood—cold, and reddish black—oozed from the stake wound in its chest, where her trembling finger remained jammed. Every instinct inside her was telling her to do something to get away from him, but she couldn't. Pain radiated up her arm like fire licking at her nerves—his pain.

No—I'm not taking this on, asshole.

She dug another finger inside even deeper, and he let out a guttural roar. Sure, he could pass on lingering wounds, or fresh injuries could be pushed onto another person. But ongoing pain, pain actively inflicted in this moment? That was going to be harder for him to shift onto *anyone else.*

If she even let up for a moment, he'd kill her.

The knife. I need the knife.

She had seconds, if any time at all. The knife was in her breast pocket, pressed against her ribs beneath the heavy robe.

But with one hand buried in his ribs and the free one on the same side as the knife—reaching for it felt impossible. Unless, she managed to get out from under him.Which was a longshot, but she had to *try*—and she had an idea. An awfully, stupid idea.

God help me.

Manny shifted her weight, slamming her knee into his abdomen. He buckled, he was still angry—but that was good, anger was disorienting, anger would take time to control, and all she needed was a few well-executed seconds. She kept her fingers in the wound, two fingers inside, as he lashed out at her, his claws grazing her shoulder, as her other hand found the knife and she drove it upward.

The blade slid through his ribs and she stared at it in disbelief—Shepherd's eyes whitened, his brows knitted together as he stared at the knife in his chest, as though the concept of death or dying had never occurred to him. Thick, reddish black blood erupted from the wound, splattering her hands and face, the warmth of it almost scalding.

"That's for Tammy—and everyone else you bled dry," she spat, her voice raw but steady.

Shepherd let out a strangled gasp, an animalistic, high teakettle like whine. Blood bubbling from his lips as sluggish rivulets wetted her hands, life draining from him with every passing second. Then slowly what little light in his eyes that remained dimmed like a dying ember.

He crumpled, and she shoved him off, his corpse collapsing into a heap on the cold concrete. His body convulsed once, twice, then fell still, the pool of blood beneath him spreading thick and viscous, staining the ritual circle, and at the same time, the three students released a unified sigh. Their pain was over—and so was the ritual.

Manny sat up, staring at Shepherd's corpse, her chest heaving.

She could hardly believe what she was seeing.

He was dead. She'd won. It was over.

that with one hand buried in his ribs and the other [illegible] as the knife—reaching for it would be impossible. Unless she managed to get out from under him. Which was a longshot. But she had to try and she had no idea. An awfully stupid idea.

God help me.

Monty shifted her weight, slamming her knee into his [illegible]. He bucked; he was still angry—but that was good; anger was distracting. Anger would take time to control, and all she needed was a few wasted seconds. She [illegible] her fingers [illegible] and two fingers [illegible], as he [illegible] her shoulder [illegible] and [illegible] the knife and she drove it [illegible].

The blade slid through [illegible] ribs [illegible] through. Shepherd [illegible], his breath [illegible] the same [illegible] thought the concept of [illegible] living [illegible] never occurred to him. Thick, reddish-black blood [illegible] from the wound, splattering that [illegible] and face, the [illegible] of it [illegible] swelling.

[illegible] somehow [illegible].

[illegible] gray [illegible] [illegible] hands [illegible] from him with every passing second. The [illegible] that [illegible] that [illegible] him.

The [illegible] and she [illegible] him off, his corpse [illegible] in the cold [illegible]. His body convulsed once, twice, then fell still, the pool of blood [illegible] him [illegible] and [illegible] the [illegible] that same [illegible] students [illegible] was [illegible] the [illegible].

[illegible] Shepherd's corpse [illegible].

She could barely believe what she was seeing.

He was dead. [illegible] it was over.

Chapter 49
January 14th

Manny heard footsteps, but didn't look. She continued to stare at the corpse because part of her worried, if she looked away, he would get up. Or she would wake up, and it would all have been a dream.

But then someone moved into her field of vision, crouched down in front of her—Damiel. He grabbed her chin, his other hand streaked with the same dark ichor as hers, but his expression was soft as he stared at her. "You're shaking," he murmured, his voice low and steady.

"I'm fine," Manny rasped, though her hands were trembling. She stared passed him, over his shoulder, at the corpse.

He helped her to her feet, but she didn't take her eyes off the corpse. "Victor went to get the others to help with the body. They'll find a way to handle the fire."

Manny managed to nod.

She wanted to breathe normally, to think, but her body refused. Somewhere in the flames, was Tammy's laughter, their silliest conversations and their warmest memories. She stood there, remembering it all.

Damiel moved her away from the corpse, and she let him.

"Come here," Damiel said, pulling her into his chest.

She hadn't expected it, but the solidity of his frame cut through her shock. Slowly, her muscles relaxed, and she gripped the front of his shirt, breathing him in.

His chin rested on the top of her head, his voice low. "It's okay."

"I'm not sure I believe you," she managed to say. "The baby—"

"Is fine. You're both safe—I was monitoring your heartbeats."

Manny looked up at Damiel. "How?" She asked, exhaling a shaky breath.

"Whenever there's a fight that's how I manage," he explained, calmly. "I want to know who is living, and if we've lost anyone…both yours and theirs are still there. Beating—I think they might've been scared."

She heard more footsteps, and nuzzled his arm, letting one eye see the corpse while he held her. He stroked her hair—she was still shaking, warm tears rushing down her cheeks.

She wiped them away again, she could make out Alexandrov and Icarus speaking to Victor and gesturing toward the corpse, but somehow, she couldn't hear them. They were only a few feet away from them, but it was as if her mind refused to listen to them. She could assume it was five vampires debating how to best separate a body.

"How did you know they were scared?" Manny asked, turning her attention back to the conversation she *could* hear.

"What?" Damiel asked.

She watched as Icarus grabbed Shepherd's arm, twisted, and pulled it from its socket. A *crunch*, then the severed limb dangled, its torn flesh, dripping—*that* she could hear. Victor took hold of his leg, claws sinking deep into muscle and with a single, brutal yank, tore the limb free with a wet, tearing sound that made her stomach lurch.

"How did you know they were scared?" She repeated.

Damiel hummed. "Hmm…I think they called out to me," he explained to her. "I knew it wasn't your voice, but it was coming from your direction."

"When?" Manny asked him, trying to distract herself from what her right eye was seeing.

Piece by piece, they were dismantling him—Icarus, Victor, Eliza, Alexandrov, Callum—their movements deliberate and unrelenting. She could faintly hear the macabre symphony of *crunching* bones, *snapping* muscles, and an occasional wet *squelch* of flesh being ripped apart. But not their voices—that was only Damiel.

"After I tore off my brother's head—" Damiel hesitated, pausing as if remembering the moment. "I believe North had kicked you…and it frightened them."

"Yeah, that makes sense."

She could understand how that might scare a child, something suddenly disturbing their resting place, but it was strange to think that the fetus inside her could call out to *anything*—especially *Damiel.* How much more advanced were dhampir children? Was she ready for that responsibility?

Bile rose in Manny's throat. Eliza held up Shepherd's severed head. His lifeless eyes stared back, and without hesitation, she tossed the head in the fire Callum had started. The flames hissed and crackled as the flesh burned, filling the air with the acrid stench of charred meat.

Manny turned to Damiel, completely focused on him, her voice caught somewhere between a laugh and a sob. "Is there anything you don't know?"

"Well, I don't know anything about being a father," he said softly.

She smiled at him, tears stinging her eyes, and hugged him again. Manny shut her eyes, keeping them closed, even as she knew they were tossing all of Dr. Shepherd's dismembered limbs into the fire, and that around them, the flames were dying down, having devoured the evidence of the horror they'd survived.

Chapter 50
January 15th

Manny walked with Damiel carrying most of her weight when they made their way out— she didn't know how long they walked and trusted him to guide her to safety—but somewhere behind her, Eliza was helping Isla, because Manny couldn't help anyone else tonight. Between the smoke she was still coughing up, the dull ache in her ribs, and the sheer relief of finally stepping out into fresh air—there were sirens.

Shrill and insistent, over the crackling flames roaring at their backs, somehow holding out against the torrents of rain pounding the ground beneath their feet. Somewhere in the smoke, she could distinguish between the vehicles arriving, and somewhere in the distance fire engines *blared*, police cars *chirped*, and ambulances were already on the scene.

Rain washed over her skin, cooling her down, washing away the blood, the sweat, the ash—like God himself was trying to scrub off the aftermath.

Manny stood there, blinking against the downpour, turning back only to take in the wreckage for a moment. But only for a moment, because Damiel turned her back forward, taking her past their surviving allies, including a few of her closest friends. Victor was doing a good job of keeping the police from swarming them.

"This way," Damiel muttered to her, veering her toward an ambulance.

You want me to get checked? I thought you said everything was all right?

"They'll be suspicious if you aren't checked," Damiel insisted. *"And I need to speak to the others, and hope they have enough energy to deal with the police."*

Deal with?

"Compel them to believe our story about three students taken by a professor under false pretenses—"

Your staging a kidnapping and then what—

"Cult."

What?

"We're going with what has already been suspected by the media. They're part of a cult—and that cult is responsible for the student's murders," Damiel explained.

They were only a few feet away from a soft-eyed concerned looking female EMT.

"We never stretch the truth further than necessary."

Then what are you going to tell her?

"Easy," Damiel said aloud, as they approached the paramedic. "She's pregnant and needs to be checked. She may have been harmed in the attack."

Manny was shocked he was so blunt about it, but the paramedic didn't question it, instead she immediately went into medic mode.

"My name is Barbara, what's yours?" Barbara the paramedic asked.

"Manny," Manny answered, glancing between Damiel and Barbara the paramedic.

Barbara nodded. "How many weeks along are you?"

"Um…14, maybe," Manny answered. "I lost count."

"Does anything in particular hurt?" Barbara asked.

Manny nodded. "My stomach, a little."

The woman began to drone on and on, about how she hadn't been on the scene of something '*this bad*' in Millfield in a few weeks, which she insisted was both a blessing and a curse. But Manny could hardly hear her as she watched Damiel speaking to the other vampires, who nodded intently at whatever he was saying. Then when two police officers approached them, probably for questioning—the glamouring began. She knew from the way their shoulders drooped, releasing all undue tension, and the goofy grins slowly spreading on their faces—it wasn't hard to tell.

Glamouring, or *compulsion* was more than mere charm—it was influence through words—shaped by *language*. Manny could only liken it to her mother telling her to not *waste her words,* which she'd understood before as anything she said being a reflection of herself and her community.

But compulsion was the supernatural mirror of language and culture—shaping and feeding the other—at best it could heal humanity, at worst it could damn them all. And like words wielded with intent, compulsion could bend minds, rewrite truths, and reshape its victims' beliefs and behaviors. It was a power that demanded careful wielding, for the line between influence and violation was perilously thin.

Manny had thought she understood the extent of the danger, but perhaps she never would, and maybe she would have to be okay with that. She could sit in the back of this ambulance with a paper-thin blanket draped over her shoulders and pretend to be okay. Barbara pressed a damp cloth to a cut on her temple, murmuring something about stitches, but her mind was elsewhere.

Across the lot, her friends huddled near another ambulance, their faces exhausted but they were alive. They'd made it out alive.

Then, a voice cut through the din.

"...a murderous cult perhaps rivaling the Manson family, uncovered right here at the heart of—"

Manny's head whirred toward the nearest Millfield news van, where Larry Bennett stood in front of the cameras, his expression serious as he spoke.

"Authorities have confirmed that the arrested individuals were responsible for a string of disappearances and ritualistic murders targeting Millfield University students with potentially more victims throughout North America. And in a bittersweet revelation, justice has finally been served for the MillU Murders including those of—"

Manny's heart lurched as the man rattled off name after name, and then—

"And basketball star, Tamara Moore, who was killed over one year ago. For so long, their murderers remained unknown, but tonight, the truth has finally come to light."

A lump rose in Manny's throat. She pulled the blanket around herself tighter. It didn't bring Tammy back. But for the first time in a long time, she let herself smile at Tammy's name—a small, tired, smile.

"I'm Larry Bennett from Millfield News, signing off."

A small flutter inside her stomach—so faint she almost missed it. Then, a firmer nudge, just below her ribs.

Manny blinked, startled, and pressed a hand to her stomach. Another kick, insistent, as if to remind her: *Hey, I'm still here.*

Manny smiled down at her stomach, because she was still here, too.

For the first time in a long time, that thought didn't send her spiraling. For so long she'd been anxious, uncertain or afraid of the future. For once, she wasn't drowning, she was *floating*—she was *alive*. If she could survive all of this, she could survive telling Dean, telling her family—she'd have to tell them. She'd have to explain. She was *okay*.

Not great. Not untouched. Not fully healed. But *okay*—which meant she could get there.

I should definitely book a session with Dr. Carter, she thought laughing at herself. *Maybe several.*

Since their last call she'd been turned into a familiar, seen someone get decapitated, set a bunch of newborn vampires on fire, killed her program's Associate Dean and somewhere in all that, realized she was going to be a mom. It had been one hell of a semester.

And, because the universe has a twisted sense of humor, she still had two essays due on Monday.

Of course, Manny didn't know what came next. But for the first time in a long time, she couldn't wait to find out.

Manny glanced Barbara the paramedic taking her vitals again, as she said. “Your baby’s heartbeat sounds great. My little one moved around quite a bit when I was pregnant. Does yours?”

“Oh, plenty,” Manny said with a smile. “They’re practically nocturnal.”

After

Soft? Each time Manny rubbed a thumb over her son, Nikolai's skin, she knew it wasn't quite the right description. His skin was softer than rose petals—like it had been specifically engineered to make silk feel insecure. Touching it made everything else seem rougher by comparison, even the blankets on top of her.

To her left, Damiel was cradling their daughter, Amara in his arms. She lay against his chest, impossibly small, her tiny hand curled into a fist near his heart. She stared past them, out the window, where the soft light of dawn was slowly creeping over the horizon.

Manny's life had changed so much in just a few months. Her first semester of grad school felt like a lifetime ago, and now here she was, finished with her second semester, with two tiny humans to show for it. Finishing her portfolio early and turning it in had been well worth the risk. Especially, given that she needed the time to adjust to *everything*.

Dean, however, wasn't in Millfield anymore. He had woken up from his coma, groggy and confused, his voice raspy as he tried to piece together what had happened—and what being glamoured was like. *Pure ecstasy,* he'd told her over the phone when he called. She managed to tell him then, so he could hear it from her. It was one of the hardest conversations she'd ever had. But he wasn't angry—she was grateful for that—and after a long pause, the first thing he said was, *I don't blame you.* His voice had been hoarse, raw from weeks of disuse, but he repeated it. "I don't blame you. You didn't know if I'd ever wake up. Hell, I'm amazed I did wake up."

It wasn't going to be easy for him to process, she didn't expect it to be. "I just need some time," he'd said eventually. "I'm going to head back home for a little bit. We'll take some space—while I figure things out."

She nodded, even though he couldn't see it. "I understand."

And she did. Dean had gone into the ice, under the water, thinking about how they were building a future together, trying to figure out how to push back a vampire that had taken control of his mind. Then he woke up from a coma, and found the future had taken a completely different shape—without his permission. He deserved time, deserved to figure out if he even wanted a future attached to hers anymore.

Manny had an easier time explaining it to her parents—the coma, the ongoing break between her and Dean, the pregnancy, the sudden, whirlwind nature of everything sans witches, vampires and the like—over a video call. Her mother had pursed her lips in that way she always did when she was trying not to judge people, looking over at the good old 'WWJD' (What Would Jesus Do) plaque on their living room mantle, and her father had just nodded, saying something about "life being *unpredictable*." And that was that. They accepted it in their own way.

She sighed, her arms were heavy but she wasn't going to set her son down, not yet. It wasn't how she thought her life would go. But then again, nothing about this year had gone the way she'd thought it would. Of course, now there were twins in the mix.

Her son's weight was comforting, even though her body still ached with the rawness of childbirth. Her son's soft, downy hair tickled her chin, and every rise and fall of his tiny breaths warmed her from the inside out.

Damiel's voice finally broke the silence. "They're so quiet. If I couldn't hear their heartbeats, I'd be worried—"

"Don't sound too upset. We should probably savor it," Manny

whispered back to him, a tired smile tugging at her lips. "And I thought there'd only be one."

Damiel laughed, a warm and unexpected sound, and she caught the glint of his fangs when he spoke. "Let me dream a little." He looked at their daughter like she was the most precious thing in the world—and it made Manny's chest tighten. "I guess I should have specified how many heartbeats I was hearing."

This moment felt surreal, this fragile family they'd created. A familiar and her vampire, holding two lives they had brought into the world together. Maybe months ago that would have terrified her, but right now, she was at peace.

Her midwife had told her to rest, and had promised to return in a few hours to check on her stitches, her pulse, her milk. But she wasn't ready for sleep. She kept remembering every moment of the past days: the ever-painful, ever-cresting waves of labor, the steady reassurance of Damiel's voice, the firm yet gentle hands of the midwife guiding her through it all—and then, their son came out first, then their daughter, but their cries came in unison.

Damiel had pulled her close to him, holding her like she was made of glass, his cold skin pressed against her cheek. Her head resting against his chest, and for a moment, she swore she'd heard his heartbeat—grounding her, drawing her back to a place where she was safe and he wasn't going anywhere.

"How are you feeling?" Damiel asked, his eyes meeting hers, snapping her back to reality.

It wasn't like he needed to ask. He could just pop into her head, know what she was feeling or think in an instant, but he wasn't—though it had taken him time to get to this point. A point where he could trust her to tell him everything, if he did the same.

Manny hesitated. She knew she was somewhere between exhaustion and joy, but settled for. "Tired," she said with a shrug. "But…*happy*." She looked down at her son, his tiny face calm and completely oblivious to the world around him.

The twins stirred almost in unison, and she smiled at their

synchronicity, at how the two little lives seemed bound together in a way no one else would ever understand.

"Do you think they'll look alike when they grow up?" she asked, her voice barely above a whisper.

He smiled. "I don't know...but I think we have a lot to look forward to."

"Shame about the vampire messiah though."

Damiel laughed, which made her laugh then he said. "It is a shame, isn't it?"

And in that moment, as they sat together with their children safe in their arms, she swore the future felt just a little brighter. At least, for now, she could relax.

Thank you! I hope you enjoyed the book!😊

Your Feedback Matters! Reviews make a huge difference for authors like me, helping new readers discover my work. If you enjoyed the book, I'd be so grateful if you could take a moment to leave a review!

Please leave a review: Amazon, Goodreads, StoryGraph, and/or any other platform where you share your reading experience!

Scan this to leave a review (on Amazon):

You can find more of my books at here:

or visit https://www.aminahfox.com/all-novels

You can also sign-up for my newsletter at: www.aminahfox.com/newsletter

Acknowledgments

This book has been with me for a long time. Since 2021, it's lived in notes, voice memos, and late-night ramblings with friends. It's a story about trauma, perception, and what it means to survive when the world insists on defining you before you get the chance. It's about a girl who returns to the place that broke her, only to realize the past doesn't stay buried.

To my family—thank you for your unwavering support during the long, winding road it took to finish this book. Writing this book alongside my own healing—through cognitive processing therapy—was not easy. But knowing I had people in my life who were rooting for me made all the difference.

To my partner, who listened, laughed, encouraged, and reminded me that I was capable of finishing this—thank you for believing in me when I couldn't see the end!

To my writer friends, who have been endlessly supportive (and very *very* patient)—your excitement has meant everything to me. You've cheered me on for *years*, and I'm so grateful that this is finally the year I get to share this book with you.

To my cover designer, Atima Kim, who designed the stunning ebook cover! I absolutely loved this premade cover when I came across it, and knew it was perfect for Threads of Fate!

To my brilliant editors—Faye and Belle Manuel—thank you for your care, clarity, and dedication. Your feedback challenged me in all the right ways and helped this story become sharper, stronger, and more honest. I'm so grateful for your time, your patience, and the way you treated this book with such thoughtfulness.

And finally, to you—*the reader*. Thank you for picking up this book, for staying with it, and for making space in your world for this story. I hope it made you feel seen. I hope you found something in it to hold onto. And honestly, I hope the main character made you laugh at least once.

Thank you for reading!

Aminah Fox

ALSO BY AMINAH FOX

ALL THE OTHER GODS NOVELS

The Eleventh Hour

Twenty-one-year-old witch Hermione must travel back in time to prevent a horrible tragedy, when growing conflict threatens to destroy her world even if she doesn't know what she might lose.

THE MOURNERS

The Mourners trilogy is the story of Elide Hester, a young woman in dystopian Texas, who discovers she possesses telepathic abilities that could end the centuries-old war plaguing her world. The companion and prequel novels explore the journeys of two other characters.

The Mourners: The Deadly Elite

The Harlots: The Devoutly Corrupt

About the Author

Aminah Fox is an American author, born in June 1998 in Oakland, California. She is an alumna of the University of Toronto (MI in Library & Information Science) and Hofstra University (BA in English, Creative Writing & Literature). Her novel, The Mourners: The Deadly Elite, was published in 2022. She lives in Texas and Toronto.

www.aminahfox.com

www.ingramcontent.com/pod-product-compliance
Lightning Source LLC
Chambersburg PA
CBHW020451310726
48979CB00016B/2605/J

* 9 7 9 8 9 8 7 0 4 0 9 8 0 *